Kismet Knight, Vampire Psychologist

'A very modern and mature approach to the subject genre that elevates itself from the standard vampire story . . . a refreshing and a likeable heroine . . . an enjoyable series [that] promises even more to come'　　　　　　　　　*British Fantasy Society*

'This is a fresh take on the fantasy trope . . . It's dark, sexy and very human'　　　　　　　　　*SciFiNow*

'Jam-packed with action, horror, and romance . . . *The Vampire Shrink* is a vivid, modern, and imaginative new take on the everyday vamp novel . . . Hilburn's writing flows off the page and leaves you breathless with laughter and anticipation. In other words, *The Vampire Shrink* is a must-read!'　　　Gravetells.com

'Ms Hilburn packs her story with all the action, romance and suspense readers are looking for'　　　　　*Darque Reviews*

'You will want to take the phone off the hook and lock the doors for the entire time it takes you to read from cover to cover'　　　　　　　　　boomerangbooks.com.au

'Everything you could want – a gripping storyline, intriguing characters, humour, romance'　　　　　*Book Monkey*

'Action-packed and sexy, with a sprinkle of humour . . . a really good book'　　　　　　　　　*Affaire De Coeur*

'Fresh and fun, smart and witty, always sexy and occasionally very scary. *The Vampire Shrink* will keep you up all night'　　　　　　　　　Freda Warrington

Also by Lynda Hilburn

The Vampire Shrink
Blood Therapy

BOOK III OF
KISMET KNIGHT,
VAMPIRE PSYCHOLOGIST

Lynda Hilburn

Crimson Psyche

Jo Fletcher
BOOKS

First published in Great Britain in 2014 by Jo Fletcher Books

Jo Fletcher Books
an imprint of Quercus Editions Ltd.
55 Baker Street
7th Floor, South Block
London
W1U 8EW

A CIP catalogue record for this book is available
from the British Library

ISBN 978 0 85738 725 7 (PB)
ISBN 978 0 85738 727 1 (EBOOK)

10 9 8 7 6 5 4 3 2 1

Typeset by Ellipsis Digital Limited, Glasgow
Printed and bound in Great Britain by Clays Ltd, St Ives plc

To my sweet little brother David Hilburn.
I'll miss you forever.

CHAPTER 1

'Welcome back, Denver! Carson Miller here, host of *Wake Up, Denver!*, WOW Radio's top-rated talk show. We're continuing this week's theme of whacked local celebrities. Is it just me, or is Denver crazier than ever?' His laugh sounded like a rusty chainsaw.

What the hell? Whacked local celebrities? I agreed to come and counsel his listeners!

'I've got self-proclaimed vampire psycho – oops, I mean vampire psychologist – Doctor Kismet Knight in the studio with me today. She's ready and willing to answer all your bloodsucker questions. Give us a call. The phone lines are open. Welcome, Doctor Knight.' He gave a wide, tobacco-stained smile.

'Thanks, Carson.' I spoke into the microphone on the long folding table in front of me. 'I'm happy to be here.' Barely catching myself before I tacked a question mark onto my response, I adjusted my headphones and peered around at the unexpectedly low-tech, dungeon-like studio.

Piles of newspapers, men's magazines, CDs, DVDs and promo flyers fought for supremacy against empty pizza boxes and Styrofoam coffee cups. Fast food bags overflowed the rubbish bin. The pleasant decor and posters of contemporary talk-show personalities on the walls in the outer office hadn't prepared me for the primitive reality of Carson World.

As he read out an ad for an auto parts store, I inched my microphone further away from his, noting the long cord curling at the base of the stand in case I needed to put even more space between us, and scanned the electronics in the engineer's booth. Not only was the equipment modern, but through a glass wall I could see yet another studio on the far side of the booth, and even from here that one looked to be state-of-the-art. Why would the station stick Carson in such a miserable hole?

He rotated his head in my direction and wiggled his eyebrows, still talking into the microphone. 'Let me start by saying that you look finger-lickin' good this morning, Doc. Seriously babe-o-licious.' He ran his thick, lumpy tongue slowly around his lips in a horror-film version of what I supposed he thought was a sexual come-on.

Gak.

'Uh, thanks?' I couldn't quite squelch the question mark this time. I studied his stained, too-small T-shirt and unfashionably torn jeans. His voice, which had sounded pretty sexy through my car radio, wasn't even close to being an accurate representation of the man himself.

'And now that I've eyeballed the merchandise, I'm going to do my best to talk the Doc here into taking off her clothes before the show's over. Then I'll post photos on my Facebook page,' he said, laughing at my alarmed expression.

'I don't think so.' *Oh, great. Another Howard Stern shock-jock wannabe, except fat and bald – what is it with all these talk-radio assholes? Miserable-hole question answered. At least I'll get a good case-study article out of this experience: Demented, Ageing Radio Hosts and Mental Illness.* 'We can take that option off the table.' I glanced at the door that led from our tiny sound booth to the engineer's studio to calculate how many steps it would take me to escape.

'Don't be so sure, Doc. I can be pretty persuasive when I put my mind to it.' He pointed at the engineer, who hit a sound effects button and filled the airwaves with loud clapping.

Young spectators were visible through a large window, lining the hallway and blocking the exit. They high-fived each other and bumped fists, laughing at something I was obviously not cool enough to understand.

Does he have those fans jammed in there on purpose to keep me from leaving? He probably does. What a creep!

I caught a movement from the corner of my eye and shifted my gaze towards a young male who'd materialised, stepped through the bystanders and sauntered over to stand next to me.

Perfect. A haunted radio station. Just what I need.

The slender man wore a glittery jacket with bulky shoulder

pads and sported spiked 1980s hair. He grinned and saluted me with a beer can.

'Ladies and gentlemen,' Carson continued, 'I have to tell you that it's a shame we aren't on TV because Doctor Knight is a feast for the eyes. She's wearing a clingy black dress that hugs her curves in all the right places. Legs that go on for ever. Big blue eyes. And she's got this great long, dark hair.' He reached out to touch my curls and I smacked his hand away. He lowered his voice and gave it an extra layer of smarm. 'It gives a guy ideas, if you know what I mean. Anyway, Doc' – he returned to me – 'so what the hell is a vampire psychologist? Are you a vampire?' He laughed and his belly flopped against the table, making the microphone wobble. When he moved, the smell of cigarette smoke wafted from his T-shirt.

'No, Carson, I'm not a vampire.' I scooted my chair and microphone even further away from the host, tilted my head and attempted a professional smile while I focused on his ridiculous question. *If he only knew.* 'I'm a psychologist who works with the subculture of individuals who believe they're vampires. Or who want to be vampires – people seeking meaning through role-playing and exploring the dark side of themselves – the unknown – and by flouting society's ideas of good versus evil.'

'Wow, Doc – that sounds pretty sexy,' he oozed. 'Are you saying that Denver has a lot of these people? These "pretend vampires"?' He reached one of his hands out towards me, making grabbing motions.

I shoved it away, giving him the evil eye.

This moron's not going to rattle me. I'm here for the listeners.

He waved three fingers at the engineer and a chorus of 'Carson! Carson! Carson!' burst from the speakers. Then, while the voices raved, he laughed and pointed to the microphone, expecting, or maybe daring, me to continue my interview despite his obnoxious behaviour.

I glanced at the studio clock on the wall, imagining pushing my way through the crowd at the door and regretting the fact that I'd agreed to be a guest for an entire segment. In retrospect, I definitely should've done more research to determine which media appearances would actually help my career, which ones had disgusting hosts, and which shows just wanted to exploit the fact that I'd been involved in a heavily reported serial murder investigation – a case dubbed the 'vampire murders' – six months earlier. Who'd've guessed finding blood-drained bodies would generate so much interest?

Carson sliced his finger across his neck, signalling the engineer to stop the chant, then said, 'Hey, Doc, wasn't somebody killed in your office a while back?'

'There was a death, yes – but I'm sure your audience would rather have me address their personal issues as we agreed.' I stared at him until he smirked and pointed to the engineer, who pressed another button on his console, unleashing the sound of a roaring crowd.

I wasn't about to discuss the death in my office – very few people knew the truth: that the perpetrator had been a mentally defective vampire, diagnosed with what used to be called Multiple Personality Disorder, and whose rotted corpse finally sloughed off his immortal coil a few weeks ago. Those select few who did know included one Denver police lieutenant, one cocky FBI agent, a bunch of vampires, a half-undead psychologist colleague, a transgendered hypnotherapist and me. Everybody else believed the cover story about a mortal perpetrator.

'80s Guy bent close to Carson and waved his hands in front of the oblivious host's face.

I'll just ignore the Billy Idol clone and he'll get bored and go away.

The sound effect stopped again, leaving empty air, and after a moment Carson realised and jumped back in. 'It seems the Doc here needs more coffee – she's a little slow on the uptake this morning. Okay, so let's go to the phones. Studio lines are open.'

He gave me an innocent smile and shrugged, as if to say I shouldn't hold him responsible for his radio persona. I notched up the ice content in my glare and pushed my chair back a couple more inches.

Maybe he's off his meds.

The studio phone had two rows of buttons and all of them were lit up and blinking. He pressed the closest one.

'You're on the air. Give us your first name and your question for the luscious Doctor Knight.'

'Hello? Doctor Knight? This is Susan in Aurora. I want to know if you've ever worked with any *real* vampires?'

Why, yes, Susan. I actually chopped the head off one, was locked in a coffin by another, met the most famous bloodsucker of them all, and have sweaty, wild, and crazy sex regularly with yet another. Nope. Better not say that.

'That's an interesting question, Susan.' I settled into my counselling mode while tracking Carson out of the corner of my eye. 'Why do you ask? Do you think vampires are real?'

'Not exactly – but I guess I wish they were real.'

'Hmm. Why do you wish they were real?'

'Well, it would just be so cool to be with a guy who could read your mind and who could make you live forever – a guy who would want to be with you all the time. A guy who wouldn't cheat on me.'

'Ah. It sounds like you've had a painful experience with a man recently. A non-vampire, right?'

'Yeah – this tarot reader told me my boyfriend was a psychic vampire. I bet you work with a lot of those, too.'

'I do come across a lot of psychic vampires.' I stared over at Carson. 'They're everywhere. For listeners who might not know what that is, a psychic vampire is someone who feeds on the emotions and energy of others, psychologically speaking. We all know people who suck on our energy, who manipulate and control things to their advantage. We can't make them stop trying to feed on us, but we can take ourselves off the menu. We can create healthy boundaries for ourselves, so that no one can drain our energy without our permission.'

Carson leaned into his microphone. 'Hey, Doc – why would people give permission for some psychic vampire to feed on them?'

I glanced towards him, keeping my expression neutral. 'Well, sometimes we don't realise we're dealing with a psychic vampire until they've already stuck their psychic fangs in our necks. They can be very clever, manipulative – extremely self-absorbed. We're bespelled before we even realise what happened. Or sometimes a person with inadequate boundaries, or maybe a poor self-image, unconsciously invites a predator into his or her life. Psychic vampires sense the vulnerabilities in others and they prey upon them. They go from one victim to another, feeding and draining. Isn't that right, Carson?'

'How would I know, Doc?' He frowned, pursed his lips. 'Are you saying that I'm a psychic vampire?'

Duh.

'Whatever gave you that idea, Carson?' I smiled and batted my eyelashes.

Okay, so my Inner Bitch is good and healthy.

'Well, I want my listeners to know that I'm not any kind of vampire – although I wouldn't mind doing a little sucking on various parts of your bodacious bod, Doc.'

I gave him a bland stare.

What an idiot.

He smirked and punched another button on the telephone. 'You're on the air.'

'This is Crystal, Doctor Knight, and I'm calling because I have terminal cancer and the doctors say I only have a few months left to live. They've done everything they can. I'm only twenty-four, Doctor, and I don't want to die – I want to live at least a normal number of years. If I can find a real vampire to bite me and turn me into one of them, will my body be cancer-free?'

Shit. They never taught this stuff in ethics class in graduate school. Do I tell her the truth, that yes, her body would be cancer-free, but she'd be the walking dead? Or do I pretend that the vampire thing is a fantasy and just let her die? Which is better, dead or undead?

'I'm so sorry you're sick, Crystal. According to vampire legend, if a vampire brings you over, you no longer have a mortal body, so, yes, you'd be cancer-free. But you'd also be dead. Since there aren't any real vampires available at the moment to ask' – *Hey, that's true, they're all dead 'til sundown* – 'I do have a medical suggestion for you. My office phone number is on my website. I'd like you to call me so we can discuss options. Will you do that?'

'Sure. I don't think it's going to do any good, but why not? I'll call you later today. Thanks, Doctor Knight.'

Ah, Crystal, be careful what you ask for, because you just might get it.

'That's great. I'll talk to you then.'

Carson edged closer to his microphone, making loud sniffing and sobbing noises, pretending to cry. 'Gee, Doc, that was heartbreaking, wasn't it? I wonder if she'd be willing to have some hot sex before she bites the dust? Could you ask her when she calls you?'

'80s Guy punched Carson in the head.

Beyond the glass, his spectators jumped up and down, slapping high-fives again.

My face twisted with disgust and he chuckled. Apparently

he'd wanted to see how far he could push me – but for what possible purpose? There was something very foul about Carson Miller. Lucky I was trained to handle mental defectives.

'Keep those calls coming in, Denver.' He clicked the next flashing button on the phone. 'You're on the air with the succulent Doctor Knight and the humble Carson Miller. Speak now, or forever hold your . . . whatever.'

'Hi, Doctor Knight! This is Amber. Me and my girlfriends are cosmetologists, and we're listening to you at our hair salon, along with our customers. We think you're cool.' Clapping and cheers sounded in the background.

Carson slumped back in his chair, a wicked grin on his fat face.

'Thanks, Amber.' I put a smile in my voice. 'I appreciate that. How can I help you?'

'Well,' she began, her voice breathy, excited, 'we're rabid vampire fans. We read every vampire book that comes out, and there are lots of vampire romances these days. Why do you think women get aroused by the idea of having sex with a vampire? I mean, aren't their bodies cold and hard like statues? How arousing is that?'

I chuckled. 'Let me begin with your first question. I think women are intrigued with the notion of having sex with vampires because vampires are extraordinary. They're immortal, and they desperately need the woman's blood in order to exist. Imagine being needed that intensely: that's a pretty powerful metaphor, don't you think?'

Be still, my heart . . .

'Wow,' Amber said, 'I never thought of it that way . . .'

'And,' I said, 'it's doubtful that a gorgeous vampire would be sitting in front of the television night after night, drinking beer and ignoring you, like an undead Homer Simpson, right?'

She laughed. 'You better believe it!' More catcalls and cheers from the salon.

'Women fantasise about males who are heroic, mysterious or non-ordinary, as well as gorgeous men with bodies to die for. What's wrong with a good fantasy?'

I should know. Devereux is definitely fantasy material.

'Woot! Woot! Woot!' came from the speakers.

After they calmed down, I continued, 'As far as vampires having bodies like statues, some of the popular books do portray their immortals that way, but I definitely agree with you. I probably wouldn't find a cold, hard body appealing. I prefer the authors who give their bloodsuckers warm, almost-human characteristics. If I were going to write a vampire novel, I'd have my characters retain control of their body functions: heartbeat, breathing, warmth, state of sexual readiness . . .'

The softest, warmest lips imaginable . . .

'Yes! Sex at the drop of a . . . fang!' Wild cheering floated across the airwaves.

With a loud click, Carson disconnected the call and barked into his microphone, 'Damn! That's enough of the sex talk.' He cupped his equipment. 'You guys are turning me on and I won't be responsible for what happens. Next call.' He punched another button on the phone.

'Doctor Knight? My name is Betsy Whitmore and I'm a social worker in Denver.'

'Thanks for calling, Betsy. How can I help you?'

'I remember reading about the murder case you were involved in a while back when a couple of young people were killed. Vampire wannabes, the media called them. The murderer was never caught. I'm wondering if you've seen the numbers of kids getting into the vampire lifestyle decreasing or increasing since then. I would've thought the negative publicity would scare them off, but I'm finding more and more kids are getting lured in. Do you offer any groups or educational classes I can refer the kids to? Is there any validity to the talk about some kind of evil energy getting stronger in Denver?'

'Those are great questions, Betsy,' I said.

Carson stood and walked behind my chair, clamped his sausage-sized fingers on my shoulders and began to roughly massage them. '80s Guy stepped back to observe. The engineer on the other side of the glass shook his head frantically, gesturing at Carson to return to his seat, but he ignored him. As his hands inched away from my shoulders, heading down towards my breasts, I bolted from the chair, grabbing my microphone before slipping out of his reach.

I guess I'll get to find out how far this cord will stretch, and maybe how he'll like a pointy toe to the crotch.

'Yes, I do offer both groups and educational classes, so have them call my office.'

Speaking of evil energy, what was up with this fool? I couldn't remember the last time I'd seen such a disturbed person out in public. Was he on drugs as well? Did he have a death wish? He'd be a midnight vampire snack if he didn't chill out pretty soon. There was more than one benefit to hanging out with the undead.

'I *have* noticed an increase in people of all ages joining these cults.'

I leaned against the glass separating the on-air room from the hallway, where Carson's audience continued to appreciate his antics. I tried to focus on Betsy's concerns while making sure I stayed out of Carson's reach.

'It doesn't make sense, because there's been so much negative publicity about the dark underside of the vampire lifestyle.'

He jumped up and started dancing around the studio while I spoke, lifting the front of his T-shirt and pointing to his protruding, hairy stomach. His audience licked the window with their tongues. I tried not to lose my breakfast and worked on keeping my voice steady.

This is fascinating – like watching a nightmare train wreck. I'm almost sorry for him – but not quite.

'There does appear to be an escalating interest,' I told Social Worker Betsy. 'I've also heard the talk about Denver being one of the places where evil is growing. A police friend said recently that all forms of violent crimes are up here. People seem to be losing control of themselves. I admit I don't understand what could be causing the changes.'

Well, at least not anything I can talk about.

Carson leaped back into his chair, drew his microphone close and affected a whining, high-pitched voice, squeaking,

'Oh my, goodness gracious, help me! There's *evil* in Denver. Somebody save me! That's enough with the social worker.' He punched the next blinking button. 'You're on the air, and I insist you be more interesting than the last caller.'

Seconds of silence ticked by . . . although *silence* didn't begin to cover it. The hairs on the back of my neck rose and goosebumps swarmed over my arms. It was like someone – or some*thing* – had sucked all the air from the room, or opened a black hole – cold, bottomless, *terrifying*. I could see even Carson was entranced, for his facial muscles slackened.

Then a deep, sonorous male voice spoke. 'Doctor Knight. I have been looking forward to meeting you.'

The ghost visibly started, causing phantom liquid to shoot up from the beer can. His eyes wide, he vanished from the studio.

My solar plexus tingled, as it always did when a vampire was near.

Whoa – what's going on here? This guy has the vampire voice for sure, and his vibe is definitely bloodsucker, but it's daylight, so he can't really be a vampire. I shouldn't be able to feel a vampire over the telephone, right? Shit. I don't trust myself any more to make judgements about who's a vampire and who isn't. Only six months ago Brother Luther slipped right under my radar and that mistake almost got me killed.

Carson snapped out of his mini-trance and wheezed into the microphone, 'Hey, Doc, I think we got us a live one here! Or a dead one! I'm a riot – I really crack myself up. I'll bet this guy's a vampire. He sounds like a vampire. So, Mister Vampire, what's your name, and what's it like being a creature of the night?' He slouched back in his chair, grinning, waiting for the next straight line to be supplied for his comedy routine.

The caller whispered, 'Silence, tedious human.'

Carson's eyes slammed shut. He slumped in his chair, his chin bouncing on his fleshy chest.

I stared at the DJ. I had seen this kind of hypnosis-like state before, but always from vampires. *Real* ones.

'Doctor Knight?' the deep voice purred.

I gasped involuntarily, for his voice was distractingly arousing. It caressed my skin like warm fingers, reminding me of intimate encounters of the gorgeous undead variety. *What the hell is going on?*

I cleared my throat. 'Yes. I'm here. There does appear to be something *unique* about you. Something . . .'

'Vampiric?' he whispered, the resonance of the word vibrating like a hand stroking my body.

Yikes. I think I moaned. *Pull yourself together, Kismet. You've been through this before. Now's not the time to re-explore the 'V' spot. Take a deep breath and cross your legs. Tight.*

He gave a devilish chuckle.

'You're a vampire?' I blurted a bit too loudly.

'I am indeed.'

And hopefully, all the listeners will assume he's either a wannabe or a nutter.

'How can you be a vampire and be awake during the day?'

'I am very old – older than anything you can understand. I no longer have any limitations on my abilities. As long as my body is sheltered from the direct rays of the sun, it is pleasant to move about – although I much prefer the night. Each vampire has his or her own special skills. You have had only a small *taste* of mine.'

And when he said 'taste' I felt something tongue-like move between my legs. I pressed my thighs even tighter together.

I glanced over at Carson to make sure he wasn't witnessing my discomfort, but he was still out cold, drooling down the front of his shirt. Judging by their loose jaws and glazed eyes, his spectators were entranced too.

This can't be good: the entire radio audience is listening to me talk to a real vampire. Is this some kind of set-up? I've never known a vampire this powerful before, not even the librarian, Zephyr, or insane Dracul—

'They will not remember a thing, Doctor Knight. Do not trouble yourself about the humans. They are in a light trance. We can chat freely,' he said, apparently reading my thoughts.

Oh, no! I quickly started practising the sound-magic hum I'd learned from my psychic friend Cerridwyn, which keeps my brain safe from vampire influence. Well, the hum and my yearly ancient-vampire-blood cocktail. *How can he be reading my thoughts? The elders intervened. They said my brain can't be accessed or harmed any more. I'm supposed to be protected from bloodsucker influence!*

Then I had a horrible thought, that whoever this creature was, maybe he'd caused hundreds of cars to swerve off roads all over the Denver Metro area as listeners dozed at the wheel. He'd obviously scared the ghost away.

'Of course I can read your mind.' He laughed, the sound tightening my stomach. I wasn't sure if the sensation was pleasure or pain. Maybe it was both.

'I am unique in all the world. Nothing the elders do can impede me. And as for the fate of your listeners, one might expect a psychologist to be the compassionate type – but never fear; the populace is safe from me, at least for the moment. They are merely hypnotised. For a vampire, creating an altered state is not dependent upon proximity. It is quite simple to insert a mental suggestion into the radio waves. While we speak, your mortals believe they are listening to a pleasant tune. They will resurface in due course remembering a relaxing daydream. No harm will come to them – until it suits me, anyway.'

'What do you want?' I finally managed to mumble. The sound of his voice made my head fuzzy, and that sent another jolt of fear through my body. I wasn't supposed to be overwhelmed by vampires any more.

'Just to introduce myself. I am a remarkable soul, even in the vampire realm. Lyren Hallow, Vampire Hunter Extraordinaire, at your service. You may call me Hallow.'

His disclosure momentarily threw me and I spluttered, 'What? A vampire hunter? But you're a vampire. How can you be a vampire hunter? Aren't there rules about that?'

'A fiend has to make a living, yes?' he replied, the sound caressing all my pleasure centres. 'Even ancient vampires are not immune to the delightful siren song of money. Surprisingly superficial, I admit, but the acquisition of gold has always been an intriguing game. And in my own defence, I challenge you to keep uncovering reasons to crawl out of the tomb every night after thousands of years. Existence can be such a chore. Hunting down and killing my own kind, now there is something a nightwalker can really sink his fangs into.' He gave a wild laugh, as if he found himself highly amusing.

I cleared my throat, stalling for time. Ever since I had stumbled into Denver's hidden vampire underworld, I'd been struggling to regain my balance – to find some sort of sanity to cling to while reeling from one absurd revelation to another. 'Why are you telling me this?'

'I have been hired to harvest someone you know and I thought it only sporting to tip my hand ever so slightly, just to keep things interesting. And of course you have become very well known in the bloodsucker community. I simply could not resist strolling through your brain, even if from a distance. I expect you will make the quest much more tantalising for me. The link between us is open now, so it will be easier for us to communicate in the future. But, alas, I must leave you, for duty calls. Oh, and by the way, you might notice some changes in your behaviour – fewer inhibitions, a bit more passion, stronger emotions. Nothing to worry about; just consider the adjustments to be my gift to you. Until we meet again, lovely Doctor Knight.'

There was a click and the line went dead. So to speak.

Changes in my behaviour? And what the hell does he mean by 'harvest'? Is he going to kill someone? He can't mean Devereux – this must be a sick joke.

I hadn't noticed that the engineer on the other side of

the glass studio partition had been staring off into space until he suddenly jerked back to awareness. So did Carson, who managed to startle himself out of his chair, which rolled away from him and crashed into the wall as his flabby ass hit the floor with a dull thud.

He wiped the pooling saliva from his chins and stood up, looking around, a stranger in a strange land.

'What the hell just happened?' he bellowed, scratching his bulging belly.

The engineer knocked on the glass, then pointed to the clock to show Carson that he needed to announce the station ID and the time. Several minutes had passed and our interview was over.

Glaring at me, Carson grabbed his microphone and slipped back into his on-air personality. He gave the required information, deepening his voice into a sexy growl. 'I'd like to thank our guest, the boob-dacious Doctor Kismet Knight, for being on the show today. Aliens must have abducted me because I sure as hell don't know where the time went. Stay tuned, and I'll be right back after these words from our moneymakers.'

He clicked off his mic and turned suspicious eyes to me. 'I don't remember shit, and I don't know what you did, but I know you did something.' He clutched his stomach, his harsh voice for once in alignment with his actual character. 'I feel it in my gut. There was that weird phone call and then – nothing. Maybe you slipped something into my coffee. This isn't over, Kismet, baby. You'll be hearing from me again. I smell a story here, and I intend to be the one to exploit it as only I can.' He made a sucking-in-air noise with his mouth that reminded me of Hannibal Lecter.

I grabbed my briefcase and headed towards the studio door. I hurried past Carson's fans, who were standing propped against the wall, looking dazed.

I had been tempted to tell the slimy host what a nasty coffin of worms he'd opened, but I decided not to. He'd been the worst kind of abusive jerk to me during our interview and I wasn't in the mood to go out of my way to save his neck. Even if he was obviously sick.

Besides, if he wanted to step into an episode of *Supernatural*, who was I to interfere?

I shook my head to clear some of the remaining mental cobwebs and hustled down the carpeted hallway towards the lobby, moving fast enough to generate static around the bottom of my dress. The material sealed itself to my knees and I stopped, resting a hand against the wall next to the reception desk, watching tiny electrical sparks dance along the fabric as I tugged it away from my legs.

Carson's voice slithered out of the invisible speakers built into the ceiling of the lobby, announcing his next guest: the former Miss Denver, who'd been disqualified when her breast enhancement surgery had been discovered. As if everyone and her sister wasn't lining up for augmentation these days.

But I felt a little sorry for the poor beauty queen. I wondered if she was as clueless as I'd been about Carson's crazed personality, or if she would be expecting his own personal brand of insanity.

I must have mumbled something out loud while I was

bent over the hem of my dress, because a voice answered me.

'Carson Miller is an oozing wart on the ass of humanity – no, wait: he's what gets sucked out of Porta-potties after sports events. No, wait, he's what you squish out of an abscessed pimple.'

Chapter 2

Surprised, I jerked my head up to discover the source of the horribly accurate descriptions and found a hand reaching out in my direction.

My gaze travelled up – way up – to settle on the amused face of the tall woman standing in front of me.

Instinctively I straightened, grasped the proffered hand and matched her smile. Despite her comfortable running shoes she towered above me. She had to be well over six feet tall, because I'm just four inches shy of that in my bare feet and today I was wearing three-inch heels.

But it was her hair even more than her stature that caught the eye: an amazing waterfall of silky white that fell almost to the back of her knees.

My dark brown hair is very long and curly, but compared to hers, I've got a crew-cut.

I stared rudely at the Arctic avalanche flowing down her body, trying to figure out what sort of genetic glitch could give someone so obviously young such pure white hair. After a few seconds, my good manners reappeared and I offered a nod of apology.

She laughed, a warm tinkling sound, and released my hand. 'Yeah, don't worry about it. Everybody has that reaction first-off. I'm the Winter Queen, otherwise known as Maxie Westhaven, the Maxie part being short for Maxwell. My parents definitely wanted a boy.' She laughed again and spun around in a circle. 'Ya think they were a little disappointed?'

I added my laughter to hers, my inner therapist glad she had a healthy sense of humour about her Victoria's Secret body. Her curvy shape wasn't something you could successfully hide under a Denver Broncos T-shirt and jeans.

'It's nice to meet you. I'm Kismet—'

'Yeah, I know who you are. I saw your picture in the paper a few months back when you were embroiled in all that vampire stuff. I even tried to interview you then. I just heard you on the radio. Oh, by the way, I'm a reporter for *National Cynic* magazine. Have you heard of us?'

My smile dissolved. Unfortunately, I *had* heard of the rag – and so had anybody else who ever went to a convenience store, gas station or Laundromat. It was impossible to miss the latest edition, which featured an absurdly fake photograph of a two-headed alien on the cover and a story about the merits of treating depression by exorcism, rather than seeing a psychotherapist.

The magazine was positively schizophrenic: it devoted as much space to publicising ludicrous 'cures' and practitioners as it did to debunking fakes, charlatans and New Age gurus in so-called 'exposés'.

Disappointed, because I'd found myself immediately liking her, I wrapped my professional aura around me again and reminded myself that I had to be very careful with the media. I'd definitely been there and done that and now I knew better than to say *anything* that might put my vampire – or vampire wannabe – clients in danger. Not to mention a certain master vampire who revved my heart rate and jump-started my libido every time he materialised in my room.

I fired up my formal therapist's voice and answered her question. 'I have, yes.'

Maxie apparently noticed my attitude change and distancing manoeuvre. 'Hmmm. I can see that my occupation doesn't fill your heart with joy. Well, let me ease your mind. I didn't approach you for an interview. Really,' she said at my raised eyebrows, 'I just wanted to meet you. You sound interesting – I think we actually might be kindred spirits, because I'm sure you spend a lot of your time convincing confused people that they don't want to pretend to be vampires, and I spend a lot of mine debunking the ones you can't talk out of it.'

'Those are polite words for what you do.'

She shifted her weight from foot to foot as if she were impatiently waiting to blast off to the next location. 'What can I say? I give them a reality check – just like you do. See?' She shrugged and flipped a thick handful of that long white hair over her shoulder. 'We're on the same side here. And I'll bet you thought my description of Cretin – I mean, Carson

– was on the money.'

I smiled before I could censor myself and met her blue eyes, which were just a shade lighter than mine. The irises were ringed with a thin line of indigo. Golden eyebrows and lashes were evidence of what her original hair colour might have been. I studied her face for a couple of seconds. I'd been so distracted by her amazing mane that I hadn't even noticed the perfect features. The pandemonium with Carson and Hallow must have thrown me off my game more than I realised.

Gee, Kismet, you're losing it. Aren't psychologists supposed to be observant? Wouldn't you say that's a handy skill for a therapist to have? I'm definitely slow this morning.

'You're right. It was on the money, if understated.'

Of course, I didn't believe for a minute that she hadn't come over to interview me – my intuition was shooting up flares to get my attention. She definitely had an agenda, and now I was curious.

Thanks to my vampire-elders-enhanced emotion-sensing skills, it was easy for me to read the intentions of most humans and immortals. In Maxie's case, I wasn't picking up any negative intent. In fact, she gave off an appealing, whimsical vibe. If she really was just prowling for a story lead, I could hold my own; she'd get nothing from me. I was getting better at playing the media game.

She smiled wide, exposing perfect porcelain. 'Can I buy you a coffee?'

I pasted on a pretend-shocked expression. 'And you were saying *what* about not wanting to interview me?'

She held up one hand, as if she were preparing to be sworn in for testimony in a court hearing. 'I swear on a stack of *Dracula* novels that our conversation over coffee will be off the record. You're perfectly safe from the creeping tentacles of the Fourth Estate. What do you say? There's a Starbucks on the twelfth floor. Is that neutral enough territory?' She pointed to the elevator and plastered an innocent expression on her face.

Despite my usual tendency to retain an aloof, professional distance with anyone I met who might be even peripherally involved with my psychotherapy work, I was uncharacteristically tempted to relax my guard a little with Maxie. Surely it wouldn't hurt to be more open-minded? Probably – maybe. After all, I *had* been thinking about making more human friends lately, to balance the alternative. I wouldn't ever build any new relationships if I didn't step out of my therapist role occasionally. There's a fine line between being careful and being paranoid – a line I frequently tripped over.

'Coffee? Okay, that sounds good.' Now that I'd made the decision and opted for what would be a novel experience for me, I was actually excited about the idea of a few minutes of chitchat with another woman around my own age – and species – no matter what her ulterior motives might be. As fascinating as it was to spend so much time with the undead, I always felt like an outsider – an *other*. Not that I needed any help with that to begin with. 'I've got a couple of hours before my first client session of the day, so what the hell?'

'Great!' she said, and punched me lightly on the arm. 'I think we could both use a little more caffeine.'

I grabbed my coat off the pegs next to the elevator, and all the while we rode down to the twelfth floor Carson's sleazy, frantic voice squealed through the speakers, going on about 'mondo tits'. Comparatively speaking, I guess I'd got off easy.

'This is some good shit,' Maxie said as she held her coffee mug in both hands and inhaled the aroma. She closed her eyes and smiled, obviously in the midst of a religious experience.

I laughed and took a sip from my mug. Another coffee junkie: at least we had that in common.

As I waited for her to complete her euphoric java worship and open her eyes, I scanned the people in the room. Maxie was attracting a lot of attention, which wasn't too surprising when you factored in the outrageous hair, the model's face and body and some indefinable energy that radiated from her. And even though I'd got used to generating a little notice in a room myself lately – consorting with vampires tends to bring out a woman's wilder side – it was actually pleasant to be out of the spotlight.

'So. You want to know about the hair, right?' Maxie blurted, distracting me from my people-watching.

Suddenly, distant laughter echoed in my mind and something moved along the edge of my vision. I swivelled my head to investigate, but nothing was there. Goosebumps ran a marathon up my arms and I stared into my coffee, wondering if the special-blend-of-the-day contained an extra ingredient, or if I was simply having an anxiety attack. It was probably just another ghost – they'd become my constant companions. But after my unnatural experiences, I no longer took anything for granted, not even my sanity.

Especially not my sanity.

'Doc?'

'What?' I said as I surveyed the room and reminded myself I was in the 'normal' world – sitting in a restaurant. For the time it took to drink one lousy cup of coffee, I wanted to pretend there were no paranormal creatures waiting to jump out at me, nothing lurking in the shadows. Just regular nine-to-five types, dressed for corporate success, indulging in a bit of overpriced caffeine. Yeah, but what about the vampire who'd called the radio show? He'd really *felt* like a vampire, and a powerful one, at that. Thinking it was possible for one of them to walk around during the day blew all my carefully constructed denials out of the water. Months ago, acknowledging they existed in the first place had been mind-numbing enough. I didn't need the terrifying realisation that safety was a bigger illusion than I'd already assumed. Part of me longed for the innocent days before I fell into the crack between the worlds.

'Hello, Doc?' Maxie tapped my arm. 'You still with me? You're a little spacey.'

'Huh?'

My gaze snapped back to her fish-eyed stare and for a couple of seconds I couldn't remember where I was. I blinked and reoriented myself. What the hell was wrong with me? I did have a tendency to daydream, but not usually when I was speaking with someone. I'd worked really hard to learn to stay present with clients. She was right: I definitely needed more caffeine.

'Oh, sorry, didn't mean to float away on you. Not enough sleep, I guess.' I wiped the corners of my lips with a napkin. 'Yes, absolutely. I'd love to know about the hair. You've got to admit it's unique. When did it turn white?' Forcing the vampire thoughts aside, I relaxed into my chair, appreciating the opportunity to discuss something I wasn't required to give advice on or have an opinion about.

She scrutinised my face for a few seconds longer, one eyebrow raised, then grinned and scooped the thick whiteness back into a tail, holding it with both hands. 'When I was a kid, my hair changed overnight, from blonde to white. I simply woke up one morning with old-lady hair. Let me tell you what a shock it was to my family.'

Hmmm . . . she believes her hair changed overnight. Interesting. I wonder what really happened?

'There's no way your hair could ever be described as old-lady hair. It's gorgeous.' I studied her, guessing her age to be late twenties to early thirties, then asked, 'You simply woke up with white hair? Nothing in particular caused it?' If her hair had really transformed that quickly, there had to be a traumatic precipitating event. Maybe she'd been struck by lightning or experienced a severe fright – or, even worse, suffered an abusive incident. Changes that profound didn't just *happen*.

She stared off into the distance for a few seconds, then turned back to me. Her eyes serious, she said, 'Not that I've ever been able to remember.'

Okay, I didn't want to be interviewed, but I couldn't help turning the tables on Maxie. Once a therapist, always a therapist; lift up the rock and see what's underneath, that's my motto. I've never been good at small talk. And, besides, turn-about was fair play: I knew I was sitting with a reporter, and she knew what I did for a living. 'Were you examined by a medical doctor?'

'Sure – scads of them. Medical doctors and shrinks and hypnotists; nobody could come up with an answer, and since there weren't any negative effects – except for a few vague nightmares – beyond the colour shift, I just learned to live with it.'

A psychological mystery: did she know that offering such an intriguing interpersonal tidbit to a psychologist was like waving a red cape at a bull? I suspected her strange situation had been the real reason she'd sought me out. Maybe she'd begun to recall unwanted memories.

I opened my mouth to ask more questions and she scooted her chair closer to the table.

'So, do you believe in vampires?' Maxie fixed her eyes on mine, her lips spreading in a Cheshire-cat smile. 'Strictly off the record, of course.'

Talk about a quick change of topic – not to mention a masterful evasion. Apparently we were finished talking about her hair.

I smiled in appreciation of Maxie's tactics; she was probably a very good reporter. Since I definitely didn't want to discuss vampires, the wheels in my brain started spinning, kicking up mental dust, as I tried to think of something innocuous to say. I'm sure my inner struggle was obvious, because I felt various emotions surf across my face.

I must have hesitated long enough that she thought she'd better try something different, because she said, 'Okay, I'll go first. No interview, honest, just a simple conversation, two ordinary businesswomen talking about their daily lives. A couple of regular professionals, discussing alien abductions, vampires, werewolves, reincarnation, demonic possession and other everyday occurrences. Regular run-of-the-mill rock-and-roll.' Her voice picked up speed and volume as she spoke.

'I've been writing for this magazine for five years and I've heard every preposterous story you can imagine – I think I could surprise even you. In all that time, as I've investigated each bizarre allegation thoroughly, I've never come across anything that could be even remotely considered paranormal. Not one real vampire. No werewolves. No aliens. No demons. Just a lot of sick, weird, fucked-up humans craving attention or behaving very badly. I now know for a fact that what you see is what you get. There is no magic. There is no *Wizard of Oz*. Just the demented little man behind the curtain, pulling the levers.' She flopped back in her chair, breathless.

Her passionate diatribe had captured the attention of everyone in the coffee shop and the room was so quiet you could hear a vampire fang descend.

Noticing she was centre-stage, Maxie smiled, stood and spread her arms wide, acknowledging one side of the room, then the other. Her long veil of hair swayed as she moved.

'Thank you, America. Thank you for this honour. They like me! They really like me!' she said, imitating a famous old Academy Awards acceptance speech.

I straightened in my seat. *Holy crap – bipolar? Borderline Personality Disorder?* Either Maxie was a certifiable candidate for a rubber room, or she was the most free-spirited – definitely exhibitionistic – person I'd met in a long time, maybe ever. I really hoped it was the latter.

'Give 'em hell!' yelled a young man wearing a backwards baseball cap. He thrust his fist into the air and the other customers applauded.

She bowed dramatically, lifted her hair out of the way and dropped back into her chair.

'If I hadn't found fame and fortune as a magazine reporter, I woulda gone into acting. And who knows? If this job doesn't pan out, I still might.' She slapped her thigh with her palm, threw back her head and howled like a wolf.

Shit. She howled! Maybe we should head over to my office . . .

The other Starbucks customers applauded again, some howling back at her. Apparently they were used to her theatrics.

Temporarily setting aside my concerns about her mental health, I clapped along with the rest of the audience, giving her the benefit of the doubt.

'Don't mind me, Doc.' She drank from her mug, then patted my arm. 'I don't get many chances to perform, so I take my opportunities as I find them.'

I watched her bask in the adulation and decided she was probably normal-weird as opposed to clinically weird. 'Wow, you're passionate about your scepticism. No fence-sitting for you, eh?' I sipped my cooling coffee.

'Yeah, that's me. The Opinionated Cynic, the Know-It-All Pessimist. The Been-There, Done-That-And-Found-It-Boring Mocker. So, what about you? Are you a sceptic, or do you really buy all the stuff your clients try to sell?' She lasered her gaze to mine for a moment, then leaped up. 'Off to the powder room. Be right back.'

Yikes. Another mood shift.

'Okay,' I said, watching her hair disappear towards the bathroom. I played with the corner of the napkin, curling and uncurling it. Was I a sceptic? Tricky question. If she'd asked me six months ago, I'd have honestly said I agreed with her assessment completely: vampires, wizards, witches, ghosts, and all those other preternatural phenomena were all imaginary – or delusional. No rational person could believe in fairy-tale or horror-movie creatures of the night; no reasonable, sane person would give credibility to nocturnal creepy-crawlies.

But in the last half-year I'd peeked under the bed and found the monsters. There really was a vampire tapping at my window. Hell, forget tapping – Devereux didn't bother with a window, he just popped in wherever he wanted and dazzled me with his platinum hair and turquoise eyes. Scepticism was no longer an option.

Unless, of course, I'd gone completely bonkers and all my experiences could be explained away by a brain aneurysm or epileptic seizures. I took the possibility of medically-induced insanity very seriously – I'd actually gone as far as to have myself tested, just to rule out those probabilities, as the scientific part of me stubbornly refused to acknowledge what appeared to be happening. As glad as I was to find myself aneurysm-free, that meant the simplest explanations were probably true, or to paraphrase Sherlock Holmes, when analysing a complicated situation, after you remove all the unnecessary elements, whatever is left – no matter how peculiar – must be true. Not being able to blame the vampires on a brain disorder meant that the simple fact – that vampires exist – must be accurate. But just because I understood that twisted reality didn't mean I'd totally made peace with it, no matter how many vampire clients I had, or how enmeshed into the bloodsucking culture I had become.

Maxie waved her hand in front of my face and tapped my nose and I jumped. My gaze reconnected with hers.

'Shit, Doc, where'd you go? Does dementia run in your family? That was another long pause. You must drive your clients nuts with that silent, staring thing. I've never understood how you shrinks do that.'

'Sorry. I'm just distracted.' *I got enough sleep last night. What the hell's going on?*

'Should I go all Freudian and read something into it? Are you avoiding the topic?' She smiled with her mouth, but her eyes were serious, calculating.

'No, I'm not avoiding the topic.' I straightened in my chair and ignored the questions I saw in her eyes. 'I'm just thinking about how much I want to say. No matter what my personal opinion might be about vampires, I do have clients who either believe they're bloodsuckers or who want to become one. Even if you aren't interviewing me right now, it's possible you might be tempted to use what I tell you in a future article and I can't take the chance that my clients might be harmed. If I say I don't believe in the undead, that could crush the trust I'm building with my clients. If they think I'm humouring them, they'll feel betrayed and our progress will stop. So I can truthfully say that I'm keeping an open mind about whether or not vampires exist.'

Not bad – actually sounds plausible, especially as I'm keeping more than my mind open to the idea.

Maxie took a breath, maybe getting ready to ask another question, but I was on a roll now. 'I *will* say that I've seen things that shake my notions of what's real and what isn't. Even in my non-vampire-wannabe clients, the mind is capable of creating astounding things. Think about all the horrors humans have caused throughout the ages. It raises the question of who really are the monsters.'

'Yeah.' She sat back in her chair. 'You'll get no argument from me there. People definitely suck. Monsters are everywhere. I hear what you're saying about your clients, so I'll respectfully stop talking about vampires.' She clicked her spoon on the side of her coffee mug and absently ran her tongue over her front teeth for a few seconds. Her eyes were still riveted on mine, but she appeared deep in thought. 'This whole discussion has given me a terrific idea. Are you free this evening?'

My eyebrows crawled up my forehead. I hadn't expected that. Despite my intention to respond in my habitual way, with my standard 'I'm already committed' speech, I surprised myself by saying something totally different: 'Maybe. My plans are flexible. Why do you ask?'

Perhaps I really *was* willing to make some changes – to step outside my rigid social comfort zone. Whaddya know? Therapist, heal thyself.

She smiled widely. 'I've been invited to a vampire staking. Wanna come?'

CHAPTER 3

A vampire staking.

My mouth dropped open and I stared at Maxie. How silly of me to assume she'd suggest something totally inappropriate, like meeting for dinner, or going to a lecture, or maybe listening to a local jazz band. What was I thinking? That would've been the height of boredom, the epitome of the mundane, so pitifully human – why settle for routine when we could watch vampires being killed?

No, thanks. I've already seen that movie.

I closed my mouth and cleared my throat. 'Run that by me again?'

She threw back her head and laughed. 'Wow. I wish I could read minds right now, because I'd pay money to know what just flashed through your brain. You should've seen your face! Like I kicked your puppy. Or you thought the topic was serious.'

'You mean you were kidding about being invited to a vampire staking?'

'Oh, hell no – I get invited to that sort of weird shit all the time. Vampire stakings, werewolf hunts, devil-worshiping ceremonies, exorcisms, witch burnings – any and every freaky thing you can imagine. Welcome to my sick little world. It's all bullshit: blatant cries for attention from the perverts and deviants who populate my journalistic universe.'

'So you're covering the event for your magazine?'

'I am indeed. I've got to admit that sometimes the costumes and fake monster props are worth the price of admission. I know you're dedicated to helping the terminally confused, but in my line of work, the mentally ill can be downright entertaining. I thought you'd enjoy exploring another aspect of the vampire wannabe community. Wouldn't the Vampire Psychologist want to understand as much as possible about her potential clientele? Who knows, some of these folks might end up on your couch.'

If she knew how crowded my couch already was, and who – or *what* – regularly came to sit on it, she'd be in yellow-journalism heaven. As much as I wanted to make some new friends, I was pretty sure that Maxie's idea of fun dangled a little further over the abyss than mine.

She did have a point, though. Maybe it wouldn't hurt me to explore the twisted layers of the vampire community, wannabe and otherwise. I couldn't always just wait for the lost souls to show up at my office – after all, I still had a book to write. I wasn't willing to completely ignore the academic portion of my professional responsibilities, and a chapter about an alleged vampire staking could re-energise my muse.

Or not.

Now that I'd considered the possibility, even thinking about going to some vampire-inspired event with a reporter made my head hurt. I knew I was asking for trouble, even without my radar flashing.

Nope. Definitely need to stay home and wash my hair tonight.

I started to decline the invitation but I was interrupted by a small, rodent-like bald man who bounded into the coffee shop and scurried over to our table.

'Hey, Maxie. Boss wants ya, pronto. Deadline, ya know; chop-chop.'

He reversed direction and sprinted out as quickly as he'd entered.

'Yeah, thanks, Dave,' Maxie shouted at his retreating form.

'How did he know you were here?' I asked.

'I hide here as often as possible.'

'Why didn't they just call you?' I didn't see a phone, but she could have had one in her pocket.

'What's the good of sneaking off somewhere if I'm going to carry my cell phone with me? That sort of defeats the "hiding" part, doesn't it?' She gave an exaggerated sigh and tapped the tip of her index finger against the end of her nose. 'Officially putting nose back to grindstone now. I'll see you tonight.' She stood in a fluid motion, beamed me a mischievous smile and danced gracefully to the exit.

'Maxie, wait!' I leaped up out of my chair. 'I don't want to go to a vampire staking!'

The room went still.

I heard Maxie laugh as she reached the exit. She raised

one hand in the air, waving good-bye. 'No chickening out now, Doc. I'll leave directions to the vampire deal on your voicemail. See you there at 10 p.m. Hey. Nice ta meetcha.' Her last words were muffled by the closing door.

'Dammit to hell!' I slammed my palm down on the table, sending a spoon clattering to the floor. The metallic sound echoed in the silence, and immediately embarrassed by my theatrical overreaction, I eased down into my chair, folded my arms across my chest and scanned the sea of raised eyebrows. It was as if a cosmic *pause* button had been pushed. Everyone in the room was posed, frozen in place, staring at me. Maybe they were waiting to see what other temperamental outbursts I had up my sleeve. Too bad I couldn't make my head spin all the way around or levitate off my chair.

As far as I was concerned, the show was over. Elvis had definitely left the building.

The silence persisted for a few seconds longer and then, as if an invisible switch had been thrown, the noise volume resumed its normal level of controlled chaos.

I lifted my half-full mug and took a healthy swig before discovering it was cold. I glared at the cup like it was the cause of my meltdown. What the hell had I got so angry about? The radio show with Carson had been irritating and the conversation with Hallow disturbing, but I'd handled worse before without losing my cool.

It had recently occurred to me that my professional training had a downside. All my therapeutic reserve and ability to remain silent while integrating client information was great in a clinical setting, but it sucked big-time in interpersonal situations. I'd let Maxie manipulate me and it pissed me off, though I was angrier with myself than at her.

Of course I wasn't going to some pathetic gathering of attention-seeking occultists and rebellious goth teenagers. It didn't matter what Maxie thought was going to happen; I didn't owe her anything, and I'd made my decision blatantly clear. To my credit, I'd been open to doing something normal with her – something relaxing. It wasn't my fault that she was obsessed with her job.

Yeah, like I'm not obsessed with mine.

I slid the coffee mug to the centre of the table, gathered my things and strode to the door, grumbling under my breath.

In the hallway, the elevator doors popped open as soon as I pressed the *down* button, and Carson's voice blasted, 'Take it off! Take it all off!' from the speakers.

I cringed, reminded that no matter what kinds of para-normal monsters might be hiding in the closet, we humans were capable of spewing our fair share of ugliness into the world.

I felt a chill that had nothing to do with the temperature.

The downtown skyscraper housing the radio station was only a few blocks from my office. The thick fog and overcast skies of the morning had magically transformed into another of Denver's famous sunny, clear masterpieces. I rolled down my car window, trailed my hand through the brisk air and allowed the tight muscles in my neck and shoulders to relax. I hadn't realised how stressed out and tense I'd been. Evidently handling a brain-dead radio host and discovering the existence of a self-proclaimed day-walking vampire punched the needle on my weirdness meter higher than usual.

Springtime in the Rockies was as unpredictable as an adolescent's mood. The blizzard that had paralysed the area a few days ago, blanketing the Mile High City in several feet of snow, had retreated east, leaving us with an already melting winter wonderland, some much-needed moisture and postcard-perfect mountain scenery. Days like this reaffirmed why I chose to live here.

I pulled through the underground parking lot and cruised into my very own space, a smile easing across my lips. Even the garage was immaculate. I'd had my doubts about moving into Devereux's building when he offered last Hallowe'en – after all, who knew how long my relationship with the mysterious bloodsucker would last? But so far things had worked out well – better than well, actually, especially now that my mind was no longer an open book to him. Everything about my new arrangement – the architecture, furnishings, location – was a perfect reflection of Devereux's style and elegance.

Thinking about the scary, humiliating circumstances surrounding the move from my old office flipped my smile into a frown. I'd actually been kicked out – which was not something I'd be adding to my *curriculum vitae* anytime soon. Discovering the dead body and blood-soaked walls and carpets, a parting gift from the violent and mentally ill Brother

Luther, had left a bad taste in the building manager's mouth, and I couldn't really blame him. I hadn't quite forgiven myself for completely misreading the cues about the emotionally disturbed vampire, even though I hadn't yet accepted the possibility then, much less the reality, of vampires. Denial can be such a comfortable place to hide.

Of course, Brother Luther – and his murdering alter ego Lucifer – was no longer a problem, since his ectoplasmic mate had shown up in the nick of time to prevent him from draining me dry. Then she retrieved his soul and yanked him from the land of the unliving. I reckoned that experience had to rank as my most strange to date.

Soft Celtic music caressed the airwaves during the elevator ride to the main level of the building, where the doors parted without a sound, ushering me into an architectural marvel. Five months in residence hadn't yet dulled my appreciation of the breathtaking beauty of the gold and marble lobby. Devereux had spared no expense in creating a stunning space, filled with exquisite furniture and incredible artwork, including his own. The fancy address was the headquarters for most of his business enterprises. My counselling practice was the only 'outside' company allowed in, and I still wasn't comfortable with getting such special treatment, especially as I knew the 'reasonable' rent he charged me was a mere fraction of the market value. Luckily, as I said, denial is my friend.

I walked across the lobby, listening to the echoing clicks of my heels on the imported marble tiles as I made for the reception area. Victoria Essex waved a hand in greeting and gave a wide smile from behind her ornate desk. Of all the positive aspects of moving to this office, meeting Victoria had definitely been one of the highlights.

'Kismet! Isn't this a marvellous day?' Still smiling, Victoria shot out of her chair and glided over to me with her arms extended in preparation for one of her friendly hugs. Gathering me close, she squeezed enthusiastically, then stepped back, grasping my upper arms. 'Are you okay? I heard that Carson idiot on the radio this morning. Was he as big an asshole as he sounded? He made me seriously reconsider my vow to do no harm!' Her eyes sparkled with humour.

I leaned forward and gave her a quick peck on the cheek. '*Asshole* is an understatement. He's definitely toad material. Are you sure I can't talk you into casting just one little spell?' We both laughed.

'Can you come and sit for a minute? I haven't seen you for days.' Without waiting for my answer, she grabbed my free hand and tugged me over to a nearby couch.

Victoria was a study in contrasts. Her face always reminded me of a Shirley Temple doll I'd once seen in an antique shop: her naturally curly, golden-blonde hair was chin-length, with tight spirals framing a heart-shaped face. Sharp cheekbones, dimples, a straight nose and round, peridot-green eyes gave her the appearance of the exotic girl next door. Her body was a different story. It was voluptuous in the richest sense of the word – wide hips, rounded belly and generous breasts: the self-identified Wiccan Mae West. She was several inches shorter than me, but she favoured very high wedges, so we usually saw eye to eye.

Half the fun of coming to my office was checking out Victoria's daily wardrobe choice. She had a vast collection of flowing goddess dresses in vibrant colours and a never-ending supply of gemstone jewellery, much of which she made herself. Today's gown was vibrant green velvet.

In addition to being Devereux's building manager, she was the high priestess of a local coven of witches, and the owner of an Internet-based Wiccan ritual supply business.

She locked eyes with me, her face serious. 'Are you going to tell Devereux about the vampire hunter who called the radio show or do you want me to?'

The question took me by surprise and my jaw dropped – not only because Victoria had never mentioned vampires in any form before, but because the scary on-air bloodsucker had been very clear that none of the radio listeners could hear him.

My facial expression must have said it all, because she answered, frowning, 'Yes, I heard him. Every evil word. He's very powerful.'

My brain spun for a few seconds, questions lining up, elbowing each other as they all tried to cram through the doorway to my mouth. *Of course* she had to know about vampires – how could she work for Devereux for so many years without being aware of the fanged elephant in the room? 'I'll tell Devereux.'

Then I focused on the important point. 'Wait a minute. If you could hear him, then he lied about nobody being aware of our discussion. So why should I believe he was a vampire? He was probably just another lost soul nut-case seeking attention.'

She clasped my hand. 'No, he's exactly what he said he is. I could hear him because I have the unique ability to resist the powers of the undead. That's one of the reasons Devereux hired me – I'm his bloodsucker bullshit detector.'

I stared at her, speechless. Once again my reality basket turned out to be nothing more than a sieve, allowing trickles of long-held truths to stream away into oblivion. I'd been so eager to leap to my erroneous conclusions about sweet Earth Mother Victoria that I'd missed yet another train leaving the parallel universe station. Like everyone, I saw the world through my own expectations, beliefs and limitations, but I was continually astounded by the evidence of how narrow my lens really was – and how relentlessly I still clung to my notions of 'real'.

She grinned. 'New information, eh? I'm not exactly what you thought I was, right?' She patted my hand. 'I figured we'd get around to telling each other the truth one of these days. The vampire hunter showing up has just kicked the schedule's butt a little. I spoke up because I wanted to make sure you realised what you're dealing with. I think it's highly meaningful that he wanted to talk to you specifically.'

I licked my lips and cleared my throat, finally shepherding my wandering thought sheep into a herdable mass. 'Why *did* he want to talk to me? I've only been involved in the vampire community for a few months. I'm no expert – yet. Why focus on me?'

'That's a good question. Wish I had an answer. One thing's

certain: he wasn't telling you the whole story, and somehow you're involved, whether you want to be or not.' She paused, studying me. 'I guess being the love muffin of the most powerful vampire in Denver has its downsides, eh? You probably had no idea about all the undead drama you'd get tangled in. I'd be willing to bet nothing in your education or training even remotely prepared you for the last six months.'

I thought about responding, then pressed my lips together, still watching her. Victoria was giving me an opportunity to vent some of my frustrations – to share my confusion with someone else involved in all this freak-show weirdness. Working as a therapist was a lonely occupation to begin with, and choosing such a 'unique' clinical focus meant I couldn't even consult with colleagues, except for occasional phone calls with FBI profiler Alan Stevens or brief meetings with Ham the hypnotherapist and Michael the half-vampire clinician, who all knew the truth. It was getting harder and harder for me to censor myself with my own therapist, Nancy – I was certain she would be sending for the men in white coats if I really levelled with her. Having no ongoing healthy outlet for my own issues was a recipe for professional disaster.

And it wasn't as if I didn't like Victoria. From the first moment we'd met, the day I came to see the office Devereux offered, she and I had clicked – our Inner Children had bonded. However, something made me hold back. Maybe it was just my suspicious nature, but since she worked for Devereux, discussing my lover with her felt like crossing a mental field strewn with hidden psychic land mines.

She chuckled. 'I hope you're not a poker player, because your face reflects your every emotion. You wouldn't last ten minutes at the gaming table. Of course, I'm more perceptive than most, but you'd be a lamb to the slaughter.' She smiled softly. 'I just want you to know that I'm available anytime you need a shoulder or a pal. Yes, I do work for Devereux, but my first allegiance is to myself. I'm a very loyal friend. And I do happen to know Himself very well – warts and all. I'm aware of his intense personality. He's been a powerful immortal for so long that it doesn't usually occur to him that others might have different needs and desires. He tends to wear people down – like charming Chinese water torture!'

I relaxed and smiled. That was a perfect description of how Devereux continued to behave with me, even after our long discussions about his domineering nature and *healthy* ego a couple of months ago. I hadn't yet come to terms with all the dissonant emotions his gentle bulldozing caused, so maybe it wouldn't hurt to share a little.

'Charming Chinese water torture? What a great description of Devereux's communication style. You know, he's wonderful in so many ways – handsome, intelligent, creative, thoughtful – the man of my dreams, who just happens to be a walking corpse. But he wants me to acknowledge that I'm his long-awaited 'mate', and he isn't shy about pushing me in that direction. For some reason, my acceptance of that title is incredibly important to him – far more important than it should. I don't understand why it's such a big deal.' I shook my head. 'Why can't he just let our relationship develop slowly, so I can get used to it?'

'I don't think the word *wait* is in his vocabulary,' she said kindly. 'At least not in regard to you.' She lowered her voice and bumped my shoulder gently with hers. 'What's he doing, girlfriend?'

I smiled at the unfamiliar word, and appreciated her for it.

'Oh, just the usual – he's always popping in unannounced, doing his best to convince me that his plan for the evening is better than mine. I know he's gorgeous, and he smells good, and the sex is *great*. And there's no question that travelling through thought is amazing. But he's so . . . so *bossy!* He's always digging up yet another thing I need to be protected from or coming up with one more reason to treat me like his fragile possession – he just lifts that magnificent chin into the air and makes proclamations as if I have no right to have any opinions of my own. Most of the time I can't decide whether I want to jump on him or run screaming into the night.'

Victoria snickered, fanning herself.

I paused, realising I'd said more than I meant to. Apparently I really did need a friend to talk to: my therapeutic persona was definitely in danger of springing a leak. 'I'm sorry,' I said ruefully. 'I really do know better than to keep all my emotions bottled up – I know how messy it is when they finally spill out. Being a therapist is easy for me because my role is clear. It's strictly defined. Dealing with the rest of my life – well, that's what I've never been good with. And I'm definitely not myself today.'

She met my eyes and took my hand in hers. 'You're so

hard on yourself. If you think that controlled bit of self-disclosure was messy, remind me never to call you in the midst of one of my PMS-driven chocolate-fuelled pity parties. You'd have me locked up! Hey, I know. You should come to one of my coven's rituals. A little wild, sweaty dancing around a fire would do wonders for you.'

I swallowed loudly. 'Uh . . .'

She hooted out a laugh and squeezed my hand. 'Or maybe not. Since you just looked as horrified as if I'd asked you to run naked through the Sixteenth Street Mall, I'll assume your dance card for strange experiences is currently all filled up. Perhaps we'll put off your visit to Witch Central for a while longer.'

'Thanks, Vic.' *Whew. That was a close one. Barely dodged another bizarro bullet.*

'Here's some unsolicited advice about Devereux,' she said. 'He's one of the most terrifyingly powerful creatures on the planet, but he's got a loving soul. And he's trainable. If you let him manipulate you, he will; that's human – and vampire – nature. If you say "no", he'll have to deal. Stop being so nice!'

She put my hand back on my lap and patted it maternally. 'In short, don't take any of his shit!' Giving a theatrical witch's cackle, she stood and waved her arms through the air to indicate her territory. 'I'm always here, and my circle's always open to you.'

'You should've been a therapist,' I said, standing. 'You're pretty good at this interpersonal stuff.'

'I *am* pretty good at it, but therapy has too many rules.

It's too restrictive. I'm the Healer and Seer for my coven, so I get plenty of opportunities to build my skills. It's more fun to make things up as I go along. I hope this is only the first of many conversations we'll have. Remember: take no shit!'

'You're right. Take no shit!' I yelled, thrusting my fist into the air over my head and realising it felt good to get into the spirit of things. It had been a while since I'd simply had fun. Professional persona be damned!

Victoria's eyes went wide and she clamped her hand over her mouth. She was staring at the area behind me and I followed her gaze. Hesitating just inside the glass entrance door a number of people were huddled together. They appeared more inclined to bolt out of the building than to make the trek across the lobby.

My first client of the day, her fiancé and both sets of parents were right on time.

Shit.

CHAPTER 4

CHAPTER 4

The view from the bank of west-facing windows in my office was spectacular. I stood watching as the sun gracefully descended behind the high peaks of the Rockies, making its daily journey into the archetypal underworld: a solar Persephone, honouring its pledge to rendezvous with the darkness. Surreal colours arced across the sky, creating otherworldly designs, like angelic Rorschach blots.

Watching the amazing light show unfolding above the mountains helped me to put life – both mine and my clients' – into perspective. This enjoyable ritual gave me a few minutes to weave the threads of the day into a larger tapestry, to cling to the illusion of control.

Remembering the expressions on the faces of my client Deborah, her fiancé Scott and their parents I'd so startled in the lobby after my conversation with Victoria made me smile. I could've made up some excuse for the behaviour they'd witnessed, but I decided to follow the first rule of psychotherapy: when in doubt, say nothing. I've developed the 'therapist nod', that gentle up-and-down head motion performed by all counsellors, into an art form. It's like a compassionate invitation to surrender, offering the quintessential soft place to fall. There is something to be said for silent, unconditional, positive regard.

In the midst of my decompression daydream, my inner radar suddenly engaged and I sensed the change in the room's energy even before I heard the faint 'pops' that indicated the arrival of vampires.

I tensed. My next appointment wasn't due to arrive for a while, and since that client was always punctual – and came alone – I prepared myself for unexpected company.

'Hey, doll – er, Dr Knight.'

'Hello, Dr Knight.'

I spun to face the voices. 'Chain? Lucille?' My shoulders relaxed and I released the breath I'd been unconsciously holding. Comparatively speaking, the arrival of two members of the Fear of Fangs group was a lot less terrifying than any of the millions of other possibilities my brain had immediately projected onto my mental movie screen. 'What are you doing here? You're not on my schedule for tonight.'

'There was no time to make an appointment. We need your help bad,' Chain said. As always, his trademark chains were looped through his baggy blue jeans, wrapped around his biker boots and encircling his wrists. The tall vampire's long, stringy black hair framed a thin, pale, scarred face. Flat grey eyes stared from beneath bushy eyebrows and lashes so light they were almost invisible. He wore his familiar Harley jacket, as always.

'What do you mean? What's wrong?' I couldn't remember them sharing any crises at the last group meeting.

'We need to get married, Dr Knight,' Lucille replied in a quiet voice. She twisted her hands and chewed on her lower lip with her descended fangs. Her vibrant green eyes held a sheen of tears.

'Married?' I knew they had a sexual relationship, but I hadn't realised they were an actual *couple*.

Lucille must have been highly stressed because she usually dressed provocatively in short, tight clothing with theatrical-grade makeup and towering hair, but tonight she was acting out one of her schizophrenic religious delusions by wearing an orange Buddhist monk's robe. Her brown hair was secured in a tight bun at the nape of her neck.

'Yeah,' Chain replied with a deep sigh, frowning. 'We gotta.' He threw one arm across Lucille's shoulders and pulled her against him.

What? No way! That usually means a pregnancy, but these are vampires. Could it be possible?

Lucille burst into tears. She covered her face with her hands and started sobbing loudly.

Have we slipped into an episode of a 1950s sitcom?

'Both of you, come over here and sit down.' I pointed at the couch. They sat and I took the chair opposite them. 'What do you mean, "*you need to* get married"?' Wondering if I was about to hear something that would completely rewrite my knowledge of vampire physiology, I sat tensely on the edge of my seat.

But wait. If vampire pregnancy is possible, what does that mean for me and Devereux?

'It's really a downer, Dr Knight,' Chain whined. 'Both alternatives really stink.'

Tell me, already!

'Concentrate, Chain. Why do you have to get married?'

'It's a sin, Doctor!' Lucille wailed.

'No it isn't, Lucille. You're really fulla shit.' Chain jumped up and started pacing.

Oh. My. God! What the hell is it?

'Sit down, Chain. Just tell me the problem.'

He begrudgingly took his place on the couch again. 'She won't put out, Doctor Knight. She's derailed the nookie train. It's *awful*.'

'What?' I didn't know whether to laugh or scream.

'Every time she gets freaked out about something and goes all schizo, she puts on one of her religious costumes. One night she's Mother Theresa, then the next night the Pope, or Joan of Arc, then Moses – and when she's dressed like that, she says screwing is a sin. So half the time I've got blue balls. Now she says she won't come across at all unless we get married. You gotta talk her out of it because I'm too young to be tied down for ever.'

Speechless, I just stared at them, outrageously relieved that my small understanding of vampire reproduction – that they only made more of themselves by biting – remained intact. And that there would be nothing additional to worry about in my relationship with Devereux. I took a breath and cleared my throat, fighting against laughing out loud. 'It sounds like the idea of marriage is upsetting for you, Chain. We definitely need to talk more about that. Lucille—' I shifted my gaze to her. 'I hope you'll share your feelings about this situation. Did something happen to frighten you?'

Lucille sniffled, reached for a tissue, then blew her nose. 'I started having more visions, Doctor. I keep seeing myself burning in Hell. They started right after Chain caught me having sex with one of my human donors, when he pulled the guy off me, drained him and called me a whore.'

Hold on – he drained him?

'Chain! You killed a human?' I couldn't keep the shock off my face or out of my voice. 'You know Devereux's policy about feeding on humans. You can't kill them—'

'No! I didn't drain him. She's lying, as usual. But I admit I sucked his ass almost dry. He was alive when I threw him out the door and I saw him a few days later at The Crypt, so I know he's okay.'

Shit. These vampires are going to give me a heart attack.

'But you called her a whore? That's pretty harsh. I know that neither of you are sexually exclusive. Why would you say such a terrible thing to her? No wonder she had a psychotic episode. We've talked about this in group. You know better.' *And why does that word only apply to women?*

Chain sank down into the cushions and pulled his jacket over his head, covering his face.

'Lucille, why do you think you need to marry Chain? Do you love him?'

She rubbed her puffy, red eyes. 'I have to marry anyone I have sex with, whether I love him or not.'

Great. Guilt and shame for eternity.

'Anyone? Will you marry them one at a time or all at once?' I couldn't believe the ridiculousness of that question, but I wanted to shake her out of her anxiety trance.

She paused, tilted her head and stared. 'I never thought of that. Since I have sex with lots of people, I guess marrying all of them would be pretty messy.' Her expression went dead. 'I remember being called a whore when I was a mortal. It wasn't even true then, but I was punished. The word makes me afraid.'

Chain pushed the coat off his face. 'Well, shit, Lucille. I didn't mean to hurt you. I only got mad because I wanted to have sex with you right then and you were already busy. It pissed me off.' He leaned over and kissed her cheek.

Lucille squealed with delight, stood and wiggled out of the orange robe then, naked, jumped, onto Chain. 'I guess we don't have to get married if you won't call me that name any more.'

He licked one of her nipples and smiled. 'Okay. Let's go screw. Bye, Dr Knight! See you at group!'

'Yeah, bye!' Lucille said.

They vanished.

'Yeah. Glad I could help. Drop in any time,' I said to the empty couch.

I rose and walked to the window, shaking my head. Had that bloodsucking mini-session been any more clinically alarming than many of my human appointments? Truthfully, no. I could count on the fact that all my clients, alive, dead or undead, would come up with one preposterous thing after another. But at least the humans couldn't physically pop into my office. I made a mental note to remind myself to strengthen my boundaries with my nocturnal clients.

But all that aside, I had to admit, on a theoretical level, that contemplating the possibility of a vampire pregnancy had been exciting: the scientific discovery of the century. If I could ever tell anyone, of course.

There was another *pop* and a rich voice spoke. 'Good evening, Doctor Knight.'

My hand extended, I moved towards the elegantly dressed man who'd appeared in the centre of my office. He clasped my hand in his. 'Hello, Mr Roth. It's good to see you. Perfectly punctual, as always. Please, be seated.'

He gave a brief nod before settling himself in the middle of the nearest couch and arranging his ever-present briefcase next to his feet on the carpet. Then, as was his habit, he closed his eyes in meditation for a couple of minutes before speaking.

I used the time to shift from dealing with the chaos of Chain and Lucille to Mr Roth's sedate dignity.

A successful Denver attorney, he wore a handsome grey, Italian-designed business suit, a crisp white shirt and a red tie. His short black hair was slicked back from his wide forehead, Bela-Lugosi-style, and his dark brown eyes shone with intelligence underneath thick, arched brows. His nose was slightly too small for his slender face, and his chin a bit too large, almost as if he'd been taken apart and put back together using the wrong parts.

Although he gave the impression of being serious and businesslike, I'd discovered his sense of humour during our first session, when I'd asked about his decision to practise law after decades of being a vampire – he'd said it was natural for a bloodsucker to be an attorney. In fact, he'd said, the words were synonymous!

Since vampires had no need of lawyers, he represented the worst kind of human perpetrators – murderers, rapists, child molesters, mortal monsters of all varieties. When I asked why he represented the dregs of humanity, he told me he enjoyed the game, and corrected me when I wrongly assumed he meant the legal game. For him, it was all about winning the case – and seeing the person set free – before taking matters into his own fangs and draining him dry.

Justice, vampire-style.

Let's hear it for instant karma.

He'd come to therapy after resisting the urge to drain one of his fouler clients. He was afraid that had set an unhealthy precedent. We're currently exploring the issue.

I'd wondered how he managed his profession in the day-based legal world, but he told me he had a human colleague. His inability to function during normal business hours was inconvenient, but it wasn't an insurmountable problem. Apparently, Denver has a busy night court system.

I gathered my writing pad and pen before sitting in my usual chair.

He opened his eyes and lifted his index finger. 'Before we begin tonight, Doctor, I must apologise.' He paused dramatically. The combination of his entrancing vampire voice and the skills he'd perfected while orating before human juries when he was still mortal was impressive. It took all the grounding techniques I knew to remain unaffected. I didn't think anyone could resist his arguments. He had one of the most persuasive voices I'd ever heard, and tonight it was especially hypnotic.

I got the chills. *Whoa. Is he apologising for something he did, or something he's going to do? Sometimes I wish religious symbols really did affect vampires. It sure would be convenient to hide behind a cross or a Buddha statue once in a while.*

'Apologise, Mr Roth?' I smiled to mask my reaction to the sudden tingling in my solar plexus. He'd never done anything out of order, but he *was* a vampire and I'd be a fool to forget that, even with my enhanced protections. After all, nothing could mute the normal biological reactions triggered by being in the vicinity of a predator.

He shook his head, folding his hands in his lap. 'Ah, now I must apologise twice. First for needing to cut our session short this evening due to a rash of unexplained deaths, and second for allowing my distress over those deaths to cause my energy to become so intense that I made you uncomfortable. Please forgive me.'

My deodorant just said 'fuck it'.

I wouldn't even bother to claim I hadn't been afraid. He'd obviously sensed – or maybe *scented* – my fear, and I'm sure my heart was pounding loud enough for him to dance to.

'Devereux told the members of his coven your mind can no longer be read – he said it is to protect your brain because the elders hold you in high regard, and they intervened on your behalf. He asked us to do nothing to cause your emotions to spike, which might render the extra protections useless. So for the third time, I do most sincerely beg your pardon. I would not want to do anything to harm you. I rather enjoy our sessions. You've been exceptionally helpful.'

Holy shit! Devereux told his coven – some of whom are my clients – my personal business? What's wrong with him? Oh, wait, remember who I'm talking about. He simply does whatever he wishes.

'There's nothing to forgive.' I shook off the annoyance Mr Roth's revelation had triggered and willed the corners of my mouth to rise. 'I'm happy the sessions are beneficial to you.' Whatever I'd felt from him earlier had dissipated and my radar quieted. 'Tell me about these deaths.'

He gave a brief nod of acknowledgment and crossed his legs. His brow furrowed. 'It's all very strange: most vampires, especially young, weak ones, have little control over their appetites and impulses. Their world is violent, harsh, and dark. It isn't until we survive beyond the first few years that our true personalities emerge once again, and we start to have choices. Most of us can't even regulate our heart rate, breathing or body temperature for centuries.'

'Centuries? I hadn't realised the extent of the limitations.' *At least somebody is forthcoming with undead details.*

'Indeed. Newborns are relatively fragile. So, given that environment, new bloodsuckers occasionally turn up truly dead for one reason or another, although it's usually only a few per week, at most.' He uncrossed his legs and leaned forward. 'Over the last month, though, there have been scores, all over the city, dying like flies – vampires, and some humans, too.'

Uh-oh: déjà vu.

'How are they dying?' My stomach muscles contracted. What a coincidence that a certain vampire hunter had recently arrived in town.

'That's the odd part: there's no cause of death. None of the victims were drained of blood, and they had no apparent wounds. They simply ceased existing.'

My notepad fell onto the floor. 'But how is that possible?'

'That's the question, and I don't have an answer. In the meantime, I now have the uncomfortable task of defending clients who are actually innocent, who simply managed to stumble across a dead body in the wrong place at the wrong time.' He checked his watch and stood. 'But as I said, I must end our session early this evening. So much carnage, so little moonlight. Oh, but before I forget' – he opened his briefcase, removed a thick book and handed it to me – 'here's the reference material I said I'd bring tonight. I'm sure you'll find it enlightening.' He bobbed his head in a brief, formal nod. 'I will see you at our regular time next week. Hopefully, I will have good news. Until then.'

He vanished.

Even after months of watching vampires move via thought, it was still an exciting – and discombobulating – occurrence. I didn't expect to ever fully acclimatise to it.

I examined the weighty textbook he'd given me, *Sociopathic Lawyers: Monsters in Plain Sight,* and said aloud, 'Yikes. Definitely grist for the therapeutic mill.'

Deciding I'd deal with Mr Roth's love-hate relationship with his legal persona at our next session, I set the book on a table, retrieved my notepad from the floor, rose and walked over to the window, contemplating the disturbing information he'd shared. Was Hallow powerful enough to kill vampires and humans without leaving a trace? Devereux probably knew, but he was unavailable, so I couldn't tell him about the new bloodsucker in town. Yet.

The unexpected change in schedule left me feeling disconnected. I hated to admit it, but I'd come to rely on Devereux's companionship, and when he was off being Master of the Vampires or International Mega-corporate Genius, I missed him.

'You're pitiful, Kismet. Time to get a life,' I said aloud.

An enticing aroma caressed my nostrils, I heard a familiar *pop* sound behind me and a velvet voice inches from my ear whispered, 'What kind of life would you like? The possibilities are limitless.' Soft lips trailed kisses down my neck and my brain cells scrambled.

Devereux . . .

I began the mental hum, which had become automatic in the presence of vampires. So far, it kept me from getting killer headaches or turning into a lobotomised zombie around powerful bloodsuckers. My breath caught and it took me a couple of tries before I found my voice.

'You're back. There's something I wanted to ask you. If I could only remember what it was . . .'

Or why I'd want to use my mouth for talking when it could be put to much better uses.

'Later.' He kissed my jaw and I was undone.

As always when Devereux was near, my body rolled out the hormonal red carpet. I relaxed against his chest and savoured his arousing fragrance, and the softness of his hair tickling the side of my face. My heart rate increased and my breath went shallow. Formerly functional knees softened. I was never sure if my reaction to his presence was excitement or fear, or a little of both. I used to wonder if my body responded to him only because of his powers as a master vampire, or if I was simply *that* attracted to him. After having his mind-muddling effect muted by the elders, it was a relief to know that my feelings – and lust – for him were purely natural.

He couldn't read my thoughts any more unless I was in the throes of some intense emotion – and I tried to keep myself calm to avoid that – but he'd become very good at interpreting my visible cues.

I closed my eyes and enjoyed the moment. Even though I was no longer unduly influenced by his presence, I still thought there *had* to be something wrong with how powerfully he affected me. It couldn't possibly be psychologically healthy for me to think about leaping on him within seconds of his approach or to want to cling to him like a cheap Spandex suit. I'd got better at reining in my impulses, but it was still a struggle.

Nobody should have a face that gorgeous. Or eyes so magnetic. Or a body so enticing. It just wasn't . . . *normal*.

Right, Kismet. He's a vampire – as if anything about him could ever be normal.

He slid his hands up and down my arms, then stroked my hips through the soft, form-fitting fabric of my dress and moaned softly. His tongue flicked along my neck and I lifted my chin to give him better access to his favourite pulsing vein – allowing Devereux to drink my blood while we have sex pushes my orgasm into the stratosphere. I shivered, acting like a shameless addict, jonesing for the sharp needle-points of his teeth to pierce my skin and provide the fix I craved.

Instead of biting, he just nibbled gently, then let go.

I groaned in disappointment.

He whispered against my ear, 'I love how you desire me. I can feel your need.'

I could feel his . . . need . . . too, pressing against me.

Shouldn't I be annoyed by his ego, his arrogant assumption that I want him? The fact that it's true is beside the point, isn't it? I think I'm going to need to sit down soon. Or maybe lie down. Yeah, lying down would be much better.

'Look at me, Kismet,' he whispered.

Geez. What is it with that voice?

'Look at you? Nope, that's always trouble. I think I'll just stay right where I am, rubbing myself against your *throbbing manhood*, as they used to say in romance novels.'

'My throbbing manhood?'

Something about the way he'd said those words, with his old-fashioned manner of speaking and his European accent, made me laugh – in fact, I laughed so hard that he gasped as I vibrated against his erection. Since he rarely sucked in air on purpose, much less allowed anyone to catch him by surprise, I was intrigued; I simply had to look at him.

I turned, and the view was worth the trip.

He'd tilted his head back, closed his eyes and parted his lips just enough so that the tips of his fangs glistened. His beautiful light blond hair flowed down his chest, soft and touchable. He was dressed in his usual snug black leather trousers, and a vibrant blue silk T-shirt clung to his well-toned body, displaying it to perfection.

I studied him, my heart pounding in lustful anticipation. He truly was an unusually beautiful man. He opened his eyes, and I felt myself falling, almost as if the carpet I'd been standing on had liquefied, and I sank into a blue-green universe. I'd never been totally sure what colour his eyes were. What's the difference between turquoise and aqua, anyway? Obviously arousal brought out the best in his devilish orbs, because they sparkled like gemstones. Or maybe it was a vampire thing. He gave a slow blink and a wicked smile quirked his lips. He slid his arms around my waist and pulled me close for a kiss.

Without any more hesitation I looped my arms around his neck, fitted my body tightly against his and kissed him back. His mouth was wonderful; as he teased his tongue through my lips I opened for him, inviting him to take more. Regardless of any doubts I might have about my relationship with Devereux, our sexual chemistry was never in question.

Part of me was lost in the delicious things his tongue was doing, but another part noticed the fact that we were standing in front of the window for all of Denver to see, and as soon as I thought that, I broke the kiss and nodded towards the glass. 'Maybe we should take our reunion somewhere more private,' I suggested.

'Yes. Privacy. I totally agree.'

The office suite consisted of several rooms, one of which was a bedroom. Clients would never know what was behind that door, but Devereux and I had made ample use of it since I moved in, and I knew just what he had in mind when he scooped me up into his arms.

He thought us into the bedroom. Moving through thought used to jar my equilibrium, but now I found it energising. For some reason, I'd had far more difficulty believing bodies could shift through time and space than acknowledging the surreal fact that the world was populated with horror-movie creatures. Thinking of it, I really did have to give my brain credit for learning to deal with the impossible on a daily basis.

Lighting the candles scattered throughout the area with his mind, he deposited me onto the large bed, which was covered with a white silk comforter. I sighed with pleasure as my body relaxed into the soft cloud of fabric.

Oozing sexuality, Devereux stood next to the bed, staring at me. He tugged his T-shirt over his head in one smooth motion, leaving his pale chest bare except for the unique medallion he often wore. The necklace appeared ordinary enough, but I'd seen it flare like a beacon. I didn't care what tricks it could perform, though. I was more interested in the muscular body it was nestled against.

I thought about the near-true-death experiences he'd had since I met him, though he never mentioned them, and something in my expression must have drawn his attention, because he cocked his head and smiled.

'Even without the ability to read your mind, it is easy to interpret the expression on your face, my love. You need not worry about me. I have fully recovered, and am stronger for all my challenges.' He slid his hand down the flat plane of his stomach and popped open the button on his trousers. 'Let me prove it to you.'

Various parts of my body grinned, jumped up and down, and yelled, 'Yippee!' The rest of me held my breath, reaching for the mental popcorn.

He hooked his thumbs into the waistband and guided the leather down his legs. His long platinum hair fell forward like a silky curtain, and I had a sudden urge to grab that curtain and pull him down on top of me, but I resisted. It was much more fun watching him disrobe and crawl onto the bed – much more arousing.

His naked form definitely qualified as eye-candy: long and lean, with muscles in all the right places. He was always comfortable in his own skin, so at ease with his nudity – I guess it was to be expected that he'd enjoy it after all the centuries he'd inhabited that skin.

'Eternity as a sex object. What man could ask for more?' I put my thoughts into words.

'I am interested in being a sex object only for you,' he said as he lay on his side and stretched out next to me. He braced his head with one hand and smiled, watching me. Then he trailed a finger across my lips. 'You are wearing entirely too many clothes. What might we do to correct that situation?'

Bursting with ideas, I rolled towards him and let my gaze slide down his body, allowing my eyes to take detours in order to appreciate the natural wonders along the route. One monument in particular stood out from the scenery and my hand reached over to explore.

Devereux groaned. There simply was nothing like a lusty Devereux groan. His voice was always enticing and magical, but the erotic sensuality he layered into that deep, growling sound sent waves of pleasure through my body, hardened my nipples and caused moisture to pool in my nether regions, it was so good.

I tightened my fingers around his erection, then slowly released my grip. 'I know just what to do with all these clothes,' I whispered. I kicked off my shoes and heard them land on the lush carpet. Then, pretending to be a stripper popping out of a cake, I sprang to my feet on the bed, peeled the soft dress over my head and tossed it onto the floor. Next went my black lace bra and matching panties. I bounced up and down on the mattress a couple of times, just for the fun of it – causing the bloodsucking hunk at my feet to bark out a laugh – then threw myself down on my back. Smiling, I fitted my naked body against his. 'So, where were we?'

His eyes sparkled mischievously. 'Let me see if I remember.' He smoothed the palm of his hand over my breast and pinched my painfully hard nipple, then he leaned in, caught my lower lip between his teeth and descended fangs and gave me a playful nip.

I gasped and he pulled away, probably thinking he'd hurt me, so to show him the error of his conclusion, I circled his neck with my arms, guided him in closer, pressed my lips to his and eased my tongue into his mouth. I'd been surprised to learn during our first sexual encounter that Devereux loved to have his fangs sucked on, as much as another part of his anatomy – in fact, sliding my tongue up and down his canines had much the same effect as what I planned to do next.

I started to slide my fingers down towards the hardness pushing against my stomach when he captured my hands, raised them over my head and climbed on top of me.

He used his legs to nudge mine apart and with no more foreplay, slid deep inside, and I moaned. *Oh, yeah. That's a good plan, too.*

He lifted his mouth just enough to mumble, 'I have missed you these last few days. I hate it when I must be away, but it cannot be helped. All I could think about was this – filling you, having you wrap your legs around me while I make love to you. Listening to your heartbeat. Possessing you.' He lowered his lips back to mine.

Whoa. That was pretty much all I could think about at that moment as well.

His wish came true as his thrusts grew more vigorous, and I tightened my legs around his hips and took him as deep as I could. Within seconds, a delicious orgasm built and I felt his subtle contractions as he approached his own edge.

Giving another marvellous groan, he broke the kiss and whispered, 'Will you give me your blood, my love?'

'Definitely yes,' I mumbled, turning my head so he could lick the welcoming vein in my neck.

Geez – what is it about that question? Why does it always melt me into a puddle of hormonal goo?

He angled his head, kissed his way down my exposed throat and gently pushed the tips of his fangs through my skin. His soft hair flowed across my breasts and we both moaned.

Having him thrust inside me while sucking blood from my neck was the most extraordinary feeling, and wave after wave of pleasure pulsed through my body. The sense of being separate dissolved and we became one being, completely merged, soul to soul, each experiencing the other's arousal and release. Vampire sex with Devereux was an off-the-chart thrill.

I screamed as my body spasmed in bliss, my muscles contracting around his erection as he came too. After a few seconds more he lifted his mouth from my vein, slid his tongue over the tiny holes to stop the bleeding and brought his lips back to mine.

Tasting my own blood on his lips had become exciting – intimate. I'd grown accustomed to the flavour – I even wondered occasionally what it would be like to sample his on purpose. Of course, I wouldn't do that – the elders had warned me about drinking Devereux's blood. They said that because I had drunk it during a protection ritual, now they couldn't just cast a spell on me to protect my brain. So I certainly didn't want to complicate my life any more than it already was. And even though Devereux had assured me that the process of becoming a vampire was much more intricate than portrayed in books or movies, I didn't want to take any chances.

How could I possibly exist without margaritas or chocolate?

Sensing him staring at me, I opened my eyes.

He raised his head, slid his tongue over his upper lip and smiled down at me. 'I apologise for being so impatient, for leaving out the delightful *foreplay*, as you call it, but I simply could not restrain myself.'

'Well, I guess I'll forgive you this time.' I pretended to be serious. 'Although I wouldn't want you to get into the habit of ignoring the appetiser in favour of the entrée.' Devereux definitely gave good appetiser.

'Not to throw cold water on this tender moment,' I said, 'but you're getting a little heavy there, Fabio. Do you think you could scoot that delicious body of yours over a little so I can breathe? Some of us don't have the choice of whether to suck in air or not, you know.' Calling him Fabio was a little joke between us. He didn't really resemble the ageing cover model but he understood what I meant by the reference.

In the blink of an eye, he was lying next to me. 'How careless of me. I would not want to suffocate the love of my life.'

'The love of your life?' I turned to him. 'That's an odd thing for a vampire to say, isn't it, since you're not really *alive* in the normal sense of the word?'

He frowned. 'Are you still troubled by the state of my existence? Is that why you will not accept your role as my mate and take your place in my world?'

Here we go again. Shit. I pressed my lips together.

'I do not wish to upset you with these discussions,' he continued, 'but we must resolve this issue.'

'Why?' I sat up. 'Why is it even an issue? What aren't you telling me?'

He shifted his body to sit in front of me. 'It is not a matter of that; the truth is that I am still attempting to understand your importance to me. The urge to bond with you is great, but the explanations elude me.'

'*Bond with me?* What the hell does that mean? You haven't mentioned that before.'

'No, you are correct; I have not expressed it in those exact words, but I have spoken of our deep connection and our destiny.'

'Wait.' I wagged my finger at him. 'Are you talking about the portrait of me – one you claim to have painted eight centuries ago? *That's* what you're basing all this on?'

Okay, I do believe he had a psychic vision of me eight hundred years ago and he painted a portrait where I wore the blue silk blouse I've owned less than a year, but I'm making a point here . . .

'My claim?' His frown deepened and he raised his chin. 'As if I am not telling the truth?' He glared at me, his eyes darkening. 'The painting is part of it. I have since gone back in time to explore the lifetime you and I shared prior to that—'

'What?' My eyebrows shot up my forehead. 'Are you talking about reincarnation? You've got to be kidding.' *Oh, please! Time-out on the weirdness.* 'There's no scientific proof of any such thing—'

'Yes,' anger heated his voice as he interrupted me, 'just as there is no proof for the existence of vampires, yet anecdotal evidence has apparently been enough to convince you of that reality.' He grabbed my hand and pressed it against his chest. 'I am proof that there are more things than your science can understand.'

He had me there, but I wasn't interested in being logical. He'd had eight hundred years to accept all the mind-bending information he'd thrust upon me during the past months. My brain hadn't finished processing all I'd already discovered, and there he was, adding more straws to the camel's back. The camel was getting pissed off.

Taking a long, slow breath to calm myself, I withdrew my hand from his chest. I didn't want to have the same old argument with him, but I was determined to stand my ground. My recently acquired ability to sense his emotions was both a blessing and a curse. It was easy to get distracted by what I knew, if it contradicted what he said; in this case, his heated words masked dread.

Why does this topic upset him so much?

'Okay.' I locked eyes with him and kept my voice dispassionate. 'I'll concede the possibility of reincarnation, and anything else you've got tucked away in your supernatural bag of tricks, but you've got to stop pushing me. You're trying to force me to accept a role that I've had no part in creating, and it's my decision to make. I understand that you've been around for ever and you're used to calling the shots, but I'm not one of your minions. I'm not a handmaiden to the Master. I know things were different when you were human, but in my world, a woman isn't property. I'm a professional. I'm my own person, and I intend to remain so. Is that something you can – er – live with?'

His expression went flat, as if all his feelings had been swept under a mental rug. 'It was truly never my intention to bully you in any way. Nothing is more important to me than being with you.' His eyes softened and he slid his finger across my cheek, nudging a stray hair. 'You are absolutely correct, I am used to giving orders and expecting obedience. It is only recently that I have come to realise that might not be an effective way to create a modern relationship.' He paused as an expression of sadness shadowed his face. 'Often, it is like I have existed for ever, and for ever can be a very long, lonely time. I give you my word that I will work hard to join the twenty-first century.'

I couldn't help but smile: a gorgeous vulnerable, sad fallen angel was just too much for my Inner Therapist to ignore. I had asked him early on to explain why he was so stuck in the past, why he spoke with such a heavy accent, and used antiquated words. He told me he'd always preferred the past until he met me; he had spent most of his time there. I thought he was talking about reliving memories, but he meant it literally. He said it was a matter of splitting his attention – of holding aspects of himself in both times and places. *Uh-huh. Right.* I added that to my list of things to figure out later. Soon I'd need a degree in Quantum Physics to be able to understand him.

'Okay, oh, great and all-knowing Master, let's kiss and make up. We'll agree that I won't psychoanalyse you and you won't coerce me. Do we have a deal?'

He lifted my hand and kissed the palm, his shining aqua eyes gazing at me from beneath long dark eyelashes. 'We do, indeed.' A devilish grin slid across his lips and he leaned forward, pushing me back against the bed with his motion.

I laughed and wrapped my arms around his neck, pulling him close for a deep kiss. In the midst of appreciating the little lust fires breaking out all over my body, I *heard* a husky voice in my mind.

'Doctor Knight. I had no idea you were so . . . passionate. What a conquest you will make.'

What? That's impossible – vampires can't access my conscious-ness any more. I froze in mid-writhe, reeled in the tongue I'd been exploring Devereux's tonsils with and said against his mouth, 'Conquest? Hallow?'

Devereux jerked up and stared at me, a horrified expres-sion on his face.

'Why did you just say "Hallow" – are you talking about Lyren Hallow? How do you know the Slayer? What conquest?'

My head spinning, disoriented, I mumbled, 'Oh, yeah, I was supposed to tell you – I can't believe I forgot . . . A day-walking vampire named Lyren Hallow called the radio pro-gramme I was on this morning and said he'd come to kill someone I know. He said he'd heard of me, and—'

Devereux vanished.

CHAPTER 5

'—wanted to meet me. Hey! What the hell?'

I rolled off of the bed and walked from one side to the other, lifting the corners of the bedding to peek underneath, although of course I knew that was stupid, that Devereux wouldn't be there. But I couldn't stop myself from searching. I had to do something. After a few seconds, I stood naked in the centre of the room, hands on my hips, scowling.

He'd done lots of popping in and out since I'd known him, but he'd never simply vanished when I was in the middle of a sentence. How rude! Then I laughed at myself: as if vampires ever worried about impressing Miss Manners.

His clothes were still on the floor where he'd left them, which meant – wherever he was – he was nude. I chuckled out loud, thinking about him showing up somewhere in the altogether. He must have been really upset about Lyren Hallow to suddenly blink out like that. It was rare for him to have such a strong reaction to another vampire.

The edgy voice in my head a few moments ago had caused the same fuzzy reaction as it had during the radio programme. The unusual tone of his voice had an oddly intoxicating effect on me, even more so than the vampire voices I was used to – and it was only after the fact that I felt creeped out by my uninvited visitor. I hadn't been in any hurry to show him the door while he was slithering around inside my brain. So what did it mean, that a vampire could invade my mind anytime he wished, despite the protections I'd been given?

'And what *did* he mean by conquest?' I asked nobody.

Devereux popped back into the room a few inches in front of me. 'He meant exactly what he said.' He collected his clothes and began dressing. 'You should have told me immediately that you had been contacted by that madman and I would have taken steps earlier to protect you. I have been so distracted by having to mediate in a feud between two vampire covens that I did not realise Hallow had arrived during my absence, although I am certain he planned it that way. But that cannot be helped. I have made arrangements for you to move into my penthouse. We will go to your place first to gather clothing and supplies. You may return to your home when Hallow has been dealt with.'

He bent down and retrieved my dress from the floor. 'Here, put this on while I find your shoes.'

Fetch. Heel. Roll over. Play dead.

I took the dress, stomped to the bed and sat. Here he was, doing it again: proclaiming yet another crisis I needed to be protected from, exactly like the two thousand previous dramas that had turned out to be much ado about nothing.

'Ignore him,' said the disturbing voice in my mind. 'He is trying to control you again.'

Huh?

Devereux picked up my shoes and walked towards me. 'Kismet, you are not dressed. What are you waiting for?'

'I'm waiting for the courtesy of some answers,' I said, trying to keep my voice calm. 'What was it you were saying earlier about not wanting to bully me? What do you call this?'

An arrogant expression on his perfect face, he made a dismissive gesture with his hand. 'We have no time for this now. It is important that you be somewhere safe – somewhere I can watch over you.'

Imprison me, you mean. If I'm not careful, you'll stick me in one of those old dungeons underneath The Crypt – entirely for my own good, of course. No way do you get to flick me off so easily.

'Well, make time, your Majesty, because I'm not going anywhere,' I said with a strained voice, struggling to hold back a sudden tidal wave of anger. When had I lost control of my life so completely? I'd obviously been too accommodating. 'Who is Lyren Hallow, and why is he such a big deal?' I demanded. 'You called him the Slayer. What did you mean by that?'

He glared at me, his own anger spiking. 'You need to stop being unreasonable. I will tell you everything as soon as we are in my penthouse where there are magical protections in addition to vampire security. This is no time for you to misbehave.'

My jaw dropped. 'Excuse me? *Misbehave?*' My voice acquired banshee overtones. 'You're treating me like a naughty child again. Being older than dirt doesn't give you the right to be condescending.' I redoubled my concentration on the hum, even though it hadn't kept Hallow from intruding, and forced myself to calm.

Devereux opened his mouth to say something, changed his mind, and sighed impatiently. 'Please, put on your dress and shoes. I do not wish to transport you naked, but I will if necessary.'

Okay, he's still bossy, but at least he didn't just zap us out of the room whether I liked it or not. Is that progress?

I simmered, studying him for a moment, trying to figure out why he was so spooked. It would have been easy for me to launch into the next verse of our familiar song about his domineering attitude, but the expression on his face, his taut body language and the anxiety rolling off him in waves made it clear I wasn't going to win this one.

'Okay,' I said, sliding my dress over my head, 'I'll let you take me to my townhouse, since that was my destination anyway, but when we get there, we're going to talk.'

He gave a quick nod, then without even waiting for me to put my shoes on, he wrapped his arm around my waist and we rode the vampire express.

We materialised in my living room and I swayed gently when he let go. It usually took me a moment to become steady on my legs. The experience reminded me of roller-skating when I was a kid: after wearing the skates for so many hours, navigating flat surfaces always felt weird.

My depth-perception was out of whack now, my eyesight fuzzy.

I padded over to the couch and flopped onto the cushions.

Devereux followed me and gave me an annoyed glare. 'What are you doing? You should be gathering your clothing – we must go to my penthouse.'

I pasted on my best bland expression and spoke conversationally, trying hard to keep my inner she-beastie in her cage. 'I told you: I'm not going anywhere until you tell me what's going on. You've got to admit that you've declared several emergencies in the short time I've known you, and all of them – since you disposed of Lucifer – were false alarms.'

He opened his mouth, but I held up a finger.

'For example, what about the time you woke me in the middle of the night, insisting I was in danger from one of your ex-lovers who happens to be a real Goddess? You said she threatened to set me on fire—'

'Yes, I was given that information on good authority. Maeve is mentally unstable. I have seen what she has done to rivals in the past—'

'But she didn't do anything to me. And then shortly thereafter you stuck me in a sub-basement of The Crypt because you heard a rumour about a nonexistent vampire uprising. Or later, when you burst in on one of my evening therapy sessions, insisting the client in question was about to kidnap me so he could ask for a huge ransom.'

He continued to glare.

'Isn't that true?' I stared up at him expectantly. 'Or the time you hid me under the Eiffel Tower—'

'The number of averted crises is irrelevant. All that matters is that you were safe.'

'There were no crises to avert, and you know it. Every time, I argued that there was no cause for concern, but you wouldn't listen. Admit it, you overreacted.'

'I admit no such thing.' His chin jutted into the air.

'You are essentially teaching me not to take you seriously.'

'What? Do not be ridiculous – you must take me seriously. This situation is different.'

'Yeah, that's what you always say.' I patted the couch beside me. 'Why does this Lyren Hallow upset you? Who is he? You might as well sit down and tell me, because nothing else is going to happen until you do.'

He scorched me with his gaze for a few seconds, then raised one perfect eyebrow, sighed theatrically and sat next to me.

'Well, maybe you can teach an old dog new tricks.' I grinned.

'Dog?'

'Never mind.' I imitated the dismissive gesture he'd used earlier. 'Tell me about Lyren Hallow.'

He held up his hand, palm towards me, his voice cold. 'You must stop saying his name. In the magical world, speaking someone's name is an invitation. It is especially important for you not to call him, since he has already accessed your thoughts and influenced your behaviour, despite your reinforcements. You must discipline yourself to avoid even thinking it.'

'What are you talking about?' I asked. 'Nothing's wrong with my behaviour; this is my normal reaction to your bullying.'

'Is that so, Doctor Knight? You would not say your tone of voice is irregular?'

'Hell, no!' I said, too loudly.

'See what I mean? That is not your usual manner of speaking.'

'Bullshit. Wouldn't I know if I was behaving differently?'

'Really? Were you aware of my effect on you when we first met last October? Did you realise that your heightened interest in sex and your increased awareness of men in general were caused by dormant desires I had awakened in you? At the time, you said you found yourself attracted to several men – in fact, you judged yourself harshly because of it.'

'Are you saying you did something to me?' My fists clenched. 'You caused my reactions?'

'Yes – but not intentionally. I simply enhanced your . . . repressed . . . sexuality.'

I *had* thought it was odd that I was attracting so much male attention back then, and he was right about me being repressed, so I couldn't really take issue with what he was saying. But how irritating that he hadn't told me then – and how *arrogant*.

'You could've said something, you know, instead of letting me beat myself up about it.'

'Yes.' He shrugged. 'I suppose I should have, but there has never been an appropriate moment.'

My heart pounded. 'Never an appropriate moment?' The pitch of my voice rose. Inhaling deeply, I took a few seconds to talk myself down from the rage cliff. 'But you have plenty of time to warn me about this hunter guy? And why *can* he read my mind? I thought I was protected – that was the whole point of drinking that horrible blood smoothie Zephyr gave me.' I shuddered at the memory of the taste.

Devereux closed his eyes for a few seconds, probably mentally counting to ten, or whatever vampires did to soothe themselves, then he refocused on me. 'This individual is the oldest vampire on the planet – so old that I cannot even imagine the mind of such a creature. Something happens when one lives so extraordinarily long: a change occurs and time itself begins to distort the neurons, causing a stronger reliance on the old brain – the primitive mechanisms.'

A tingle ran through me as I suddenly remembered what Dracul had said about there being another immortal much more powerful than he: his maker. *Holy shit.* My stomach clinched. A brain-damaged, nuclear-grade bloodsucker running loose, and focused on me. Could things get any worse? 'Oldest vampire in the world?' I whispered.

'As far as we know.'

'What's he doing here?' I asked.

'Hunting, just as he said.'

'You communicated with Victoria?' *Did he contact her in his mind, or make an impromptu naked visit? She's probably used to that.*

'Yes, we spoke mentally. She is amazingly good at cutting through vampire lies and deceit.'

'Tell me about him.' I knew that sounded like a therapy line, but I really wanted to know why everyone was so nervous about this particular immortal.

Devereux gathered my hand into his. Lecturing always calmed him. 'Humans are predators, of course, and vampires even more so. In this ancient's case, the rapacious instinct has been heightened beyond all known limits. The thinking part of his brain continues to evolve and expand, but it is governed by a dark, evil nature. He is, in essence, the perfect killing machine, but as the centuries wear on, he has become more violently sadistic. Merely destroying his human food no longer satisfies him. He requires ever-greater stimulus, and takes particular pleasure in torture and misery, so he has switched to butchering his own kind. To all intents and purposes, he is no longer a vampire, for he has mutated into something unknown: a malevolent *other*. He has a stable of female slaves to serve his needs, and he adds to it frequently.'

He paused briefly before speaking, his eyes blazing murderously. 'I believe he plans to add you.'

My mouth fell open and goosebumps crawled up my arms. *Will this frickin' nightmare never end? Is every deranged bad guy in the universe after me?*

I reclaimed my hand and hugged myself to ward off the psychic chill. 'Add me? Why would you think that? Hal— That guy hasn't even seen me. What possible reason could he have for wanting me? Is it because of you?'

'Perhaps partially, but you should not underestimate your

notoriety in the vampire world. You are well known and it is quite possible that he is simply curious about you. Taking you from me would be icing on the cake, as they say. He might see you as a toy, a temporary distraction. Of course, by the time he finished with you, there would not be much of *you* left.'

'What do you mean?' I asked, my mouth dry. I was afraid I already knew more than I wanted to.

'I have seen the empty shells of the women Hallow leaves in his wake.' Devereux jumped up and started pacing, his hands clasped behind his back. 'Their minds are useless and their bodies wasted. They have described their captivity in ways that sound like human heroin addiction: euphoria, pleasure beyond belief, followed by an aching need that never ends. Apparently, he can create such ecstasy that his victims would rather die than leave him. Inevitably, their bodies deteriorate as he depletes their life-force and thrusts them into madness.' He returned to the couch, his expression solemn. 'That is why I became so upset when you said his name.' He tipped his head in a slow bow. 'I apologise if I resorted to caveman tactics.'

I squeezed his hand and gazed into his eyes. 'Apology accepted. So, let's say the energy sucker does intend to add me to his harem: are you seriously suggesting that I hide out in your penthouse indefinitely? That I never leave the building?' I spoke playfully, because of course it was beyond the realm of possibility that Devereux would propose something so unacceptably ludicrous.

'Yes,' he said eagerly, 'you understand! That is the only

way for you to remain safe. Your office is only an elevator ride away, so there is no real reason for you to go anywhere else. I do not wish to curtail your freedom, but you see that it is necessary, and I must insist that you follow my guidance.'

'Oh, my,' the strange intruding voice said. 'The lad has really stepped in it now. I'd be angry if I were you.'

Damn right!

'You must *insist*?' I clenched my hands in my lap and scowled. 'So, you're only willing to restrain your chest-beating instincts when it suits you? You really don't see me as an individual at all, do you? Someone with her own goals and needs and desires? No: you see me only as some fated extension of yourself. What about all the other times you forced me to rearrange my life and my work because you thought I was in danger? Nothing bad ever happened, did it? So why should I listen now? How do I know this isn't just another excuse for you to stroke your ego? Do you know for a *fact* that he's interested in me? Nope, sorry. You're just crying wolf – *again*. I won't allow anyone to make my decisions for me.'

I leapt up from the couch and stomped around the room, and Devereux followed, then stepped in front of me. He grabbed my upper arms and tried to give me a shot of vampire voodoo with his eyes.

'It is distressing that you cannot see how unlike yourself you are right now. But I am willing for you to be angry with me if it means you will remain unharmed,' he said, sounding calm and rational. 'And even if I were "crying wolf", which

I am not, I could live with that. We can return for your things later. I am taking you to safety now.'

His gaze was no longer producing the usual hazy, entranced feeling it used to. Instead, it sharpened my awareness of my anger, which felt pretty good.

He slid his arm around my waist and I twisted away, pulling him off-balance. The shock on his face was almost comical and I laughed out loud. The Master wasn't used to disobedience!

Stress is an amazing thing: all that adrenalin pumping and cortisol surging.

He reached for me again and I pivoted, shoving him with my hip. He growled and lunged and we performed a sweaty little grapple for a frantic few seconds. He tried to hold onto me without hurting me while I struggled to get away – I don't know how we remained on our feet. At one point we each had handfuls of the other's hair, and lots of snorting and grunting ensued.

'Ahem.' Luna, Devereux's hostile femme fatale assistant stood a couple of feet away, sneering. She had a habit of showing up unannounced and uninvited.

'Forgive me for interrupting your disgusting little mating ritual, but the Master is needed. The truce between the covens has been breached and they're at each other's throats again. If you don't mind, I'll just go and stake myself now, which is the only way I'll be able to rid myself of the grotesque scene I just witnessed, since it's burned into my brain.' She vanished.

Devereux disentangled himself from me, straightening

his clothing and patting down his hair. I leaned forward, braced my hands on my knees and tried to catch my breath.

Wow – my visits to the gym have really paid off. I've got muscles!

'We will follow Luna,' Devereux proclaimed, and he slid his arm around my waist again, preparing to transport us to his penthouse.

I screamed, 'No!' I wanted to stay put and appreciate my new strength.

Of course, he paid no attention. Then something strange happened. There was the usual hair-raising sensation always present when we blink from one place to another, but instead of landing in Devereux's elegant living quarters, there was an itchy, tingling, *pulling* along my back, and then we were standing in my living room again.

Whoa. I wasn't an expert at undead transportation, but I didn't think Devereux had planned that.

'How did you do that?' he demanded, turning to glare at me.

I'm sure I looked as confused as I felt. 'Do what? I didn't do anything.' Unless thinking I didn't want to go and screaming *No!* counted – but why would it, since it never had before?

He took a step back, his eyes distant and cold. 'You forced us to return. How could you possibly know how to do that?' He growled low in his throat. 'It was *him*. The situation is even worse than I feared. He has lent you his power, strength-ened your mental and physical capacities, which were already amplified by the elders' blood. He is not merely influencing you. He is *controlling* you.' He made an obvious effort to calm himself and stroked his hand over my arm. 'You can rest assured that I will not allow him to interfere in this way; I will not allow him to change you. But while I consider the best course of action, I would like you to come with me, of your own free will. I can probably still force you to accompany me, but it would be highly unpleasant for both of us. Will you come?'

I reached up and took his face in my hands, staring into his eyes. 'Devereux, nobody is controlling me. You're such a worrier. I know you want to protect me, and your actions are well-meaning. You don't think I can take care of myself, and you're probably right that I have a lot to learn about your world – but how will I ever learn about this twisted reality if you don't let me make my own mistakes and explore my abilities in my own way? If you try to hold me captive, even kindly, I'll come to resent you, and neither of us wants that. I need to stay here, in my own home, and make my own decisions, even if I screw up.'

He wrapped his fingers around my wrists, brought my hands to his mouth and kissed one palm then the other.

'For an intelligent woman, you are being incredibly obtuse.'

My mouth opened and closed in indignation. In the middle of my inadvertent fish imitation, I tried to form a coherent sentence and failed. I pulled my hands away.

Devereux stared down at me and I felt like a schoolgirl being reprimanded by the principal. 'You have no idea what that lunatic can do, and instead of listening to me – someone who actually does know what the beast is capable of – you dig in your heels and resist. Your careless actions could cause both of us pain – or worse. Now, *please*, be the sensible woman I know you are and come with me.'

'Being sensible is highly overrated.'

Where did that come from? I didn't mean to say that.

I backed away and slammed into a strange vampire who'd just materialised behind me. The visitor didn't even react to my stomping on his feet.

Let's see how many more vampires we can cram into this room.

'Master, you are desperately needed. Things have taken a turn for the worse. They are calling for you.'

Devereux snarled at the newcomer, 'Yes, yes. Tell them I am on my way.'

The messenger departed and I crossed my arms over my chest. My body language was as clear as it could be: as far as I was concerned, the topic was closed. I needed a break.

'This discussion is not over – far from it – but I must go. The conflict between the covens is fuelled by those wishing to restore vampires to the top of the food chain again, those who support Dracul's campaign. No doubt you remember that issue was at the heart of the battle between us.'

'How could I forget when he almost sucked me dry?' I hugged myself to ward off the sudden chill. 'I thought the problem had ended with Dracul's death.'

'No. He created a growing cancer, so to speak, and as the leader of the opposition, I must intervene in person.'

'Should I be surprised that you never mentioned a word to me about this continuing threat to mortals? What about

your promise to tell me more about the preternatural world
– to keep me in the loop?'

'I tell you what you need to know.'

'He doesn't treat you like an equal at all, does he?' the
voice whispered in my head.

No, he doesn't.

'I see. So *you* determine what I need to know.'

'Let us not speak of this now. I must subdue the trouble-
makers. At least promise me that you will remain indoors
tonight.'

I smiled, promising nothing, and he grumbled something
harsh-sounding in the strange language – Druidic? – he
sometimes used. 'The Slayer has made you incapable of
rational thought, so I will take matters into my own hands.
Like it or not, you will be protected.'

He disappeared.

Devereux's suffocating behaviour had got to the point
that I had to take a stand, even if it seemed self-destructive,
stubborn and stupid. I couldn't continue to hide behind
him. It had been my decision to involve myself in the vampire and vampire wannabe worlds, so there was no point in
cowering and playing the Damsel in Distress. I had to learn
to take care of myself or I'd spend the rest of my life being
a victim.

Thinking about cowering made me remember my unnatural altercation with Devereux. Something was definitely
different. I remembered eagerly holding up my end of the
tussle, even taking a sadistic pleasure in grabbing handfuls
of that platinum hair. My temper had slipped its leash and

run amok, and that was new for me. I wasn't sure how I felt about it, but I couldn't deny I'd enjoyed the exhilaration.

'Hell, yes! Kismet Knight, Ass Kicker!'

After the flurry of chaos, being alone in my townhouse was odd. The silence pressed against my ears, and the lack of drama felt empty rather than peaceful. Had I become addicted to the soap operas of the bloodsucking world? Was I hooked on the neuro-chemical rollercoaster?

With those disturbing thoughts in my mind, I wandered over to my desk and sat. Extensive paperwork was a staple of my chosen career. As I started to rummage through the insurance forms and consultation requests on my desk, I suddenly remembered I'd left my briefcase, containing my current client files, at my office.

Did I want to drive back over there, or—

Damn! My driver's licence was in my purse, which was also still at my office. Then another revelation rolled over me: driver's licence, hell! – my *car* was still there! I pounded my fist on the desktop and belted out a primal scream. Good thing my neighbours were in Mexico. I should've stopped thinking about Devereux's hormone-kindling face and body long enough to gather up my personal belongings. 'Crap!' I slapped the desk again. 'I wish I could just think myself there. A few minutes ago it was Vampire Central Station – where's a vampire when you need one?'

I could even envision exactly where I'd left my possessions.

As soon as I pictured them in my mind, there was that familiar swoosh, and I found myself in my office. Or I should say, sprawled on the floor of my office. It was like somebody had opened a cosmic door, positioned a foot on my ass and pushed me inside.

Stunned, I sat up and gazed around. I'd landed next to the desk where I'd left my purse and briefcase. Apparently, just imagining the place I wanted to be was all it took to get me there now. I patted myself down, making sure all of me had arrived and reassembled in the correct order.

After I mentally scratched my head for a few seconds, I burst out laughing. Devereux was going to have a stroke when he found out – well, maybe not a stroke, because one had to be alive for that, but he'd surely suffer some kind of undead affliction. The idea that his destined beloved had developed her own superpower and might be able to survive day-to-day without his constant intervention would be as welcome to him as a broken fang.

When my laughter died down, I sobered. I'd just done something impossible, and the cautious part of me pursed her lips and shook a finger in my direction. She didn't think this situation was funny at all, and she was very concerned about the source of these new skills. She thought I ought to contact Devereux immediately and tell him about this surprising development. She was worried.

Whoa. This is getting crazy. She? Isn't she me? I should definitely *call Devereux.*

But apparently not all of me agreed. In the midst of the anxiety, another opinion forced its way into the discussion and I felt myself smile, almost as if my facial muscles had a mind of their own. Why tell Devereux anything? Yes, the pleasure of watching the shocked realisation blossom across his face would be entertaining, and there was no mistaking how exciting his temper tantrums could be, but why tip my hand? Why share this radically unexpected turn of events? An unfamiliar confidence filled me.

Okay. The fact that my new skill allegedly came from Hal— from the ancient vampire Devereux had mentioned - was unsettling news. That would be the part my blond Adonis would hate the most. Who knew how long my ticket for Air Vampire would last? Shouldn't I keep this little bit of freedom to myself? I wasn't thrilled about how I got this ability, but as long as I had it, shouldn't I use it? Besides, there was a more immediate issue to deal with: I had to find out if travelling via thought was a one-shot deal, or if it had a longer shelf life. Could I get myself home the same way I came – and would I be able to take my briefcase and purse with me? Burning questions, all. But if I popped home, my car would still be parked in the underground parking of the office building, so shouldn't I simply take the easiest path and drive home, just be a normal human? Boring but practical.

That's what I did.

On the ride home, I fantasised about thought travel – as outrageous as it sounded, it really wasn't any more out-landish than most aspects of modern quantum physics. In fact, Einstein had speculated about the possibility of that very thing, so it really wasn't surprising that vampires could manipulate energy. What *was* really odd was the fact that vampires existed, period. Devereux had promised to tell me the story of the original vampire, but so far he'd changed the subject whenever I'd raised it. Another mystery?

It also occurred to me that I'd forgotten to ask Devereux about the deaths Mr Roth had mentioned. I made a mental note to find out what he knew.

When I arrived home, my townhouse was as quiet and bloodsucker-free as I'd left it. I strolled into the kitchen, rummaged through the refrigerator and grabbed the least rancid leftover container of Chinese food, found a lone fork in the sink and leaned against the wall to eat. I glanced down at my lovely black dress, now crumpled and covered in lint and dust, and groaned. A greasy fat noodle dangling on the end of the fork made a run for it down the front of the soft fabric. Perfect.

I pitched the empty box, stashed the fork in the dishwasher and shuffled over to the staircase leading up to my bedroom. A hot shower would feel like heaven.

I'd climbed just a few steps when the doorbell rang. In my pre-vampire life, someone coming to my door was a normal, natural thing, no cause for alarm, but since I'd fallen into this alternate universe, nighttime visitors could be extremely bad news, sometimes downright hazardous to my health.

I tiptoed over to the door and eyeballed the peephole. Someone was definitely there, but I couldn't make out who it was. I reached over and flipped on the porch light, then peeked again. A tall woman with a waterfall of white hair stood there, smiling and waving.

CHAPTER 6

'Maxie? What are you doing here? How did you get my address?' I was sure the frown in my voice matched the one on my face.

I'd cracked my front door open enough to stick my head out, but I hadn't invited her in. What the hell was a reporter doing on my doorstep?

Her smile widened. 'I can find anybody's address – I'm a bit of a computer geek. Actually, yours was easy. Did you know that the American Psychological Association actually lists member contact information online? And it's only protected by the flimsiest of passwords – it's child's play, really. Can I come in?' She didn't try to hide the fact that she was inching her shoe into the door crack.

I tightened my grip on the handle and shifted my hip against the door. 'I don't think so, Maxie. I'm tired, and I've got a lot of paperwork to do. Why don't you call me tomorrow?'

She stuck her lower lip out in a pout. 'I've left you several messages today, Doc – remember? We're going to the vampire staking? I gave you directions, but then the location was changed, so I left you another message, asking you to call me, but you didn't, so I thought I'd better hightail it over here and see if anything was wrong. Just being a concerned citizen, ya know?'

Maxie's energy was intense, chaotic.

When I continued to stare at her, she pulled her foot away from the door. 'I'm sorry, Doc,' she said contritely, 'I do tend to come on too strong sometimes. I just got back from interviewing a paedophile and I had to hammer him with every aggressive interrogation technique I could think of. He finally caved, and it wasn't pretty. I guess I haven't finished decompressing. I've been meaning to work on my polite social skills. It's on my list.' She smiled and studied me. 'Seriously, I do apologise. I'd kill for a glass of wine.'

If she really had just come from such a horrible interview, I could understand why I was picking up so many mixed energy signals from her. I was probably even sensing the perpetrator's residue as well. I supposed it wouldn't hurt to ask her in for some wine. In fact, that sounded pretty good to me too.

'A paedophile? That had to be one miserable interview.' I pulled the door open in invitation. 'How can you do what you do?'

She stepped inside and gave a melancholy smile. 'I could ask you the same thing, Doc. You have to listen to shitty stuff all the time. Mostly I just talk to people who claim they were experimented on in a spaceship or who saw Bigfoot – just your standard flaky loons.'

I laughed, thinking about some of my clients' fanciful tales.

'Sit down, relax.' I pointed to the couch. 'I'll get the wine. Which do you prefer? Red or white?'

'Red.' She sat, and I noticed for the first time that she was dressed in black leather – quite a change from the jeans and football T-shirt she'd been wearing earlier. There was no mistaking the model's body in those tight clothes. *Interesting choice for a work outfit.* I wondered if the creepy interviewee had been intimidated by all that leather. Maybe that was why she'd worn it: dominatrix reporter. I glanced down at my dress and discovered the noodle that had made a suicide leap off my fork had sealed itself to my left breast. Although I don't usually pay much attention to fashion, I do generally make an effort not to wear my food. I suddenly felt insecure in my messy threads next to Maxie's easy perfection.

I peeled the pasta off my chest, poured the wine and brought the glasses to the couch.

'I take it you've never been to a vampire staking before?' Maxie asked.

'As I already told you,' I sat on the other end of the couch and gave her a blank face, 'I have no intention of going. We both know it will just be a lot of goth children, vampire wannabes and the mentally ill. No purpose would be served by my attendance.' Plus, I'd *really* had it with people forcing their opinions, desires and expectations on me. This was as good a place as any to put my foot down. I prepared myself to argue with Maxie, waiting for her to lob the next sally over the net to try to convince me that she was a better judge of how I should spend my evening than I was.

She sipped from her wineglass. 'Can I level with you, Doc?' *No! Please don't. I'm off-duty. Oh crap.*

Recognising the same emotional vulnerability in her voice that I was picking up intuitively, I slipped into my professional persona and gave her my attention. 'Of course.' Her vibrant personality crumbled in front of me and she suddenly looked very tired.

She met my eyes and hers shone with moisture. 'I don't want to go to this ridiculous thing, but I have to. I'm in trouble at work – my job's on the line. That's why I asked you to go with me. I was just hoping for some company. For someone to . . . be there. I have lots of acquaintances, but nobody I can trust. I've got myself in some hot water financially – I made some stupid decisions – and if I lose my job, the whole house of cards will come tumbling down on me.'

She heaved a sigh. 'You seemed like such an understanding person that I guess I got carried away. I just wanted to hang out with someone I could be myself with – whatever that is. I'm great at putting on a tough façade, and I'm good at never letting anyone know how I really feel – shit, I don't even let myself know. But I can say for sure that I'm both burned out on my job and at the same time worried I'll lose it – in other words, I'm totally screwed. And don't even get me started about my boyfriend . . .'

Apparently she'd sought me out – consciously or unconsciously – because of my job. It wasn't the first time it had happened, and it wouldn't be the last. I had to acknowledge that her seeking unofficial counselling was marginally better than just trying to use me to get a story. *Everybody has an agenda.*

One fat tear slid down her cheek and she glanced around, then plucked a tissue out of the box on the table in front of her and blew her nose, making an unusually loud, multi-octave honking noise.

The unexpected sound caused us both to stare at each other for a moment, then we burst out laughing.

'Whoa! Where'd that come from?' Maxie said, smiling. 'Do I know how to lighten a mood, or what? Barnum and Bailey, sign me up!'

I'd put my hand over my mouth in a futile effort to muffle my own laughter. It was terrible of me to have such an inappropriate reaction after someone had shared something so emotionally intense, but it was why people sometimes laughed at funerals: stress can cause some really unexpected reactions.

I caught my lower lip between my teeth to force myself to stop chuckling, but all that did was cause me to snort too, and we both lost it again.

After an endless amount of time, the frivolity calmed and we each reached for a tissue. I fanned myself with my hand, shaking my head, grinning.

'I think we both needed that, don't you?'

'Hell, yeah! I'm already better just being around you. I think you've got the healing touch, Doc.' She sipped her wine, not making eye contact any more.

Well, apparently she needs to talk. I gave a mental sigh. 'Do you want to tell me about your situation? And your boyfriend?'

Her anxious gaze quickly shifted to mine and away again before she set her glass on the table. 'I didn't come over to spill my guts, Doc. Denver's full of shrinks if I need one.'

Uh-huh. I relaxed back into the couch cushions and waited.

She glanced at me a couple of times before twisting her body to face me. 'I'm just a fuck-up, Doc. Everything I touch turns to shit.'

'Hmm. Give me an example.' I retrieved my wine glass and sipped.

'You want actual specifics?' At my *go ahead* gesture she started, 'Well, my job for one. I screwed up a while back and slept with the boss, then I asked him to front me some cash to pay off a debt. After he gave me the money I managed to lose that, too.'

'Are you saying you have a gambling problem?'

'Bingo, Doc.' She picked up her glass and took a healthy sip. 'I love casinos – I'll bet on anything. And sometimes I even win, but I can't walk away, so I end up broke and swearing I'll never do it again.'

'So you lost the money the boss gave you?'

'Yep – but it was worse, because that wasn't the first time. He gave me an ultimatum: get my shit together or get out.'

'Are you still in a relationship with him? Is he your boyfriend?'

'Nope – I only had sex with him a few times to keep him in a good mood. If my boyfriend found out, he'd go berserk.

In fact, he'd probably beat the shit outta my boss, which wouldn't help my employment situation.' She finished her wine. 'Can I have a refill?'

'Sure.' I pointed. 'The bottle's on the kitchen counter. Bring it back with you.'

At least if I listen to her, maybe she'll forget about the vampire staking plan.

She came back to her place on the couch, filled both our glasses and lifted the bottle to read the label. She burst out laughing. 'Perfect, Doc! Vampire merlot. You *do* have a sense of humour!'

'I can't take credit for it,' I chuckled. 'It was a gift from a friend.'

She set the bottle on the table. 'You must have some strange friends.'

You have no idea. 'A few. So, back to your boyfriend. Tell me about him.'

She frowned. 'We've been together, on and off, for years – he's gorgeous, smart and funny.'

'That sounds pretty good. So why are you frowning? What's the problem?'

'Can't put anything past you, Doc.' She paused while she drank more wine, then she admitted, 'There's a problem – a few of them, actually. He just can't keep his cock in his boxers – and he's got a hair-trigger temper.'

Uh-oh. 'He's violent? With you?'

'Sometimes.'

Shit! 'Maxie, what the hell are you thinking?'

'I don't know – like I said, I'm a fuck-up. Trust me to find the biggest asshole in town, and to keep believing his stupid apologies.'

'But what—'

'Ya know,' she bolted off the couch, 'I really don't wanna talk about this any more. There's nothing you can do. I just have to stop being a coward and make a new decision.' Her face was pale and her eyes dull. She drained her glass before replacing it on the table. 'I've taken up enough of your time. I'm gonna head over to the meaningless event and let you get on with your evening. I'm sorry I vomited my dramas over you like that. It wasn't fair, since that's the kind of crap you have to listen to all the time. I hope you'll forgive me for being such a loser.'

Damn. I can't leave her like this . . .

I emptied my glass and set it on the table alongside hers. It wouldn't kill me to spend a little time with her, give her some resources, encourage her to get help.

'I don't think you're a loser – in fact, just the opposite. I think you're a survivor.'

'Yeah.' She gave a cynical laugh. 'Survivor – over and over again. I think I've got a theme going.'

And maybe it *would* do me good to get a firsthand taste of Denver's occult underworld. Maxie had been right this morning when she suggested I could use the material in my private practice and for my book. And if I was really serious about expanding my social horizons, here was a perfect opportunity for me to step outside my rigid routine – to follow my own therapeutic advice and take a chance. After all, I was client-free for the weekend, and I had no other plans.

'Why not change the theme?'

'As if it's that easy, Doc.'

'It isn't easy at all, but it can be done.' I stood, because staring up at her was putting a crick in my neck. 'You seriously want me to go with you?' I frowned. 'My being there will make things easier?'

Her face lit up like a kid on Christmas morning as a huge smile curved her lips. 'No shit? You'll actually go with me? Well, hot damn! Maybe I should whine more often.' She laughed. 'Thanks so much, really – how cool! I have a pal – someone to share the bullshit with!' She plopped down on the couch again with a wide grin, back to her effervescent personality, all angst sufficiently repressed.

I watched her for a few seconds, waiting for another mood shift. *Borderlines are such amazing manipulators . . .*

'Are you going to change clothes?' she said. 'I don't think a dress would be the best choice for the lunatic festivities, but if you're going as you are, I have to say I really miss the fat noodle you had on your tit when you opened the door. Maybe we could fish it out of the garbage and stick it back on? I thought it made a powerful statement. Sort of a metaphor about being willing to bend, or knowing when to cling to what you have . . .'

She hooted out a laugh as I picked up a cushion from a chair and sailed it at her head. She deflected the fluffy assault and continued laughing.

I folded my arms over my chest, grinning. 'If you're going to make fun of my fashion accessories, I'll have to rethink my offer.'

She stood and bowed from the waist, her silky hair cascading to the floor. 'Many humble apologies, my new buddy, for my thoughtless remark about your . . . noodle. I promise never to have another opinion about whatever you plaster to your tit. Unless it's some hot guy's hand, then I might have to speak up . . .' She gave a mini wolf-howl and flopped onto the couch again.

I paused for a moment, reconsidering my decision to spend the evening with a crazy woman, but her words gave me a quick memory-flash of Devereux's hand on that very tit and I smiled. Maxie was clever – wounded and probably nuts, but clever. She reminded me of Alan Stevens, a certain cocky FBI agent I'd befriended a while back. He was out of the country with his mother the vampire now. I missed talking to him. Maybe it would be fun for me to spend some time with someone else who enjoyed laughing. It was no secret that I tended to take things way too seriously – definitely another downside to my profession, and a downside I wouldn't mind uplifting. And there was no time like the present.

'Yeah, you're a laugh riot. I'll go upstairs and change. I'll be right back.'

We walked out of my front door onto the street still arguing about whose car to take. Maxie was insisting on her Jeep, saying it would come in handy.

'What do you mean? Are we going off-roading?'

She tugged on my coat sleeve as I veered off in the direction of the garage to fetch my BMW, pulling me over to the beat-up vehicle at the curb.

'Not exactly.' She grinned. 'But I gather from my infor-
mant that our destination isn't car-friendly. Apparently, the
"staking" is happening in some abandoned area, so we might
have to camouflage the Jeep and walk to the main event. I
like to make a surprise entrance – that way I get to see more
than they intend for me to see.'

'So?' I shook my arm loose. 'How does that put my car out
of the running? My comfortable little ride can hide in the
shadows as easily as yours. You're just prejudiced against
slick cars.'

She opened the passenger side and shoved at me until I
was all the way in.

'Hey! No pushing! You'll wrinkle my favourite suede coat.'

She circled around the front of the car and slid behind
the wheel.

'Sorry,' she said, not appearing sorry at all. 'Are you
saying my baby's not slick? I'll have you know this vehicle
has got me out of more tough spots than I can count. Take
a look behind you.' She clicked on the inside light and
twisted in her seat so she could reach into the back, and
lifted a tarp.

I goggled. The back of the car was filled with an assort-
ment of shovels, tools, junk food, beer, cold weather supplies,
a tent, outdoor cooking equipment, flashlights, candles,
what appeared to be sharpened stakes, and weapons – guns
and knives.

Guns. Knives.

I slowly turned my eyes to hers, my stomach tightening.
'What the hell, Maxie? Are you some kind of survivalist?

Why do you have guns? And what's with the stakes? I thought you'd never encountered a real vampire?'

'Chill, Doc! You've obviously led a very sheltered life. In my line of work, I deal with all manner of slime-bags. Before I figured out the degree to which I needed to take care of myself, I barely escaped from some dangerous situations. It's impossible to be a reporter if you aren't going to follow the vermin into their holes. As far as the stakes, they're amazingly effective at scaring off vampire wannabes. I'll use whatever works.' She replaced the tarp and reached into a storage box between our two seats, then she pulled out a strip of leather and tied it around her hair, making the longest ponytail – or, rather, horsetail – I'd ever seen. She saw me watching her and smiled.

'Still fascinated with the white hair?'

'No. Well, yes, but I was wondering how you deal with hair that long. Doesn't it get in the way? Isn't it heavy?' I thought about the relentless weight of my own hair, and mine was only half as long as hers.

'Nope. I'm used to it. It's just another one of my many charming idiosyncrasies. Besides, my foul-tempered significant other likes it this way.'

'I hope you'll talk about him some more – expose the truth. Perpetrators like when you keep their secrets.'

She slanted a glance at me and gave a wicked smile. 'We'll see. I'll tell you my secrets if you tell me yours.' She started the Jeep, shut off the inside light and pulled onto the road.

'What makes you think I have anything to tell?'

'Let's just say that it isn't easy for an incredibly gorgeous, wealthy man to avoid being stalked by reporters and the paparazzi, even in Denver. Showing up on his arm once might have been explained by a casual friendship, but there were repeated sightings – and then you moved your practice into his building. The only business on the premises, I might add, that isn't owned by his international conglomerate. Demented little enquiring minds want to know, Doc, and my rag of a magazine intends to supply the answers. Devereux is incredible – odd, though, that there's no mention anywhere of a last name. He's quite the mystery man. You wouldn't happen to know what his last name is, would you?'

I glared. 'Are we back to interviewing me, Maxie?'

'*Mea culpa*,' she grinned. 'Old habits die hard.'

I had to hand it to her, that was a smooth move – masterful avoidance.

'Okay, so you know about Devereux. It's not a secret. Back to *your* boyfriend.'

'Jesus, Doc, you're relentless. As I said, I manage to screw up everything. My patterns with men are hopeless. I've always had a weakness for narcissistic cocksmen, and right now I'm mad about a man who's too busy to pay any attention to me – he travels a lot for work, but when he's on good behaviour, he's *irresistible*.'

'Will I get to meet this irresistible . . . man?' *Maybe I can sic a vampire on his battering ass.*

'Well, it's not out of the realms of possibility, but I do doubt it – he doesn't live in Denver, and I never know when he's going to show up. We make up for it with great phone sex.' She flashed another of her trademark grins at me.

'Phone sex?' *Too bad Devereux and I never talk on the phone. He has no use for them.*

She smiled. 'Yeah, but sex is certainly more fun when he's actually in the room with me.'

Appreciating the truth of that statement, I grinned myself and stared out the window at the full moon, wondering where *my* sex object was. It was probably better that I didn't know, though, since I was pretty sure he'd be furious that I'd fled protective custody. I glanced behind me, just to make sure he hadn't materialised – he could be anywhere in a multitude of universes, and yet he could still show up in a heartbeat to surprise me. And the ease with which I contemplated that bizarre thought made me shake my head. How weird was it that my vocabulary now included words like parallel dimensions, simultaneous existence, auras, aetheric bodies and Druids, of all things.

Leave it to me to fall for a guy whose mother was an apparition and whose extended family included ancient witches and wizards!

I'd recently realised that I'd stopped labelling Devereux's vampirism as the strangest thing about him. I hadn't exactly got used to it, but in the midst of all his other disturbing facets, blood-drinking didn't rate very high on the fright-o-meter any more. Amazing what one can acclimatise to – especially if it was linked with great sex.

I roused myself from my daydream and noticed we'd travelled away from the lights of the downtown area. We probably hadn't been driving that long, but I'd lost track of time. 'Where the hell is this place? Kansas?'

'Nope.' She chuckled. 'We're still in Denver. I took a back route so nobody would see us arrive. Here we are.'

She angled the car off the road, edged it between two rows of trees and killed the engine.

I leaned forward and peered through the windshield. Thanks to the moon, it was pretty easy to see. 'What is this place?' I pointed. 'That rickety thing looks like some old rollercoaster or something.' I shifted my head towards Maxie. 'This is where we're going? An abandoned amusement park?'

'You got it, Doc. I don't know how long you've been in Denver, but the fire that destroyed half of this place was the talk of the town. We wouldn't have our fancy new state-of-the-art tourist trap downtown if a little pyromaniac bugger hadn't torched this one. And are you ready for this? The jerk set the fire because he was a pyromancer.'

I frowned. 'A what? I'm not familiar with that term.'

Maxie nodded. 'A pyromancer – somebody who reads the future by interpreting flames. This is right up your alley, actually. At his trial, the creep testified that the voices in his head told him to barbecue the whole park so he could write his own book of future predictions, like Nostradamus. There's an asshole born every minute. Come on. Let's collect supplies.'

She opened her door and stepped out before quietly pushing it closed. I followed her example and tiptoed around to the back of the Jeep.

'Are you sure this is where the thing is happening?' I glanced around. 'I don't see anybody. It's so quiet.'

She popped open the plastic flap covering the rear window

and peeled it back, flopping it up on the roof. 'Shhhh. We're on the other side of the park, but you never know who's lurking.' She pointed to a broken chain-link fence. 'We'll be crawling in under that fence and skulking around to find a good place to observe.' She studied my clothes, her lips pursed. 'The jeans, sweater and hiking boots are great, but you might want to lose the coat if it really is your favourite. Leave it in the car or it'll get filthy. I have a couple of parkas – you can use one.'

I started to complain that I didn't want to crawl anywhere, but she'd already focused her attention on grabbing supplies from her rolling disaster-preparedness stash.

Well, I said I was willing to try something different . . .

I shrugged out of my coat, took my cell phone, wallet, and keys out of the pockets and exchanged it for one of the black parkas. The pillowy jacket was too warm for the mild weather, and it turned me into the Pillsbury Doughboy. I crammed all my things into one large pocket and filled the other with the flashlight, tape recorder, pocketknife, writing pad, candy bar and pen Maxie thrust into my hands.

'Okay. You have to take one of these. Which one do you think you could handle?' She held out a Taser and a pistol. She shifted her weight from side to side impatiently as I stared at the two foreign objects in her hands. 'Well? What's the problem?'

'What's the problem?' I whispered, but louder than I meant to. 'You didn't say anything about needing to be armed to attend this crap-fest – what the hell are we going to do with *weapons*? I thought we were just going to hide out and watch. Are you planning to burst in and take hostages or something? Tasers are *illegal*.' This adventure had now gone from being an interesting change of pace to something that was making fear coil in my stomach.

Maxie dropped her head and stared at the ground. She lowered the weapons to her sides, then raised her eyes up to mine. 'I'm sorry – I'm so used to doing these crazy things alone and I psych myself up for whatever's going to happen. I should've told you, there's always a chance some weirdo will freak out and do something violent. Let's face it, if these were normal, healthy people, they probably wouldn't be here, would they? You should be used to unpredictable, mentally whacked-out people.' She brought the pistol and the Taser into the space between us again. 'Maybe I'm overreacting, but I need you to choose one of these, just so I can be sure you have something to defend yourself with. You could use the pocketknife, but an attacker would have to get awfully close and personal before it would be a good option.'

She held the small pistol out to me. 'Have you ever fired one of these?'

I took the gun. At least I wasn't likely to stun myself with it. 'Just a few times, when an old boyfriend dragged me to the firing range. I wasn't very good – I'll probably shoot myself in the foot.'

In fact, I almost shot him *in the foot back then.*

'No, you won't. It has a safety. Here, I'll show you.' She demonstrated, and then handed the gun back to me. 'Take it, okay? Just in case.' She pocketed the Taser and grinned. 'I'll hold onto the illegal device.'

My hand tingled when I took the weapon, as if my skin was trying to reject all the emotions trapped in the handle.

'You're going to owe me big-time, Maxie. Crawling around in the dirt, carrying a gun, prowling through the burned-out remains of an amusement park – next time we listen to jazz and drink margaritas.'

She grinned and patted my shoulder. 'Way to suck it up, galpal. What a trouper. This will be an adventure you'll never forget.' She strolled over to check out the back of the Jeep again. 'Yep, I think we have everything we need. Let's rumble.' She re-fastened the flap over the rear window, did up her jacket and trotted off towards the fence.

She shot me a glance over her shoulder. 'Hey, you'd better zip up unless you want dirt and soot all over that fine rack.'

I heard her laughing as she glided to a gaping section of fence. Still walking fast to catch up with Maxie, I glanced down to zip the parka and tripped over an exposed tree root. Thanks to the foamy coat, I made barely a sound as I hit the ground. 'Fuck!' I said under my breath and raised my head in time to watch Maxie crawl under the fence, stand and stride off. She disappeared behind the ruins of a building.

'Uh, Maxie?' I croaked.

CHAPTER 7

There was silence as I struggled to my feet, brushing off dirt, twigs and a used condom. The damn coat was so bulky it was like wearing a fat suit. I finished tugging up the zip and jogged over to the fence. I stared at the curled-up corner, then squatted and examined the small opening, talking to myself.

'How the hell am I supposed to cram this hot-air balloon of a parka through that hole in the chain-link? Of course Maxie's leather jacket had slid right through. What was the point of dressing me up like the Michelin Man?'

I peeled off the jacket, dropped to my hands and knees and pushed it through, then slid under on my stomach. The ground was relatively smooth, indicating that many other people had made the journey before me.

Emerging on the other side, I stood and rotated my shoulders. I hated to put the parka back on again, but if Maxie thought it was important for me to have a gun, I probably should at least keep my hands free. I retrieved the fluffy beast, slipped it on and walked tentatively towards a maze of building remains. The full moon shone large and bright, like a cosmic lantern. It should have been easy to find Maxie, but she was nowhere in sight.

Thinking it would probably be better if I weren't quite so visible, I detoured along a partial wall and scanned the area. This was definitely a weird place, and not only because of the scorched landscape – although that definitely qualified as creepy – but because of the ominous vibe.

Suddenly the scene burst into flames and I stumbled back, startled. The smell of burning wood and flesh was so strong that I pressed my hand over my mouth and nose and started breathing as shallowly as I could. Thick clouds of black smoke blanketed the park, blotting out the sky, and screaming spectral people ran from the buildings as they tried frantically to extinguish blazing hair and clothing. Several of them crossed through me, causing my stomach to cramp and goosebumps to swarm over my arms and legs. I coughed, and tasted the smoke at the back of my throat. Willing my legs to move, I darted towards a cement-block building and huddled against the wall. My rational brain knew it wasn't real, that it was yet another ghastly replay, apparitional memories that had become an unwelcome part of my freakish life. But my animal brain wasn't listening; it was cowering in fear.

The vision was so overwhelming, it took me a couple of minutes to remember how to make it go away. I lowered my hands from my face, stood straight and whispered as loud as I dared, 'Stop!'

And it did. Everything vanished, and I was once again standing in an abandoned, destroyed fun centre.

'Shit, Kismet,' I mumbled, angry at myself for not stopping the grisly movie as soon as it had started. But the truth was, the ghostly visitations had become more intense ever since I drank the elders' blood, and I hadn't had enough time yet to get used to their unexpected appearances.

And where the hell was Maxie?

I slumped against the building, forcing myself to relax my muscles and practise breathing. I threw in the mental hum for good measure, since it always calmed me.

Then everything went still – unnaturally still, with not even the sound of a cricket – and I held my breath as something triggered my inner alarm. I couldn't identify what was *off*, but the air hung heavy, dangerous. I waited for another horrifying memory to burst forth, but whatever this was had a different texture.

Maybe Maxie was right about whackos hiding in the shadows. I reached into my pocket and wrapped my fingers around the gun, but instead of reassuring, it terrified me. I turned my head slowly from side to side, watching for – what? Nothing else had happened to make me anxious, but my gut clenched and my breath caught, as if I was sensing something or someone I couldn't see.

'Maxie?' I whispered, barely audible. Dread washed over me and I froze, trying to figure out where the threat was coming from. If there even *was* a threat. I was torn between thinking my imagination was working overtime since I was now constantly waiting for the next ghostly shoe to drop, and wanting to trust my intuition. My heart pounded and my temperature spiked so high that I unzipped the coat and used the edge to fan myself.

What was happening to me? I'd never had a panic attack before, but whatever was happening to my body fit all the symptoms. Maybe I was holding onto the energy echoes from the chaos of the fire – I'd prefer that explanation to thinking I was losing my mind.

Then I heard a groan and I gazed around, searching for the source of the low sound. I heard it again, closer this time, but still I couldn't see anyone near me. I jumped as a hand stroked the side of my face and gasped as fingers trailed down my neck. I heard another groan and my whole body contracted in terror. I reached up to swat the invisible hand away, but there was nothing there – and yet I could still feel it, as real as my own skin, and the longer the phantom hand touched me, the more my muscles cramped.

Footsteps pounded towards me. 'Kismet? Where are you?'

I must have been holding my breath because so much air escaped from my mouth that I coughed and doubled over. The unseen hand disappeared. 'Maxie? Here. I'm over here.'

She crouched, grabbed my upper arms, and pulled me upright. 'Where the hell did you go? I thought you were right behind me. What's wrong with you? Why are you all sweaty and shaky?' She pivoted, waving the Taser she carried. 'Did someone attack you? What happened?'

I closed my eyes for a moment to calm myself. Either I'd

been fondled by an invisible *something* or I was going mad. Neither option was acceptable.

My fingers still had a death-grip on the weapon in my pocket and I forced myself to let go. My palm was so slick with sweat that the gun slid out of my hand easily once I relaxed my muscles.

I opened my eyes, took a deep breath and let it out slowly. Maxie half-turned her body so she was still able to catch anyone approaching, while whispering furtively, 'Kismet? What the hell's wrong with you? Tell me what happened.'

I certainly wasn't going to tell her about the spectral fire. Nobody but Devereux knew the extent of my immaterial visions. My hand rose to the spot on my face where the invisible fingers had stroked me. 'I don't know what happened. Somebody touched me.'

She spun around, pointing the Taser in one direction and then another. 'Who? What did he look like?'

I licked my dry lips. 'He didn't look like anything.'

'What do you mean? Did he have a bag over his head or something? A pointy white hood?'

'No – I mean, nobody was there at all, but I swear there was a definite hand on my face. And there was a groan – a male-sounding groan.'

She lowered her weapon and raised her eyebrows. 'Lay that on me again: an invisible hand and a manly groan? Do you realise how nuts that sounds? Doc, help me out here. Get a grip. Don't go Looney Tunes on me now. Maybe you've been listening to too many schizo stories from your clients.' She retrieved a small flask from one of her many pockets, flicked off the attached lid and offered it to me. 'Here. A little brandy to calm the nerves.'

I shook my head. 'No, I don't want any more alcohol. I feel strange enough as it is.'

'I insist, Doc. I can't have you flake out on me.' She stepped closer and held the flask out to me. 'There's nothing like a little brandy – for medicinal purposes only, of course – to set the world right.' As I continued shaking my head, she said, 'Here, I'll go first.' She took a swig, then licked her lips.

When I didn't say anything she gave me a light punch on the arm and a concerned look. 'Your turn. Trust me, you need it. Liquid courage.'

Spoken like a true addict. Well, why the hell not?

I grabbed the flask, took a small swig and swallowed and as warmth spread down my throat and into my middle I realised I was a bit steadier.

Hmmm. Funny-tasting brandy. I don't even want to think about how long Maxie must have had that in her car.

She watched me and nodded, her face serious. 'Okay, that's better. You scared me, Doc. I barely recognised you there for a minute. Under different circumstances, I'd walk you back to the car and let you wait there for me, but I've found the location of the main event and I need you to cover my back. Are you going to be able to be there for me? Can I count on you?'

Damn. Where in my job description did it say anything about scaring myself to death while trailing mentally defective role-players? What exactly am I trying to prove? I really wanted to crawl back under that fence and head for the Jeep, but Maxie had pressed

my guilt button – and my coward button. Either she'd figured me out very quickly, or I was horribly easy to read.
Regardless, she had me.

'Yeah, sure. You can count on me. Let's go.'

'Are you okay to walk? Seriously, Doc, you looked like you
were having some kind of breakdown.'

Welcome to my world.

'I'm good.' I took a couple of awkward steps before my
legs solidified beneath me. My knees were still a little wobbly,
but they held.

She walked alongside me, casting glances every few seconds to make sure I wasn't going to pass out or bolt. Great.
My intuition had decided to reappear. Where had it been
when I was in the midst of the panic attack? Why couldn't
I read the emotions and intentions of whatever the hell it
was that touched me?

'What did you find?' I whispered. The silence was especially thick again.

Speaking softly, she gave me a verbal tour of the demolished site, then pointed to the hulking edifice in front of us.
Soft light shone from the broken windows. 'So many people
died here.'

'Sounds grisly.'

'Yeah. The funhouse had world-famous twisted mirrors,
scary monsters and bloody exhibits, and a large area was
left open in the centre where reenactments and horror-
theatre-type presentations were held nightly. People lined
the upper balconies to watch the orchestrated mayhem.
Performances still take place in the centre circle, but the

morons are in charge now. I wonder how the idiots managed to generate light in there. You don't think they're dim enough to light a bonfire or something?'

I hoped not, because the last thing I wanted was more fire.

Speak of the devil: just as Maxie finished explaining, excited voices sliced the air. She grabbed my arm and pulled me behind a corner of the large building and we crouched there, watching as a group of men dressed in theatrical versions of occult chic carried a wooden box – a coffin? – across our line of sight. As they approached, I heard a muffled voice screaming from inside.

I started to stand, but Maxie tugged me down again, vigorously shaking her head. I didn't know what I thought I could do about the person trapped in the box, but doing nothing was the unacceptable choice. I followed the goth caravan with my eyes, waiting for any helpful ideas to form in my brain, until Maxie tapped me on the arm and mouthed 'per-form-ance' and flicked her thumb in their direction. My mouth formed an O, and I nodded, relieved. I'd forgotten we'd come to observe role-players. After my horrifying experiences with violent bloodsuckers, I tended to overreact – just a little Post-Traumatic Stress Disorder, nothing to worry about.

Maxie jerked her head towards the rear of the building, signalling me to follow her as she crept through the shadows to an old-fashioned fire escape hugging the wall of the colourful funhouse. The bottom rung was only about six feet from the ground. Maxie examined it, then bent over, lacing the fingers of both hands together to form a foothold.

'Put your foot here and I'll boost you up,' she said, her eyes constantly scanning the environment for unexpected company.

'Hold it! What do you mean? Boost me up where, Lucy?'

Maxie straightened. 'You're such a stick in the mud, Ethel. Put your fucking foot in my hands, get on the damn ladder, and climb to the top floor.'

We grinned at each other for a few seconds, enjoying the old *I Love Lucy* joke, then I remembered where we were and that I really did want answers to my questions.

'Why do we have to climb to the top floor? I thought you were invited to this thing. I didn't volunteer for a black-ops assignment. What's the purpose of hiding?'

'I told you. I like to sneak up so I can see the things they don't want me to see. That's how I've got my best stories.' She laced her fingers together again. 'Jesus, Doc – do all psychologists have to know every fucking detail all the time, or is it just you? Has anyone ever mentioned that you're a bit . . . controlling?'

Why yes, they had, as a matter of fact – but I wasn't the one doing all the bossing around. In this case, Maxie made me look like a slacker.

'*Me*, controlling? Hey, you're the Dominatrix from Hell today, not me! I think I've been very polite and accommodating, while you—'

She put her hand over my mouth, leaned in and whispered, 'Somebody's coming. Either climb the fucking ladder or run over there and hide in those bushes while I go up.' She removed her hand from my face, laced her fingers again and waited a heartbeat.

Now I could hear the footsteps approaching too, and almost without thinking, I put my boot in Maxie's hands, she gave me a boost and I grabbed a rung and scurried up the ladder.

Maxie was athletic, or at least in good shape, because she quickly moved up close behind me.

We'd climbed almost to the top before I peered down to check on our visitors. It was hard to make out details, even in the light of the full moon, but it looked like two guys had sneaked off for some private time and were in the midst of shucking the lower portions of their costumes in preparation for some . . . deeper . . . intimacy.

Maxie hadn't realised I'd slowed and her head smacked into my rear, causing me to lose my grip on the bars. I almost yelped as she grabbed my legs and whispered, 'Keep going!' Thankfully, we were high enough that the small sounds we made hadn't carried. Besides, the guys sharing body fluids below weren't paying any attention to us.

We made it to the top floor and stepped across the six feet of iron grating leading to a heavy metal door, which was locked. After I'd tugged fruitlessly on the handle Maxie shoved past me, extracting a set of small tools and a minia-ture flashlight from her pocket. She held the slender light between her teeth. I peeked over her shoulder as she worked on the lock with a small knife-like tool. 'Hmm. Breaking and entering. Should I ask what other illegal activities we might be undertaking tonight? Maybe next time we can hit an ATM, rob a gas station, maybe knock over a convenience store? Or perhaps we could freelance as drug mules.'

She let the flashlight drop into her hand. 'Shut up, Ethel. *Yes!* Am I awesome, or what?'

The door creaked open.

Maxie stuck her head into the crack, then stepped inside, gesturing at me to follow. I pulled the door closed behind me.

We'd gone to hell.

In the total blackness, glow-in-the-dark paint depicted demonic scenes, with rivers of blood, and evildoers feasting on the bodies of the previously living. The ghoulish displays had been demolished and the remnants of their wood and glass littered the floor.

My eyes adjusted to the darkness and I noticed there was a path under my feet dusted with glowing sparkles. Remembering the last time I'd been in a funhouse as a kid, when I'd slammed into an invisible glass on my quest for an exit door, I put my hands out in front of me.

'Hey! We don't know each other well enough for you to touch me there, Doc.' Maxie chuckled softly. 'Let's go.' She clasped my hand. 'The sounds are coming from this direction.'

She was right, the noise was definitely getting louder. A solid wall of chatter punctuated by shrieks, screams and laughter had a musical backdrop provided by Black Sabbath. The sound levels increased as we approached, moving ahead slowly until we reached a set of saloon-type doors.

Maxie pushed one side of the door and we dropped to our hands and knees before crawling through onto a mezzanine floor. A wild party raged below. There were large gaps in the wooden barrier between where we were and thin air, so we stretched out on our stomachs, our heads poking beyond the balcony just enough to explore the source of the noise. Maxie slipped a compact camera from her pocket and began clicking.

Torches were spread throughout the room and together with flame-filled steel barrels in the corner they provided soft respite from the prevailing darkness. The music burst from a large CD player perched on top of some wooden crates.

The building had four sets of double-doors at the entrance, and all were gaping, either because they'd been propped open with rocks, or the doors themselves were missing. In spite of the ventilation, the air inside the building was thick with smoke from the various fires plus all the cigarettes and joints adding to the mix. The sour stench of body odour floated like the bottom note of a nauseating perfume. My eyes stung and my lungs ached as I breathed the acrid air. Maxie wasn't at all bothered by the toxic atmosphere.

It was a rave: there had to be at least a hundred people in the performance space – except most of the revellers were dressed as their favourite movie or television monsters. In some cases, they wore nothing but tattoos. Maxie was going to be disappointed. This event wasn't likely to provoke anywhere near enough twisted behaviour for one of her ridiculous articles. Raves were pretty run-of-the-mill these days – just drugs, sex, alcohol, and not one mutated alien baby head to be found anywhere.

I yawned and blinked my eyes to clear away the tears caused by the smoke, and started thinking about how great it would be to go home – and then the crowd went berserk. The dancers slammed into each other and the noise level exploded as everyone started yelling at the tops of their voices and pounding on whatever was at hand. The noise was almost painful. Vicious fights broke out between couples who, moments before, had been acting extremely friendly.

'What the hell?' I said to Maxie, who paused in her picture-taking long enough to shrug.

As if by some invisible signal, a circular opening formed in the middle of the frantic dancers and two robed figures pulled a struggling, scantily dressed female into the centre. She fought in vain to free herself as the spectators began chanting, 'Kill her! Kill her!'

A third robed person pushed through the mob, heading straight for the woman, a long knife poised in the air. Without a second's hesitation, he drove the blade into her chest, and blood blossomed from the wound.

I gasped, rose to my knees and reached into my pocket to find my cell phone. My heart pounded and my hands shook. The amusement park was on the outskirts of town, so who knew how long it would take the police to arrive? As I watched, the woman fell and the robed attacker continued stabbing her as she flailed on the floor. Her thin dress was saturated with her blood. I palmed my phone, ready to dial 9-1-1, when Maxie grabbed it out of my hand.

I was shocked to see her smiling. 'You're such a Girl Scout. Get down before they see you. Everything's okay – I've seen this before. Just watch.' She pushed on my shoulder until I lay flat on the floor again, then returned my phone. 'Put this back in your pocket. You won't need it.'

The revellers in the circle stopped chanting and began cheering as the knife wielder stood and raised his blood-covered blade into the air, accepting the adulation of the onlookers. Then he reached a hand down to the woman on the floor and she grasped it, letting herself be pulled into a standing position. They took a bow and melted into the throng.

What the hell had just happened? Adrenalin flooded my body and my brain spun in stunned confusion.

Maxie shouted into my ear, 'Adolescent party tricks – fake knife and packets of red paint taped to her body. Watch; there'll be more. The children aren't very original tonight.'

That had been a *performance* . . . I was so relieved I felt light-headed. Maxie could have warned me before I had a full-on panic attack – but why hadn't my intuition given me a heads-up about the pretence? I'd been really off since we arrived. Hell, I'd been off all day.

I'd just taken a long deep breath to release the lingering tension in my body when a large hairy thing crashed through the dancers, scattering them like paper dolls.

On closer inspection, the beastie was a big guy in a shaggy bear suit, with the head replaced by a wolfish rubber mask, a sort-of low-rent lupine Bigfoot.

'Oh, eek! It's a werewolf,' Maxie deadpanned in a high voice.

The creature lunged towards a shirtless skinny guy and raked its claws down the young man's chest, leaving dripping blood trails on the white skin.

Maxie leaned in. 'Good luck getting rid of all that red stuff. There's tattoo ink stored in the fake claws.'

I glanced at her and said, loud enough for her to hear, 'You know a lot about all this insanity.'

She grinned, pointed at the hairy guy and made the universal gesture for crazy, twirling her finger next to her head.

The 'werewolf' growled, reached down and grabbed his victim's neck, tearing away a portion underneath his chin.

The attendees roared, thrusting their fists into the air in manic glee.

Were-foot stood over his victim, pounding his chest. The throat-less man remained prone for a few seconds, then jumped to his feet and executed a graceful bow.

They wrapped their arms companionably around each other's shoulders and were swallowed up by the herd.

A movement drew my attention and for the first time I noticed a tall man standing on a raised area in the midst of the crazed revellers. He wore dark, loose-fitting genie-style trousers, and his impressive bare chest was partially hidden by unusually long hair, black, or very dark brown. He had an air of authority, standing there with legs spread, hands fisted on his hips as if he were surveying his kingdom. After observing the dancers for a few moments, he raised his arms into the air and the crowd parted, making way for a cluster of black-robed figures to carry in the wooden box I'd seen earlier.

I nudged Maxie and whispered, 'Who's the genie guy with the long hair? Is he the leader of this cult? Have you seen him before?'

She lowered her camera and focused on the tall man. 'I don't know who he is. Never laid eyes on him before,' she said, grinning, 'but I wouldn't mind finding out. If he's a genie, I'd be happy to rub his bottle anytime.'

I almost laughed out loud before catching myself. 'That makes two of us.' I was too far away from the intriguing man to see if he really was as attractive as he appeared, but he certainly had . . . *something*.

A couple of the robed participants moved to either side of the wooden box and lifted the lid. 'This must be the vampire-staking portion of the evening's entertainment,' I said.

'It's about time. If nothing interesting happens soon, we can head out. This has got to be the most boring pseudo-supernatural event I've ever attended. Sorry for dragging you out to such a feeble waste of time. Maybe we can go find a margarita.'

The moment the top was off the box, the inhabitant started flailing his arms and legs, trying to sit up. The noise of the celebrants diminished a few decibels, as if they'd all quieted to listen to the prisoner screaming obscenities. He didn't disappoint.

Four collaborators lifted the struggling captive, a large, naked fellow, out of the box. Each holding an arm or leg, they carried him up onto the platform where the long-haired man waited. The noise level began to rise again as the audience swarmed closer for a better view.

The victim's limbs were stretched out to form an X as the robed lackeys lowered him to the platform's surface. They held the struggling man in place as the leader bent over, picked up four huge spikes and a fat hammer, and held them aloft. His dark hair streamed down the front of his body.

'My children!' he called, and the masses quietened to hear his voice. 'We have gathered here tonight to slay a traitorous vampire: a renegade who has been banished from his coven for disobedience and betrayal. A bloodsucker who will not follow the will of his Master. I ask you now – shall he live or die?' The man's deep, commanding voice cut through the chaotic sounds in the room with an intimacy that made me squirm with discomfort. Something about his voice troubled me, but I couldn't get a fix on why.

Then, like a scene from an old movie of the spectators at the Roman coliseum giving the thumbs-up or thumbs-down to determine a gladiator's fate, the ravers in the funhouse screamed their approval while gesturing downwards.

Wow. Role-players really take their performances seriously.

'So be it,' the leader proclaimed as he handed three of the thick spikes to a new helper who'd stepped onto the platform. He held up the remaining stake and the hammer, then leaned down and pounded it into the wrist of the man on the floor. The captive screamed and flailed, giving an amazingly authentic performance. Fake blood spurted from the wound as the man in the genie trousers pounded the spike in deeper.

The group cheered.

I leaned into Maxie, and bumped her shoulder and mouthed, 'What the hell?'

She lowered her camera, gazed in my direction, and shook her head. 'These people need to get a life,' she shouted into my ear.

I've never been much of a horror movie fan – not being able to release the ghastly images from my brain after the end of the film definitely put a crimp in my enjoyment of cinematic carnage. So why the hell was I forcing myself to watch this slasher parody?

The leader stretched out his hand, palm up, and his assistant placed another of the thick spikes there. Stepping over the victim's head, the torturer thrust it into the man's other wrist, and pounded until it appeared thoroughly wedged into his skin and bones.

The man screamed. More fake blood spewed from the new hole and spread out in a dark circle from the wound. His pain sounded so legitimate that I had to put my hands over my ears at one point and remind myself I was watching theatre. I couldn't figure out how they made the wounds so real. Maybe this production wasn't as amateur as I'd assumed.

Maxie laughed. 'What a bunch of losers.'

A high-pitched wail drew my attention back to the stage as spikes were pounded into the victim's ankles. His terrified shrieks echoed throughout the building and a familiar smell wafted into my nostrils. My head jerked up and I lifted my nose into the air, sniffing. *Blood.* My stomach tightened. I didn't have any trouble recognising the smell because I'd been swimming in it since I met the vampires.

Why am I smelling blood?

The fake version shouldn't have an odour – unless . . . had they used some kind of animal blood? One of my vampire wannabe clients had mentioned using pig blood from his grandfather's butcher shop in some of his rituals. He said they actually drank it. *Yuck.*

It was hard to hear the man's screams over the uproar of the audience, but I thought he was genuinely suffering – in fact, his performance was *terrifying*. A miserable thought occurred to me and my gorge rose. I'd recently worked with a client who belonged to a BDSM group. He enjoyed being physically abused – experiencing pain was the only way he knew to feel alive, and the only way he could have an orgasm. I wondered if the man on the stage was like my client. Had he signed up for this torture? Or was he the best actor I'd ever seen? If he was mentally ill enough to allow himself to be tortured, shouldn't I do something?

The observers were jumping up and down now, too excited to contain themselves. They'd cheered as each spike pierced the skin and more of the oozing liquid spread onto the platform. There was so much of the dark substance pooling around the man's naked body now that it began to drip off the edges and slide down onto the floor. Some, more adventurous, leaped over to the dripping fluid, slid their hands through it and smeared it on their faces before licking the remains from their fingers.

The leader stood, planted his bare foot on the victim's stomach and stared down at the bloodied man impaled on the platform. The man's screams had diminished in volume. Had he passed out for real, or was he still acting?

'Shall we complete the ceremony?'

The crowd thundered an affirmative, and became even more agitated.

'Who wants to take on the sacred role of my lovely assistant tonight? My vampiric Vanna White?' The leader scanned the room, pointed at someone I couldn't see and said, 'You – *you are chosen!*'

The room went silent, and I realised someone must have switched off the music, because it no longer blared out. From within the mass of bodies, a light-haired, full-figured woman dressed in a flowing white wedding gown made her way to the platform. Like some absurd military escort, all four of the guys who'd secured the man left the raised area and walked down to surround the woman. Was this a take-off of *Bride of Dracula*?

As the woman approached, the leader opened his arms to her. She stepped into his embrace and he swept her into a dance. They twirled and circled on the platform, the bottom of the white dress sliding through the pooled blood until the entire hem was stained.

The crowd was oddly mute.

Then, as abruptly as the dancers had begun, they stopped moving. The genie man cradled the woman's face in his hands and kissed her, then gave her what appeared to be serious eye-contact. She went limp and he guided her onto her knees, next to the imprisoned man.

The tension in the room was palpable. Everyone was so hyper-alert, so on edge, that the slightest stimulation could set them off.

The vampire staking had quickly morphed into a demented reality TV show. Maybe Maxie would be able to glean some disgusting angle to write about after all. I glanced at her, to find her staring at the spectacle, her camera forgotten. Something about the performance had riveted her attention.

The leader bent down and picked up another stake and handed it to the woman. She stared at it until he knelt down beside her, manoeuvred the spike over the bloody man's chest and enclosed her hand within his, tightening her grip on the iron.

'Hold on tight, now.'

He retrieved the hammer, stood and held the tool in the air for the approval of his audience.

They went berserk.

The leader swung the hammer, slamming the spike into the man's heart. The victim shrieked, making a sound I'll never forget, then went silent again. Blood splattered everywhere.

Simultaneously, a jolt of pain shot into my chest and my breath caught, a powerful wave of heat blanketed my body and sweat streamed down my face. My gaze was locked on the lifeless man on the stage.

Sheer terror swept through me and I snapped out of a trance I hadn't realised I'd been in. *That was no performance.*

Being drenched in blood must have startled the bride, because she became hysterical. Her fear was real. The leader lifted her into his arms, carried her to the edge of the platform and tossed her into the crowd.

The tortured man's misery had to be horrifyingly intense near the end in order for it to burst through my psychic protections. That man had just been brutally murdered in front of a huge audience.

I stared at the butchery, my brain spinning in shock, just about to turn to Maxie so we could make a plan of action – call the cops – when several things happened at once.

The leader stood on the stage, blood dripping down his body. He waved his arms through the air and almost every person in the room fell to the floor, scores of costumed bodies piling on top of each other like a Hallowe'en party massacre. A few of the leader's helpers remained standing, flanking the maniac, as if awaiting further instruction.

Next to me, two robed figures appeared from nowhere, grabbed Maxie and disappeared. 'Hey! Stop! Where are you taking her?' I shouted. Adrenalin pumping, I jumped up, not sure what I was going to do, but needing to do something, and smashed into the tall, muscular body of the long-haired murderer. He was suddenly just there, up on the balcony with me, holding my arms.

He smiled, and his silver eyes sparkled.

I screamed.

CHAPTER 8

Blood oozed down the killer's smooth chest. Some of the crimson liquid had transferred onto my parka when I'd slammed into him and the odour was so intense I could almost taste it.

'I've so looked forward to meeting you, Doctor Knight. I hope you enjoyed the show. It was performed especially for you.' His deep voice flowed into my ears like auditory silk, sending vibrating ripples across my skin.

I jerked from side to side, trying without success to break his hold on my arms. His rigid fingers were unyielding. 'What are you talking about? How do you know my name? You just *murdered* that man down there.'

'Indeed – it wasn't one of my finer spectacles, but it was a last-minute affair after all. I can always count on the mindless masses to create whatever drama I require. But where are my manners? I'm keeping you from discovering the purpose for our gathering tonight. Let us retire to the arena.'

He slid one arm around my waist. There was the slightest sense of motion, then we were standing on the platform below, next to the bloody dead body nailed to the floor.

Vampire. The sadistic madman was a vampire. What was wrong with me that I hadn't realised? My intuition was MIA.

I turned my head away from the corpse. Why did this monster want me to see his handiwork? Did he have something against psychologists? Had he been forced into therapy against his will when he was a child? Were there even such things as psychologists when he was a human child? Or was he just mad as a hatter?

'Do you recognise this man, Doctor Knight? I realise he's a bit of a mess, but his features are easily identifiable.'

I struggled against my captor, still trying unsuccessfully to twist out of his grip. 'I don't want to look. What kind of ruthless demon are you? Didn't you have a large enough audience for your insanity?'

'Yes, of course, but I went to all this trouble just for you, so I'm afraid I'll have to insist that you cooperate. Let me get rid of that shadow so you can see better.' He cupped my chin, tilted it towards the body and yelled at his helper, 'Bring one of the torches closer.'

The light was relocated and I tried to shut my eyes, but I couldn't. My eyelids refused to follow my brain's commands. Against my will, I stared down at the face. The man's eyes and mouth were wide open, locked forever in a silent scream, startled by death's sudden arrival.

There *was* something familiar about him. It took me a moment because of all the blood, then recognition crashed over me like a tidal wave: Carson Miller, the radio host. The obnoxious idiot. *The dead guy.*

My head spun, my body went clammy and my solar plexus cramped. Watching what I'd thought was a performance had been disgusting enough, but the realisation that I'd sat passively by, observing the murder of a person I actually knew, was too much for my brain to handle.

He released me, my knees gave out and I dropped into a kneeling position in a pool of Carson's blood.

'Oh, my. We are sensitive, aren't we?' the vampire said, laughing.

I was too busy trying not to vomit to react to his psychotic sense of humour. 'I'm going to be sick.'

'Well, it simply won't do to have you smelling like the contents of your own stomach, so let me make it all better.' He reached down, grasped my arms and lifted me all the way up to his eye-level, effortlessly, as if I weighed nothing. Shocked by being hefted into the air, I met his eyes, but something about them felt bad – dangerous, even – so I quickly averted my gaze. Even that brief eye-contact caused me to go fuzzy, like I used to before the elders' intervention.

'Oh, come now.' He spoke softly, in a low, rumbling voice. 'Admit that you find my eyes beautiful. You can't resist them.' He said the last four words as a command and my eyes shifted to his. I fought as hard as I could to focus anywhere else, but failed, locking gazes with his shining, silver pools and found myself agreeing when he said, 'You feel wonderful – fully restored.'

He lowered me to the platform and I stood, swaying. I

stared down at the bloody corpse and felt nothing. I was pretty sure I ought to have some kind of emotional reaction to being this close to a murder victim, but I couldn't summon anything more than distant curiosity.

'There now. Much better – although you're still a bit sweaty and pale. Let's take off that repulsive wrap, shall we?' He peeled the coat off me, undressing me as if I were a small child, one arm at a time, and threw it to the other end of the platform, away from the blood. He took a step back.

Part of me thought losing the coat was a great idea. Being near the fire had overheated my body, and the smoke made it hard to breathe. The moment the parka was gone it was like a huge weight had been lifted off my body, literally.

But immediately another part of me, struggling to regain control, freaked out that my gun was gone. Not that a firearm would subdue a vampire, but maybe it would distract him long enough for me to make a run for it. *Yeah, right – make a run for it against a creature who can think his way through time and space.*

He was staring at me. I met his gaze.

A roguish smile slid across his face. 'You're quite right, dear doctor. A gun would do nothing against me. It wouldn't even slow me down. I doubt if even the traditional methods for dispatching vampires would affect me any more. Sometimes I actually find that distressing – not to mention boring. As I told you earlier today, I am older than you can imagine.'

As he'd told me earlier today? He's a vampire. I didn't have any vampire clients today. How could he—?

The realisation of where I'd heard that voice before blasted fear through my body. My heart beat double-time and my breathing went shallow.

'I see the light is dawning for you, so to speak. I clouded your mind earlier; now I want you to know me. Lyren Hallow, at your service.' He bowed his head. 'I was your mysterious caller on the radio programme this morning. The programme where our dearly departed treated you with such disrespect.' He picked up one of the unused stakes and tossed it back and forth between his hands. 'In a nod towards full disclosure, I'll admit that I spent a little quality time with him before the radio programme, which might have enhanced some of his less civilised tendencies in preparation for his time with you – it appears I have a rather *primitive* effect on everyone. That's why he was particularly foul. But he was enjoying himself a little too much, so I had to make an example of him.'

I was stunned. My mouth had gone so dry I had to swallow a couple of times before I could speak. 'You mean you killed him because of how he behaved on the radio this morning? Is that what you meant by saying it was for my benefit?'

He dropped the spike, which landed with a loud, echoing thump, and shrugged, his face friendly, as if we were discussing paint samples. 'Why, yes, of course. Such poor breeding is inexcusable. Even more important, the repugnant human had a habit of using the burning ends of cigarettes to torment the women he coerced into spending time with him. While I don't usually concern myself with the tawdry affairs of mortals, this particular specimen was especially intriguing. His predilections reminded me of my own, so

I'm sure you can appreciate the twisted psychological plea-sure I took in destroying him. Perhaps I'll spend some time on your couch one day, and we can explore my motivations. In any case, he was merely a death waiting to happen. I accommodated him. After all, I am a vampire and killing is what we do. Although I'll admit I do a lot more extermi-nating than most. We all have our gifts.'

My brain couldn't get past the fact that Carson's murder had something to do with me. I knew I hadn't done anything myself to cause his death – the fanged Grim Reaper had made it clear he had his own sick reasons – but I was still swamped with sadness and confusion – and terror. What did the vampire have in store for me? Was I to be punished, too?

'No, my dear Doctor Knight,' he responded, reading my thoughts, 'you did nothing deserving of punishment. Indeed, I have other plans for you.'

'Plans?' I croaked. 'What plans?'

He studied me for a few seconds, his smile widening. 'You will star in the glorious unfolding – but now is not the time to speak of that. You are tired, and I have other matters to attend to.' He glanced around at all the monster-costume-clad bodies in puppy-piles throughout the room. 'I must awaken my devotees, erase their memories and send them home. I could leave them here to take the blame for the murder, but I have need of them later.'

I gazed around the room, still oddly surreal and floaty. 'Why did you kill Carson in front of all these people? If it was truly your desire to rid the world of a bad man, why not just visit him in his room and drink him dry? Why make it so public?'

He grinned, his handsome face as innocent as a child's. 'Ah, Doctor, you're applying your own limited interpretation. Don't misunderstand: there is no such mortal designation as *bad* in my mind. I have no interest in ridiculous human notions, and as far as drinking him dry in private, what fun would that be? As the saying goes, "been there and done that." Now I must excuse myself – I hope you won't mind seeing yourself home?'

He reached over and stroked his hand across my cheek. The feeling was very familiar – like the invisible touch when I first arrived in the park – and it was as if he threw a bucket of ice water on me. I suddenly came fully back to myself again as whatever he'd done to me receded, and the horror of standing next to an impaled body grabbed me by the throat. I jerked sideways a couple of steps, tripped over the unused stake and fell on my butt.

Hallow smiled, and vanished from the platform.

Even though the room was still hot and the air thick, chills broke out on my arms. My sensing system shot off its version of flashing red lights and sirens and I struggled to my feet, ran to the other end of the platform and grabbed my parka. As I slipped into it I scanned the sea of sleeping bodies and was torn between concern for their welfare and being creeped-out by their life choices.

I jumped down from the platform and ran to the open doors. Dawn was lightening the eastern sky – I must have been inside far longer than I'd thought. It wasn't until I reached the cool fresh air outside and took a deep breath that I began to wonder what had happened to Maxie. Was she still in the building? Should I go back in and search? And where the hell were the bodyguards I knew Devereux would have had tracking me? He was way too controlling to ever actually leave me on my own.

As soon as I asked myself those questions, the now-familiar voice spoke in my mind: 'Your friend is safe and well. She drove herself home, in a mild trance, of course. No need to concern yourself with her or the sleeping children.' He chuckled. 'I'm so glad you asked about your White Knight's security force. I had so much fun eliminating each one, slowly and painfully.'

I scanned the area for the source of the voice, but Hallow wasn't there, at least not physically. *Oh. My. God. What about Devereux? Why hadn't he followed me? That was so unlike him. He's too strong to be influenced by this lunatic.*

'Oh, but this is delicious! Sorry to be the one to break this to you, but your devoted warrior is having a hard time resisting me himself. In fact, he doesn't even know how accommodating he's being. He'll be shocked.'

Shit. I need to get out of here. Go to The Crypt and warn Devereux . . .

Laughter echoed in my head. 'No, I don't think so – it wouldn't do any good, anyway. Besides, he's snoozing in his coffin and wouldn't hear you if you screamed in his face. Go home now.'

'Go home? How am I supposed to do that when you kidnapped the person who drove me here—'

'Surely you haven't already forgotten the new skills I gave you?'

I grabbed the sides of my head. Something about his voice was causing my skull to vibrate and I had the beginnings of a headache, which scared me. My hands shook and my heart pounded. He was obviously able to override my protections, which meant my brain was in danger again. I hurried towards the entrance to the park, hoping his voice would fade like a cell phone signal if I put distance between us. What new skills was he talking about?

'Come now, Doctor. How could you forget something so momentous, so *otherworldly*? Surely you recall your unexpected trip to your office earlier this evening?'

'Hey!' I yelled, pain radiating through my skull. 'Will you get out of my head before it explodes?'

Silence.

Had I just scolded a homicidal vampire? Something was definitely hinky with my impulse control lately.

I stopped dead and grabbed onto the splintered wooden counter of the ticket booth at the gate as my knees almost gave out. The absence of Hallow's reverberating voice in my mind sent relief surging through my body.

The reprieve made me remember some research I'd read about using sound waves as a weapon, and how resonance could obliterate solid objects. I wondered how much pressure would have to be exerted to split open a skull? But I wasn't about to volunteer to find out. How could a disembodied voice produce sound waves anyway?

More occult bullshit.

Anger and discouragement wrestled for position in my emotional control centre. I couldn't count the times over the last five months I'd regretted my decision to involve myself with supernatural beings and metaphysical philosophies that most people only fantasised – or had nightmares – about. I often had second thoughts about wading into the preternatural muck, not only because it was terrifying, but because there was no way to make sense of anything – there was no rule book. Never knowing what lurked in the next shadow was a recipe for ulcers and insanity.

And after everything that had happened, the likelihood that the vampires would let me walk away was nil.

As I stood alone in a burned-out amusement park at the crack of dawn, I wished with all my heart I could press the *rewind* button on the cosmic video camera and go back to my simple, safe life. Okay, it was boring, but secure, predictable.

But would I really go back? Pity party aside, would I really give up my new life if I had the chance? Give up my new clientele – and Devereux? Right then I didn't have a clear answer, and I had more immediate problems to deal with.

Carson had been murdered. My first instinct was to call the police. I reached into my pocket and fished out my phone and started to punch in 9-1-1 – then stopped. What was I doing? If I did call them, what would I say? An evil vampire – yes, they really did exist – kidnapped and staked a radio talk show host in front of an audience of fake monsters, a reporter for a scurrilous rag and a local psychologist? Then the bad vampire caused the audience to pass out, ordered his servants to grab the reporter, and travelled through thought to snatch the psychologist? Send the guys with the white coats, please. Reporting another murder I had no rational explanation for would trap me into a new legal ordeal, and I'd only just begun to recover, professionally and personally, from the first situation months earlier.

Too bad Lieutenant Bullock, the lead investigator on that serial murder case, and one of the only other local humans aware of the vampires, was off training at Quantico. She would've known what to do to straighten out this mess.

But I was on my own. I paced in a circle, grasping for ideas. What if I called in anonymously from a pay phone – if there were such a thing any more? I could just report the crime, give the location – supposing they knew where the old amusement park was located, because I certainly didn't – and hang up. Yeah, I could do that.

I tucked the cell phone back in my pocket and stared at the vast sky. Barely perceptible light softened the eastern horizon, announcing the approaching dawn. All the little vampires, except the day-walking Lyren Hallow, of course, would be snug in their coffins soon, the immortal horror show concluded for another night. Of course, the human maniacs were still free to spread their own brand of ghastly chaos, impervious to the position of the hands on the clock.

As much as I hated to admit it, Devereux had been right. He hadn't been crying wolf about Hallow; the sociopathic bloodsucker was seriously dangerous. And what did he mean about *having other plans for me*? I'd witnessed his idea of fun, and remembering the sound of the large spikes piercing

Carson's limbs made the bile rise in my throat and my stomach clench. What could I possibly do to fend off such a demon?

The cautious portion of my psyche took centre stage and began reciting the reasons I should go and hide in Devereux's penthouse. She enthusiastically gave voice to my fears, and hadn't even got halfway through her arguments when the smirking, rebellious part who'd thought it would be fun to leave Devereux out of the information loop swaggered into the spotlight, pushed Caution aside and grabbed the meta-phorical microphone. They yelled at each other in my inner rubber room, attracting the attention of another indecisive group of my sub-personalities who stepped into the scene, observed the conflict and decided not to get involved, leaving Caution and Rebel to duke it out.

As I watched Caution leap onto Rebel's back and wrestle her down, I hoped she'd have the strength to retain control. Who would I be if I wasn't her? Then it occurred to me to wonder which part of me was doing the watching?

Schizophrenia, anyone?

I – whatever *I* meant at that point – concentrated my thoughts on Hallow. What if he'd lied about Maxie? What if he'd done something to her? As I thought that, I braced myself for another mental onslaught – more head-rumbling opinions from the dark hunter – but didn't receive one. Had the murderer really stopped talking in my mind just because I'd asked him to? No, I didn't believe that for a minute. Nothing about immortals was that simple. I was sure the situation would prove to have more horrifying layers than

I could anticipate; yet another aspect of vampires a human mind couldn't comprehend.

I surveyed the empty landscape with the burned-out rollercoaster silhouetted against the sunrise and wondered again how I'd get home. I could call a cab – surely the dispatcher would know where this old park was located? That would certainly be the normal, *rational*, thing to do.

Then I thought about what Hallow had said about his little gift, and I suddenly remembered my earlier experience. Why not test out the travelling-through-thought thing – what if it wasn't just a one-shot deal? It had worked before – although, granted, by accident. Was I refusing to try it just because he suggested I should? There was definitely a point to that; no good could possibly come from following the advice of a murdering psychopath. Maybe he was setting me up. My attempt to replicate my previous experience would no doubt amuse him. He'd probably get a kick out of watching me fail. Vampire or not, sociopaths shared some characteristics in common, and I was very familiar with those.

Wait a minute. What if I got caught in some weird vortex of time and space? I didn't know enough about how vampires manipulated energy to have any options for rescuing myself if I got stuck between dimensions. A particularly gruesome episode of *Star Trek* came to mind where, due to a transporter malfunction, some poor man screamed as his molecules were wrenched apart and scattered into the universe. Sometimes I wished I didn't have such a fertile imagination.

Actually, I'd be considerably more comfortable if there

was some kind of contraption to step into, like on the television show: something with solid walls and a floor to stand on, and someone in charge of the process. Just intending to blink from one place to another felt like leaping into a bottomless abyss and hoping for the best.

Despite all my rational fears about transcending consensus reality, my body was apparently eager to give it a go. My intuition chimed in, nodding its head, willing to sign off on the experiment – or maybe that was Rebel's voice. It was hard to tell; it was getting so crowded in my psyche that I wasn't sure which part of me was at the controls now. Who was I to quibble about a tiny thing like my molecules scattering to the winds?

Was this what insanity felt like?

I closed my eyes, visualised my favourite chair in my living room and scrunched my face into a serious pose of concentration. After a few seconds, when I didn't get the usual breeze against my face, I opened one eye to investigate. I was still standing frozen in the same spot, all the muscles in my body tightly contracted like I was braced for attack.

Well, shit. I was obviously doing it wrong. How had I managed it before? I'd just thought about the location of my purse and briefcase and found myself there, hadn't I? I forced myself to relax my shoulders, circled my head to release the tension and shook my hands in front of me to restore the circulation.

Okay, so all I needed to do was think about sitting on my comfy armchair, my feet propped up on the ottoman, drinking a glass of wine. Yeah, that was good. I'd just smiled at the pleasant vision when my solar plexus began to itch, my hair blew back from my face and I had the sense of being in an elevator, or falling without a parachute – just for a nanosecond, then the next thing I knew, I was flat on the floor next to my chair at home. I huffed out a breath at the rude landing, raised my head to glance around, then sat up.

The living room light was on. I must have forgotten to turn it off when I left with Maxie, though that wasn't like me. I slowly climbed to my feet, patted myself down to make sure, as before, that all of me had arrived in the same time zone and zip code, and smiled.

'Hot damn! I did it! At least there's one good thing that came from all the vampire crap!' I promised myself I'd enjoy this mysterious ability for as long as it lasted.

Caution pursed her lips and gave me a disapproving scowl, which I ignored.

I threw off the heavy parka and moved to the stairs leading up to my bedroom and bathroom, then I froze. Was my shower running? Had I left it on? What the hell was the matter with me? I'd *never* done anything like that.

Stress hormones surged through my body and the warning arrow on my radar shot from zero to a thousand, letting me know in no uncertain terms that something was wrong. My fight-or-flight instinct shifted into high gear.

Remembering the gun in the pocket of the coat, I tiptoed over to where I'd thrown the parka, retrieved the weapon and crept to the staircase. Holding the pistol in my trembling hand, I climbed the stairs, cursing under my breath at every creak. I paused halfway when I saw the light was on in the bathroom and the door open.

I had sneaked the rest of the way up the stairs when I was startled by a loud noise – and since I often made that noise myself, I recognised the clatter of the bar of soap hitting the bottom of the tub. Somebody was in my damn shower! I paused for a moment, straining to remember if any visitors were expected from out of town or if I'd given my house key to anyone recently, but no one came to mind.

I lifted the gun, held it with both hands in a futile effort to stop the shaking, and stood in the bathroom doorway.

The water suddenly stopped and I waited through a few seconds of heavy silence. A hand whisked back the shower curtain, causing a loud ripping sound, and a wet, naked man grinned from inside.

'Kismet! Surprise!'

CHAPTER 9

I automatically raised the gun with quivering hands and pointed it at the intruder's chest as he lifted his arms into the air and widened his smile. 'Hey, don't shoot me! I'm not immortal yet.'

His pale skin was lighter than I'd ever seen it, and his black hair had grown well below his shoulders, but as I slid my gaze down his lean frame, I recognised a familiar body part. We hadn't seen each other since before Hallowe'en, and it had been a lot longer than that since I'd hung out with the portion of his anatomy in question, but there was no mistaking the unique endowment of my superficial, materialistic, narcissistic ex-boyfriend, Dr Thomas Radcliffe.

I lowered the gun and relief swamped me as I stared into mischievous dark brown eyes. 'Tom? What the hell are you doing here?'

My naked visitor flashed an even-more-blinding Hollywood

smile. 'Didn't you get my message? I told you I want to talk to Devereux. Zoë tells me he's the big vampire cheese.'

I struggled to keep a stern expression on my face, but I couldn't quite manage it because 'Tom Junior', as he used to call it, was twitching and bobbing like a dowsing rod, almost as if it was trying to say hello in its own fleshy way. I couldn't shift my gaze; the kinesthetic memory was so strong that my hand almost reached out to pat the little guy's head.

To keep myself from doing something I'd certainly regret – same old song, different verse – I grabbed a towel from the nearby rack and shoved it at Tom.

He smirked as he dried his hair, fully aware of his effect on me.

I cleared my throat and glared. 'How the hell did you get into my house? I'm absolutely sure I locked the door when I left.'

He threw the towel on the floor and stepped out of the shower. Junior now displayed his best posture, apparently happy to see me. 'Zoë brought me – it was amazing. She just thought us here, all the way from Los Angeles. Hanging out with vampires is so awesome.' He chuckled. 'Listen to me telling the big vampire cheese's girlfriend about hanging around with vampires.' He scanned me up and down. 'What's that all over your sweater? And your jeans? Have you been partaking in Cow Town's favourite sport, mud wrestling?' He threw back his head and laughed. 'I would've paid money to see that.'

I glanced down at the dried blood on my clothes. Tom's

obliviousness saved me from having to give any normal explanations. 'Very funny.'

He closed the distance between us and pulled me into a wet hug, apparently not at all concerned about the 'mud' on my shirt. 'It's great to see you, Kismet. I've missed you.'

I pushed against his chest with my free hand, forcing him to back up. Saying he missed me was Tom code for 'I need something from you'.

'Dial down the Don Juan routine, Doctor Hollywood. Even if I weren't already involved with the big cheese, I'm not getting cozy with you or Tom Junior. That's ancient history.'

He winked. 'You know what a history buff I am.'

'Uh-huh. So, where's Zoë? At The Crypt?'

Tom had met Zoë the night we'd gone to Devereux's club, when he'd shown up on my doorstep and invited himself along on my date with Alan Stevens. I hadn't seen Tom for a couple of years before that; I'd been surprised to find he was genuinely interested in my vampire-wannabe research.

That night had been his first exposure to the undead underworld, and something about the lifestyle had obviously appealed to him, because he and the attractive Zoë had taken off for California without even saying good-bye.

'Are you sure you want to talk about Zoë? I'm all warm and clean . . .' He moved closer.

'You've got to be kidding,' I replied.

Not that I expected anything different. Tom and I shared a profession, and we'd spent several years together as a couple, but Tom's philosophy was 'so many women, so little time', and so we'd parted, not entirely amicably, almost three years earlier. It had taken me a while to heal, but now, aside from a little residual lust, I couldn't remember what I ever saw in him. He was the poster boy for Narcissistic Personality Disorder. In his mind, the universe revolved around Tom Radcliffe.

I pushed harder against his chest. 'So, back to Zoë. Where is she?'

He let his arms drop away from me and ran his hands through his long wet hair. 'She's using one of Devereux's extra coffins at The Crypt. She says he always keeps a few vacant to accommodate out-of-towners.'

I nodded. 'Yeah, it's a regular bloodsucking Holiday Inn.'

Tom laughed and pointed to the bathroom door. 'Hand me my clothes, will you? They're hanging on the hook.'

I grabbed his designer jeans and trendy T-shirt. 'Why did you need to take a shower? Or, more important, why did you need to take a shower *here*? Why didn't you get a hotel room?'

And where's your underwear?

He tugged on his jeans, zipped up slowly and smiled. 'Well, I came here instead of getting a room because Zoë said Devereux practically lives here and I intend to talk to him. I needed a shower because Zoë and I – well, we entertained ourselves, and I needed to freshen up.'

'Oh, *yuck!* Just exactly where did you entertain yourselves?' I had disgusting visions of DNA stains on my bedding or couch – or on my carpet! I was going to mention the blood-coloured blotches now decorating his wet chest from his contact with my ruined sweater, but he slid on his green T-shirt before I could form the words.

He frowned. 'For your information, I spread a towel on the bed in your guest room before we used it. We actually started out in your room, but Zoë said Devereux would kill us if we were disrespectful enough to have sex in the Master's girlfriend's bed. So since I didn't want to die before everything was arranged, naturally we moved to the other room. Oh, that reminds me, I need to pop that towel into your washing machine. You do have one, don't you?'

A low, rumbling voice whispered in my mind, 'Dispose of this idiot.'

Without any conscious thought, my fingers tightened around the handle of the pistol I was still holding. I stared at Tom and for a few seconds I seriously considered shooting him. Some evil part of my brain smiled as it imagined inflicting a scar that would mar the perfection of his face or a wound that would forever alter the appealing lines of his body. I'd just begun to fantasise about him falling to the floor in a spreading pool of his own blood when he snapped his fingers in front of my face.

'Hey, Kismet. Are you in there?'

I jumped, startled, and my consciousness snapped back into place like a stretched rubber band. Back from where, I didn't know, but only a second before I could've sworn I'd heard familiar laughter.

'What?' I glanced down at the gun in my hand; I was clutching the handle so tightly all the colour had leached out of my skin, and the weapon was pointed at Tom.

He smirked. 'I'm into playing cops and robbers as much as the next guy, but if you're going to hold me at gunpoint,

I can think of better rooms to do it in.' He cocked his head and frowned. 'You look like your credit card was declined, or you've just seen a ghost – what's going on?'

I'm losing my mind, that's what's going on.

I forced myself to lower the hand holding the gun. I raised my eyes to his, almost afraid my homicidal daydream would commandeer my brain again, but as he stood there staring at me, the same self-absorbed, thoughtless man he'd always been, I didn't experience any more violent urges. I might still harbour some resentment for the way he broke up with me, but we had so much shared history and so I'd long since relegated him to the category of old friend. I even enjoyed his company. Sometimes. Even at my angriest, I'd never had such ferocious thoughts about Tom – or anyone, for that matter. I didn't know how to answer his question, or why I'd overreacted. There might be two therapists in the room, but neither could help me.

'I'm just tired,' I muttered at last. 'Too much mud-wrestling.'

That elicited a smile from him.

'I need to see this infamous towel.' I marched down the hall to my guest room, flicked on the light and studied the large purple towel covering the bed. Gross. It would definitely need the heavy-duty wash cycle. Repeatedly, if I was ever going to bring myself to use it again. 'You're lucky you didn't desecrate my bed. Forget Devereux. *I* would've killed you.'

Tom crept up behind me, pressed himself against my body and rested his chin on my shoulder. He whispered close to my ear, 'See? No mess on the bed. Everything on the towel. Neat and tidy. I'm nothing if not efficient.'

I smiled to myself. What a fool the man was! I couldn't decide if I wanted to slug him or knee him in the balls – in a *friendly* way, of course. He was lucky I was too tired to act on either option.

I pointed at the towel. 'Pick up your mess and come with me.'

He retrieved it, holding the corners with two fingers, and followed me downstairs to the washing machine. I was tempted to simply throw it away, but it was one of the gorgeous plush set my parents had given me for my birthday last year and I hated to part with it.

I left him to deal with the remains of his entertainment, detoured over to where I'd dropped Maxie's parka and replaced the gun in the pocket. Then, completely wiped out, I shuffled into the kitchen and sat at the table, staring off into space. I was too wired to sleep, but so exhausted I couldn't imagine doing anything else.

Tom ambled into the room, leaned against a counter, and grinned. 'You look like hell. And you smell funky – like smoke and . . . blood? Where were you tonight, some wild vampire orgy? Wait, I've got it: you were at some mud-wrestling vampire orgy.' He laughed at his pitiful remarks, as usual thinking everything he said was laugh-out-loud funny.

It took him this long to scent the blood? All that recreational snorting must have fried his sense of smell.

He'd actually come pretty close to guessing where I'd been – the vampire orgy part, anyway – but not the way he assumed. Even if I'd been inclined to tell him anything meaningful, which I wasn't, I wouldn't involve him in Hallow's madness. Tom was a behavioural psychologist, which meant he believed 'reality' was exactly what it appeared to be. *Truths* equalled quantifiable facts and were written in stone. In my new world, that belief had proven to be a faulty assumption. I didn't know how deeply Tom had explored the vampire realm, so since I didn't have the energy or inclination to reeducate him, I opted for misdirection.

'Just out doing research for my vampire wannabe book.'

He cocked a brow. 'Still working on that? I would've thought you'd be finished by now – or you'd progressed to a sexier topic. Wait until I tell you about the deal I'm putting together for a cable programme. You'll be so impressed – I'll be the most famous shrink in the world.' He frowned. 'I just need to take care of something first.'

The man has always had an ego the size of Jupiter and now it was bloating with age. 'What are you talking about? Why do you want to see Devereux?' It occurred to me that Tom might be planning to ask Devereux for money, since the wealthy vampire was up to his fangs in it – Tom always had a deal cooking that required extra capital. But on second thought, that didn't add up, because Tom had become quite rich in his own right over the last few years.

He sat across from me at the table and I noticed again how light his skin was. I couldn't remember ever seeing him without his trademark tan. During our time together, he'd frequently told me he didn't believe the sun could damage his skin; he was certain that idea was a myth! I had chosen not to mention the fact that his skin had already begun to age – it was almost reptilian, in fact. It wouldn't have been kind of me to poke fun at such deeply-held delusions, especially as his regularly scheduled facials, skin peels and cosmetic surgery procedures had become the focus of his life.

Tom's parents had set the perfection bar higher than he could ever reach.

He stared at me for a few seconds, playing imaginary piano on the tabletop – something he always did while trying to choose the most influential words for his latest manipulation – then beamed a toothy smile. 'I've decided to become a vampire,' he announced.

My head automatically began the up-and-down motion I used to stall for time, which also functioned as an entry ramp into the silence that would encourage clients to spill their guts. 'I see.' I knew where this conversation was going.

He stopped pretending to tickle the ivories and scowled. He splayed his hands palms-down on the table. '"I see"? That's all you have to say? I share a life-changing decision with you and that's all I get?' He leaned in and opened his eyes wide, waiting.

I cleared my throat. I *really* didn't want to have this discussion. Going to bed sounded so much better – so much more *normal*. 'Well, it isn't as if I don't hear that every day.'

Right on cue, the thick vein on his forehead that always throbbed when he was angry started pulsing. 'You're comparing me to your pitiful wannabe clients? I'm being lumped in with those lost souls you counsel? You're going to treat me like some fucked-up—'

I thrust my hand up in a *stop* gesture and held it in front of his face. 'Okay. Tell me.' *I surrender. The faster I get this over with, the quicker I can crawl under my covers and pretend my excursion with Maxie was only a bad dream, a vampire-created hallucination. Then I can figure out why I almost shot my ex-boyfriend. I'm too young for menopause.*

He relaxed in his chair and maintained eye contact. 'I'm not sure where to begin – meeting Zoë that night you took me to Devereux's club changed everything.'

Here comes a long, tedious Tom tale.

'How did meeting Zoë change everything?' I asked patiently. 'You mean because she's a vampire and you were certain no such things existed?'

'Yeah, well, her being a vampire was certainly the big news, but initially I had other things on my mind. At first, it was just the obvious: she's a beautiful woman with a great body, and I'm a guy. After we danced for a while, she suggested we go to one of the small private rooms up on the second floor and get to know each other better. She was definitely playing my tune – you know me, I'm always up for a quick tumble with a gorgeous woman.' He winked suggestively at me.

Yeah, in your dreams.

'Anyway, we got naked and she started talking about being a vampire. I figured she was nuts, but I humoured her. It wasn't like I was going to let something as lame as her vampire delusion interfere with my orgasm.' He waggled his eyebrows. 'I guess I can be a little self-absorbed sometimes.'

'You think?' I laughed so long he raised his voice to regain my attention.

'*Ahem*. So she said she was going to show me she was a vampire, and she let her fangs descend, and all this time she'd been staring into my eyes, making me feel like I'd had a few tokes of good Mexican, and just as I was about to have the best climax I'd ever had—' He stopped and patted my hand. 'No offence meant, of course. Our sex life was great, too.'

I snorted again – he was so pitifully self-obsessed – but managed, 'No offence taken. Go on with your story. I'm all ears.' I was so tired I couldn't even work up any annoyance at his density.

He frowned, and I could almost see the wheels in his brain turning as he tried to figure out what was so funny. 'So, best climax, et cetera, and then she *bites* me – she actually chomps down on my neck with her sharp teeth. For a couple of seconds it hurt like hell, but then – well, I'm sure you know, since you and Devereux—'

Multiple orgasmic body rushes, soul-melding transcendence, toe-curling ambrosia . . . 'Yes, I know. Then what?'

'Well, after she convinced me she was really a vampire, we sat and talked until dawn. She told me how she'd been turned, and how lonely she'd been until she joined Devereux's coven. Evidently he's held in high regard by the vampire community. She says he's strict but fair, something that isn't common in their world. The vampire who sired her – that's the guy who fanged her – is a wuss, so she isn't as powerful as she would have been if someone like Devereux had brought her over. Apparently if she drinks Devereux's blood, she gets stronger – I guess that's one of the things he does for his coven members.'

I sat up a little straighter in my chair. I'd never heard that. Devereux was very close-mouthed about his coven. He shared his blood with them? I guessed that made sense. But something about it made me uncomfortable, although I wasn't quite sure what bothered me – was it the intimacy of it, or the fact that he hadn't told me?

Too much to think about. I pushed those questions out of my brain and shifted my attention back to Tom. 'So I still don't understand how hanging out with Zoë has made you want to die. That's what really happens, you know. It isn't glamorous or romantic. You'll be dead. A *corpse.* A blood-drinker . . .'

'Yeah, I get it.' He paused and studied me. 'Is that really how you think of Devereux? As a corpse? Or are you just giving me your therapist spiel?'

I had to ponder that for a few seconds. Devereux was unique in ways that had nothing to do with vampirism – all that magical mysticism and Druid ancestry, I guess. And I was hardly one to be pointing a self-righteous finger at anyone about drinking blood. 'No, I guess I don't think of him that way, but it's still the reality for most, and if I didn't mention that particular set of truths to my clients, I'd be lying. From what little I know about the process, it isn't as if a new vampire simply springs forth complete with powers and ancient knowledge. All that stuff comes with time – sometimes decades, sometimes centuries. And unless a powerful vampire does the turning, a newbie could spend eternity as someone's flunky. Does that sound appealing to you?'

He gave me his best nefarious grin. 'Not in the least – that's why I'm here to sign up with the most powerful vampire there is. If Devereux brings me over, I'll be in the top percentage of vampires.'

Holy shit.

'The *top percentage* of vampires?' I hooted with laughter. 'That's the stupidest thing I've ever heard you say, and you've given me lots to compare it to. If you think being a vampire is just another lifestyle choice, you're a bigger ass than I thought. Is this some kind of competition to you? Some kind of undead award you're after? Do you honestly think it's like being a member of some exclusive club? What on earth has Zoë been telling you – and why would you ever think Devereux would participate in such a thing?'

His face fell, as if he'd momentarily abandoned his performance. 'I'm getting old, Kismet,' he said quietly.

'What?' I knew he had always been fixated on staying young, but he was only eight years older than me, and that wasn't old by any rational standard.

'I'm not even forty yet and I have wrinkles,' he said, sounding almost heartbroken. 'My surgeon said I've already had too many procedures for someone my age – he said my skin is *sun-damaged*.' Tom was beginning to sound seriously aggrieved now, as if the world had lied to him. 'He refuses to operate on me any more – and he says if I go to another doctor, I'll end up like one of those scary reality TV plastic-surgery-gone-wrong freaks who don't even look human any more. My career is just starting to come together and I live in La-La land where we worship youth and beauty. Zoë says if I come over now, I'll stay as I am forever – I'll maybe even gain a little youth in the process. I could at least be a star for a few years before they notice I'm not ageing.'

I realised my mouth had been hanging open, so I closed it. 'Wait a minute – what about the current crop of television psychologists? They're not spring chickens and haven't built their empires on their physical attributes. Why are you so paranoid? Have you considered that it might be a good thing to appear old and wise?'

He sprang out of the chair and paced around the kitchen, no longer making eye-contact. 'Old and wise won't work for the project I just pitched to cable. It's an edgy reality TV show for an adult audience. I'd be counselling people, but not in a talk-show format.'

I watched him march back and forth across the room. 'Well, if not a talk show, what would it be?'

He mumbled something under his breath.

'What did you say? I didn't hear you.'

He paused in front of me, crossed his arms protectively over his chest, and cleared his throat. 'Everything's tentative right now – my people are talking to their people – but I'm going to be Doctor Sex. I'd . . . um, actively – well, counsel people who have sexual problems. Sort of – well, a glorified sexual surrogate. We'd have a tasteful yet erotic bedroom set, and all the sessions would take place there.' He eased into the chair again. 'It's going to be on one of the premium channels, and there'll be lots of full-body shots. So you can see why I need to stay young and handsome.'

I had a sudden vision of Tom at his most pompous, instructing people on how to most efficiently shove part A into part B, and then demonstrating the correct way to accomplish the task. It sounded X-rated to me.

'So what's the difference between that and a porn movie?'

He thrust his chin into the air. 'Sex therapists are *professionals*, Kismet. Obviously I'll need to get my licence for that specialty. I can assure you there's no licence needed for *porn!*'

Oops. Apparently I'd hit a nerve – he must have had some mixed emotions about the porn notion too. We both knew that making one false move, professionally speaking, could lose him his psychology licence.

'You came up with the idea for this programme all by yourself?'

He reclaimed his chair and fanned his fingers out on the table, pretending to examine his manicured nails. 'The idea was tossed around at a party I attended. You probably remember that I have a keen interest in all aspects of sex, right?' I nodded at the understatement of the year. 'Well, some friends and I were experimenting, and a couple of them teasingly asked if I knew the best position to achieve a certain goal, and I just happened to have that knowledge, so I showed them – in fact, I ended up demonstrating a number of techniques to several people. At the end of the evening someone said I was so good at it, I should go into business as a sex therapist. Not only that, but someone else had videotaped the evening and when I watched the tape back – well, I had to agree that the camera loved me. I do have a knack for sex therapy.'

Trying not to laugh by holding my lower lip between my teeth had started to hurt, and my jaw made a cracking sound when I opened my mouth. I struggled to keep a serious expression on my face. 'I'm not clear on the actual *therapy* part of this plan,' I started. 'So what else happens besides a lot of orgasms? Can you even do that stuff on television?'

'Yes,' he said enthusiastically, 'on special channels for adults – I forgot to mention that during the sessions, while I'm describing the sex techniques, I'm also talking to them about the psychological reasons for their problems, and about ways to enhance emotional intimacy. So whenever I demonstrate something myself, I'll be sharing personal issues I've conquered myself in order to become the man I am today. We had a mock session, and at the end one of the audience members was crying – it was *tremendously* moving. So you must see why I'm excited about this idea? I'd get to do two things I love – sex and therapy – as well as make money and be on television. It just doesn't get any better than that.'

He stared at me expectantly.

I didn't want to say 'I see' again, so I just stared back at him. I noticed his unnaturally ashen appearance once more. 'Why are you so pale? Are you sick? Is that really why you think you want to become one of the children of the night? Is this whole Doctor Sex story just a cover?'

He gave me a sheepish smile. 'No, I'm not sick. I really do want to be Doctor Sex and on television. I'm so white because Zoë's been trying to turn me and she just doesn't have the juice.' He lowered his gaze. 'She's getting a little worried, because no matter how much blood we swap, the only thing that happens is that I get weaker. She's afraid she's just killing me, even though we're trying to follow the transformation ritual but the thing is, she's not totally clear on how to perform it. In fact . . .' He stared down at his hands again. 'We've kind of just been making it up as we go along.'

'There's a *transformation* ritual?'

'Yeah. Zoë asked a bloodsucker she met in California for information and apparently there are a couple of routes to becoming a vampire. The most painless one has lots of steps, and it involves both the sucker and the suckee holding a *pure desire*, whatever that is.'

'Pure desire? Devereux told me that the turning process was more complicated than anything that's portrayed in movies and books, but he has never elaborated.' Devereux's dead mother had mentioned something about it being difficult to become a vampire – she'd said *intention* was needed. If I ever ran into – or *through* – her again, I'd be sure to ask what she meant – along with a couple of hundred other questions.

Then I focused on something Tom had just said and grimaced. 'Go back to the bit about swapping blood. You're *drinking Zoë's blood?*' Geez! All the chemicals in his peels, facials and hair dye jobs must have seeped through his skin and started rotting his brain. He was crazier than most of my clients. I had no idea he'd got so desperate.

He narrowed his eyes and pressed his lips together tightly for a few seconds. 'You hypocrite! You're boinking a corpse – you let him drink your blood. Are you honestly expecting me to believe that you've never sampled his? That you've never been on the receiving end?'

Since my judgemental opinion was probably written all over my face, I couldn't blame him for having such a reaction.

'We're not talking about me. I'm not the one going on a liquid diet.' I had a quick memory flash of drinking a cup of elders' blood. *Bullshit much, Kismet?*

We locked eyes for a few seconds, both scowling – then his brown eyes softened and he reached across the table and took my hands in his. 'Will you help me, Kismet? Will you talk to Devereux? Put in a good word for me? Please?'

Wow. Tom had to be desperate if he was willing to admit he needed anyone's help for anything. But I couldn't begin to imagine how the conversation I'd have to have with Devereux would go after, *Devereux, my love. Would you please drain all the blood from my ex-boyfriend Tom so he can die and rise as a vampire to become the world-renowned Dr Sex on cable TV?* Yeah, that would be fun. Time for some artful avoidance.

I stood and patted Tom's cheek. 'Let me sleep on it.'

He smiled. 'I could help you sleep on it.'

Laughing, I walked out of the kitchen, trudged up the stairs and into the bathroom. I locked the door, stripped off my bloody clothes and took the world's quickest shower. Still wet, I bolted into my bedroom, secured that door, peeled down the covers – which were thankfully still clean – and jumped into bed.

I slept like the dead.

CHAPTER 10

'I see you threw quite a party. I'm sure the Master will be amused.'

My eyes flew open. Luna, Devereux's personal assistant and undead pit bull, was standing next to my bed. It wasn't full dark, but since she was vertical, it was safe to assume the sun had gone behind the mountains. I'd slept the entire day away.

She was dressed in her familiar black leather: skintight trousers and a cleavage-enhancing bustier. Her eye makeup was sedate compared to her usual Cleopatra-inspired artistry, with only one colour of eye shadow tonight, rather than the multi-hued extravaganza she regularly painted on. The bold design was still a sharp contrast against her very pale skin. Her long, straight hair fell like a thick, black veil in an unintended salute to Morticia Addams. Her silver eyes reminded me of . . . the murdering psychopath from the night before at the deserted amusement park. I took a breath and forced myself to banish that thought. It wasn't safe to send out any unconscious invitations.

'What are you talking about? What party?' I sat up and something fell from my forehead down onto my breasts. I'd been in such a hurry to get into bed that I hadn't taken the time to put on a nightgown. Or anything else.

Without thinking about my state of undress, I flicked on the bedside lamp, squinted down at the shiny blue thong displayed on my chest and tried to remember why strange underwear would've been on my head. Unless I'd blacked out and one of my split personalities had invited someone for a sleepover, I had no answer to the mystery.

Luna bent down, lifted the thong with one finger and dangled it in the air in front of my face. An evil smile spread across her lips. 'I hope the sex was worth dying for, because the Master is going to destroy him.'

I tugged a blanket over my exposed breasts and stared at the blue fabric. I snatched the object from her finger and gave it a close inspection. There, embroidered across the front in golden thread, were the initials TR. Well, at least I knew why Tom hadn't donned any underwear when he'd got dressed in front of me – he obviously still enjoyed whipping off his skimpy thong and throwing it into the air before he got down to business. Some things never changed. While I was glad to have solved the puzzle, I was disgusted that it had somehow ended up on my head. Apparently, they'd spent more time in my room than Tom let on. I guess his fear of death took a while to kick in.

I tossed Tom's underwear on the floor and met the

smirking gaze of the Amazon vampire looming over me. 'Tom and Zoë frolicked in my guest room while I was gone last night. They must have undressed in here. Not that I owe you any kind of explanation.'

She snorted. 'I'll be sure to tell the Master. I'm *certain* he'll be understanding. He's *so* trusting of your sincerity.'

I wasn't awake enough to deal with Luna. Actually, I was never awake enough to deal with the hostile she-devil. She'd loathed me even before we'd met, for the sole reason, as far as I could see, that Devereux enjoyed my company. To Luna, humans were useful only as a food source, and she couldn't imagine any other reason to have one of us around. I'd never figured out if there was any jealousy in the mix – if she wanted Devereux for herself – or if it really was all about her belief that humans were nothing more than liquid delivery systems – and inferior ones at that.

The fact that Devereux's assistant was a cross between a Playboy bunny and a supermodel didn't make dealing with her any easier. We'd unwillingly spent time together a few months earlier, when Devereux had ordered her to protect me. She'd fought the insane vampire Lucifer to save my life and wound up on the short end of the fang. Watching Luna struggle to control her bloodlust while her body healed her battle-scars was one of the most terrifying experiences I'd ever had. She regressed to a primitive state, took control of my mind and paralysed my body, and I was at her mercy. If it hadn't been for the magic talisman Devereux insisted I wear, she'd have drained me dry – I know that, because she told me. And I believed her.

Devereux assured me he and Luna had never been intimate and I trusted him, but every time I saw her outrageous body I wondered, why not?

I frowned. 'So why are you here? What do you want?'

She lifted her upper lip in an Elvis-like sneer, showing me her fangs. She was one creepy bloodsucker.

'Never mind, I *know* what you want.' I tugged the blanket up a little higher. 'And you know you aren't going to get it. Devereux won't let you suck on me. So, again, why are you here?'

'Lucky for you I fed before I arrived, otherwise I might be tempted to drink from you, heal the punctures and erase your memory. You're fortunate I'm loyal to the Master, but never doubt that I'm counting the minutes until he casts you aside. Then all your protections will end and we will have our rendezvous.'

I glared at her, but she ignored me and added, 'He sent me to tell you he's still involved with the warring covens, so he won't be available until after midnight. He wants you to join him at The Crypt then. He also commands that you wear the protective necklace he gave you.'

She snarled and vanished.

He *commands*?

Devereux had given me the magical silver pentagram – the one that had kept Luna from my throat – when I'd been stalked by Lucifer. It hadn't kept the monster away completely, but it had succeeded in discouraging several other hungry undead predators from turning me into a buffet. I'd taken it off after the nightmare with Dracul – it was a heavy piece of jewellery – but wearing it again sounded like a great idea.

I flopped back and pulled the covers over my head.

Well, Kismet, what's it going to be? Should you get up, or just hide under the covers? Hmmm, difficult decision. Let's review the reasons to burrow in: a maniacal killer who has plans for you, a bloodsucking supermodel who yearns to drain you dry, an ex-boyfriend who wants to become the undead Dr Sex, and an ancient lust object who arranges your life to suit himself.

As much as I wanted to put my stressful world on hold, my body reminded me that no matter how crazy things might be getting, I still had to pee.

I shuffled to the closet, grabbed my fluffy pink robe and as I scurried next door to the bathroom I caught a glimpse of myself in the mirror over the sink. 'Damn! It's the Wicked Witch of the West.' I'd got my hair wet in the shower before climbing into bed and now my thick, dark curls stuck out in all directions like a fright wig. My skin was whiter than usual, but that was probably due to the shock of witnessing a murder and then being brain-slimed by the killer. It would've been unnatural to have no physical reactions to the insanity. I was surprised I was functional at all.

Craving caffeine, I headed down to the kitchen to load up my coffee machine. It felt odd to wake up this late in the day. My whole system was out of whack. I stood staring at the pot while the aromatic elixir brewed, as if my gaze could hurry it along.

I noticed my empty couch. If Tom had spent the day there, he'd left no evidence behind – no clothes on the floor or take-out food containers on the table. But I knew I hadn't seen the last of him, not just because he had his own personal vampire transport service, but since he intended to use me to ingratiate himself with Devereux.

I'd just grabbed the handle of the coffee pot to pour my first brain-stimulating dose of nirvana when there was a loud pounding on my front door. The sound startled me and I almost dropped the pot. 'What the hell now?' I muttered, stomping over to the door as the banging continued. I flicked on the porch light, eyeballed the peephole and saw white hair.

Releasing the locks, I pulled the door open. 'Maxie!'

She leapt inside, closed and locked the door, pressed her body against it and stared at me. She looked like I felt: her skin was pasty-white and there were dark circles under her bloodshot blue eyes. She had severe bed hair, and a pillow-crease across her cheek.

I touched her arm. 'Maxie, what happened to you? Where did those idiots take you? Are you okay?'

'Yeah – no, damned if I know. That's why I'm here. I hoped you could tell me what the hell happened to me.'

'Come inside. I need coffee. Do you want some?'

'Does a werewolf shit in the woods?'

'I'll take that as a yes.' We shuffled like zombies into the kitchen and I pulled out a chair at the table. 'Sit down. How do you take your coffee? Do you want something to eat? I've got bagels.'

'Black for the coffee and no for the food, but don't let me stop you.'

I filled two mugs, carried them to the table and sat across from her. We each drank in silence for a few seconds, both understanding the importance of the sacred coffee ritual, and neither of us wanting to disturb the other's ecstatic moment.

Finally she put her mug down, glanced at me and burst out laughing. 'Have you seen your hair?'

I smiled, because I had. 'Have you seen yours?'

'Yeah.' She nodded. 'I didn't take a shower or brush my hair or anything. I didn't know what else to do besides come here.' Her eyes went vacant. 'I only have sketchy memories of anything after those two satanic asswipes grabbed me from the mezzanine. I'm missing a lot of details – it's like a portion of the videotape in my brain was erased. I just woke up about an hour ago in my apartment, still dressed in the clothes I wore last night, and I'm still not sure how I got there.' She stared down into her coffee. 'Shit, Kismet. How the hell did they just appear like that? How did they get me down to my car? I have vague recollections of driving, but why would I just take off and leave you there? Jesus. I was so terrified when I woke up and thought about what they might have done to you. Especially after I guilted you into going.' She turned frightened eyes to me. 'What happened?'

Without thinking, I almost blurted out the truth. I was right on the verge of unburdening myself about the existence of vampires, homicidal rituals and the reality of one psychotic, murdering bloodsucker in particular – I'd actually gone so far as to form the first word with my lips – when I remembered who I was sitting with, and, more importantly, what she did for a living.

I held Maxie's gaze, adopted my most compassionate therapist expression and hoped Victoria had been exaggerating about my inability to bluff.

Maxie had told me she'd never found any evidence for the existence of the paranormal. She had also said she was worried about her job. It didn't take a brain surgeon to figure out what she'd do with any information I shared – even if she couldn't prove anything I said, it wouldn't matter. I'd be the story: just another chapter in the crazed adventures of a formerly respected local psychologist who'd gone round the preternatural bend. Given the rag she worked for, proof wouldn't be an issue.

No matter how much I needed someone to talk to, I couldn't put myself or my clients in jeopardy by indulging in loose lips.

I reached across the table and took her hand. 'What do you remember?'

She studied my face for a moment, frowned and broke eye-contact, staring down at the table. She extricated her hand from mine and lifted her coffee mug. I got a sudden flash that Maxie was hiding something, which was weird, because I was the one trying to avoid telling any impossible tales.

This sudden intuitive flash about Maxie made me realise I hadn't had any hits about her before – not even when we first met. I replayed our time together, trying to recall any instances where my psychic radar had given me insights about her, and drew a blank. I couldn't think of any other time in my life when I'd been unable to sense someone's emotions or read between the lines, especially since my skills had been given the elders' upgrade. So either my empathic and clairsentient abilities were on the fritz, or Maxie shielded better than anyone I'd ever met.

She raised her gaze to mine. 'I remember us lying on our bellies on the balcony, checking out the chubby guy being killed on the stage below – or pretending to be killed, whatever. Although the guy was pretty convincing. I'd just started snapping photos again when I was lifted off the floor by a couple of creeps in black robes – and there's a page missing in my memory book at that point. I surfaced later, long enough to observe myself driving – but how the hell could I "observe myself driving"? What does that even mean? Did you see them take me?' She pointed to herself.

'Yes, I did. They must have sneaked up behind us because I didn't hear them coming. There had to be a staircase up to the balcony from the main floor – maybe they'd been watching us the whole time.'

'I don't know.' She didn't sound convinced. 'I think I would've heard a couple of men creeping up behind me. I've got a black belt in paranoia – I've always prided myself on being able to sense the freaks before they get close enough to hassle me. Even if there was a staircase, that doesn't explain why I don't remember anything.'

I sighed. 'Yeah, that's true.' It was official: I sucked at lying. Dancing around the truth was making me feel like shit. Technically, I had no actual proof about why her memory was impaired, but I'd seen evidence of a certain bloodsucking sociopath's mind-control abilities, and I knew full well he'd erased Maxie's mental tapes. But as I wasn't going to risk exposing myself and my clients to another media-blitz of ridicule and scorn I'd say whatever was necessary to point her in a different direction. And maybe I could manage to convince myself that I was protecting her from horrors she really didn't need to know about.

'Do you think you might have been drugged?'

Her eyebrows shot up her forehead. 'Drugged? How the hell could I have been drugged? I didn't eat or drink anything – but hey, come to think of it, I was pretty hung-over when I woke up a little while ago.'

'It's relatively easy to administer a sedative using a syringe. You might not even feel the needle. That would explain the memory loss.'

She stared at me with her mouth open. 'Holy shit.' Her voice rose. 'You mean those bogus little perverts might have taken me for some disgusting sexual reason? You're saying they might have *done* something to me? That they—'

I raised my hands in the air and cried, 'Stop! Wait—' *Way to go, Kismet. Make everything a thousand times worse, why don't you. You are the worst liar on the face of the earth.* 'Listen, you said you woke up still wearing your clothes, didn't you? So if they'd done anything to you, they probably wouldn't have left everything on, right?'

She frowned. 'Yeah, maybe . . .'

I lowered my hands and folded them on the table, just like a regular, non-lying person would do. 'You don't think you've been violated, right?' *I'd better be careful: the last thing I want to do is plant the seeds of a false memory. I'm willing to lie, but I'm not willing to hurt her. Hallow said she drove herself home and I'm going to make myself believe that.*

'No.' She shrugged. 'At least, not physically – but if they didn't do anything to me, why the hell would they drug me? And why didn't they take both of us?'

My head spun. She was right. Why *wouldn't* they have taken me, too? Unless I wanted to tell her about my meeting with the blood-covered genie vampire, I had to come up with another pack of lies, and immediately. It couldn't be good that I was getting increasingly comfortable with creating blatant fabrications. I took a breath and waded back in. I'd need to roll my imaginary trouser legs up pretty soon.

'I did hear one of them say the word *reporter* when they lifted you up.'

'*Reporter?* How the hell would they know I was a reporter?'

I reached out and touched her white curtain of hair. 'That's a little distinctive, wouldn't you say? You said you've been covering these events for a while, so it makes sense that they'd know who you are, what you look like. Maybe they wanted you gone before they did whatever else they were going to do at their sick little performance. They could've seen you taking pictures.'

She stared at me. 'What could they have been planning that would've been worth *drugging* me? What could a bunch of low-life losers be doing to warrant such a cover-up?'

Finally, something I could be truthful about. 'I honestly

don't have a clue. You know more about their activities than I do.'

'Did you see anything after they took me?'

I shook my head, wondering if my nose was growing. 'I was pretty stunned when they took you and I just stood there for several minutes, not knowing what to do – I was hoping you'd come back, I guess. Then the crowd downstairs started pouring out the front doors, so I left the way we came. By the time I got down the fire escape, all the bystanders had gone. I couldn't remember the way at first so I wandered around for ages, searching for any sign of you or the car. When I finally got back to where you'd parked and you weren't there – that's when I called a cab. I didn't want to leave until I was sure you'd gone ... Luckily, the cab company knew where the condemned amusement park was.'

Her eyebrows rose. 'You called a cab?'

'Well, yeah – what other choice did I have? You and the car were missing, so I could either put one foot in front of the other or call a cab. Since I had no idea where I was, walking home in the middle of the night really didn't seem like a sensible option.'

Great. Throw in a little guilt to make her feel even worse.

She sighed and slouched back in her chair. 'I told you I usually manage to get myself into trouble. I'm really sorry I dragged you into that mess. You must have freaked when you couldn't find me. I promise never to nag you into doing anything you don't want to ever again.' She locked eyes with me, her lips pursed. 'Will you give me another chance, pal?

Can we go have those margaritas and listen to that jazz sometime? Or did I scare you off?'

Shit. I don't feel like much of a pal right now – more like something scraped from underneath a toenail.

I gazed at her exhausted face, found my compassion and smiled. 'I'd love to do the margaritas and jazz sometime. I listen to some pretty strange tales in my office every day. It isn't so easy to scare me off.'

'That's great.'

She grinned and rose slowly from the chair, as if her muscles were sore. 'I'm going to take off now. I've still got to come up with some kind of story for the magazine.' She snorted. 'I'll just make something up – nobody will know the difference. And I'm sure you have plans with that gorgeous blond rich guy. I hope you'll trust me enough at some point to introduce us. I promise not to ask any obnoxious reporter-type questions. If his face is half as good up close as it looks in a camera lens, I might have to give you a run for your money.'

'We'll see.' I laughed. 'Devereux's a pretty busy guy. I never know when he's going to show up, but if the opportunity presents itself, I'll be glad to introduce you.'

She hobbled to the front door. 'Thanks. You're being a good sport about the whole abandoning-you thing. I won't forget it. I'll be in touch. See ya.'

She left, closing the door behind her, and I hurried over and locked it.

I really felt terrible about lying to Maxie. I knew it was for a good cause, but I didn't care for the ease with which the fictions had rolled off my tongue. I'd always worked hard to be an ethical person, so what did it mean that I could set those standards aside so easily? What was I becoming?

I went back to the kitchen, refilled my coffee mug, and grabbed a bagel from the counter. As I sliced it, toasted it and slathered it with cream cheese I thought about all the madness that had taken place during the previous twenty-four hours – and then, like a slap to the head, I realised that I hadn't called the police about Carson's body. *I must have brain damage.* Bagel forgotten, I jumped up, found the phone and checked the time. At least sixteen hours had passed since I transported myself home – maybe someone else had notified the authorities already?

Or maybe there was a rotting DJ corpse in the funhouse.

I sat at my desk and fired up the computer. If the body had been found, there would be local news stories. I searched the newspapers' websites and came up empty. Googling Carson brought up lots of hits, but they were all about his radio antics. I even scanned the obituaries without finding a familiar name.

Since it didn't appear anyone had reported Carson missing, let alone dead, I decided to drive to a convenience store and use the pay-phone to make an anonymous call. No matter what my opinion might be about the rude radio host, I couldn't just forget his crucified and eviscerated body was dumped at the amusement park. Surely he must have family or friends, someone who cared about what happened to him?

I moved a couple of steps from the desk and once again

slammed into the chest of the silver-eyed devil, who'd popped into my personal space, grinning, silent as death.

I gasped and reflexively tried to back up, but he grabbed my arms, holding me with unyielding fingers. It was a good thing I'd recently emptied my bladder, or I would have peed on the carpet like the possessed girl in *The Exorcist*. The vampire's energy felt dark and dangerous, which pretty much described his appearance as well. He'd replaced the genie trousers with tight jeans and a red T-shirt tucked in at his trim waistline. His unnaturally long, dark hair flowed down his muscular chest. The fiend was even more gorgeous than I remembered.

He tilted his head from side to side, and studied me. 'Doctor Knight – or may I call you Kismet, since we've become such good friends?' His deep voice caused my ears to buzz and goosebumps to rise on my skin. He released my arms and stepped away, then strolled in a circle around me. 'Obviously you weren't expecting company. What on earth is that appalling pink thing you're wearing? And I must say that whoever did your hair should be gutted.' He laughed, the sound both pleasant and terrifying.

I licked my lips so I could speak. 'What do you want?'

He smiled, exposing impressive fangs. 'I want so many things, my sweet Kismet. And I intend to have all of them. But you were doing so much mental fussing about the remains of our dearly departed that I felt duty-bound to come and inform you the matter has been dealt with. There is no reason to involve human police. I might have need of that location again so I would prefer it to remain undisturbed.'

He inched in closer and riveted his gaze on mine, and I lost control of my muscles and bones. He slid an arm around my waist and caught me before I collapsed. My heart sped up, beating so frantically I feared it would burst out of my chest. My breathing went shallow and my limbs were heavy. Holding me with one arm, he untied my robe and slid the fabric off each shoulder, leaving my naked body exposed.

I wanted to scream, to fight, to do anything except stand there, frozen, but my brain was off-line. Bubble-wrap filled the places in my skull that were formerly occupied by my cerebral cortex, firing neurons and brain chemicals.

He leaned in, his soft hair streaming across my body, and kissed me. His touch was electric, literally jolting me as if I'd come in contact with a live wire. Currents of energy flowed along my skin, pulsating in the area between my legs, and I moaned. I didn't know where his other hand was – it was everywhere at once. I'd never had an orgasm while paralysed before – I wouldn't have thought it possible – but somehow it was happening. He eased the pressure of his kiss, flicked his tongue along my lower lip, shifted his mouth down to my neck, and bit me. The sensation of his fangs penetrating my vein was indefinable. If I'd experimented with hallucinogens, I might have had something to compare the sensations to, but since I hadn't, I simply surrendered into the ecstatic bliss vibrating through my body. It was as if my neck had become a hyper-potent erogenous zone. My body convulsed with the most powerful orgasm I'd ever experienced.

The rational part of me made futile attempts to gain

control, but as whimpers erupted from my lips, the rest of me wondered who was making all the noise. He drew me in tight against him while he fed. I'm not sure I would have moved, even if I could.

Then everything went dark.

CHAPTER 11

Silently arguing with myself about whether or not waking was worth the effort, I swam against the tide, forced myself to become fully conscious, and opened my eyes. For the second time, Luna's face peered down at me. She didn't speak, her expression was solemn and serious, but for a moment, her eyes sparkled with glee.

'Luna, what—?'

She vanished.

I blinked a few times to clear the fog from my vision. *What the hell?* Why did I feel so strange? Had Luna, the vampire Kali, really been here, or had I imagined it? I glanced down at myself to discover I was sitting naked in my oversize chair, my pink robe discarded on the floor. I rubbed my eyes, trying to orient myself. I didn't remember sitting in the chair. Why would I do that? I had to go upstairs and get dressed for my midnight meeting with Devereux at The Crypt. I slanted my eyes to the clock.

'Shit – it's already midnight – what the hell is wrong with me?' I murmured to myself.

I stood slowly, making sure my legs were solid enough to navigate the stairs, and shuffled in that direction. I took some deep breaths, and more of my fragmented reality coalesced. It occurred to me that my shaky state might be caused by low blood sugar due to lack of food, so I diverted to the kitchen, opened the refrigerator and grabbed the orange juice container. Rummaging for a glass was too much work, so I just untwisted the cap and drank directly from the carton – something I never did. The natural fructose had an immediate stabilising effect and I felt better. I retrieved the abandoned bagel, then sat at the table and devoured it with enthusiasm. I suddenly realised that my last meal had been almost twenty-four hours ago, and it had consisted of half a container of left-over Kung Pao Chicken. No wonder I felt so odd. Considering that, nodding off wasn't such a strange thing.

As I sat there, something nagged at my brain, distracting me, rather like a little kid tugging at the hem of my mental skirt. What had I been doing before I fell asleep? Wasn't I going to call someone about something? Yes – Carson's body – but wait— Why was I going to do that? His body had been taken care of, hadn't it? I couldn't recall why I thought I needed to do anything.

I shook my head and noticed I'd managed to dribble orange juice down the front of my nude body. I laughed, flicking the drops away with my fingers. 'You're losing it, Kismet.

Get off your ass and get dressed. The Master has commanded your presence!'

Thinking about Devereux sobered me, and reminded me that I hadn't seen him since before the insanity at the funhouse. I needed to tell him about my encounter with Hallow. I hoped he wouldn't go ballistic and try to lock me away at The Crypt.

Unfortunately, that was definitely a consideration. Maybe I shouldn't say anything yet; I'd just stay away from Hallow. I certainly didn't want to be sucked into his evil universe. He'd publicly killed Carson in a maniacal frenzy and I had no doubt that inflicting torture and pain was one of his favourite recreational activities. If it was true that he drained the life-force from all the women he collected, I wasn't about to sign up for a demonstration, no matter how amazing a lover he supposedly was.

Eewww. Why am I even thinking about what kind of lover he is?

It might be better for me to stay home, do some paperwork and then talk to Devereux about moving into his penthouse for a while. Yes, that was the answer: caution. Sensible, mature caution. I would behave responsibly, like a thoughtful professional. I was totally out of my depth with the undead assassin and nothing but misery would come from making myself available to him, even inadvertently.

No matter how intriguing I found the undead, there was no reason to get more involved in the vampire horror show than I already was. Choosing to be careful had nothing to do with giving up my independence. It was all about securing my survival. I wasn't too proud to admit I was in over my head. I'd been incredibly naïve to think I could deal with a monster like Hallow – but in my defence, I had actually learned a lot from our brief interaction. The vampire version of psychosis was beyond anything the psychological establishment understood, and I now had a front-row seat for the case study of the century.

A bloodsucking Charles Manson.

It was frustrating to have nobody to discuss my experiences with. My professional self was fascinated by the behavioural aspects of Hallow's madness, but the personal me wanted to hide under the bed. If I ever had a client in the same incredible situation as I found myself, what would I say? That was a no-brainer: I'd tell her to take the first plane out of Denver. I wouldn't be heading to the airport, but I could remove myself physically from the freak show.

Fortunately, Devereux wasn't part of what I wanted to leave behind.

With the issue firmly settled in my mind, I brushed the crumbs off my breasts, fetched my robe from the living room floor and slipped it on. I tied the belt, walked to my desk to begin the paperwork and froze. My scalp tingled and my eyes blurred.

'Fuck that! I'm going to The Crypt to have some fun.' *Fuck that? What?*

I knew the words had come out of my mouth, but I hadn't intended to say them – I hadn't even been aware of the potential thought lurking in my mind. But now, suddenly, it was clear – of course, why the hell should I stay home? I didn't need to think about any vampire's opinions or actions.

I was an adult, professional woman who could make her own decisions.

Grinning, I peeled off the robe, and strode up the stairs.

The Crypt was a gothic wonderland. Devereux had transformed an old multi-level church into a playground for the children of darkness. The huge building was magnificent, with its ornate towers, spires and archways. Grotesque gargoyles leered down from corners, loomed over doorways and peeked out from hidden architectural surprises. The extensive stained glass alone was worth the visit. The original religious-themed panels had been replaced by paranormal and supernatural renderings. Eerie, gravestone-laden cemeteries were a pervasive theme – them, and rivers of blood.

The club was open every day from dusk to dawn and it was always busy but the Saturday night crowds gave new meaning to the word *packed*. I'd left my car down the block in the underground parking my office shared and jogged towards the building, eager to join the festivities. As I approached the entrance, the usual smell of marijuana and other recreational substances wafted into my nose and the intense, pulsating rhythm from the heavy-metal band performing inside vibrated the bottoms of my feet.

A cloud of pot-smoke enticed my nostrils and I smiled as I inhaled and angled over to the group toking away under a streetlight on the sidewalk. It had been a long time since I'd got high; right now I couldn't think of a better way to start the night.

I tapped a seriously stoned, skinny, long-haired twenty-something guy on the shoulder. He swivelled his head towards me, his eyelids at half-mast and blinked a few times in an obvious attempt to focus his eyes. Then he licked his lips, and slurred, 'Uh, what?'

Giving him my brightest smile, I pointed at the joint. 'Could I have a taste of that?'

He stared at my face, the joint poised in the air partway between us. 'Wow. Cool makeup. You look like a movie star.' I didn't know about the movie star resemblance, but I had been a bit more heavy-handed than usual – so sue me. I had the urge to be dramatic. What the hell? If you hung around with vampires, it was acceptable to let one's Inner Drama Queen out once in a while.

A young shaven-headed fellow wobbling next to him jerked his body in my direction when he heard his friend's words and shuffled over to see for himself.

I reached out and lifted the joint from the skinny guy's fingers, fitted it between my lips without giving one thought to hygiene issues and took a toke. I inhaled the warm smoke into my throat and lungs and held it for exactly two seconds before the acrid substance burst out of my body in a series of hacking, gagging, fifty-year-smoker-type coughs.

My two companions leaned backward, as if my coughing had created a strong enough wind to bend the top portions of their bodies, and said simultaneously, 'Whoa, dude.'

Tiny embers from the end of the joint fluttered down onto the front of my red sparkly shirt, and Shaven-Headed Guy gallantly attempted to brush them away.

Probably fearing I'd lose what was left of the joint in my full-body spasm, Skinny Guy reclaimed the pot and pitched in his other hand to help his friend extinguish my chest.

They both froze, mid-brush, leaned in and stared at my breasts.

Another duet: 'Oh, wow, man.'

Skinny Guy said, 'Awesome. Great tits.'

I peeled off the hands that were hermetically sealed to my mammary glands, brushed away anything else that didn't belong on my shirt, and smiled. 'Yeah, isn't the blouse gorgeous? There's a matching bra that goes with it, but I just didn't want to be constrained tonight. Besides, in the dim light you have to look twice to notice the shirt is transparent. But thanks so much for the hit, and for keeping me from setting myself on fire. I'm going inside now. It was nice meeting you.' I moved towards the club entrance.

'Wait! Maybe we could hang out a while? Drink some wine? Fuck? You know?'

I cocked my head, fluttered my cosmetically elongated eyelashes and smiled. 'What a lovely offer, gentlemen. Unfortunately, I already have plans, but I do appreciate the thought.'

Continuing in the direction of the huge wooden double doors, I shifted my eyes down to my shirt. It wasn't any worse for the pot embers experience. And it was really cool: all fresh-blood-coloured and glittery. It worked great with my short leather skirt and favourite stiletto-heeled black boots. Tonight I'd be Psychologist Ho.

I reached for the door handle and paused, my head

spinning for a moment, and studied my chest again. *Psychologist Ho?* Why would I think such a stupid thing? More importantly, why was I even dressed like this – and when did I decide to go out instead of doing paperwork? My stomach tightened with fear. Had my brain skipped a page? *A chapter?* I knew what a blackout was, and there were several mental and physical illnesses that could account for one. Shit – maybe I had a brain tumour. There could be something seriously wrong with me. What if I hadn't merely nodded off in the living room earlier after all? What if it was something much more dire?

'Where am I?' I recognised my location – I'd visited The Crypt many times before – but I had no recollection of driving myself there, and I certainly couldn't recall dressing myself like a hooker – well, maybe a call girl, since I had bought the clothes and I knew they were expensive. I'd intended to model them for Devereux when we were alone, rather than for hundreds of strangers at his club.

I pivoted to head down the stairs, back to my car and an inner switch flipped from *on* to *off*. The muscles in my limbs seized and I stood like a statue, not even sure I was breathing. Terrified, I heard a familiar, low voice in my mind. 'It's time for some fun, sweet Kismet. Go into the club and explore your wild nature. Leave your inhibitions behind. Entertain me. Make me proud. Give Devereux my best. We will meet again soon.'

A mild electric current coursed through my body and my limbs regained function. A fuzzy, almost intoxicated feeling settled over my brain and I couldn't stop smiling.

'Go into the club and have some fun!' I shouted, just as Victoria, Devereux's witchy office manager, stepped up next to me.

'Kismet?' She gave me an eyeball-scan, brows raised, and her gaze locked on my chest. She frowned. 'Does Devereux know you're here? Are you aware that you're wearing a see-through blouse with nothing on underneath?' She stepped back. 'And an extremely short skirt? That's not your usual fashion style.'

'Victoria! How wonderful to see you. Did you come to have a little fun, too?'

She leaned in and sniffed. 'Have you been drinking?'

I hugged her, then shook my head. 'Not yet.'

Her nose wrinkled and she sniffed again. 'Pot?'

'I'll never tell.'

She grabbed my arm as I headed towards the entrance. 'Kismet, wait – something's wrong. You feel different to me – you're not yourself. Your aura is strange – it's got all odd, murky colours, almost like there's something extra there. Something dark.'

'Don't be silly, my friend.' I patted her hand. 'I'm the same ordinary Kismet I've always been – or at least as ordinary as somebody whose parents named her after an old Broadway musical can be. Come on. Let's go and stir up some trouble.'

I tugged on the handle and opened the door to a wall of sound. The whine of a high-pitched lead guitar screamed over the throbbing rhythm section as the players cavorted frantically on a stage at the far end of the room. The jarring aural explosion assaulted my ears and took my breath away.

The club was decorated like a Goth's wet dream. It had everything a wannabe vamp could desire: scenes from Dracula's castle, bodies rising from haunted graveyards, and enough black to make Ozzy Osbourne want to bite the head off something. The ever-present fog machine pumped out a slithering layer of white smoke, adding an eerie ambience to the shadowy interior, which was lit by modern versions of ancient torches.

The huge main room was filled with bodies – some alive, some otherwise – all dancing to the thunderous beat of the musicians. One of the many great things about The Crypt was all the cozy little nooks and crannies scattered along the walls, not to mention the ornate balconies of various sizes, some small enough to fit only one table. There were lots of places for romantic rendezvous, sexual assignations and under-the-table drug deals. In fact, it was easy to find a private space for pretty much anything you wanted.

Standing at his post just inside the entrance was Devereux's doorman – er, door*vamp*. The first time I saw Ankh, his ghoulish, creepy appearance made my skin crawl. He was very tall, cadaverously bluish-white, with badly discoloured teeth and fangs. His obsidian eyes were oddly sunken into his face and underscored with large, dark circles, making it appear as if he wore a perpetual Hallowe'en mask. His head was mostly bald, except for a thick, dark braid that burst forth from the top of his skull, reminiscent of the style Egyptian pharaohs often wore in movies. A long, black robe shrouded his lanky frame. When I'd asked Devereux why he would station such a distasteful-looking specimen at the entrance to his business, he'd said Ankh had the gentlest, most loving temperament of any vampire he'd ever met. And the large fellow provided excellent customer service. That's what I got for judging a vamp by his cover.

Ankh bowed from the waist. 'Good evening, Doctor. The Master said you were expected.' I nodded. He gave Victoria the same bow. 'And Victoria, a pleasure as always.'

'Hello, Ankh.' Victoria smiled. 'It's lovely to see you. You've got quite a crowd here tonight. Do you think we'll have any luck finding a place to sit?'

He nodded. 'The Master reserved a table for Doctor Knight. I'll just call someone to escort you.' He raised an arm into the air, signalling an invisible helper.

I grasped Victoria's hand and pulled her behind me as I headed for the throng. 'That's okay, Ankh. We'll just dive in and take our chances. Thanks.'

Victoria gasped and tried to free her hand from my grip, but she couldn't and I enjoyed the powerful sensation of towing her through the crowd. My ever-increasing new physical strength was exciting.

I navigated us to the long, sarcophagus-shaped bar ensconced along one wall of the spacious room. All the stools were occupied. I'd just started thinking about the most fun way to clear off a couple when a woman with neon-orange hair smiled in my direction, exposing tiny fangs. She slid off her stool, pulled her raven-haired companion from her perch and pointed at the empty seats. She shouted over the music, 'Please. Take our chairs. Tell the Master we were happy to help you out. My name is Dark Widow and this is Rain.

Tell him we're at his service.' They giggled and darted off into the crowd.

Devereux always managed to surround himself with female devotees who were willing to do just about anything to be in his vicinity. I guess I couldn't blame him for taking what was offered. No doubt he wanted me to become his groupie, too. Well, the Master was in for a big disappointment. But if his handmaidens wanted to kiss some Master ass by sucking up to his significant other, that was fine with me.

Victoria had been silent during our trip through the club. She'd even stopped resisting and trying to break free. Now she watched the stool swap, her lips pursed. I climbed up onto my seat, not bothering to tug the short skirt down, and patted her chair. Victoria situated herself, a very serious expression on her face, and leaned in, speaking directly into my ear because of the noise. 'Kismet, has anything unusual happened? Have you had contact with anyone . . . dangerous?'

I didn't want to spend any more time talking about such a boring subject so I chose to ignore her questions. Instead, I pinched the fabric of her shimmering black and gold goddess gown between my finger and thumb. 'Sweet. I didn't notice before. That's an incredible dress you're wearing. Are you meeting some mysterious stranger here at the club tonight?'

She frowned, no doubt understanding my distracting manoeuvre. 'Yes, as a matter of fact, I am meeting someone, but now I think I ought to stay with you. Something's not right.'

'No way, my witchy friend. I'm not letting you play mother hen with me when you could be kicking up your heels with Mr Right. Or Mr Right Now.' I laughed, and signalled the bartender. 'I want to hear all the details tomorrow.'

'Really, Kismet,' Victoria sighed, meeting my gaze, 'I don't want to be a wet blanket, but you're not yourself. I mean, *literally* – your aura is completely different, as if you're actually someone else. Have you been in touch with Hallow? Has he done something to you?'

I shook my head and grinned. 'Not that I know of, but anything can happen.'

'What can I get for you?'

I revolved towards the smooth voice and smiled. My evening had just got a lot more interesting. 'Wow. You look just like—'

'Yeah,' he said, 'I know: Johnny Depp. But trust me, I'm much older.' He smiled, the tips of fangs glistening in the overhead light.

I leaned forward, bringing my knees up onto the stool so I could get a better view. 'Hmmm. What can you get for me? Let me think.' I slid my hand on top of his and tapped my fingernail on his cool skin. 'When's your next break?'

'Kismet,' Victoria interrupted, 'I don't think Devereux would like you distracting his employees. You wouldn't want to get Nigel in trouble, would you?' She wrapped her fingers around my arm, as if she worried I'd fall.

I kept my gaze on the eye-candy in front of me. 'Would you *like* to get into some trouble, Nigel? We could just sneak away for a few minutes and discuss the issue.'

He laughed. 'Trouble I could deal with, but if I laid one finger on Devereux's woman, he'd rip my heart out of my chest before I even thought about unzipping my trousers. I think that's a little too much danger for this vampire. I'm a mellow bloodsucker. Besides, I'm happy here. I don't want to mess things up. So, what else can I get you, besides me?'

I pouted, and he laughed again. Thanks to my unexpected new muscles, I could probably drag him from behind the bar, find a cozy hideaway and indulge myself for a few minutes, but they were right. Maybe he wasn't the best candidate, but damn, he was gorgeous.

'Okay.' I smiled. 'If I can't have you, I guess I'll have a couple shots of tequila.' I asked Victoria, 'What do you want?'

'I'd like a glass of red wine, please, Nigel.'

'Coming right up.' He trotted off to fetch the drinks. The view was arousing.

'Victoria?' said a male voice from behind me.

Intrigued, I angled my head to check out the owner of the warm, appealing sound. A tall, distinguished man wearing a dark suit, red shirt, and grey tie stood behind me. My ass was still swaying in the air from my attempt to crawl across the bar, so I plopped it down onto my heels.

'Winston.' Victoria's face lit up. 'It's so good to see you. Let me introduce my friend, Doctor Kismet Knight.'

He bowed his head, and smiled. Fangs. His dark eyes twinkled. 'I have heard of you, Doctor Knight. It's lovely to meet you in person.'

I sat properly on my stool and gave him a friendly smile. Anyone who could animate Victoria's face like that was aces in my book. His shoulder-length salt-and-pepper hair made him look somewhere between forty and fifty. I hadn't met a vampire that old before – not that forty-something was old, but most vampires were brought over sooner. I wondered what his story was.

Nigel brought our drinks, winked at me and bolted away. He must have seen the gleam I was sure I had in my eyes.

I slammed the tequila shots, one after the other. 'Wow. Those were tasty. I think I'll get a couple more. You two go on and find a romantic corner.' I saw Victoria's smile slide into a frown and patted her arm. 'Honest. I'm just letting off some steam. I'll go find the lord and master shortly, but before that, I want to dance! It's been ages since I let my Inner Wild Woman out.'

Victoria gave Winston a pained smile, as if she was trying to telepathically communicate something she didn't want to share with me. 'I think we should invite Kismet to sit with us while she waits for Devereux to arrive, don't you, Winston?'

'Certainly.' He smiled, oozing charm. 'What man wouldn't be pleased to have a beautiful woman on each arm?' He extended both elbows, either waiting for us to grab on or preparing to flop his arms in a chicken imitation. I laughed, and he cocked his head, a confused expression flowing across his handsome features.

'I'm sorry,' I said, 'I have a weird sense of humour. Seriously. I don't want to go and sit with you until my owner comes to fetch me. I want to have some fun. So run along.'

They both stared at me, so I added emphasis. '*Really.*'

Winston bowed, put his arm around Victoria and guided her across the room. She glanced back once, her face an unhappy mask.

I climbed back up on my knees, plopped my chest on the bar, and hollered, 'Nigel! More alcohol, please!'

He ambled over. 'Do you want another tequila shot?'

I licked my lips. 'I'd say you read my mind, but I know you can't.'

He smiled as he poured the potent liquid into my glass. 'It doesn't take a mind reader to know that you'll probably find the trouble you're seeking. I heard that a certain ancient vampire hunter is in town and he's taken a fancy to you. If you'd heed a word of advice, I think you should be more careful than usual. Something evil is percolating, if you know what I mean. If even half the legends about Hallow are true, he's a deranged vampire. You'd do well to stay out of his path.'

I reached over and stroked his pale cheek, giving him my brightest smile. 'Are you sure you don't want to duck out for a few minutes?'

Nigel gently removed my hand from his face. 'Doctor Knight, because I know how crazy Devereux is about you, I wish you'd take my warning seriously. Hallow has come to kill someone. If the rumours are right, it might be someone close to Devereux. I'd suspect it was you if you were a vampire, but the situation is ominous. Why don't I send someone downstairs to find Devereux for you?' He stared into my eyes, making a valiant effort to entrance me. 'You really don't want to dance tonight. You want to be a good little human and stay out of trouble.'

'Woot! That was awesome, Nigel.' He backed up, clearly surprised. 'Ineffective, but awesome. I'm not that easy to enthrall, but I do appreciate your concern. I'll tell Devereux what a darling you are.'

I downed the shot, jumped off the stool and waved good-bye to Nigel over my shoulder. Then, heeding the call of nature, I headed to the bathroom.

The crowd was thick and uncooperative as I elbowed my way through.

'Hey! Watch out, asshole!' yelled one of the women whose drinks I jostled.

I raised my middle finger as I pushed past and kept it aloft as I encountered other unhappy people needing to be shoved aside. The shock on their faces made me feel good, powerful.

'Look out, world, I'm full of vampire blood!' I pushed the bathroom door with my hip and barged inside. The tequila on top of the pot had given me a nice buzz. 'Make way!' I bypassed the line of women waiting for a stall and jumped into a newly vacated one.

'Hey, bitch!' A hand grabbed my wrist before the cubicle door could close. 'Don't you see this line? Get your ass to the end of it and wait your turn like everybody else.'

I easily tugged free of the Mohawk-haired tattooed wom-an's grip. 'Oh, yeah? Who's gonna make me?' This was going to be fun.

Her lips spread in an evil smile, exposing a wide gap in the front where two teeth should have been. The surrounding dentistry featured various shades of brown and yellow. Her massive breasts spilled over the top and flowed out the armholes of a too-tight Harley Davidson leather vest. 'You're lookin' at her, whore.' She poked out her chest and stood up straight, gaining a couple of inches in height.

A collective gasp filled the room, and all the women waiting in line took quick steps towards the wall.

'Oh, shit – go and get a waitress, Candy,' one spectator said to the woman next to her. 'Jenna's gonna wipe the floor with this skinny asshole.'

A tiny woman with curly blue hair darted out the door.

'Yeah, go and get someone to save this bitch's life because I'm about to stomp her brainless,' Jenna said, and reached towards me. She looked like someone who'd had some practise at what she threatened – all the better.

'Bring it on, cow,' I yelled, and shoved her back from the door.

She obviously hadn't expected me to have any muscle, because she wasn't prepared for the force of the push. She stumbled backwards, unable to recover her balance, and went down hard on her ass with a thud. I laughed at the sound.

The last things I remember before I jumped on her and started punching were the gasps that filled the room and the big woman's startled expression. Her eyes went wide and her mouth dropped open as she raised her hands in defence.

I lost track of time, then suddenly people were pulling at me, trying to lift me off the unmoving biker. I rose to my feet and stood over Jenna, my hair barely ruffled, not even breathing hard, and glanced at the blood on my knuckles.

A waitress slammed into the room and bounced her gaze between the woman on the floor and me. 'What the hell happened?'

'She cut in line and Jenna was gonna set her straight,' a tall, emaciated woman said, pointing at me. 'But she beat the crap out of Jenna.'

Everybody stared down at Jenna, who was unconscious. She had a bloody nose and bruised eyes that would be swollen shut very soon. Her lips were split in several places and she'd lost another tooth. The buttons on her vest had gone missing, and her breasts had taken advantage of the breathing room to run amok.

The waitress studied me, her eyes narrowed. 'Holy shit. It's you. Devereux's girlfriend. No. Fuckin'. Way.' She pressed her hands to the sides of her head. 'He's going to go apeshit when he finds out that someone tried to hurt you. You're supposed to be guarded at all times – you're no match for someone like her. Or so we thought. Are you hurt?'

Everyone was watching me, waiting for me to speak.

'Hell no, I'm not hurt. She shouldn't have tried to fuck with me,' I said calmly, expressing what I thought was merely logic. 'I had to pee and she got in my way.' Silence continued as I swung around and walked back into the stall and shut the door. I peed, then came out. The crowd parted as I walked to one of the sinks to wash my bloody hands.

Turning to grab some paper towels, I scanned all the open-mouthed faces around me. 'I'm going to go dance now. See ya. Thanks for the good time.'

I walked back into the main club, which was even more packed than before I went to the bathroom.

The band was playing an upbeat, heavy-rock number and I stood on the edge of the dance floor, jiggling in place. My stiletto heels gave me the height I needed to see over the heads of the crowd, which made it much easier to search the area for potential dance partners. Lyrics from an old song my father loved – something about a stranger across a crowded room – popped into my mind as I laid eyes on a dark-haired cover boy strolling in my direction.

My face wasn't big enough to hold the smile that spread across my lips. Oh, yeah. Things were definitely improving.

CHAPTER 12

'Hey, pretty lady. I was just standing over there, thinking I'd like to find someone soft and curvy to dance with, and there you were. We must've been destined to meet, wouldn't you say?' He spoke with a subtle western twang.

I just couldn't stop smiling. The sweet young thing probably wasn't even twenty-one. I wondered how he'd got past Ankh. The band had paused long enough for the musicians to down a number of beers before launching into the next tune, so I was able to hear my new companion without any need for him to yell.

'My, my. Aren't you adorable?' I trailed a fingernail down the front of his shirt. In my stilettos, I was almost six feet tall, but my sumptuous companion wasn't at all intimidated by my Wonder Woman stance. His cowboy boots had heels that elevated him a couple of inches over me. 'What's your name, handsome?'

His jeans and black T-shirt perfectly showcased his slender, toned body. The yummy stranger ran his fingers through a mass of dark, shoulder-length hair. Warm brown eyes gazed soulfully from beneath thick lashes. I was certain there had to be a Stetson on the front seat of his truck. He grinned. Fangless. 'I'm Trevor, Trey to my friends.' He offered his hand for me to shake.

What a delicious morsel. I clasped his warm hand and held on, pulling him closer. 'Well, Trey. I don't know if you've got a thing for older women because of unresolved mother issues or if you just want to play with fire, but I'm ready.'

The drummer counted time, raised his drumsticks over his head, and the first chords of a classic Eric Clapton tune split the air.

I tugged Trey towards the dance floor. He registered surprise at my strength, but quickly boogied into the spirit of things. We elbowed our way through the fray, moving to the powerful rhythm. I could tell he was a natural – watching his slim hips undulate was a treat for the eyes. And the libido.

We rocked to the driving beat, and by the time the song ended, the temperature in the club had spiked into the tropical range. We grabbed onto each other, laughing, and I slid my hands down his shoulders, appreciating the fine muscle tone. He leaned back and grinned, shifting his gaze down to my breasts. The expression on his face made it clear he believed all his most orgasmic dreams were about to come true.

I hadn't decided yet if I wanted to slip away with the luscious lad or not, but I was enjoying his hard body next to mine. He bent forwards and kissed me on the lips. He smelled like fresh young male, and I had a quick fantasy about licking my way down his muscled frame.

The band began playing a slow song and when Trey pulled me in close, his erection pressed against my stomach. He tilted his head, aiming his lips in my direction, when an arm snaked around my waist from behind and tugged me backwards, lifting me a couple of inches off the floor.

'Hey! What the—?'

I didn't need the distinctive medallion to recognise the contours of the chest I was pinned against. Trey's eyes went glassy and his mouth slowly sagged open.

A velvet voice cut through the music. 'Thank you for entertaining my fiancée, my friend. I was delayed in arriving, so it was most kind of you to make sure she enjoyed herself. Here.' Devereux shifted me to his hip as if I were an unruly toddler and handed Trey several business-card-size pieces of paper. 'Complimentary drinks for you and a guest, for the rest of the night. Go now.'

Trey shook his head vigorously, gave a blank stare and shuffled off the dance floor.

'You can put me down now, Mr Party Pooper,' I said, pouting.

He released me. 'Pooper?'

I pivoted, all prepared to give him hell for ruining my high school fantasy, but found myself smiling instead as my hormones shouted, 'Yippee!' What a gorgeous hunk of man-hood he was: a platinum-haired, high-fashion, leather-clad god. My hands caressed his chest, sliding along the soft fabric of his ice-blue silk T-shirt. 'Never mind about pooper. Dance with me.'

He studied my face, his expression serious. 'Something is very wrong.'

'Oh, come on, Blondie.' I reached up and clasped my hands behind his neck, moulding my body to his. 'Stop whining and dance.'

He wrapped me in his arms and began swaying to the music. After a few seconds, I felt a tingling over my scalp and I leaned back far enough to meet his eyes. 'Are you doing something? My head feels funny.' I stumbled and he had to tighten his hold to keep me on my feet.

'No, it is not me. The Slayer has somehow penetrated your protections.'

I blinked a few times, trying to dissipate the woozy disorientation, and laughed. 'Here I am, all dressed up just for you, and you're talking about some other guy penetrating me.' I threaded my fingers through the long, soft strands of his hair. 'What's it going to take to get you in a romantic mood?'

The music stopped and Devereux frowned. 'Come.' He gently released my arms from around his neck, grabbed my hand and hustled me through the crowd, which parted for him like the Red Sea did for Moses. We hurried to the door leading down to the lower level of the club. John the vampire-addict, whose job it was to keep humans away from the secret portions of the building, opened the heavy door for us and we stepped inside, but instead of making our way down the steep stairs, Devereux encircled my waist with his arm and thought us into his private bedroom.

The large room was more like a combination studio, ritual space and sleeping area than just a bedroom. I had asked him if he really slept there instead of in a coffin, but he'd just smiled without answering. Funny how he was so close-mouthed about anything to do with his own life, but demanded to know every single thing about mine.

The space hadn't changed since the last time I'd visited. Devereux was an accomplished artist and his paintings filled the walls. One corner of the room was devoted to art supplies, empty canvases and easels holding works-in-progress. He'd hung the portrait of me, supposedly painted eight hundred years earlier, in a prominent place, with special lighting above and below, displayed alongside the portrait of his mother – the dead one who'd shown up in the flesh at a ritual to welcome me to the family.

A long table cluttered with bottles, ornate boxes, candles and New Age paraphernalia dominated the space between the art corner and the bed. A beautiful large amethyst ball was balanced on a golden pedestal, apparently in readiness for future casting – Devereux was a well-known seer, by all accounts. He'd told me the strange bottles contained herbs and other ingredients for his magic spells and potions. I'd thought he was kidding at first, that all this hocus-pocus was just a silly hobby, but he soon disabused me of that notion. In fact, he'd done a number of things for which I had no rational explanation – not that I had any rational explanation for vampires, either.

He flicked his fingers, igniting candles, and stepped back

to stare at me, a sour expression on his face. 'I must find a solution to this problem,' he said.

'What problem?'

He ignored me. 'If my vampire powers are not sufficient to the task, then I will create a magical resolution.' He started to move away towards the door leading to an outer office. 'I must consult my books for an appropriate spell.'

I sprinted in front of him to cut him off. 'Wait a minute, Love Buns – I didn't come down here to sit alone while you indulge yourself in woo-woo research. I have my own agenda – a woman has needs, you know.' I batted my eyelashes and gave what I hoped was a naughty smile. 'Let's go and sit on the bed and talk for a while.'

Pain radiated through my skull, making my legs tremble, and I grabbed the sides of my head. 'Ow, dammit – knock it off! You're giving me a headache. If my brain explodes, I'm holding you personally responsible.'

Devereux lifted me effortlessly into his arms. 'It is not me, Kismet, truly. Hallow has infiltrated your aura. He must be visiting your dreams in order to create such blockage. I cast a very strong protective spell on your home after I left yesterday so he could not accost you there, and since I told you not to leave, you should have been safe.' He walked over to the bed and deposited me on the multicoloured duvet, then sat on the edge and removed his boots before crawling up beside me.

I smiled even wider and scooted over, giving him room to sit next to me. I smoothed my hand along his leather-clad leg, heading north. 'That's more like it. Less talking, more sex.'

He stared at me. 'Victoria and Nigel are correct: you are indeed behaving like a hormonal adolescent. I must find a way to counteract Hallow's influence, for I fear for your safety. This new personality you are exhibiting is mindless and dangerous, just like the one who contaminated you.'

'What new personality?' My fingers reached the zip of his trousers. I'd just started making him much more comfortable when he grabbed my hand and lifted it away from his crotch. 'No. We have important matters to discuss. Personal pleasure can wait. Tell me what you remember of the last twenty-four hours.'

I stuck my lower lip out in an exaggerated pout, but when I got no response from my undead judge and jury I said grumpily, 'I don't remember anything.' And then, having said that, I realised the last couple of days *were* rather fuzzy. I had the sense that I *should* remember something, and something important at that, but I just couldn't bring whatever it was into focus. I could recall the clients I'd seen on Friday, but after that, everything was gone.

Devereux shook my arm. 'Kismet? Are you listening to me?'

I started to tell him that I'd been trying to remember something that might be helpful, but different words came out of my mouth. 'No. You've finally bored me into a coma.' I scrambled onto my knees and climbed on top of him, pushing him flat on the mattress. As I straddled his hips, my short skirt rode up even higher, collecting around my waist and displaying my lack of underwear. I peeled off my transparent shirt and threw it on the floor. 'Personal pleasure *can't* wait.'

I untucked his T-shirt from his trousers and shoved the fabric out of the way as I bent to lick his nipples. He wound his fingers into my hair and yanked my head up. 'Where is your protective necklace? I instructed Luna to tell you to wear it – did she fail to convey my message? She will be punished if that is the case.'

He released my hair and I sat up. 'You have the most annoying one-track mind. Yes, the she-fiend told me, but I guess I forgot – or maybe I decided I didn't *want* to wear the damn thing. It *is* up to me, you know. Now, be a good little vampire and let me have my way with you.' I'd never heard him threaten Luna before. Maybe there was something going on that I didn't know about – but if it meant Evil Vampira would be out of the picture, that definitely worked for me.

Before he could start on the next lecture, I opened his fly, crawled to the foot of the bed and tugged forcefully on the leather until he lifted his ass enough for the trousers to slide off freely. He made a squeaky completely unmaster-vampire sound which I attributed to his surprise at my strength.

I held his leather trousers in the air, grinning at my success and appreciating the rigid erection stretching across his abdomen.

He sat up, a wicked smile spreading his lips. 'So, you wish to play rough, yes? In that case, I believe I can accommodate you.' Faster than my eyes could track, he grabbed my arms and dragged me up his body, and still holding on, he wrapped his legs tightly around my hips, effectively restraining me.

It was my turn to make a noise, but mine was one of plea-sure; I certainly liked being trapped this way.

I wiggled against his thick erection. 'Lay it on me, Fang Boy.'

He growled and flipped us over. 'As you wish,' he mur-mured as he landed on top of me, his platinum hair covering my face for a couple of seconds before he jerked his head from side to side, flipping the lustrous strands behind him. He'd obviously had a lot of practise with that move, because the hair cooperated. I wondered how many thousands of women he'd had sex with in his long, *long* life, and smiled as I considered the educational possibilities.

It occurred to me that things might be more interesting if I put up a bit of a struggle, so I twisted my body until I was able to free an arm. A shocked expression flashed across his features before he narrowed his eyes, reclaimed the escaped limb and pulled both my arms tightly over my head and secured them in one of his large hands.

'Feel free to fight and struggle, my little psychologist. I know it is the maniac's influence causing this aggression in you, but I can assure you that I am not without experience in this arena. Be very careful what you ask for, my love, for you might receive it.'

I stared up into twin pools of aqua quicksand and batted my eyelashes. 'I'm counting on it,' I purred.

Wicked-fast, he forced my legs apart, and I could feel his erection lying heavy against me. I struggled to lift my hips high enough to put out the welcome mat, but he ignored my invitation. Instead, he filled his free hand with my hair and held my head in place, then, all the time watching me with his psychedelic eyes, he raised his upper lip, showing me his fully extended fangs.

Little moans erupted from my mouth as my body trembled. He smiled and lowered his lips to mine, but instead of the full-on passionate kiss I'd expected, he caught my lip between his teeth and fangs and bit down gently. He groaned as the blood flowed, and the coppery liquid slid across my tongue, driving me wild with need. 'Please,' I begged. I wanted him so badly, to touch me, to fill me—

But he didn't. Instead, he lifted his head, his mouth smeared with my blood, and licked his way down to my breast. He began sucking roughly on my nipple and that sensation was somehow directly connected to the hot, tingling area between my legs. 'Oh, *yeah* – that's what I want,' I groaned and he paused for a second, then sliced his fangs into the tender skin around my nipple and resumed sucking.

I screamed – it was horribly exquisite – and struggled to break free, not because I wanted him to stop, but because I wanted to take matters into my own hands. But even with my newly enhanced strength, I couldn't budge him. As he drew the blood from the fang holes on either side of my nipple rushes of ecstasy shimmered through my body and I continued to scream until my throat was raw and my mouth so dry, all I could do was whimper.

Finally, he lifted his head and locked eyes with mine. A circle of red surrounded the normal turquoise-blue-green of his irises and the colours swirled together. He licked his lips slowly, his tongue darting out to catch the crimson drops dotting his chin.

Jesus. He was astounding, all that shining blond hair and dazzling eyes. Just seeing him with my blood on his face made me crazy. My breath came in rapid pants and I continued trying to twist out of his grip, still with no success, but at last he smiled, raised his hips to alter his angle and thrust deep inside me in one smooth motion. I was so wet, it was perfect. Still holding my wrists captive in one hand, he used his other to grab my hair again and this time while keeping my head immobile, he kissed me, as if he were feasting at my mouth, pulling the life-force from my body, all swollen lips and probing tongue.

It was awesome.

Devereux pounded himself into me with fierce determination, and now we were both making animal grunting sounds as we pressed our lips even tighter together. My orgasm was building, and I matched his rhythm with my hips, the ferocity of his thrusts causing a mixture of pleasure and pain. He contracted inside me as he raised his mouth and spoke in the strange, lyrical language he sometimes used. The power of his release pushed me over the edge and I made strangled croaking noises, all my lacerated throat was capable of.

His pale skin was flushed, maybe from all the blood he'd taken from me, and his heart beat fast and loud. An almost-goofy grin slid across his perfect face. 'Would you like more?'

Yes! But . . . maybe not right now.

The area between my legs was tender and raw. I'd had sex

with Devereux more times than I could count, but he had never been quite as large before. He'd said it was possible for a vampire to transform aspects of his physical appearance. Good to know it was true.

'I think I'd better rest a while.' I grinned up at him. 'You have made your point. You are indeed the Boink Master.'

He released my wrists and fell on the bed next to me, lying on his back. I examined, then rubbed, the red skin on my arms where he'd held me, before shifting my gaze to the nipple he'd gnawed on. The skin around it was bruised and swollen and the tiny fang holes still oozed. There'd be a rainbow of colours by morning. I turned my head. 'Geez, Blondie – you really did a number on my body. I think I like this side of you. I'll bet you have lots of sexual tricks to show me.'

He gave a lazy smile and balanced onto his side, facing me. He propped himself up with an elbow and rested his head against his palm. 'I am always happy to find ever-more-creative ways to make love to you, but I wonder how *wild* you will wish our coupling to be after you are freed from the monster's influence. I plan to do whatever I must to remove you from his power.'

'You keep saying I'm under someone's power. I think you're losing your marbles. I'm no different than usual, maybe just in a better mood. Are you complaining?'

'Of course not. I was happy with our sexual relationship before your personality changed, so you need not worry about my expectations.'

I laughed. 'Your *expectations*? Do you believe I'll ever be one of your handmaidens?'

He readjusted his position, lying on his back, his fingers laced behind his head. 'No, but I am hoping you will respect the fact that I have been around much longer than you, and I usually know what is best for you.'

'What?' I sprang up and glared at him. 'Like some undead daddy? You think you know what's best for me?'

He angled his head towards me. 'Yes, I do. I am very old and you will have to admit that I was right to protect your home and to order you to remain there until our appointment here at midnight. My actions kept you safe from Hallow's madness. I wish to compliment you for your willingness to trust my judgement.'

'So, you're saying that you just tell me what to do and then trust that I'll follow your instructions?'

'Yes. I am very powerful. I offer protection. How could it be otherwise?'

'And you think I want to be protected?'

'Regardless of whether or not you wish to be protected, I intend to make it so.'

I couldn't remember a large chunk of my recent past, but something about Devereux's assertion that he'd ordered me to remain at home and I'd followed his commands wasn't quite right. He sounded so confident that he could take my actions for granted. I didn't know why that struck me as amusing, but it did.

He climbed on top of me and smiled, flicking his long hair out of the way. 'Let us not argue. All will be well soon enough. Hallow will be taken care of, your personality will return to its normal charming self and we will continue to forge our future.' He kissed me sweetly.

I enjoyed the kiss, prolonging it as long as possible. After he pulled away, I gazed up at him and smiled. 'So, let me just make sure I'm clear on the game plan, Gorgeous. Because you're the undead Methuselah and one of the most powerful bloodsuckers on the planet, you get to decide what I will and won't do with my life? You'll make my choices for me?'

'I would not put it exactly that way,' Devereux said carefully, 'but I will certainly give you the benefit of my expanded knowledge and experience. I will take very good care of you. You will never want for anything.'

Except freedom.

'Uh-huh. And what is the benefit to you for having me as your subjugated female? What's the payoff for keeping your *mate* under your thumb?'

He appeared genuinely surprised by the questions. 'Subjugated? Under my thumb? How could you think such a thing? You will be revered and cherished. Your life will be enhanced. The benefit to me of having my mate by my side is too complex a topic to discuss in your unnatural state of mind.'

'Hmmm. I see. Too complex. Well, what about when my physical body ages, rots and dies? What's the plan, then? Will you have me mummified and displayed in your penthouse? Maybe alongside my portrait?'

'There is a ritual.' His expression became serious. 'You will be able to share some of my gifts – but we will speak of this another time.'

'Does it involve me drinking more of your blood? Are you talking about turning me into a bloodsucker?'

'I have told you it is not easy to become a vampire. For optimum results it must be freely chosen. Now, no more talk of this tonight.' He rubbed his erection against me. 'Are you too tender from our previous lovemaking, or shall we have an encore?'

I grinned. 'I'm ready if you are, Maestro, but this time I'm on top.' I straddled his hips, then impaled myself on him. I clenched my vaginal muscles, gripped him as tightly as I could and got a rhythm going. He planted his hands on my waist, holding me in place while he pumped his hips. He stared at me with those hypnotic aqua eyes as his tongue played with the tips of his fangs.

I gave him my best innocent smile. 'Do you want more of my blood, my Dark Prince?'

He hissed and pulled my upper body down to his. His soft, warm lips plundered mine, our tongues dancing, then he kissed his way to my neck and bit, and we moaned in concert as our shared orgasm built between us and exploded.

When the aftershocks quieted, I sat up and gazed down at him. 'Drinking blood must be good. Why is it that you won't let me drink yours?'

He studied me for a few seconds. 'Have you forgotten what you learned from the elders about drinking from me? The negative consequences? Even the fact that you do not remember such an important thing is evidence of your altered mind. You are currently incapable of making considered decisions, so I will take charge. I will not let you harm yourself. You have no need for vampire blood.'

'He is lying.' A familiar deep voice floated through my mind. 'Break the glass on the nearby table and cut him – drink, and see for yourself.'

Really? Well, why not?

I glanced at the bedside table and saw a small vase sitting there. Moving oddly fast, I grabbed it, tossed the lone flower and its water onto the floor and smashed the glass against the table edge. A large piece broke away, leaving a sharp corner, and without hesitation or thought I drew the jagged edge of the vase along Devereux's stomach and watched the blood blossom from the cut. I caught a fleeting glimpse of his shocked face before I bent, licked the blood with my tongue, then sucked hard on the wound.

Devereux grabbed a handful of hair and jerked my head up. Anger and fear fought for dominance in his face as he cried, 'Stop – what have you done? My blood is *poison* for you – it could *kill* you!'

CHAPTER 13

Devereux jerked into a sitting position and knocked the splintered glass from my grip. I watched the piece of vase sail through the air. He released my hair, snarling, and recoiled as if he'd been clutching Medusa's snakes.

I swiped the back of my hand across my mouth, smearing his blood along my cheek.

'I don't know about it killing me, but it sure tastes like shit.' I stuck my tongue out. 'How can you drink that crap all the time? Do me a favour and stake me right away if I start to turn into a vampire. I'd rather be dead.'

Devereux's scowl clued me in to the fact that he was no longer in a playful mood, but that was okay, because I'd started feeling weird. Suddenly, everything was too bright. My lips tingled, and my throat contracted, making it difficult to swallow. I could see Devereux's mouth moving, but the sound dissolved into the abyss stretching between us before it could reach my ears. But even without the volume, it was easy to read his anger.

I slid off him and tried to say, 'I think I've had enough fun for one night. I'm going to go home—' but my numb lips weren't cooperating. 'Uh-oh.' My head flopped onto the bed. The room spun and my stomach was cartwheeling.

I must have nodded off for a few minutes because the next thing I knew, I was loosely wrapped in the bedspread, lying in the centre of the colourful pentagram etched into the marble-tile floor of Devereux's room. Chanting bodies encircled me, their voices rumbling in a soft, monotonous drone. Lit candles cast soft light and deep shadows and a strong aroma wafted from incense burners scattered around the space, reminding me of a Christmas Mass I had attended as a child.

I recognised Luna, who was standing next to a Johnny Depp look-alike, but the rest of the participants were strangers. Scanning the expressions on their faces told me that whatever the purpose for their gathering, it wasn't good.

Devereux knelt next to me and looped something around my neck. I shifted my gaze down to see what it was. My protective necklace. He must have retrieved it from my house.

'What's going on?' Still slightly dizzy, I tried to sit up. 'Why are you all standing around me?'

Devereux pressed me down to the floor with his hand on my shoulder. 'No, Kismet, do not move yet. My blood had a

seriously debilitating effect on you – you have been unconscious. We have discovered the situation is much worse than
I had feared: drinking from me has somehow deepened Hallow's influence over you, which is why he commanded you
to do it. We have been attempting to remove some of the
psychic tendrils he thrust into your aura, but he is more
powerful than I ever imagined. I have called every master
vampire, healer and wizard available to assist – they are still
arriving and we will work through the night. *I will not let
him have you.*'

'Have me? What happened? Why do I feel so terrible? I
drank your blood?' My voice sounded feeble.

He frowned. 'What is the last thing you remember?'

I tried to concentrate through the fuzz in my head. 'I was
at home, getting ready to do some paperwork. I'd decided
to spend a quiet evening there – how did I get to The Crypt?'
I glanced down again. 'Where are my clothes?'

Devereux gazed at me with such tenderness that it frightened me. It was almost as if he pitied me, or was avoiding
telling me an unpleasant fact I needed to know.

Panic overwhelmed me and I tried to wiggle out from
under his restraining hand. 'Why are you staring at me like
that? Tell me what happened – am I dying?'

He gave a gentle smile and stroked his hand along my
hair. 'No, you are not dying. I will not let anything bad
happen to you, but this is a serious situation and it is best
if you return to sleep for a few more hours.'

What did he mean, a few *more* hours? Was he saying I'd
already been out that long? I opened my mouth to argue

and met his eyes. He spoke some odd-sounding but strangely familiar words and I drifted away.

I'm in a hazy, surreal, sunset-tinted landscape, standing in a structure surrounded by many white columns high on a mountaintop. A fragrant breeze blows through the open building, causing my white filmy gown to mould itself to my body. I stare out at the expansive horizon, mesmerised by the ethereal, magical view, breathing in the rarified air. I am light – free.

Sensing a presence, I shift my gaze away from the stunning scenery and turn to the handsome figure lounging against a column.

'Ah, there you are, Doctor. It took me a while to break through all your saviour's spells and incantations. I must tell you, this adventure is turning out to be even more exciting than I expected. I had no idea Devereux had become so powerful. What a treat for me to defeat and control such a vampire. It's almost a shame he isn't the one I've come to harvest.'

'Hallow? Where am I?'

He ambles towards me, smiling, his long hair fanning out in the wind. 'Mount Olympus, of course. The home of the gods. Or at least one god.'

'You're a god?'

His smile spreads wider. 'Unavoidably.'

'Why am I here?'

He saunters in a circle. 'I'm preparing you to be my next lýtle.'

Wary, I turn to follow his motion. 'Your what?'

'Lýtle. It's an Old English word. It translates as female slave, but I've given it much richer meaning over the centuries.'

I shake my head. 'This can't really be happening. I'm not going to be anybody's slave. This is a delusion – a dream, right?'

He stops moving and stands in front of me. 'Let's just say it's a dream dimension. The actual explanation would raise too many questions, and I must return you to your body before you become too attached to this reality. It isn't your time to transition yet, but I couldn't resist claiming you again, just to confound the magicians. And speaking of your knight in shining armour, I have masked your memories from our time together. He will not find them.'

He steps close, pulls me against his body and stares at me with his shimmering silver eyes. 'I am perplexed by my unexpected interest in you. I had not anticipated I'd find you so intriguing. It appears that I desire more than your blood and obedience and that makes me curious. My reactions to you are odd – it isn't often that any-thing surprises me.'

'Don't you already have a harem of women who do whatever you want? Why would you want someone who would rather die than willingly submit to you?'

He laughs. 'That is no doubt one cause for the fascination. It will be exciting to break you.'

He cocks his head and lowers his mouth to my neck. The sharp points of his fangs slice through my skin and I groan, my muscles melting. He wraps me more tightly in his arms and at the pressure of his lips sucking blood from my vein a full-body orgasm radiates through me. I writhe in his arms, gasping. He raises his mouth from the punctures and brings his soft, warm lips to mine. They taste of my own blood, and that excites me. My heart pounds madly, my breath comes in rapid pants.

He releases me and I stumble, grabbing onto a column to steady myself. A depraved smile quirks his lips. 'I'm afraid I'm spoiling you for anyone else, my dear doctor. Fantasy sex is definitely in our future, and it will be long and slow – but, alas, not today. Go back now. Return to your body. And remember my touch. Yearn for it.'

I opened my eyes feeling like I'd dived into deep water, then fought my way back to the surface. It only took a few seconds to recognise I was wearing a bright red satin nightgown and lying on the huge bed in Devereux's room. Soft light glowed from candles hovering in the air. I would have assumed I was still dreaming – or insane – if I hadn't seen a similar impossibility previously at vampire rituals.

Remnants of the odd dream flickered across my inner movie screen. In my mind's eye I could still see the achingly beautiful colours flowing, one into another, along the celestial canvas. My body remembered the caress of the soft air against my skin; my eyes had memorised the brilliant white of the marble columns. And my soul yearned for . . . what? Hallow? How could I yearn for him? No; that couldn't be possible. Even the thought of desiring the beautiful demon filled me with shame. What had the murdering psychopath done to me?

Raised voices – familiar voices – floated into my awareness, jarring me out of my reverie. I lifted myself onto my elbows and watched Dr Sex pace back and forth in front of Victoria, who sat in the large, throne-like chair Devereux had once claimed was almost as old as he was.

Since the room was apparently vampire-free, that meant the sun was up. I had no idea how long I'd been sleeping, or what day it was. I had a full schedule of clients for Monday, and I was worried I'd abandoned them.

'It wouldn't hurt him to listen to me for a few minutes. This is very important. I'm certain if he lets me explain my situation, we could come to a mutually beneficial outcome. I'm not used to being dismissed that way,' Tom ranted.

Victoria tried to whisper, but her anger made her voice louder than she had probably intended. 'You're lucky he even let you stay here while Zoë sleeps. If I hadn't convinced Devereux that despite your complete and utter self-absorption, you're Kismet's friend, you'd have had your memory altered and be on your way back to Los Angeles. Count yourself lucky that I was here to speak for your pitiful self.'

Tom flicked his hair behind his shoulder and adopted his most pompous tone. 'I'm not self-absorbed. I'm focused. There's a difference.' He paused, planting his fists on his hips. 'And why the hell can't I get out of this dungeon? All the vampires are dead to the world, even the one everybody is afraid of. Why are there guards on the doors? What good are human guards going to be, anyway?'

Victoria stood and faced him. 'Has anyone ever told you that you have an annoying habit of talking when you have no knowledge to back up your words? You ramble endlessly and pointlessly. It's very irritating.' She stepped closer into his much-cherished personal space. 'The guards are on the doors for Kismet's protection, you idiot. The grotesque vampire in question doesn't follow any rules, including being unable to function during the daylight hours. There is no limit to what he can do. He can crawl into her mind and make her behave in ways she ordinarily wouldn't. She could try to leave – from what I've seen, she might even attempt to overpower us. We're here to protect her.' She poked her finger into his chest and he swatted her hand away.

'Don't touch me!' He scowled.

'Of course,' she said, 'the idea of doing something for someone else is probably a foreign concept to you, but if you want to go through with your absurd plan, you should probably pay attention to what Devereux says. No matter who turns you, you'll still start out at the bottom of the undead totem pole, and that means you'll be somebody's flunky, for at least a little while. I suspect that will be a humbling blow to your astronomical ego.' She shook her finger in his face. 'I barely know you and I've already been tempted to turn you into various barnyard animals – I certainly don't understand how Kismet tolerates you. Or Zoë.'

'You don't know me well enough to speak to me that way.' Tom's voice rose in pitch. 'You're just a receptionist, aren't you? Where do you get off—?'

Their argument was getting old. It was time to press the *pause* button. I lifted my head. 'Hey! You two are going to wake the dead.'

Both their heads swivelled towards me, and Victoria scurried to my bedside.

'Kismet!' She wrapped her fingers around one of my hands. 'Thank the Goddess you're awake! We were all so frightened. Nobody knew what the psycho had done to you. How do you feel?'

Tom peeked around Victoria, stealing little glances at my face.

'I'm fine. I don't understand why I'm in Devereux's bed instead of my own.' Tom still hadn't moved any closer to me. 'What are you doing, Tom? You're behaving even more eccentrically than usual. Why are you hiding?'

He sidled next to Victoria, frowning. 'I just wanted to make sure you weren't going to attack anyone else like you did Devereux.'

'What?' I glared at him. 'I didn't attack anyone, especially not Devereux. Victoria, what's he talking about?'

She cast a frosty gaze at Tom. 'As usual, he's just yapping to hear the sound of his own voice.'

'She did attack him! Are you going to lie to her?'

I sighed. Their quasi-sibling rivalry was making my head hurt. I fell back onto the pillow. 'Okay, *stop*. Please. Victoria, just tell me. I don't remember anything. Did I have some kind of breakdown? Did someone spike my coffee? Did Devereux bring me here? What day is it?'

She paused, a conflicted expression on her face. 'It's Sunday, late afternoon. You're probably afraid you missed your client appointments ~ don't worry, you didn't. Everything's fine. Besides, even if you had, I would've contacted all of them to reschedule.'

Relief washed over me. I patted her hand and smiled. 'Thank you for being such a good friend. So, what about the rest of my questions?'

'I don't know how much I should tell you.' She frowned.

'I don't want to upset you or make things worse. All I know is what Devereux told me.'

I raised my eyebrows. 'Well?'

'Do you remember Devereux saying that Hallow had already begun influencing you? That you weren't . . . yourself?'

'Yes. I remember he said that, but it didn't make any sense. Are you saying that's what happened? Lyren Hallow has been controlling me?'

'My theory is that he began entrancing you when he called the radio show. Devereux agrees with me.' A thoughtful expression crossed her face. She pursed her lips and asked Tom, 'Doctor Radcliffe, would you mind telling the guards at the door that we need human food and drink down here? Ask one of them to go upstairs with you and bring supplies.'

He raised his nose into the air. 'You don't give the orders around here. Why don't *you* go?'

Victoria shifted her eyes in my direction, then to Tom and receiving her unspoken message, I said, 'Come on, Tom – help me out here. I really am thirsty.' I gave him my best puppy-dog look.

'Yeah, sure. Don't think I'm buying that story for one minute. I know you want to talk about me when I'm gone, but I'm used to that. I often inspire jealousy.' He stomped off towards the door.

The expression on Victoria's face gave me a good idea about what she intended to say, so I beat her to it. 'Yes, I know. He's a complete ass and an insufferable egomaniac. We've known each other for so long, believe it or not, he's actually my oldest friend. Strangely, he's the closest thing to a brother I have – well, okay, maybe a third cousin twice removed who'd sell me to white slavers for a shot of Botox – but for now let's both pretend he's not the biggest dickhead in the universe.'

She shook her head. 'Come on, Kismet, level with me. How could you ever have lived with someone like Tom? I know he's handsome, but didn't he drive you insane?'

I thought for a moment. 'Yes, he really did.' I grinned. 'But I met him when I was in grad school, when I was young, insecure and shy. He was already the Wunderkind of the psychology department and I was incredibly flattered by his attention – a bit shocked too, actually. He was so popular. I mostly just trailed around after him, allowing his life to become mine. It took me a while to realise how empty the relationship was. It wasn't his pomposity that broke us up; it was his infidelity. He never could resist a pair of perky breasts.' I paused for a few seconds. 'After we broke up and I stopped pretending not to see the obvious, I actually started to enjoy him. Mostly. He's much worse when other people are around than when it's just the two of us. Maybe he doesn't think I rate the full obnoxious act. Sometimes he can actually be fun to spend time with. But if you ever tell him I said that, I'll lock you in a room with him!'

We both laughed. Then I became serious again. 'So, what did you want to tell me?'

She scooted a chair to the edge of the bed and sat. 'We both know that Devereux, delightful soul that he is, has a tendency to be a little arrogant. It never occurs to him that his view of something might not be universal. He's convinced that Hallow's only communications with you have come through your dreams.'

I nodded, recalling the mountaintop scene. 'Hallow *has* been in my dreams.'

She folded her hands on her lap, nodding. 'I can't read your mind, but I have various psychic abilities, and my strongest gift is the same as yours: clairsentience. I simply know things. And sometimes I'm clairvoyant – and that's how I'm aware that you've had more contact with Hallow than merely through dreams. I saw you on a stage somewhere with him, both of you covered with blood. Then I saw him again in your townhouse. I watched him bite you.' She hesitated, frowning. 'That part was very sexual. Despite what Devereux might believe, Hallow appears to have unlimited access to you, no matter how many magic spells and vampire enchantments are involved. Do you remember any of what I described?'

I stared at her as the memory came flooding back. The stage was at the amusement park – *how could I forget witnessing a murder?* I drew a blank about him being in my house.

'Yes.' I nodded, licking my very-dry lips. Anxiety twisted my stomach and I couldn't make eye-contact with Victoria. 'I do remember being in an abandoned building with Hallow. He killed the radio host who'd been so obnoxious to me that morning. He made me look at the body. He said he'd done it for me.' I raised my gaze to hers. 'But I have no memory of him being in my home. Are you sure you saw that? Maybe you were just afraid it might happen and you imagined it?'

'I wish it was my imagination, but unfortunately I'm sure. Do you remember coming to The Crypt last night and being rather . . . rowdy?'

'What do you mean?' I grabbed her arm. 'Are you saying I came to the club under my own power? Why don't I remember? Did you come with me?'

'No. I met you on the front stairs. You definitely weren't your usual self.'

'What did I do? Pick a bar fight? Take off all my clothes?' I cringed and briefly covered my eyes with my hands. 'No, wait, I'm not sure I want to know. Just tell me that I didn't do anything to humiliate myself personally or professionally.'

She shrugged. 'One fight. No nudity. You were simply . . . uninhibited.'

'Oh, my God! *One fight*? I don't understand. I *never* fight. Are you sure?' I glanced down at my unblemished hands.

'Absolutely. You were the talk of the club. A waitress who came in at the end said you mopped the floor with a large woman named Jenna.' She laughed. 'You should have seen Devereux stalking into the women's bathroom. He erased all the memories of the women in the room and gave away free drinks, then he planted the idea in Jenna's mind that she had fallen down drunk and slammed her face against a table edge.'

'Oh, shit.' I covered my face with my hands. 'Is that the worst of it?'

'Pretty much. You did a fair bit of flirting, but there was no harm done. All of Devereux's employees are aware of

Hallow's presence and his effect on you.' She paused. 'And I need to confess something: Nigel and I were so worried about you that we went to find Devereux and – well, I'm afraid I'm the one who said you were behaving like a hormonal adolescent. He told me he mentioned it to you, although I know you don't remember anything that happened while you were at the club. But still.' She lowered her gaze and shook her head. 'I'm so sorry – I just wanted Devereux to understand that the demon's influence had caused you to regress to a younger, more primitive part of your consciousness, rather than have him think your normal personality had made those decisions. Do you forgive me?'

I pulled a corner of the blanket up and flipped it over my head, as if trying to hide from my misbehaviour. 'Of course I forgive you,' I mumbled through the cloth. 'I'm sure the label was accurate. I'm just confused – I don't know whether to be embarrassed that everyone knows what's happening to me except me, or happy that I didn't do any irreparable damage.'

She tugged the blanket away from my face. 'You have nothing to be embarrassed about.' A slow smile slid across her lips. 'You were certainly enjoying yourself. You've got quite a way with men – you were just about to add another boy-toy to your collection when Devereux showed up and brought you down here. Then, from what I heard, things got a little . . . out of hand.'

A way with men? Not in this universe.

My heart started to beat faster. Dread trickled through

my body. 'Is that what Tom was talking about? Did I actually attack Devereux?'

She shook her head. 'I don't think so – at least, not exactly. Devereux didn't tell me everything, but at some point in your . . . intimacies . . . you broke a glass vase, cut his skin and drank his blood. That's why you were unconscious.'

I jerked up like my upper body was spring-loaded. 'Holy shit! Did I hurt him?'

'No – he probably healed immediately, but you were knocked out, and Devereux doesn't know what other longer-term effects his blood will have on you. He did discover that for some odd reason his blood has deepened Hallow's control over you. Devereux said he could perceive an even more powerful presence in your energy field.'

I stared at her, frowning silently for a few seconds. 'Is Lyren Hallow controlling me now? I don't feel anything different – I've been aware of everything since I woke up a little while ago. Is he just taking a break from making me do inappropriate things?'

'Devereux and the others worked all night to remove as much of Hallow's influence as possible,' Victoria said, trying to sound reassuring. 'Your protection necklace has been strengthened and enhanced, so it *should* be harder for Hallow to enter your mind while you're awake – but nobody knows for sure. Unfortunately, I doubt if anyone could restrict him from your dreams. He's a force unlike any other, but for now, you're mostly back to being the Kismet we're all familiar with.'

Suddenly anxious, I chewed on my bottom lip. 'But *why*

would I want to drink Devereux's blood? I'd never do such a thing in my right mind – or maybe that's the problem. Perhaps Hallow is driving me mad. What if I reach a point where there's no going back?'

Since neither of us had an answer to that question, we just stared at each other.

A commotion near the entrance drew my attention. Ankh, the cadaverous door vamp, was holding a struggling Tom aloft by the back of his shirt. 'He was trying to crawl out the storage-room window. I thought I'd check with you before I disposed of him.'

'Thank you, Ankh,' I said with a laugh. 'You can just leave him here.'

'Yes, indeed.' A commanding voice floated through the air a second after a golden-robed Devereux manifested at the foot of my bed. 'He wanted my attention. He now has it.'

CHAPTER 14

Ankh lowered Tom slowly to his feet, then bowed to Devereux. 'Will there be anything else, Master?'

Devereux smiled at the tall vampire. 'No thank you, Ankh. You may return to your post.'

With a tiny *pop* sound, Ankh vanished.

Ignoring Tom, Devereux greeted Victoria before gliding over to sit beside me on the bed. He gazed into my eyes a few seconds before speaking. 'I am glad you are awake. How are you?'

I blinked a couple of times, waiting for Hallow to flip the switch on my personality again, but nothing happened. I still felt normal – whatever that was. 'I'm okay,' I said a little nervously.

Devereux's calm confidence had reappeared. I wondered how he'd take the news that Hallow had got through all his spells and enchantments. I wasn't looking forward to that conversation.

My gaze fell to his ornate golden robe and I grinned. Devereux usually dressed in high-fashion contemporary clothes. Or his bare skin. I'd never seen him decked out in such Grand Poobah raiment. There were no moons or stars on the fabric, but the neckline boasted enough gemstones to finance a small country. He was as gorgeous as ever, but it was certainly a different style for him. Did he really sleep – or die – in such a fussy get-up?

He matched my grin. 'My robe amuses you?'

I opened my mouth to answer and was distracted by an intrusive, repetitive sound: Tom had crossed his arms over his chest and was impatiently tapping his foot against the marble tile floor. 'I thought you said I had your attention. It would be common courtesy for you to speak with me for a few moments. I have a serious issue to discuss.'

Devereux lifted my hand and kissed the palm. 'Excuse me, my love. I must attend to an annoying detail.'

So fast my eyes registered only a blur, Devereux grabbed Tom by the front of his shirt, hefted the shocked man into the air and locked eyes with him. All of Tom's muscles loosened and he collapsed into a Dr Sex ragdoll. Devereux growled, his voice low, 'You forget yourself, Doctor Radcliffe. You are in *my* world now and you have no power here. You have been allowed to remain only because you are Kismet's friend.'

Devereux closed his eyes for a few seconds and Zoë appeared next to him. He acknowledged her arrival and refocused on Tom, speaking very slowly, anger dripping from his words. 'Doctor, I have a low tolerance for nonsense, and you are fast becoming a nuisance. My staff tells me you have been frequenting my club every night, asking questions and causing difficulties. Zoë has been ordered to inform you that I no longer transform humans, and even if I did, your ridiculous reason for wanting to join the ranks of the undead would not sway me to your cause. I have also forbidden her from attempting to bring you over herself.'

I was stunned by the rage in Devereux's voice. I'd completely missed his animosity towards Tom. I wondered what else I'd been oblivious to over the past couple of days.

I wasn't sure what I intended to do, but I leapt out of bed and hurried over to Devereux. I pressed my body against him and slid my arms around his waist, hugging him from behind. I caught Zoë's frightened eyes. 'Devereux, please, let him go. Don't hurt him. He's behaving badly because he's afraid for his future. He's not thinking clearly. Please – I'm sure he'll apologise for whatever he did to upset you.'

We all stood, frozen in our weird tableau for what felt like aeons, but was really only seconds, then Devereux stroked my arm. I released the breath I'd been holding and my contracted muscles relaxed. I surrendered my grip on his midsection and stepped sideways. He lowered the boneless Tom to the floor. His enticing voice whispered, 'Sleep,' and Tom closed his eyes, pulled his knees up to his chest like a baby and followed the instruction.

Devereux spoke to Zoë, a sharp edge to his voice. 'Take him to Kismet's townhouse and do not let him out of your sight. I am willing to be tolerant this time, but do not try my patience. He is not to visit my club or show himself here in any way. Is that clear?'

Zoë nodded, her lips pressed tightly together, her pale skin even whiter than usual.

'Do you understand the danger to Doctor Radcliffe if you continue your attempt to transform him? You will not succeed, and he will simply die.'

Her shoulders slumped and she stared at the floor.

'Go now.'

Zoë slanted a quick and grateful glance at me, then bent to lift Tom into her arms. She mouthed 'thank you' before they vanished.

I stepped in front of Devereux. 'Are you going to tell me what that was about? And why you told Zoë to take Tom to my house?' I'd rarely seen him behave so aggressively. Maybe I wasn't the only one splintering under the heightened stress.

Devereux shifted his gaze to Victoria, who'd waited silently during the impromptu drama. 'Victoria, please make sure everything Kismet requires is brought to my penthouse. I will leave all the details in your capable hands.'

Victoria rose and smiled at me before exiting the room.

I wiggled my index finger in his face. 'Have I suddenly become invisible, or are you just ignoring me?'

'Come.' He grabbed my hand and tugged me over to the bed, where we both sat. 'I am happy to tell you anything you wish to know.' He paused before speaking again. 'Your friend has overstepped his bounds and I had to take action, for his sake as much as anyone else's. I regret that you were distressed by our . . . disagreement. I had Zoë take Tom to your townhouse because it is a safe haven for him. He will sleep for hours. And, regarding my penthouse, I hope you now see the benefit of living there temporarily. Even though I can cast protective spells at your townhouse again, it is easier for me to take you to a fortified space. You will be even safer there.'

I wasn't going to argue with him about stashing me away in his building. I didn't remember large portions of my recent past, and accepting his plan seemed prudent for everyone – although after my discussion with Victoria, it was probable that Devereux was the only one who thought I'd be safe anywhere.

'It is good to have you back. I have missed you.' He lifted me onto his lap, smiling. I felt his warm breath on my face as he enveloped me in his arms and kissed my cheek with his soft lips.

I knew what he meant, but being curious about my other personality, I fished for more information. 'What do you mean? I never left – I was here all the time.'

Apparently aware of my tactic, he raised a brow. 'Why not simply ask what you wish to know?'

I enjoyed studying his face for a few seconds, then brushed aside a few long blond strands of his silky hair and tucked them behind one of his perfectly shaped ears. 'Just tell me if I did anything to embarrass myself or anyone else in any way. Victoria said I was *uninhibited*. I suspect that's an understatement. How bad was I?'

'You were not *bad* at all – merely not yourself. Or at least not the self you normally show the world. You were very influenced by the one who tainted you. He has little regard for others. He is a violent sexual predator, often crude and sadistic, and you exhibited mild aspects of his tendencies. According to my staff, you behaved as if you were youthfully intoxicated, nothing more.'

'That's what Victoria said, too.' Ridiculously relieved, I blew out a breath. 'It's very upsetting to lose chunks of memory. I feel as if I've crashed and my personal black box is still missing.'

'I do not understand.' He tilted his head and frowned. 'Did you misplace a black box?'

'I'm sorry.' I chuckled. 'That's an aeroplane reference. Since you have no need for conventional transport, you've probably never heard about the recording devices used on aircraft. Never mind, it's not important. It's just a metaphor.' I kissed his chin. 'So, what's the plan? We're going to your penthouse, right? I have clients tomorrow morning.'

He grinned, his beautiful eyes twinkling. 'What is the rush?' He lifted me off his lap and tossed me onto the centre of the bed, and in a heartbeat, I was pinned under his body. I opened my mouth to complain about his weight and got a mouthful of hair. I sputtered, pushing at the strands with my tongue, all the while listening to him laugh. As quickly as the sweet-smelling mane had covered my face, it was gone again as he flung his platinum veil behind him with a masterful flick of his head.

'Hey, are you trying to suffocate me?'

He braced his arms and feet to lift his body, lessening the pressure on my chest. 'I am sorry, my love.' His voice still held traces of his laughter. 'That was not very romantic, was it? In the future, I will remember to tie my hair back before jumping on you.'

I inhaled the delicious scent of his skin and sighed in satisfaction. 'I guess I'll forgive you this time.' I wrapped my arms around his neck, pulled his body against mine and tenderly kissed him.

He deepened the kiss and moaned softly.

We explored each other's mouths, tongues joyfully caressing, as we reignited the romantic flame between us. As much as I craved Devereux sexually, I was blissfully content to press my lips to his and revel in his presence. For the moment, all I needed was the closeness – the touching.

Finally coming up for air, he rolled onto his side, and balanced his head on his palm. He watched me, his face serious. 'Kissing you is always as amazing as the first time. You cannot know how incredible it is for me to share your life-force – to lose myself in you. It is as if you were created especially for me. I am very grateful that the ritual restored you to me.'

'Well, I don't know where I was, but I'm glad to be back, too.' I trailed a finger along his lower lip. 'You certainly know how to raise my heart rate.' I laughed. 'I never could resist a guy in a sparkly dress.'

He smiled. 'That is the second time you have mentioned my robe. Druids are fond of such garments. Why does it make you laugh? I wear it merely for convenience.'

Visions of a rhinestone-studded Liberace swept into my mind. My parents had taken me through the flash pianist's museum in Las Vegas when I was a child and I never forgot the outrageous capes and robes displayed there. I wondered if he and Devereux had the same tailor.

I toyed with the gemstones circling Devereux's neckline, still smiling. 'I guess it's because I'm used to your tight leather and the robe makes you look like a monk in drag.'

'Is that a bad thing?' He frowned. 'What is a monkindrag? I am fluent in many languages, but I am not familiar with that word.'

I hooted out a laugh. 'It's English – three words, not one. Monk. In. Drag.'

He appeared completely confused. 'Drag? What is drag?'

'It's just a joke – being in drag means dressing flamboyantly like the opposite sex.'

His lips pressed into a tight line and he raised his chin. 'Are you saying my very expensive, custom-designed robe makes me look like a *woman*?' He lifted the hem of the robe, gathering the fabric in his hand until it exposed his lower body. He nodded at the thick erection straining upwards. 'Is *this* the body of a woman?'

I could have soothed his indignation and doused the fire with some calming words, but the expression on his face was so perfectly outraged, so theatrically appalled – the lord and master had been insulted – that I couldn't stop smiling.

I shook my head. 'No, that's most definitely not the body of a woman, but in that fancy robe you could be acting out the drag-queen role in the vampire version of *The Birdcage*.'

I really didn't want to upset him, but he *had* asked me why I kept smiling at his robe. If we couldn't be honest with each other, what did that mean for the longevity of our relationship? A sense of humour was crucial – although apparently I could've been more tactful.

'What? Drag-queen? Birdcage? I do not understand. No one has ever before expressed any such opinion about my attire.'

I didn't think his chin could lift any higher and still be attached to his neck. He flung the bottom of the robe down, covering himself. He was obviously waiting for me to apologise – or grovel.

Instead, I opted for logic. Reaching out, I stroked my hand down his arm. 'Devereux, we have to be truthful with each other. You said you want a twenty-first-century relationship with me, and that means we *communicate*. We have *differences of opinion*. We can tease each other in a loving way.' He lowered his chin just enough to acknowledge he was considering what I said. 'My comments about your robe were not meant to be insulting; I was being playful. You have to admit all that sparkly gold with the gemstones is rather . . . *unusual* in today's world. It just took me by surprise.' I thought a little flattery wouldn't hurt. 'I love your body in all that sophisticated leather. It's so . . . *you*.'

He stared at me, his eyes narrowing. 'Are you attempting to sweetly manipulate me, my love?'

'Maybe.' I leaned in and kissed his lips. 'Is it working?'

He flashed a brilliant smile. 'It would appear so. I understand what you mean about communication. So, in the spirit of compromise, I am willing to overlook your amusement about my wardrobe. In fact, I will wear other robes that are even more majestic and you can acclimatise. And, to be fair,

I promise to be naked as often as possible, for I would not want my gender to be in question for you in any way.'

I slid my hand over the bulge under the gold fabric and batted my eyelashes. 'You know you're all male. You've definitely got the alpha thing down. After all, you're the big cheese vampire.'

'That is true.' He nodded, smiling. 'And I can assure you that you have only just begun to understand how my *alpha thing* can benefit you.' He peeled one of the spaghetti straps of my red satin nightgown down my shoulder with the tip of a finger.

The touch sent a pleasant shiver along my arm. 'Oh, yes. I like the way your mind works.' I was glad his good humour had returned.

Effortlessly, he stood, pulled the robe over his head, and tossed it on the floor next to the bed. He noticed I was enjoying a slow scan of the lean muscles of his pale frame and waited for a few seconds to allow me to complete the review. His platinum hair tumbled over his shoulders and down his chest, creating a shining veil of silk. Some men looked silly with long hair, but Devereux's suited him perfectly. He always managed to be the 'after' photo in a shampoo commercial. He did have a vast array of soaps, shampoos and gels in his bathroom – and they were clearly responsible for a portion of his excellent hygiene – but I'd become convinced the perfect state of his body and his wonderful aroma were by-products of his mystical transformation from mortal to undead. He'd once told me that his aroma was another vampire enticement, that humans were attracted to his fragrance and unable to keep themselves from responding. I could personally vouch for that.

He went down on his knees next to me, flicked a couple of fingers at the levitating candles and extinguished a few, creating even softer light and deeper shadows. My attention was drawn to a drop of moisture glistening on the head of his erection.

As if drawn by a magnet, my finger slid over that pearl-drop and massaged the liquid into the surrounding skin.

I rose to my knees facing him, lifted the gown over my head and tossed it next to the Liberace costume on the floor. The protective pentagram necklace nestled between my breasts.

We leaned towards each other, our lips meeting. The kiss started out sweet, then became more intense with every passing second as our mouths moved together, our tongues caressing and thrusting. We embraced, pressing our bodies tightly against one another, both of us moaning. The feeling of his thickness pulsing against me was making me crazy with need, so I pulled Devereux to me as I let myself fall backwards into the fluffy duvet. Still feasting on his mouth, I immediately wrapped my legs around his hips and ground myself into him.

He broke the kiss, licked my lower lip with his warm tongue and gazed into my eyes. 'The last time we were in bed together, we had sex. It was wonderful, if enthusiastic. This time I wish to make love. Slowly. Deeply.' He'd whispered the last two words, the timbre of his voice caressing my ears.

'Well,' I murmured, 'if you insist.'

It's a tough job, but somebody's gotta do it.

Since not all of me had been present for the last encounter, and I didn't have any memories of my alter ego's sexual performance, I wouldn't have anything to compare our lovemaking to. I was sure I wouldn't be disappointed.

He was as good as his word. We touched and stroked each other's bodies, using our hands and our mouths, and he licked his way from my nipples down to the wet, hot ache between my legs. His tongue slowly laved my clitoris, torturing me with ecstasy, bringing me to orgasm unexpectedly. I moaned and bucked my hips as he held me in place, and by the time he slid himself inside me, I was ready to explode again. Devereux had an astounding ability to remain hard for an unusually long time, his thrusts maintaining the deep, fast rhythm we both loved. Each time he shifted his angle ever so slightly, my body spasmed with pleasure. I gave new meaning to the words *multiple orgasms.*

Sated, he finally rolled over, which surprised me because we usually ended our lovemaking sessions with a blood donation. I heard him chuckling softly and I moved towards him, not sure if laughter was the most appropriate after-lovemaking response. 'What's so funny?'

He lifted a hand in the air and let it drop heavily onto his chest. He laughed louder. 'I simply feel good. As if every muscle in my body, every fibre of my being, is content, peaceful and satisfied. If I slept like a human male, I would be blissfully snoring right now.'

Vampires don't snore. Check. Breathing is required for snoring, and no breathing while dead.

I frowned. 'What's funny about that? I'm sure you've been *content, peaceful, and satisfied* thousands of times before – I can only imagine how many devotees you've had at your disposal. I still don't understand why that would make you laugh.'

He climbed onto me and pressed his lips to mine for a quick kiss. 'You of all people should understand, Doctor Knight. It requires a great deal of trust to be emotionally safe enough to release all of one's defences and protections around another individual. I have never done it before you. It is a heady, addicting and quite unfamiliar sensation. I have indeed had more sexual experiences than I can remember, but quantity has nothing to do with intimacy. I continue to be in unknown territory with you.'

'Why didn't you take any blood from me?' I stroked his hair. 'You always do. I was ready to have a few more of those brain-numbing orgasms.'

'There is always tomorrow.' He smiled wide. 'I can promise you an endless supply. You were so depleted, both physically and emotionally, that I did not wish to stress your resources any further. You need time to build up your blood again.' He kissed me. 'Come. It is time to travel to the penthouse. You require sleep before seeing your clients in the morning.'

'Yes, I suppose you're right. Should I get dressed first?'

'There is no need. The penthouse is empty, awaiting our arrival.'

He slid off the bed, scooped me into his arms and the familiar sensation of air blew against my face. We materialised in Devereux's sumptuous living room to find Luna standing in front of the wall of windows, staring out at the lights of the Denver skyline. She turned and gasped as we entered.

'I told you to stay away from me!' Devereux bellowed.

CHAPTER 15

'But you must listen to me – don't let her ruin everything. If you would simply allow me to explain–'

'Have you forgotten to whom you are speaking?' he growled. 'There is nothing that I *must* do. Get out of my sight, and do not return until I send for you.'

'Master, please–'

'Be gone!'

Eyes wide, Luna vanished.

Whoa. What the hell?

What was going on between Devereux and Luna? He'd always treated her respectfully, and always spoke highly of her, despite the fact that she made my life miserable. Whenever I'd joked that I wouldn't mind if she relocated to Transylvania or had a personal encounter with a sharp stake he'd always insisted that I didn't understand her. Personally, I thought I understood the snarly bloodsucker perfectly: she was in desperate need of the vampire equivalent of electroshock therapy and some heavy-duty mood-stabilising medications – not that any of those interventions would actually be effective with the mysterious animating systems of the undead. Since the relationship between them had always been friendly before, something had to be terribly wrong.

Devereux's expression was as angry as I'd ever seen it, and his grip on my body had tightened uncomfortably. Obviously distracted, he stared off into the distance, his mind elsewhere, unaware that his strong hands were pressing into my flesh. I wiggled in his arms, finally catching his attention and causing him to remember he had a passenger. He gazed down, released the tension and mumbled 'Many apologies, my love,' then lowered my feet to the pristine wood floor. 'Luna's presence was an unpleasant surprise.'

It felt weird to be standing naked in the middle of Devereux's luxurious penthouse, but I wasn't about to say anything that might give him an excuse to change the subject. I wanted to know what had happened. 'I don't understand. Why are you so angry at Luna? What did she do?'

He gave a slow blink, then met my eyes, his posture rigid, mouth tight. 'It is a long story, and one I am not at liberty to share at the moment.'

I'm sure my face registered surprise. '*Not at liberty?* You mean you're not going to tell me?' My stomach tightened, sending alarm signals to my brain. I couldn't remember any time since I'd known him he'd refused to tell me something about Luna. In fact, he usually enjoyed discussing his minions. Whatever the secret was, it didn't bode well.

He visibly relaxed, smiled and floated two fingers towards

my breast, capturing my nipple. Pinching the tender nub, he chuckled as I twisted away.

'Hey!' I covered my breasts with my hands in case he intended to poke or prod them again in his pitifully transparent attempt to hijack my focus away from the subject of Luna.

He smirked and held his hands up, feigning innocence. 'Do not trouble yourself about Luna. As you have often mentioned, she is not your favourite . . . individual. Just enjoy her absence.' He bowed from the waist, then straightened, offering me an elbow. 'Let me show you to your room.'

Step into my parlour, said the spider to the fly . . .

I studied his face, seeking signs of an ulterior motive, and found a mischievous angel staring back at me. That was one of his hardest-to-resist aspects. I gave up and took his arm and he guided us through the absurdly large room.

Since the penthouse belonged to Devereux, of course it was stunning. But unlike his personal room beneath The Crypt, which was filled with his artwork, magical potions, books and mystical symbols, this huge space was sparsely furnished; it had an unlived-in look. It was perfect enough to be featured in an interior design magazine, but it was sterile, empty. The black leather couches and chairs created a lifeless façade of sophisticated elegance, rather like a never-visited funeral parlour or the dentist's waiting room from Purgatory. Large, abstract sculptures, beautiful but soulless, sprouted from the polished wooden floors in random patterns throughout the rooms.

The window glass was invisibly tinted, shielding the

interior from outside view while leaving the panoramic vista unobstructed from the inside.

He led me into a large bedroom.

'Wow.' The last time I'd seen it, the style had been lovely but generic, everything white, but now the room appeared to have been designed with my particular tastes in mind. Blue was the predominant colour, and varying, complementary shades could be found in every detail.

A flick of his fingers illuminated the room. He sailed his hand through the air, indicating the lovely furnishings. 'I hope you like the décor. My staff worked very hard to create a welcoming sanctuary. I wish for you to be comfortable while you are here. My home is your home.'

I stepped around so I stood in front of him and raised my eyebrows. 'Do you sleep up here?'

He blinked and lowered his chin, gazing down at me from beneath those dark eyelashes. The corners of his lips curled into a gentle smile. 'As you will notice' – he glided towards the walk-in closet – 'much of your clothing and accessories were brought from your townhouse, and various new items have been added. Please call for anything additional you need.'

Very slick. He was getting entirely too skilled at ignoring me. 'Why do you always avoid answering that question? Is it possible you don't trust me with your physical safety while you're dead to the world?'

'No.' His face was serious. 'Keeping the location of my daytime chamber unknown is simply a deeply rooted habit, and not disclosing that information to any living soul has kept me safe for centuries. I trust you implicitly, and after we are bonded, I will share all my most intimate secrets. You are not the only one who must adjust to new conditions.'

His comments effectively slammed the coffin lid on that discussion. I didn't want to talk about the bonding issue again, and the fact that he brought it up probably meant he knew exactly what he was doing. I was too tired to try to figure out the next pothole on the vampire-boyfriend highway. Devereux had been right earlier when he said I needed sleep. Fatigue had begun to be my constant companion. If I didn't zone out for a few hours before seeing my clients, I'd be worthless.

I glanced up at his serious face and smiled. 'Okay, I won't ask you about your hiding place. It's more fun to imagine you lying in a red-silk-lined coffin anyway. More Bela Lugosi-like. I am tired. Would you like to tuck me in?'

A devilish glint sparkled in his eyes. He lifted my hand and sucked one of my fingers into his mouth. 'It would be an honour, but I must regretfully decline. I have many business details to complete before the dawn arrives, and time is short. If you desire anything, simply lift any of the telephones in the penthouse and someone will satisfy your needs. I will come to you tomorrow evening when I rise. Sleep well, my love.' He leaned in, pressed his warm lips to mine, then vanished.

I chuckled as I thought about picking up the phone to have someone satisfy my needs. Just how far did Devereux's hospitality stretch?

Waking in Devereux's extravagant penthouse was a delicious experience. The potent aroma of fresh coffee caressed my nostrils, drawing me like a java junkie towards the dining room. The table was spread with all my breakfast favourites. I could definitely get used to Master-style room service.

When I had finished luxuriating in the spacious, dual-stream shower, I wrapped myself in a thick bathrobe and perused the contents of the huge closet. My eyes skimmed the familiar garments that had been transplanted from my own humble abode before locking on to a fashion masterpiece: an ankle-length dress of sky-blue silk waved hello and winked at me. Celtic patterns hand-stitched in silver thread adorning the neckline and along the sleeves glittered softly in the light. Next to the gorgeous dress was a matching jacket.

The outfit was a step up from my usual work attire but I couldn't resist slipping the soft material over my head. Naturally, it fit perfectly – a slim column, encasing my body with elegant style. I didn't have to search far to locate the matching shoes. The Master certainly had taste. I spun in front of the three-sided mirror a few times, enjoying the sensation of the smooth material against my skin.

After indulging myself, I completed my morning tasks, grabbed my briefcase and headed towards the hallway.

I strode to the elevator like I was walking a Paris runway, and rode the mirror-walled box to my office a couple of floors below. I always enjoyed my morning conversations with Victoria in the lobby, and it was odd, not following the familiar routine. When I got to the door of my office I held out my keycard – and found my door open a crack.

My stomach tightened. The last time I'd found my office door ajar, bloody carnage had awaited me inside. Of course, that was at my old building, where the security was nonexistent and underpaid cleaners often left the doors unlocked. All of Devereux's properties had state-of-the-art alarm systems, hidden surveillance cameras and both human and undead guards, depending on the location of the sun. In the five months I'd been in the office, there'd been no problems. Maybe Victoria had opened my door for some reason.

Using one finger, I pushed the door gently. Sitting on one of the cream-coloured leather couches in the waiting area, her feet propped on the magazine table, was Maxie. She grinned when she saw me, threw her copy of *Psychology Today* onto the pile and stood.

'Hey, Doc! It's good ta see ya – wow, snazzy outfit! I didn't know you were the Psychologist to the Stars. I'm impressed. If I'd'a known, I woulda dressed for the occasion.' She glanced down at the faded black T-shirt and baggy jeans she wore. Her white hair was gathered into a braid that brushed the backs of her knees.

I was deeply relieved to find neither a corpse nor the police waiting for me – but how the hell had Maxie got into my private office? 'What are you doing here?' I asked, ignoring her comments. 'How did you get in? This door needs a keycard to open it.'

'Yeah – I expected to find a receptionist or someone down in the lobby, but nobody was there.' She waggled her eyebrows.

'You'd better complain to the owner – I could've been anybody. I waited around for a while, because I've been in the building before, and last time there was this New-Agey chick sitting behind the desk, so I figured maybe she went out for coffee. But she was a no-show. Your name's on the directory so it was dead easy to find your office, and when I didn't get any answer to my knocking I went back downstairs and rummaged through the reception desk to see if there was a master key.' She grinned wide and held up a keycard. 'So I let myself into your waiting room and – well, waited.' She handed the card to me. 'I imagine you want this?'

I took it, making a mental note to ask Devereux to change the lock codes. The breaking-and-entering adventure of a couple of nights ago was fresh in my mind; Maxie wasn't above taking more than one master keycard – or copying this one – so she could keep one. But more importantly, where was Victoria? She'd never leave the lobby unattended, especially not with all this vampire weirdness afoot.

'It's not that I'm unhappy to see you,' I started, 'but I have a client in a few minutes. Is there something you wanted to talk to me about?'

Maxie plopped down onto the couch again, her expression serious. 'Yeah, I need to tell you something I heard. About Devereux.' She stared at me, obviously waiting for my reaction.

I tried not to visibly tense. 'What about Devereux?' What could Maxie possibly know about him? It simply wasn't possible that she'd uncovered anything dangerous, but if she had . . .

She jumped up and stood in front of me. 'It's too long to go into right now – can you get away for a while at lunch?' She appeared agitated, and she started pacing, unable to stand still.

'What's this about, Maxie? You're rather nervous.'

She rested her hand on the doorknob. 'Too much caffeine.'

'Spill. What's really going on?'

Her gaze slid to the floor. 'I'm the bearer of bad tidings and it kinda wigs me out.'

Bad tidings for whom? For Devereux? I argued with myself while I mentally reviewed my schedule for the day. It wasn't unusual for me to meet clients outside the office – I sometimes found being in the fresh air calmed them. Maxie wasn't a client, so that wasn't a concern, but she was acting odd – anxious – and I wasn't sure moving our discussion to a public location was a good idea. 'I can take a half hour around noon. Do you want to meet here?'

'I don't think we should talk here, not in *his* building – let's go to the café down the block.' She pointed out of the window. 'That one over there. I'll see you at twelve, then. Have a good time listening to the loons.'

She left and closed the door behind her.

We shouldn't talk in Devereux's building – what did that mean? I didn't know if Maxie was being a paranoid drama queen, or if she genuinely knew something, but whatever she was going to tell me, I knew I wasn't going to like it.

'. . . and there he was, tapping on my window, brazen as you please.'

I glanced surreptitiously towards the clock. 'What happened then?'

Shirley scooted to the edge of her chair, excited. There was a manic edge to her aura. She always saved the most outrageous portion of her tale for the last ten minutes of our sessions. Lowering her voice, she leaned towards me. 'I opened the window and he smiled like the devil himself and climbed into my bedroom. Before I had a chance to think, I was unbuttoning my nightgown. The lustful demon must have taken over my mind, because I'd never have shamed myself without his satanic control.' She thrust herself back against the couch cushions and wrapped her arms around herself. A visible shudder quaked through her body.

'How did you shame yourself, Shirley?' I used my most soothing therapy voice.

Her chin quivered as she tried in vain to resist the memory. 'I let him have his way with me,' she whispered, sobbing in earnest now. She swiped the back of her hand under her runny nose, spreading slime along her cheek. Then, jutting her chin into the air, her voice became louder as she rocked back and forth. 'I didn't try to stop him – I didn't fight him – so it was all my fault. He told me so himself. I'm a bad girl – a very, very bad girl. I must be punished.' Tears streamed down her face.

Recognising the glassy-eyed stare of a self-induced regression, I angled my chair close to hers, plucked a couple of tissues from the nearby box and gently patted her arm. 'Everything's okay, Shirley. You're a wonderful girl, and you didn't do anything wrong. Here, let me wipe those tears away.' I took the opportunity to wipe her runny nose as well as her face, then curled her fingers around a clean tissue. 'You're safe now, Shirley, and no one can hurt you. No one can make you do anything you don't want to do.'

She turned vacant eyes to me. 'He was a monster, you know: a bloodsucking demon waiting to sneak into my room. I can't sleep because he'll come again. He always comes.'

I spoke softly. 'He can't come any more, Shirley, because he's dead. Your father is long-dead, and he can't ever hurt you again. Do you believe me?'

She nodded, scraping her lower lip with her teeth. 'What about the aliens? Are they going to abduct me again?'

'No, the aliens won't return either – but Shirley, you've got to promise me that you'll take your medication every day. It helps to keep the monsters and aliens away. Will you promise?'

An innocent expression flowed across her sixty-five-year-old face and she smiled sweetly, appearing almost childlike. 'I promise, Doctor Knight. You take such good care of me.'

I met her eyes, letting her see the compassion in mine. 'It's my pleasure. I'd like your permission to call your daughter later today, to talk about your medications. Is that okay with you?'

Tilting her head, she thought for a moment, then smiled again. 'That's fine. My daughter Sonia is such a good girl. No vampires or aliens will ever hurt her, will they, Doctor Knight?'

'No, Sonia's safe and well.'

She licked her dry lips and I shifted my gaze towards the water cooler. 'Would you like some water before you go?'

She stood and flexed her hands, which had been clenched so tightly the veins almost popped out. 'No, thank you. I'll see you next week.'

I rose and walked her to the door. 'Shirley, do remember, you can always call me if you have a bad night. You don't have to wait for our next appointment. I'm always here for you.'

She said thanks and left.

I went to my desk and thought about Shirley's delusions, the results of her horror-filled childhood, as I jotted notes in her file. As was so often the case, her psyche had compensated for the painful traumas by creating metaphorical fantasies – frightening, *non-ordinary* males who invaded her life and assaulted her body: beings who overpowered and victimised her.

Vampires had nothing on sadistic bastards like Shirley's father.

The café was busy, with a queue snaking out the front door. I started by being polite, asking the people blocking the doorway to please excuse me, and when that didn't work, I began pushing my way through. In the end I managed to get inside the actual restaurant with only a tender arm to show for my efforts. I searched the area for Maxie, who was so much taller than most of the other people milling around that she was easy to spot. I headed in her direction, but instead of greeting me and taking me to her table, she grabbed my arm and towed me behind her as she ploughed through the swarms of people back towards the entrance, stopping only once we'd reached the sidewalk in front of the café.

'Hey, Doc, good ta see ya. You're lookin' righteous today. Love the outfit.' She gestured over her shoulder. 'This place is a madhouse – there's no place to sit. There's some kind of meeting going on – Adult Children of Fucked-Up Alcoholic Vegetarian Alien-Abducted Cross-Dressers or something. Let's head out. I know a place where we can have a private conversation.'

That's the second time she's mentioned my clothing. She's definitely acting strange.

I glanced at my watch. The nervous energy radiating from Maxie was definitely increasing. 'Where is this place? I have a client in forty-five minutes. Maybe we should just stop at a deli, grab a sandwich and talk in the park.' I shaded my eyes from the sun and scanned the horizon. 'It would be great to sit outside for a while. The weather's perfect.'

She tugged on my arm again as she motored down the sidewalk. 'Naw. I need a beer and the dive we're going to is filled with low-life scum, which is appropriate for our topic of conversation.'

Low-life scum appropriate for our topic of conversation? What the hell did that mean? Was there even a dive bar in this trendy part of town? I'd never had any reason to know the answer to that question and I was even less interested in finding out now. I wrenched my arm out of her grip. 'Maxie, stop. I don't want to go to some crappy bar. I'll wind up smelling like cigarette smoke. Some of my clients are allergic to it.'

'Nope.' She mimicked smoking a cigarette. 'No ciggie smoke – haven't you been paying attention? Almost the entire state of Colorado is smoke-free now. It's illegal to light up anything in public. Although I can't promise you won't emerge wearing *Eau de Low-Life*.' She laughed at her own joke and took a right turn into an alley.

I stopped at the opening of the narrow passage. 'No shit, Maxie, cut it out. I really don't want to go to a bar. I need to go back to my office. What the hell is wrong with you?'

She breathed fast, then pursed her lips and stared off for a few seconds while she visibly struggled to calm herself. 'Okay. Have it your way, Doc. I thought you might need a drink after I tell you my news. I'm clumsy with this pal stuff, but I just wanted to be supportive. I meet a lot of my sources in that bar, so I'm a familiar face and they leave me to my business. Plus it isn't likely we'd run into any of Devereux's flunkies in that kind of shit-hole.'

The alley was in the shade, and the sudden lack of the sun's warmth caused me to shiver. Of course, the chills might also have been triggered by the creepy, somewhat sinister ambience of our off-the-beaten-path location. My solar plexus tightened and a headache which had just started poking my eyeballs with a screwdriver picked up a jackhammer and got serious. I was becoming more annoyed by the second. Being surrounded by so many domineering people was getting very old. Did I have a sign on my back that said: 'Easy mark, take advantage'? My voice held a layer of frost. 'Well, what's the big announcement? I can't imagine you could have heard anything about Devereux. He's a very private man.'

She raised her chin and crossed her arms over her chest. 'I wonder how well you really know him. Rich guys have a tendency to think they own the world, that they can do whatever they please. And mostly, they can. I just happened to be at The Crypt, interviewing a vampire wannabe who hangs out there, and I overheard a couple of goth types talking about a dangerous guy who'd come to town. Sounded like they were talking about a hitman. Anyway, one said he'd heard Devereux hired the killer – there's some bad blood between the gorgeous rich guy and one of his managers, a woman named Luna. They told me Devereux hired the thug to erase his problem. They said it wouldn't be the first time he had someone killed.' She paused, studying my face. 'I'll bet you didn't know any of that stuff about your *private man*.'

My stomach clenched with anger and I pressed my lips together and matched Maxie's arms-across-her-chest stance. Why the hell did she need to repeat these ridiculous rumours about Devereux – was she trying to upset me? Was she jealous that I had such a romance? She kept mentioning his money; was she fantasising about hooking a wealthy fish?

But right behind the anger was distress as I allowed the remote possibility that her assertions might be accurate to wash over me. The mention of trouble between Devereux and Luna made my head hurt, for he *had* been treating her harshly of late – but he couldn't possibly have hired

Lyren Hallow to kill Luna. I refused to believe Devereux could hide something so important from me – although he did have a habit of not telling me the whole story about anything, and there was no doubt strangeness was definitely afoot. Did he want me to stay away from Hallow so I wouldn't stumble onto the truth? Was that why he went nuts every time we talked about the psychopath? I shivered. If Devereux could lie to me like that, then I didn't know him at all.

My face must have reflected the emotional rollercoaster I was riding because a self-satisfied smile spread across Maxie's lips.

'Well, well.' Her arms relaxed. 'I see my little newsflash didn't come as a complete surprise to you.' She paused, frowning. 'Hey, I know it's not my place to be asking a psychologist questions like this, but if Devereux is doing anything to you physically, I hope you'll trust me enough to tell me – after all, I came clean about my own bad-tempered boyfriend.'

I experienced a moment of confusion before her meaning sank in, and with that realisation, my eyes opened wide. 'Doing anything physical – are you talking about *violence*?' I shook my head from side to side. 'Devereux would *never* do anything to hurt me. In fact, he's—' Once again, I found myself almost spilling my guts to Maxie, very nearly disclosing the truth about the strange universe in which I now lived, and details of its undead inhabitants. Either she was one hell of a good reporter, or my boundaries were well and truly ruptured.

She leaned in, her eyes riveted on mine, smelling a story. 'He's *what*?'

I heaved a sigh, determined not to be overwhelmed by my emotional reactions to what Maxie was saying. 'He's very gentle and loving – overprotective, in fact.'

Unless I'm deluding myself.

'I don't have to tell *you* that isolating and dominating the woman is part of the cycle of abuse.' She frowned and shook her head; she must have seen something on my face. 'Don't get more pissed off, but this isn't the first time I've heard something negative about Devereux. It's common knowledge that he's a powerful figure – dangerous mobster eye-candy. So far, nobody's been able to come up with any firm evidence to link him to organised crime, but it's only a matter of time.'

Organised crime? Holy shit, is she ever tuned to the wrong channel!

I smiled. 'Devereux isn't a mobster.'

Maxie smirked and raised one eyebrow. 'And you know this because—? Wait, I know. Because he *told* you. The standard line. Damn. So even a psychologist can be taken in by a great face and a hot body.'

I was tempted to defend Devereux – and myself – but there was no point. I couldn't disclose the truth to Maxie, and the explanation she'd come up with was as good as any. 'You can think what you like. He isn't abusing me, and I've seen nothing to lead me to believe he's involved in organised crime.' I paused, then, adding some razor blades to my tone, said, 'Not that it's any of *your* business, but right now, we're simply enjoying each other's company. We've made no commitments for the future.'

At least I haven't.

An emotion resembling sadness shadowed her eyes. 'Okay, I get it. It's none of my business – but I care about you, Doc. Don't shoot the messenger here; I'm just trying to be a friend. Yeah, I'm doing a fucking bad job of it, but I'm trying. I told you about Devereux because I don't want you to get hurt.'

I'd been holding myself so tightly that I was getting pins and needles from where the circulation in my arms had been cut off. I shook my hands to restart the flow. I studied Maxie, trying to determine if she was playing me for future journalistic reasons or if she really cared. I was usually good at reading people, at sensing whether someone was telling the truth or not, but Maxie had been a challenge from the moment I'd met her.

She was either the best actress in the world, or I'd put my foot in it. Since I hadn't made the best decisions lately, I decided to give her the benefit of the doubt. 'I appreciate that – and I'm not mad. I want some time to process everything.' I checked my watch again. 'I've really got to go. Next time, no mystery. If you have something to tell me, just blurt it out as you usually do.'

As I started to leave, Maxie hollered, 'Hey, Ethel, are we still buds?'

'Yeah, Lucy,' I yelled over my shoulder, 'we're still . . . something.'

CHAPTER 16

'. . . and I'm wearing a black silk teddy underneath this gorgeous dress. Would you like to see?'

The visual was so potent that I had to pretend to cough into my hand to cover the smile that quirked my lips. 'No, thank you, Kenneth, but it's great that you gave yourself permission to act on your desire to cross-dress. That's a huge breakthrough.'

He peeked up at me coquettishly from beneath theatrical-grade false eyelashes and gave a shy smile. 'Are you sure? I know we've only talked about my fantasies up until today, but I brought all my clothing and supplies with me – just in case I had the nerve to become Dolly, and at the last minute, I dashed into the bathroom down the hall and changed.' He laughed. 'And I mean *really* changed.'

It was easy to smile at the mild-mannered bank executive who now sat before me dressed as his alter ego Dolly Parton, and not merely because of his costume. He'd only shared

his secret a few weeks earlier, and I was glad he'd come out
of the cubicle because he got such obvious pleasure out of
the ritual of applying makeup, putting on his huge blond
wig and stuffing his two hundred and fifty pounds into a
low-cut, form-fitting, sequined outfit. We hadn't yet discussed
where his interest might lead.

'How does it feel to be Dolly?'

His face lit up. 'It's amazing – but I'm not wearing all the
props today. When I'm home alone, I paste on long red fingernails and I use them as guitar picks to play my guitar,
just like *she* does.' He slid his hands under the drooping fake
breasts and lifted them with a sigh. 'I need to find a much
better bra. Dolly is very well-endowed, and most undergar-
ments simply aren't up to the task.'

'I'm sure you'll find what you need. Maybe Victoria's Secret
would be a good place to try.'

Does Victoria's Secret lingerie come in husky?

I checked the clock on the wall. 'We're out of time for
today.' We both stood and he extended his hand for me to
shake, as he always did. 'I really appreciate you letting Dolly
come today. It meant the world to me.'

*I wouldn't have missed it for anything. A little lighthearted relief
in the midst of bloodsucking madness? I should be paying you!*

'The session was powerful, Kenneth. I'm very proud of
you.' I noticed he wasn't carrying anything and wondered
where his 'regular' clothes were. 'Did you leave your business suit in the bathroom?' I smiled. 'Your employees at the
bank probably aren't quite ready to meet Dolly yet.'

He chuckled. 'Yes, all my stuff's in the bathroom.' He

pressed one hand to his bulbous breasts, fanned himself with the other and, in a high-pitched Southern accent, cried, 'Gosh, golly, I hope it's all still there!'

I walked him to the door, smiling. 'See you next week,' I said as he wobbled down the hallway on his size-twelve stiletto heels.

A two-hundred-and-fifty-pound Dolly Parton with a moustache and goatee definitely qualified as the highlight of my day so far, but the sun hadn't yet set, so who knew what the vampire portion of the programme might offer?

Haunting harp music floated from invisible speakers in the elegant elevator as I rode downstairs to the lobby. After updating Kenneth's case file, I'd wandered restlessly around my office, unable to settle, fretting about Victoria. It wasn't like her to abandon her luxurious domain. True, I'd only known her for the few months since I'd moved into Devereux's building, and in my line of work I was used to uncovering previously unknown aspects of people's personalities, but I trusted my gut about her. And even if I disregarded my intuition, according to the vampire grapevine, her dedication and responsibility were legendary. She'd said she was fiercely loyal to her friends, and I knew she counted Devereux among that number, so she simply wouldn't leave his building unattended.

Something bad must have happened. I couldn't shake the idea that she was in danger.

Victoria's beautiful, hand-carved desk sat forlorn, like an abandoned ship in a sea of imported marble. Thanks to

the nocturnal requirements of most of the building's ten-
ants, the lobby was often semi-deserted, but Victoria's
absence exaggerated the emptiness. Her desk was the nerve-
centre of the realm, for Devereux counted on the clever
witch to keep his mysterious universe functioning while
he sequestered himself away during the daylight hours.
He'd mentioned once that discovering Victoria was an even
bigger workaholic than himself was an unexpected bonus;
she thrived on juggling multiple projects, and had even
shown up for work once covered with fur from a spell gone
bad.

My heels clicked on the polished floor as I approached
her vacant desk and I paused for a moment, staring through
the floor-to-ceiling glass that framed two sides of the lobby.
The soft light reflected off the peaks of the distant mountains as the sun retreated. A rush of heat suffused my body
and everything slowed. Victoria had once told me about an
experience she called *stepping behind the veil* – entering a
time-out-of-time. Her coven often created sacred space for
spell-casting, and there was a distinct sensory trace left
behind by the ritual. For the first time I understood what
she'd been talking about: while I stood there, not one car
drove through my line of sight on the busy street. As I cen-
tred myself in that odd stillness, my heart began to race and
my stomach tightened with anxiety.

Fear.

The very air in the lobby was saturated with it.

Had Victoria left an energy echo for my benefit?

I circled the desk, studying the clutter of papers covering

its usually pristine surface. Her favourite mug, which read, 'My other car is a broom' sat half-empty on a napkin, next to a partially eaten muffin, and all of the drawers were open to varying degrees. Someone had obviously been rummaging for something. I had a sudden recollection of Maxie saying she'd gone through Victoria's desk, searching for a keycard. Had she caused this mess? Was she that thoughtless? The distasteful possibility sat heavy on my chest. I really liked Maxie, but could she ever be trustworthy?

Without thinking, I sat in Victoria's chair, and immediately sank into her energy. It surrounded me like warm water and I closed my eyes, dropping into the powerful vibe. Strobe-light visuals flashed through my mind like fragments of an LSD trip. None of the pictures made sense, but even though I couldn't focus on the content, I was certain the scenes were about Victoria. The imagery was chaotic, surreal – darkly occult. I had no idea whether I was picking up her old memories or receiving information about her current where-abouts, but it felt ominous.

We needed to find Victoria, and quickly.

Maxie was right about my tendency to drift away because by the time I blinked and roused myself, the sun had gone completely behind the mountains and the orange-pink light show had morphed into red-purple. The coming of the night meant gearing up for the arrival of my first san-guinary client of the evening. Since they transported them-selves directly into my office, I usually tried to be present to greet them. I shook my head to clear the cobwebs and scooted the chair back to rise. As I grabbed the edge of the desk, my gaze locked onto a long hair stretched along the scattered white papers.

I lifted it, letting it dangle down in front of my face. 'Damn! I could make a hair sweater out of all the strands I shed in a single day.' Then I peered closer. My hair was long: even curly it hung halfway down my back. This hair was a similar colour to mine, but much longer. And straight. I held it by both ends. If it wasn't mine, and it wasn't Victoria's – her mane was golden – and it wasn't the snow-white of Maxie's, then whose was it?

Like a physical slap, a memory of Lyren Hallow leaning against a white column in my dream crashed into my awareness. His hair had been blowing in the breeze – his *very long, dark* hair.

I tensed. No – Devereux said the building was magically protected, so the murdering psychopath couldn't have got into the building, could he? I couldn't allow myself to believe that Hallow had anything to do with Victoria being missing-in-action, because if he was involved, the possibilities were too horrible to imagine.

I glanced at the ever-darkening sky, wrapped the long hair around my finger and hurried to the elevator. I pressed the button for my floor and closed my eyes, concentrating on sensing whether Devereux had risen yet. Damn him for not telling me where he spent his days. He knew I had clients this evening, so he wouldn't stop by right away. 'How am I supposed to tell him about Victoria?' I said to nobody.

'What about Victoria?'

I sagged with relief at Devereux's voice and almost threw

myself on him when he strode towards me, wearing his normal dark leather and a light green silk shirt. I wrapped my arms around his waist, crushing my cheek against his chest for a few seconds, breathing in his spicy fragrance. He held me close. It was wonderful to touch him. I hadn't realised how frightened I was for Victoria. 'She's gone,' I said quickly. 'Something awful has happened – I know it.'

Rallying from my mini-panic attack, I remembered what I'd found, released my grip on him and backed up a step. I held out my finger and unwound the dark strand. 'Here. This was on her desk. Her morning tea and muffin were only half-finished, and everything was a mess. Someone had rifled through her papers.'

His face serious, he lifted the hair from my hand and studied it silently. Then he rubbed it between his thumb and first finger. 'There is no life-force present. This hair did not come from a mortal.'

'It's Hallow's hair, I'm certain.'

His eyes narrowed as he raised them to mine. Strong negative emotion radiated from him and he spoke slowly, his voice low. 'And how is it you are certain of this?'

Psychic abilities weren't necessary for me to pick up that he was working hard to control his anger, and I considered taking another step back, but decided to hold my ground. Devereux was probably going to blow a fang because I hadn't told him about the dream where Hallow declared himself a god – and I honestly didn't know why I hadn't told him – why it hadn't even *occurred* to me to tell him, but none of that mattered now. The only important thing was finding Victoria alive and well.

My lips had gone dry and I had to lick them before I could speak. I didn't think any explanation would satisfy him, but I pressed on, 'It's logical, because when I found the long hair, I remembered dreaming about him after you held the ritual for me in your room beneath The Crypt. In the dream his long hair fanned out in the wind, and it's too coincidental to find such a hair on Victoria's desk when she's gone missing.'

He appeared deceptively calm, but his energy had sharp claws. 'And why did you not inform me of this dream? We spent hours together last night – you had ample opportunity to share this information with me.' He paused, his features tightening. 'Is it because you enjoy your time with him?' He tilted his head, studying me.

Startled by his intuitive question, I cleared my throat to give myself a few seconds to regroup. 'No – of course not.' I gazed into his beautiful turquoise eyes, and recognised pain – and disappointment – there. 'I just didn't want to talk about Hallow any more. I didn't want you to get upset again, like you are now.'

Devereux walked me to the elevator and extended a hand, frowning. 'Come. See to your client. He is in your office. I will take care of everything else and we will continue this discussion later.'

I started to ask another question, but he vanished.

My stomach churning, I rode upstairs, then walked slowly to my office door. I'd forgotten to tell him about Maxie using the keycard to get into my office, and her theory about him hiring a hit man – but he'd been so upset, maybe I simply hadn't had the courage to raise more issues.

Was he right about Hallow – was I enjoying my time with the devil? I couldn't deny that studying such an ancient vampire was intriguing, and I probably wouldn't get such an opportunity again – but were my motives only professional? For some reason, even thinking about Hallow caused my nipples to harden. Victoria said she'd seen us together at my house, and that it was sexual – so maybe I had been with Hallow and didn't remember. Was that why my heart pounded at the thought of him? Was it a simple attraction to a handsome male, or was this beyond my control? Devereux said Hallow made women desire him like addicts craved heroin. It was terrifying to think that the madman might still be controlling me. Had he planted thoughts of himself in my psyche? How much freedom of choice did I really have? *Who was in charge of me?* I shook my head at the strangeness of those questions.

As I walked through the waiting room and into my office, I plastered a pleasant smile on my face. Every light in the room was blazing, illuminating a small, thin man who sat huddled at the far end of the couch. He had the same haircut he'd originally got at school in the 1940s, parted on the side and slicked down. Even though he appeared to be in his thirties, he had never developed socially or psychologically beyond late adolescence. He was afraid of everything – or at least he believed he was. He reminded me of the death-obsessed young male character in that quirky old cult classic *Harold and Maude.*

'I'm so sorry to have kept you waiting, Jerome. I'm glad you made yourself comfortable.' I closed the door and sat in my chair. I swept my personal problems aside and focused on my client. *The professors who trained us to cultivate a dispassionate professional mask would be so proud of me now*, I thought, *even if they'd never envisioned this particular clientele.* But was I proud of me? I used to be so pleased at my ability to emotionally disengage, and now I found myself distressed by that same skill. I was certainly changing, but I wasn't sure that was a good thing.

'Is the hypnosis helping your fear of the dark?' I asked him. And then, 'Are you still keeping a light on in your coffin while you sleep?'

Jerome shuddered visibly. His large brown eyes stared, unblinking, from his pale face. 'The hypnosis isn't helping yet. I keep telling myself that I'm not afraid of the dark, but *myself* isn't listening. So, to answer your question, yes: I am keeping a light on. In fact, I saw a portable lamp on television that runs on batteries, so I sent away for several, and they're working really well. Since my coffin is extra-large, I can pretty much stay in there all the time – except for when I need to get blood, of course.'

'Yes,' I agreed, 'I suppose you could stay in your coffin all the time, but that's not going to help your agoraphobia. Let's talk about how you get blood now. Are you still ordering pizzas and feeding on the delivery people?' His expression told me what I needed to know. I couldn't figure out why the pizza restaurants didn't notice their drivers always came back in a dazed state from one address. Jerome must be better at entrancing humans than he let on.

He lowered his gaze to the floor and mumbled, 'Yes – I know I promised I wouldn't do that any more, but I get so *hungry*. I don't kill anybody, honest, but I *can't* go out, Doctor Knight. I try to make myself, but my legs won't work. Even though I live in a perfectly good basement apartment in one of the Master's buildings, most days I can't even make myself get out of my coffin. I think my depression is getting worse.'

Poor Jerome. We revisited the same emotional territory every session. Psychotropic medications didn't work on the undead, so all I could offer were some behavioural techniques, which hadn't been very helpful so far. 'Do you *want* to get better, Jerome?' I asked suddenly. 'Are you happy with the way your life – er, your existence – is?'

He sat silent for several seconds, then raised sad eyes to mine. 'You know I never wanted to be a vampire. I'm simply not equipped for this kind of life. I was always a morning person. My stepfather only bit me to get rid of me. He thought I wouldn't survive the transition.' He got up and moved towards the window. 'I wish I hadn't. I'm miserable.'

Since none of my usual interventions were at all useful, I felt justified in grasping at straws. 'Jerome, is there *anything* that would make you happy? Something you could get excited about? Life without a purpose, for mortals or vampires, can be empty. Is there anything that you have passion for? Anyone?'

He turned to me, an odd expression on his face. 'I'll tell

you if you won't get mad.' He pursed his lips. 'You aren't going to like it.' His voice sounded even younger than usual, and when he sat down again he almost physically shrank into the cushions of the couch.

'Tell me,' I said gently. He was treating me like his mother again, which was normal in therapy, but I needed to figure out what had triggered the transference.

'I am passionate about figuring out a way to end this terrible existence.'

I nodded. 'Well, if you're miserable, I can understand wanting to relieve the pain.' I paused. 'Have you figured it out yet?'

Does he have a plan to off himself – and is it even suicide if the person is already dead? How could I stop him, anyway? There's no 9-1-1 to call, no undead suicide hotline. I'm not trained for this!

He suddenly became agitated, shifting his gaze back and forth between the carpet and my face. 'I think so.'

The air thickened. My stomach clenched and goosebumps prickled my arms. *Holy shit. What's going on now?*

'What are you doing, Jerome?'

He stood and moved with vampire speed, looming over me, effectively trapping me in the chair. I tried to slide off the seat and onto the floor, but he jammed one of his legs between my knees. 'You probably don't know what Devereux said he'd do to anybody who hurt you. He was quite graphic about providing a quick and non-negotiable death. I'm sorry to involve you in this, because you've been very nice and I've enjoyed our time together, but it's the only way. I just can't take any more.' Dark red replaced the brown of his eyes and his fangs descended. 'And if I am totally truthful, I've had a few passionate fantasies about you, too.'

Fear tackled me. My heart began pounding and I started sweating as dread washed over me like a tidal wave. 'Stop, Jerome! Don't do this. I can help you. Things really can get better – please—!' I pushed ineffectually against his chest, but just as his teeth scraped my skin, he was suddenly gone, lifted away from me.

'I hate to interrupt this tender moment, but that had to be one of the biggest piles of melodramatic bullshit I've ever heard.' Hallow laughed, holding the struggling Jerome in the air by the back of his shirt. 'I suppose I could be a good sport and turn this pitiful specimen over to Devereux for disposal, but I've never been a team-player. Killing is so rewarding – I never waste an opportunity to revel in the thrill of the slaughter.' He glared at Jerome, who was making high-pitched keening sounds and flailing his arms and legs. 'This whining sot is a blemish on vampires everywhere. He's not even fit food. Besides, Devereux's off following the trail of crumbs I scattered for his benefit – although as I recall, he's never really got into the spirit of the hunt. He's always taking the joy out of everything with his lofty philosophies. But he's good and confused this time. He really doesn't know how powerful I am, and that I'm confounding his magic. He's a puppet on my string – he hasn't even noticed how erratically he's behaving. I say, what good is being a vampire, if you're not going to be the meanest predator on the block? I like to set a bloody example.'

Hallow grabbed a fistful of Jerome's hair and jerked my

attacker's head to the side with such force, and so quickly, that with a wet, bone-crunching, sickening sound it was ripped away from his body. Blood sprayed in all directions and I gasped as the viscous red fluid hit me in the face.

I screamed and frantically wiped at the blood dripping down my nose.

Hallow watched me for a few seconds, then gave an evil grin. 'I always have such fun when I'm with you. It's a pity we can't leave today, but I have responsibilities to take care of. I'm sure you understand.' He glanced down at his hands, chuckling, as if he was surprised to find himself holding two parts of a ravaged vampire. He threw Jerome's body on the floor and raised my former client's severed head aloft, staring up at it. 'Do you want this as a souvenir? After all, the unfortunate boy was just about to commit suicide by draining the therapist.'

He angled Jerome's bloody head over his open mouth and drank the dripping liquid. Crimson streams spread down his face, through his hair and onto his shirt, saturating the dark fabric. He enthusiastically licked his lips and his fangs glinted menacingly from between them.

The horror of what Hallow had done upended my brain and I sat there silently, numb and staring. I stared at a ragged portion of Jerome's spine protruding from the torn skin and my head spun. Realising I was in shock and dangerously close to throwing up, I lowered my head between my knees and tried to breathe. I heard something hit the floor with a squishy crunch and the gleeful monster laughed. I shifted my gaze just in time to see Jerome's head roll against the toes of my shoes. I groaned.

'I keep forgetting what sissies you humans are. One unexpected beheading and you're reaching for your barf-bags. Let's get you some air. I prefer your natural, sweet-smelling aroma.'

He lifted me from the chair, balanced my limp, nauseated body in his arms and transported us to the rooftop patio. Along with everything else about Devereux's building, it was both lovely and utilitarian. Motion-sensing lights illuminated the space, which wasn't really necessary since the moon hung low in the clear sky, only a couple of days past full.

I'd just cleared my throat to demand he release me when he did exactly that. My feet hit the floor and I steadied myself and stared at the bloodied fiend standing in front of me.

'Blood agrees with you, Kismet.' He grinned. 'It brings out the blue of your eyes and the ivory tone of your skin. Of course, your beautiful dress is damaged beyond repair.' His silver eyes glistened. 'I hope it didn't have any special significance for you.' He stroked his hand down my breast over the ruined silky material. It didn't take a huge mental leap to understand he knew the garment had been a gift from Devereux. Disgusted, I recoiled from his touch and jerked backwards a step. 'Get your hands off me, you bastard,' I gasped through the fear contracting my throat. My voice came out thin and high-pitched. Hallow's energy was suffocating.

His grin expanded, and he grabbed my upper arm, hauling

me closer. 'I don't think I will. As much as I enjoy your keen mind – and you know I'm looking forward to exploring your abilities – it's probably time to shift to the next level of my plan.'

I tried, without success, to free my arm from his grip. 'You're not exploring *anything* about me, you homicidal psychopath. I'm not participating in any of your sick plans. You're a delusional monster.'

His eyes wide, he shook his head, adopting an expression of innocence. 'Is this all the thanks I get for keeping that irritating boy from tearing your throat out? Name-calling? My dear doctor, I would've expected much more gratitude – and subservience. Oh well, it's clear I have my work cut out for me.' His eyes narrowed. 'You will make a marvellous *lýtle*.' He leaned in. 'And perhaps more.'

I kept struggling, but his fingers were steel. He stared at me with his cold eyes and my awareness fragmented. His hypnotic gaze locked on mine, pulling like a magnet, enticing me into his dark aura, and my knees buckled. Only his grip on my arm kept me from falling. One part of me remained conscious of the fact that I was on the roof of Devereux's building, held prisoner by a killer, but another part – the one with the hard nipples and damp crotch – eagerly dived into the mercurial lure of his eyes, unable to concentrate on anything but the need for his hands on me. I was sentient enough to understand my level of danger, but unable – or unwilling – to turn away.

He held me tight against him, entwined his free hand in my hair and tugged my head back, exposing my neck. The smell of blood overwhelmed me.

'Soon your only purpose will be to serve me,' he whispered, his mouth against my ear, 'and you will do so willingly, craving me above life itself.'

The words sent rushes of pleasure down my body. Almost painfully aroused, I groaned, surrendering the use of whatever bones still remained. The sane part of my brain frantically screamed, 'No! I don't want this! Stop!' The inmates had taken over the asylum.

Want this . . .

His soft tongue licked down my neck before he plunged his fangs into the rich vein pulsing there, and I screamed with the beginnings of an almost overwhelming orgasm that rumbled through my entire body, bombarding me with chaotic emotions. As the pleasure intensified, my muscles spasmed, shaking me violently, as if I were having a seizure.

I never wanted it to end.

Loud voices startled me from my erotic dream and I opened my eyes – which I hadn't realised I'd closed – to find several vampires in a circle around us. I tried to focus my eyes and hadn't even time to wonder if Devereux was there when he leaped on Hallow and grabbed him from behind.

I collapsed.

CHAPTER 17

I lay on the ground as orgasmic aftershocks reverberated through me, my mind as boneless as my body while my brain smoked a mental cigarette.

A series of crazed noises finally penetrated the fog in my head and I shifted my gaze towards what sounded like rabid wolves fighting over a deer carcase. I goggled at the sight of Devereux and Hallow locked in immortal combat.

Their mouths were stretched in lethal snarls, their long, sharp fangs exposed, their silky hair, dark and light, flying about their heads.

In the face of so much preternatural insanity, all I could think about was how beautiful they both were.

I rolled onto my side and raised myself into a sitting position, but even that small movement was harder than it should have been, as though my muscles had forgotten their programming, or the bridge between the thought and the action had been washed away in the unnatural hormonal flood.

The lustful part of me – the hormonal adolescent, as Victoria called her – was still quivering in the afterglow. She wanted to leap into the fray, seize Hallow and force him to pierce my neck again with his paroxysm-inducing fangs. She was annoyed that her good time had been interrupted.

But the logical part, my Inner Psychologist, was scowling, arms crossed.

My psyche was at war with itself again, but it had reached a temporary impasse. I honestly wasn't sure which part of me would prove to be the victor.

There was no telling what would have happened if I hadn't got distracted. One of the vampires in the circle, a male I hadn't seen before, reached out to help me up. I stared at the pale hand for a few seconds before grabbing onto it. I didn't hesitate just because he was a stranger, or because I was busy having a lust-instigated psychotic break, but also because I wasn't sure my legs would hold me if I managed to become vertical. His hand was unpleasantly cool and I released it as quickly as I politely could, after giving him a nod of acknowledgment. I had a momentary thought that it was no longer unusual or frightening to be surrounded by vampires. *That couldn't be good.*

I backed against the railing and gawked at the spectacle.

Inhuman growls, snarls and hisses erupted from the fighters, and the grotesque sounds caused an itching sensation on my skin, like hundreds of tiny bugs crawling on the surface. That wasn't too much of a surprise, since I'd already seen lots of evidence of how a vampire voice could elicit pleasure or pain.

One part of me found watching them very exciting, for the other, it was quite terrifying.

Devereux and Hallow tore at each other's throats, carving great bloody gashes that immediately healed, only to be ripped open again. They were god-like zombies, one second wrestling on the ground, then the next levitating in the air before they smashed one another savagely into the nearest wall. I'd never seen anything as viciously, violently primitive. Their shirts were soon shredded, then discarded.

In the midst of the carnage, Hallow laughed, which obviously infuriated Devereux. With renewed vigour, he wrestled his opponent to the ground, displaying truly impressive skills and power, and a flash of confusion shadowed Hallow's face at Devereux's unexpected abilities. Watching the two of them, their muscles straining and rippling across sculpted shoulders and chests, was horribly confusing. My wild side found it arousing, but my more rational aspect – the one who couldn't imagine life without Devereux – was terrified that the ancient monster might prevail. I gasped in fear.

My inadvertent sound must have distracted Devereux, causing him to shift his gaze to me and to lift his hands from Hallow's neck, where he'd been gouging at the flesh of the maniac's throat, and in that instant, Hallow vanished, and reappeared across the room. That was odd – couldn't Hallow transport himself while Devereux focused on him? Was Devereux's physical touch keeping Hallow from blinking from one place to another? Or was it Devereux's attention?

Hallow shook his head, blood spraying from his long hair

like water shaken off a wet dog, and in a booming voice cried, 'What marvellous entertainment you've provided, Devereux. I can't remember when I've had such a rousing time. I look forward to our next rendezvous, but I have much to complete before ending my work here.' He materialised next to me, grabbed my hair and pulled my face to his, pressing his lips forcefully against mine before releasing me just as abruptly.

Fear flooded my brain and at the same time Lust donned her party dress and grabbed her coat, ready to check into Hotel Hallow, the other, cautious, part held a metaphorical bucket of cold water at the ready.

Devereux sprang to his feet, growling. He recaptured my gaze and, chanting in the strange language he used when working magic, stalked like a dangerous predator towards us. Hallow bowed from the waist and laughed again, pointing at me. 'I will leave her in your care for a while longer.' He raised an eyebrow. 'If she's willing to stay. But don't get too comfortable. She's mine now.' He disappeared.

Enveloped in a strange fugue, I experienced that odd, dissonant sense again: the schizophrenic need both to be with Hallow and to run from him. My conflicting parts jockeyed for position while arguing in my head. Having two clear aspects taking centre stage was definitely new to me, and it was frightening. I'd always been aware of my inner cast of characters, and comfortable with them. Like everyone, I had certain characteristics that dominated my psychic landscape, but my sub-personalities usually took turns sitting in the driver's seat. I now had dual pilots in my consciousness cockpit, and neither wanted to relinquish the controls.

I had to believe the compassionate, wise part of me would find a way to triumph. All other outcomes were unimaginable.

Victoria's description of my behaviour at Devereux's club, and my inability to remember the time in question, was classic dissociative amnesia – that was bad enough, but this was different, for I was fully aware of both parts of myself, and their differing agendas. I feared I'd detoured onto the entrance ramp to madness.

Devereux looked like a bomb-blast victim at a cover model convention. He studied me for a few seconds before flicking his fingers in a dismissive gesture at his companions. 'Leave us,' he ordered, and they vanished.

The remaining scraps of clothes were torn and bloody and his hair and skin were coated with thick red blood, but his body showed no physical damage from the undead brawl he'd just participated in. He slid his arm around my waist and propelled me towards a wooden bench against a brick wall. When we sat, I slumped against him, mentally and physically exhausted.

Lust strolled over to a shadowy corner of my psyche and stood waiting, an amused expression on her face. She let me know she wasn't going anywhere, but she would allow me the illusion of control, for the moment. I wondered what would happen if I couldn't retain my portion of our joint reality. Would she simply take over my whole personality, or would the entire structure collapse?

I shifted my gaze to Devereux's serious profile. Lust peeked over my mental shoulder to leer at his glorious bare chest before she retreated back to her patch of darkness, laughing.

'What the hell just happened?' I raised my fingers to the throbbing bite on my neck and they came away bloody. Touching the wound caused my body to spasm dramatically, as if the memory of the orgasm was still there, eager to rejoin the party. Devereux grabbed me, steadying me on the bench. I held my breath, waiting for my alter ego to do something outrageous, but she only watched, her impish smile in place. What was she up to?

Devereux smoothed a strand of hair from my cheek. 'The demon has reestablished his influence over you. I can sense the chaos in your energy field.'

I shivered, either from the cooling temperatures of the evening or in reaction to Hallow's bite, and Devereux lifted me onto his lap, holding me tight against his chest. 'Come. We will return to the penthouse.'

'No. Not yet. Let's sit here for a moment.' I didn't want to go back inside the building. Breathing the fresh air was great, and the open sky gave me the illusion of normality, whatever that was. Lust stepped forward inside our shared mind and tapped an imaginary watch on her wrist. What the hell was that supposed to mean? How bizarre was my mental meltdown going to become?

If I survived having two radically different personalities running my body, I'd never again question my dissociated clients' accounts of their experiences, I told myself fervently.

I wondered if Dr Jekyll had to consciously live through the exploits of Mr Hyde.

Devereux rocked me gently for a few seconds before he spoke again, his cheek resting against my hair. 'I must accept full responsibility for what has happened to you. I refused to see what was clearly in front of me. I knew Hallow was powerful, and that he used his wiles to ensnare women, but I believed my own vampiric abilities and magical skills could keep him in check. Even surrounded by my security force, you were not safe. He is more dangerous now than he was the last time I encountered him. I was overconfident, and you have paid the price.'

I started to sit up, intending to assure him I knew he'd done everything he could, but he pulled me close against his body.

'Wait, Kismet. Please, let me finish.'

I shut my mouth and relaxed. He obviously needed to talk.

'Victoria shared some of her concerns with me about Hallow. She spoke of her visions – how she had seen Hallow in your townhouse, and on a stage of some kind with you. She said she saw him bite you. I was so certain that my spells would protect your home that I did not consider the possibility that Hallow is not subject to any rules – human, vampire or magical. Even after she shared her insights, I did not take action quickly enough.' He was silent for a few seconds. 'I am angry because I do not know how to protect you from his malicious intentions. In all my eight hundred years I have rarely been bested, and it is a bitter fruit to swallow.

Even now, I doubt that I am immune to his powers. Like you, I have recently found myself behaving in ways that are unusual for me, as if the choices were not mine. My consciousness has been hazy. But I will continue to fight against his influence.'

Shit. That's very bad.

He went totally still, his breathing and heartbeat growing faint. Those human-like functions were under his direct control, and I wondered if he'd simply forgotten about them. In a bid to break whatever introspective spell he'd woven around himself, I said, louder than necessary, 'Can I sit up now?' He'd been holding me so tightly, I was having a hard time breathing.

He released his grip and heaved a huge sigh. 'Yes, of course. I apologise. Once again I have behaved obliviously. You must truly think me a thoughtless cave dweller by now.'

His heart jolted back to life in his chest and his breath wafted against my skin. He'd told me he only bothered with things like breathing when he was around me or other mortals. I appreciated his efforts, because I certainly took breathing for granted and didn't think I was ready for him to remind me constantly of his corpseness. There was no need for me to give him any lectures about his previous arrogance, or his tendency to gently bulldoze, because he was being harder on himself than I would've been, so I tried to lighten the mood.

'Oh, yes. You're a regular Fred Flintstone,' I teased.

'Fred Flintstone?' He lowered his voice and locked eyes with me, as if the topic warranted the utmost seriousness.

'Is he one of your clients?' Articulating the words very clearly in his antiquated manner, he imbued them with great importance. How he'd managed to become the successful billionaire he was, functioning in this modern century, was a mystery, since his education about anything he didn't consider pertinent was meagre. I guessed someone of Devereux's age and temperament might find society's focus on the superficial to be uninteresting.

He obviously doesn't have a television in his coffin.

'No – he's a cartoon character, but that's not important.' I knew he was going to take offence and ask if I thought he was one, and that wasn't what I meant. 'I don't think you're a thoughtless cave dweller, although if you'd asked me that a couple of days ago, I might have given you a different answer.'

He recognised the humour in my face and smiled. 'Yes. And I would have deserved it.' His expression became serious again. 'I have since discovered that Hallow created the trouble between the two vampire covens I have been attempting to resolve.'

'What do you mean?'

'His mind-control abilities are second to none. He knew exactly how to distract and manipulate me, and I was a fool not to recognise it. In my mistaken belief that as Dracul's previous adversary, I was the only one who could settle the dispute, I walked right into Hallow's clever ruse, just as he intended. It is true that the factions were in need of mediation, but only because of his intervention. I should have realised this much sooner – and I should have been more available to you. I should never have left your side.' He kissed my forehead.

My therapeutic lecture on the parental roots of the tendency to 'should' oneself sprang to mind. Apparently I couldn't ever stop being a therapist, even in the midst of a psychic brain split, but I didn't think he'd appreciate the unofficial counselling session. He was being so sweet and beating himself up so badly, I thought it was time for me to own up to my own participation in the problem.

'Well, as fascinating as your self-flagellation is, I have to admit I didn't make it easy for you to remain by my side. And I didn't listen to you when you said Hallow was influencing me. I had no idea what you meant then, but I do now. I wasn't aware of his ability to force me to forget my logical, practical self and to become a more primitive aspect of my nature. I didn't realise he was a literal monster until I watched him kill the radio show host in front of my eyes.'

He froze again. His relaxation immediately morphed into rapt attention as his body adopted a rigid posture. 'What? When did you witness such a thing?'

The cool air and the energetic buzz of Devereux's impending anger had become uncomfortable. I needed a few minutes to organise my thoughts. For the first time I noticed my feet were bare, as if my brain wanted something simple to focus on. I wondered what had happened to my shoes. 'If we're going to have that discussion, I want to go back inside.'

Without a word, he gathered me into his arms, stood and transported us effortlessly to my bedroom in his penthouse.

I expected him to launch right into demanding to know how I'd seen Carson die, but he surprised me by changing the subject. He was taking the news very well. I didn't know what to make of the rapid mood shift, but since I was currently the Queen of Split Personalities, I didn't see how I could point any fingers at him.

His gorgeous eyes twinkled. 'We are both blood-covered, which I am sure is a greater burden for you than for me. I am, after all, very comfortable in this state.' He gave a dazzling smile. 'Perhaps we should discard our soiled garments and shower before we continue our discussion.'

No matter what else is happening, a guy is always a guy.

My eyebrows shot up. 'Is that your way of asking me to have sex with you? In the midst of all the insanity we're dealing with? After the fight you just had?' Lust drew my attention by jumping up and down, clapping her hands. She started unbuttoning her blouse, a wide smile on her face.

I thought he'd make a lighthearted remark, perhaps toss out a *double entendre*, but he became serious again, almost sad.

'At this moment, I am at a loss to know how to proceed. I want to keep you safe, yet short of holding on to you physically, I am without options. I will, of course, cast all the appropriate spells and strengthen your protective necklace – which, by the way, is probably the only reason Hallow was not able to completely take you over again tonight. I will station vampire guards at each entrance, and I have ordered the building's security heightened in every way. The truth is that I need to reclaim you, physically and emotionally.

And I need to find myself again. I know that sounds primitive, maybe like something your Fred Flintstone would do.' He grinned when he said the last. 'But I need to rebuild our emotional bond, to soothe my own yearning as well as protect you. And, yes,' the brilliant smile was back, 'of course, I always want to have sex with you.'

Gazing up into his sparkling aqua eyes and blood-clumped platinum hair, I couldn't help but smile back at him.

'So, this would be sex for magical purposes?'

He gave a brief nod. 'It could definitely be considered such.'

'Some men would be too upset after the evening we've had to concentrate on sex.'

He gave a slow blink, the corners of his mouth curving. 'I am not a man. I am a vampire. A very old vampire. Rest assured that concentration will not be a problem.'

His tone of voice played along my body like warm hands. Butterflies fluttered in my stomach. At that point it didn't matter to me which personality was rolling out the welcome mat. Our nipples were hard.

The scientist part of me remembered that I'd often had discussions with clients about the difference between male and female sexuality, and how men felt most connected during the sex act. Devereux needing to reconnect that way made total sense. As always, his self-awareness was impressive. How could I resist such a perfect male – even if he was a chest-beater on occasion?

'Well, then.' I gave what I hoped was a come-hither look. 'I wouldn't want to be accused of not holding up my end of our emotional bond. I guess I'll have to suffer through another glorious Devereux orgasm. Only in the name of soothing you, of course.' Maybe he was more brilliant than I thought. Was he suggesting sex to positively distract me?

He threw back his head and laughed and the sound tickled over me like soft feathers. He walked us into the lovely bathroom. 'Of course.'

Returning me to my feet, he cocked his head. 'Your clothing is ruined. That is another score I will settle with the demon. A replacement will be arranged.' He bent down, grasped the hem of my dress and began to tug it up my body. I raised my arms in the air, letting him pull what was left of the masterpiece over my head and he dropped it on the floor, leaving me standing in my blue silk bikini panties, matching bra and protective necklace.

With an easy motion he removed his boots, then unbuttoned the waistband of his black leather trousers, staring at me as he slowly lowered the zipper. As I watched the downwards movement, I was reminded that the reason Devereux always wore leather was so blood could be easily cleaned off the surface. With that in mind, I'd recently added more leather to my own wardrobe; I wished I'd had the forethought to dress in that this morning instead of the wonderful designer dress.

He slid the trousers down his legs and kicked them aside, then covered the short distance between us. His tall, muscular body was beautiful, even dirty and blood-covered. I let my gaze meander down his chest and over his flat stomach, finally reaching the erection jutting from between his legs.

It was blissfully unconcerned about any vampire or human melodramas; it knew exactly what it wanted, and my hand moved on its own to grant its wish.

Devereux groaned as I stroked him and wrapped his arms around me. The fingers of one hand effortlessly unfastened my bra in the back and I closed my eyes—

—and a sharp pain radiated from between my brows. I gasped, my body trembling.

Devereux jerked back from me, staring, his face a mask of concern. 'Kismet? What has happened?'

I smiled – at least, I think it was me, it was my body – but the drivers had switched seats. Or, more accurately, they still shared the seat, but the positions had been rearranged. The psychologist couldn't reach the brake pedal or the steering wheel any more. The part I thought of as my usual self was still present, but she'd been pushed aside and now she could only observe. But I was clearly both.

'Love Buns!' I threw my bra on the floor and stepped out of the panties. 'It's so good to see you – I thought my old ball and chain would never get things rolling. Come to Mama.' I dropped to my knees and sucked Devereux's erection into my mouth, and was reminded of the joy of licking a Popsicle as a kid. I used to like to shove the whole frozen treat into my mouth, creating a vacuum with my lips and tongue. He grunted in surprise. If I'd only known what those lazy summer days were preparing me for.

I'd barely got a good suction going when Devereux yelled, 'Stop!' and wove his hand into my hair. He grabbed on and held me immobile.

I mumbled, 'Wha—?' through a mouthful of penis and relaxed my jaw muscles just enough for him to slide his erection through my lips as he backed away.

He released my hair and loomed over me, scowling, the family jewels still at eye-level but, annoyingly, slightly out of reach.

'Hey! What did you do that for? I was just getting warmed up!'

Devereux spoke slowly, his voice almost a growl. 'Return her. Now.'

I shook my head, plopped my ass onto the cold floor and sprawled, opening my legs to make sure he understood the offer. 'No way. I'm out and I'm staying out. You can't stand there with a hard-on the size of a giant redwood and tell me you don't want to have some fun.'

He smiled and bent down, his blood-soaked hair falling forwards in clumps.

Well, damn. That was easier than I expected. He wants me bad. 'All right! Let's do this!'

Too fast to see, he hefted me up into his arms. 'I said return her. *Now.*'

'So, Rhett Butler, playing hard to get, eh? Well, have it your way.' I wiggled free of his grip, looped my arms around his neck and planted a wet kiss on his luscious mouth. Before he could dislodge me, I managed to chomp down on his lower lip, sucking hard on the small puncture I made.

He swung me onto my feet and wiped the back of his hand across his mouth, smearing the line of blood dripping from his lower lip. He glowered. 'No. I will not help him strengthen his control. You will not taste my blood again.'

I folded my arms across my breasts and pouted. 'What's a girl gotta do to have a good time around here? What kind of bad-ass vampire are you, anyway, afraid to share a little blood. It isn't like you can't just go out and get more. What's the problem?'

He leaned in, locking eyes with me. 'Return. Her.' His voice vibrated dark and low. 'Now.'

I gasped as a wave of heat flowed through my body. Closing my eyes, I had a vision of Lust, walking naked, hips exaggeratedly swaying, through my inner landscape. She spoke over her shoulder. 'Don't even think this is over. I'm not finished with him. Ciao for now.' She laughed as she skulked off into the shadows.

Forcing my lids open, I stared up into Devereux's eyes.

'Is it you?' he asked.

For the first time in my life I didn't know how to answer that question.

I blinked, licking my dry lips. 'That was awful – like being locked behind a glass wall in a soundproof room. Is this what it's like to go insane?' I grasped the hand he offered.

He held me close. 'Are you all right?'

'I don't know how I am.' My arms circled his waist. 'I'm pissed off that some ancient monster was able to splinter my brain and cause me to lose control. I'm terrified that I'll never be myself again, and that things are only going to get worse, that I'll lose everything about myself I value. I'm powerless, like a frightened five-year-old. I want to run and hide, but there's nowhere he can't find me.'

Devereux tightened his embrace. 'I will not let him have you. I swear it. Do you remember any of what happened?'

I mumbled against his chest, 'Every moment of it – but only as an observer. I didn't get to experience anything directly.' I let go of him and stepped back, giving a weak smile. 'I appreciate you saying no. It was strange watching her trying to seduce you. I know she's me, but that aspect is usually mediated by the rest of the team. She's raw. Primal. It really was like having my id run wild. I don't even want to think about the kinds of professional and personal trouble she can cause.'

'Is there anything you can explore as a therapist that might help you remain in control?'

I shook my head absently. 'I'm not aware of anything like this in the psych literature. This situation is so totally outside the realm of – well, wait a minute.' I paused, holding my index finger in the air. 'I do remember reading a popular novel – what was the name of that book? Oh, yes, *Sybil* – about a multiple personality patient with one alter who was aware of everything. She was present, watching, remembering everything for all of them, while other aspects blacked out when they weren't on centre stage. Hypnosis was helpful in that case.' I walked in tight circles in the large bathroom, ideas sparking, speaking more to myself than to Devereux. 'Maybe Ham could hypnotise me – oh no, wait, he's out of town. Or Tom – he's pretty good at it when he's not being a pompous ass. What if the wild part is suggestible enough to be modified?'

Devereux gently grasped my upper arm, freezing me in my tracks. His expression was both incredulous and concerned. 'You want to entrust your mind to someone who wants to become a vampire so he can be a pornography star?'

I raised my hand and patted his cheek. 'I know you don't have much use for Tom, but underneath all his narcissistic idiocy he is a talented clinician, and I'm willing to try anything that might keep Hallow from dragging me further into his psychotic hell.' Thinking about Hallow caused my body to contract in fear and tingle with excitement all at the same time. Frowning, I gazed up at my avenging knight. 'What did he *do* to me? How could he possibly have caused this mind split?'

Devereux shrugged in frustration. 'He is incredibly powerful – and completely mad.' He touched my protective pentagram necklace. 'As I mentioned earlier, I believe he was unable to take you over completely due to the power of the spells in this talisman, so instead of replacing your normal personality with a more uninhibited version as he did before, this time he could only give the primitive equal footing.'

I didn't think the footing was equal. I thought her feet were huge, and getting bigger.

CHAPTER 18

Devereux adjusted the water temperature in the luxurious dual shower while I tried to intuit whether my inner trouble-maker was revving up for an encore. My body – *our* body? – was exhausted, and the last thing I wanted was to be pushed aside again while the Fellatio Queen forced herself on my man – er, vampire. Not to mention that thinking of myself in the third person was becoming too weird for my brain to deal with.

He slid one panel all the way open in the expanse of etched glass. 'Shall we?'

When I hesitated, he raised an eyebrow in silent question.

I pressed my palm against his chest, simply needing to touch. 'Are you sure we should shower together? I don't want to do anything to tempt her into reappearing. She lacks boundaries around men, and I've had enough surprises for one day.'

'You are safe with me.' He lifted my hand and kissed my

knuckles. 'I will give her no cause to overwhelm you. I have complete control over my body and its reactions.' I glanced down at his flaccid organ to find out if it believed what Devereux said about control and he smiled in reassurance. 'Tonight is about comfort and safety. We have plenty of time for lovemaking after our current problems are dealt with. There are many other ways for me to express my love. Allow me to soothe you.'

Even though he wasn't supposed to be able to read my thoughts any more, I worried that my emotional upheaval had opened the door to my mind again, because everything he'd said was exactly what I needed to hear. If he truly was unable to read my thoughts, then he was much more perceptive and intuitive than I'd imagined.

I stuck a hand in to test the warmth before stepping into the large enclosure and sighed with pleasure as the just-hot-enough water flowed down my body.

Devereux joined me, closed the shower door and stood under the second stream.

Wonderful aromas filled the air as he lathered his hair with shampoo, then smoothed the rich liquid soap over his body. The smells were earthy, spicy – his signature fragrance – and just inhaling the scents relaxed me. I enjoyed watching him run his hands over his hard-muscled, lean frame.

I was fascinated by his lack of erection. Even as he washed his genitals, his penis didn't so much as twitch. In all the time I'd known him, I couldn't remember one instance where we'd been naked together and he'd remained unaroused. He smiled as he caught me checking.

'I told you: I have complete control over every aspect of my body. Just as I am able to remain erect for long periods of time if I so desire, I am also able to choose not to rise to the occasion, so to speak. And now, if you will indulge me, I would very much like to wash your hair.'

Oh, yeah. I love this part.

He stepped behind me, reached for the bottle of my favourite shampoo and poured the thick gel into his hands. I moaned before he even touched me, remembering the last time he'd used his magic fingers to massage my scalp. Muscles I hadn't even realised were tight started to relax and my jaw sagged. My head tipped back against his chest and he chuckled as he tilted it upright again.

'Good. The tension is leaving your body.' He spread the lather through my hair before piling it into a soapy clump. His amazing thumbs pressed little circles towards the base of my skull and along the back of my neck, and when he focused on the area between my shoulder blades, I thought my bones would liquefy and spiral down the drain.

'I'll give you an hour to stop that,' I mumbled. Whatever he'd been doing with his fingers ceased and I groaned, thinking he'd misunderstood my comment. Sometimes modern humour sailed over his head. Then I smelled the scent of my own bath gel and realised he'd simply switched from my hair to my body. He smoothed the aromatic soap down my arms and onto my hands, massaging each finger. Ordinarily, that would have made me very happy, but I was still concerned about my uninvited visitor's reaction.

'You are tense again, and it does not take a mind reader

CRIMSON PSYCHE | 311

to understand why.' Devereux twirled me and I automatically gazed up into his beautiful eyes. 'While I cannot keep him out of your mind, I can use my magic skills to keep you in a state of pleasant relaxation. You will be completely aware, and totally in control of yourself, merely too comfortable to allow worries or memories to upset you. Would you like me to do that?'

The idea was appealing, but I'd spent enough time under someone else's control recently, and it made me doubt even Devereux's intentions. 'Just relaxation? And it would keep my wild companion at arm's length? I could become a basket case again any time I want to?'

'I swear it. And, because I wish to ask you questions about the radio show host, the more calm and relaxed you can remain, the better.'

My solar plexus tightened even thinking about my time at the amusement park. I stared harder into Devereux's eyes, trying to discover any hidden agendas or ulterior motives, and when I found none, I said, 'Okay, since even the thought of talking about that subject makes me nervous, and I don't want to invite my alter ego to the discussion, go ahead: zap me.'

He laughed. 'That sounds like a word some of my young friends use to describe their victories or defeats with one computer game or another. No zapping. Perhaps I will simply ease you with an incantation. Much more appealing, yes?'

I had to smile at that. 'Yes. Much more appealing.'

He muttered some odd-sounding words and before I could even wonder what his spell would do to me, my muscles

surrendered and a delicious warmth spread along my skin.
'Oh, you're good. Very, very good.'

His lips spread in a dazzling smile. 'I have heard that
before.'

I intended to lift my hand to swat him for his cockiness,
but that was way too much work. Instead, I moaned as he
smoothed bath gel around my breasts and started heading
lower. The touch of his hands on my breasts was wonderful,
but for the first time I didn't have the urge to jump him. He
was right about my still being aware yet unconcerned. If he
could bottle that spell, he'd make millions. Oh, wait: he
already had millions.

He rubbed the skin around my nipples with such tender
dedication that I had to take a quick peek to see if any of
his relaxed muscles had regained their tension. Nope, still
soft and dangly.

I closed my eyes, revelling in the sensation of his fingers
sliding the gel on my body, and made whimpering noises as
he briefly stroked a certain spot. Too bad I was so relaxed,
because otherwise I'd have encouraged that finger to stay
right where it was for just a few more seconds.

'So, as I spread the soap over your skin, and you are safe
and calm, you may tell me about the death of the radio host.'
His mesmerising voice sent warmth radiating down my
spine.

I opened my eyes and smiled at him. 'That's some pretty
smooth hypnosis there, my night-walking guardian angel.
Maybe I could just have you hypnotise me instead of Tom
– your methods are certainly much more fun.'

'I have had years of experience using my abilities and skills to create desired outcomes. I discovered early that using certain words and phrases in conjunction with the power of my vampiric voice was an elegant and effective tool. But while I would not choose Tom as my clinician of choice for any purpose I can conceive of, he might actually be better suited to your needs this time. After all, I have no psychological training and I am not willing to take chances with your well-being.' He spoke more nonsensical words and another wave of heat rushed through my body. 'As you become even more relaxed, you may now share your recollections.'

'Slick, Fabio, real slick.'

The words poured out of me as he massaged my body with his talented hands, almost singing melodious phrases at sporadic intervals to enhance my relaxation. I told him everything I could remember about what happened after he left my townhouse: my discovery that I could move through thought, Maxie's visit, my decision to go with her to the vampire staking, the creepy amusement park, the events inside the funhouse – including Carson's murder, Tom's unexpected arrival and pitiful tale, and waking up naked in my living room chair.

It felt like I'd been talking for hours, but my skin hadn't pruned, so we couldn't have been in the shower for as long as I imagined. When I finally finished my tale and took a deep breath, I noticed Devereux had switched from smoothing on the soap to using a washcloth to wipe away the lathery remnants. I'd been so distracted and relaxed I hadn't even noticed the difference.

He discarded the cloth and held my face in his hands, his expression solemn. Love filled his beautiful eyes. 'I am very sorry I did not comprehend the gravity of the situation. Even had you wanted to tell me about any of those experiences as they were happening, I was not available to you. I allowed myself to be distracted. I deeply and humbly apologise.'

'Uh . . .' Well, damn. Losing the ability to speak while staring up at Devereux's sublime face hadn't happened for months. Before I got used to his outrageous good looks and powerful vampire vibe, and before the elders' involvement, I frequently found myself reduced to monosyllables in his company. Maybe it was the mystical relaxation or the cumulative effect of all the metaphysical and preternatural madness, but the neurons in my brain refused to fire.

He gave one of his slow blinks and the corners of his lips curled up: a mischievous angel. 'Does that mean you accept my apology?'

I mentally threw cold water on myself and quickly shook my head to clear the cobwebs. 'Yes, of course – I just spaced out there for a moment. I must be more tired than I thought. I apologise, too.'

'You have nothing to apologise for. Being under Hallow's influence meant you had no choice about your actions. It is he who will be sorry.' He paused, staring out through the shower glass, as if he were listening to something. 'We must dress and prepare for the rest of the evening. Our guests have arrived.'

Guests? Immediately more alert, I pivoted to stare through the glass, expecting vampires to pop into the bathroom, but there was nothing but empty silence. I quickly washed the shampoo from my hair and added conditioner to tame the tangles.

As soon as my hair was rinsed, Devereux slid the door open, stepped out and extended a hand. I frowned up at him. 'Guests? You didn't mention anything about guests. What's going on – is this another ritual?' As adorable as Devereux was, his idea of acceptable activities often bordered on the absurd, and I didn't think I was ready for another trip down the nightmare yellow brick road just yet.

'I have invited some powerful vampires to assist me to raise power, both to protect this penthouse and your office, and to surround you. I also instructed Zoë to bring Doctor Radcliffe so that he can hypnotise you, if you still wish it. Perhaps it would be good for you to have an old friend near you.' He smiled. 'A human friend, such as he is.'

'Thanks for that.' I slid my hand down his chest. 'I know he's a pain, but he's a familiar pain.'

We wrapped ourselves in big soft towels and walked over to the multi-sink vanity stretching the length of one wall. While Devereux used the dryer on his shining platinum hair, I bent over and towelled my curls dry. It was weird to be doing such normal, human things with a vampire. The first time I'd watched Devereux brush his teeth I was fascinated. I guess I hadn't thought about the undead having dental hygiene routines, but it made sense. How else would one get rid of blood-breath?

The towel covering my body fell away as I leaned into the mirror to finish putting on my makeup. I felt Devereux's gaze on me before receiving verification in the mirror. He met my eyes, a wicked expression on his face.

'Don't look at me like that, or we'll never get out of here,' I said.

He grinned as he brushed his long hair. 'Oh, yes, I meant to ask about the reporter you mentioned – Maxie? She must be quite a unique person for you to befriend her so quickly. What is it about her that caused you to let down your guard? You are usually more reserved and introspective about new people.'

Reserved and *introspective* were understatements. Sometimes I got so overwhelmed by the intense psychic energy in my environment that I exhibited all the symptoms of Social Anxiety Disorder. It wasn't that I didn't *like* people – there were many therapists who didn't – or even that I was afraid of them; it was more that I couldn't shut them out. I couldn't turn off my emotional radar. The more extreme the situation, and the more people in the room, the stronger my reaction. Being constantly bombarded by a continuum of feelings was oppressive, but he'd asked a good question: what *was* it about Maxie? Why *had* I let her in? I must be lonelier for human connection than I realised.

For some reason, I'd been dreading this discussion. What did I want to tell him about her? I didn't really know much about the crazy woman. If her 'organised crime' theories were any indication, she obviously didn't have a very good opinion of him. I probably should have mentioned her journalistic speculation about the source of his wealth and power, but I couldn't, and I wasn't sure why.

'Maxie is a character – she's sort of wild and uninhibited. I never know what she's going to do next. Since I'm more reserved and structured, maybe that's her draw for me – someone to nag me out of my comfort zone.' I grinned and glanced at him. 'You'd probably like her. She's very beautiful: tall, and built like a swimsuit model.'

He paused in his hair brushing and raised an eyebrow.

'But the main attraction is her knee-length white hair,' I continued.

'White hair? I somehow got the impression that she was a young woman, perhaps your age.'

'Yes, she is – she said something caused her hair to turn white overnight, but since that can't really happen, I'm assuming there was a trauma at some point, severe enough to trigger such physiological changes. She hasn't shared that secret with me yet.'

He dropped his towel, which was highly distracting. 'I imagine it would take a powerful situation to change a mortal's hair that way. I know of cases where physical transformations have occurred due to magic, but I am sure there is a less mystical explanation for your friend's situation.' He faced me, his tall, muscular frame reflected in the various mirrors, and I felt the need to fan myself.

'Please excuse me while I transport to my room on the other side of the penthouse and dress. I shall return.' The spot where he stood was suddenly vacant.

If it wouldn't have messed up my freshly applied makeup, I would have splashed cold water on my face. Devereux was temptation incarnate, but since we obviously had company to greet and runny mascara wasn't an option, I opted instead to stroll into the closet to find something appropriate to wear for the occasion – whatever that occasion might be.

Devereux enjoyed assigning his female devotees the task of filling my closets with expensive clothing. When I first discovered my fashion bounty, I was annoyed; I thought it was simply another way for him to exert control – to override my choices in favour of his own. And when his helpers disclosed they'd been spying on me – following me in person and observing my dreams – I thought he'd crossed the line between indulging me and manipulation. But it didn't take long for me to understand this wasn't about control; he really did derive great pleasure from showering me with gifts. Several of his undead elves mentioned the fun they'd had in the process too, so I stopped complaining about my constantly growing wardrobe. I accepted the clothes in the spirit they were offered and counted myself lucky. If truth be told, my own fashion education left a lot to be desired. I'd long ago faced the fact that, while I had many skills and abilities, choosing the best clothing for my body type wasn't one of them. Somehow I'd missed the junior high class on 'Being a Cosmo Girl'.

Who knew I'd turn out to be Alice in a twisted Wonderland instead?

After debating between a sophisticated ankle-length dress of dark blue velvet or my version of hipster black leather trousers that matched Devereux's, I chose comfort and pulled on a pair of probably overpriced jeans. Strappy sandals and a pale blue cashmere sweater completed the ensemble.

Never confident about my clothing choices, I stood in front of the three-sided floor-length mirror to make sure I really was acceptably attired, and tried a few moves I'd learned in a jazz dance class once. I'd just glanced down to pull the protective necklace from underneath my sweater when I sensed someone behind me. Fearing the worst, my head jerked up and my breath caught – until I saw Devereux's grinning reflection. I blew out so much air my lips flapped like a horse. I pressed my palm against my heart, as if that would slow down the frantic rhythm.

'Shit, Devereux!'

'Forgive me for frightening you.' His grin melted into a frown. 'I did not try to sneak up on you; you were so engrossed in your selection process that you did not hear me reenter the room. And truthfully, it was very pleasant watching you when you were not aware of my presence.' The grin reappeared. 'I especially enjoyed the dancing. I have only seen you dance once before, so it is always a pleasure. But I do apologise for causing you distress.'

'You scared ten years off my life. Next time clear your throat or cough or something, would you?'

He was dressed in dark brown leather trousers and a black silk T-shirt. Nobody could fill out a T-shirt in the elegant way Devereux could.

He bowed from the waist, his silky hair falling forward. 'I will endeavour to make more noise, and I will see what I can do to return the stolen ten years to you.'

I started to laugh, but his overly serious face stopped me.

'What do you mean? You're joking, right? That's just an expression.'

'As we have discussed before, time and space are not the rigid constructs mortals believe them to be. Some time in the near future I will be pleased to demonstrate – but now we must go.'

He took my hand and we walked together through the bedroom, along the hallway and into the large living room I'd previously described as the dentist's waiting room from Purgatory. It was anything but sterile and empty now: the room was filled with people – er, *individuals* I'd never seen before. All eyes locked onto us as we entered.

'Thank you for coming, my friends,' Devereux said, his presence dominating the room. 'You are aware of the current situation, and I appreciate your willingness to help strengthen our protections.' He released my hand and placed his palm in the centre of my back, gently urging me forward. 'For those of you who have not yet met her, I am pleased to introduce my mate, Kismet. It is for her safety we gather tonight.'

I curved my lips in what I hoped was a sincere smile.

His mate.

Hearing the words surprised me, because I thought we'd agreed to discuss the ramifications before going public with the title. I was still trying to understand what it meant to him and why it was so important.

As one, the group of strangers bowed or curtsied. 'Lady Kismet,' they said in unison.

Lady Kismet? What the hell was going on now – were all

vampires so melodramatic? Why was I always the last to get the memo?

I glared at Devereux, and he gave a subtle shake of his head, indicating I shouldn't say any of the hostile words struggling to explode out of my mouth. He'd definitely been around his minions and handmaidens too long.

One minute I was his equal and the next his property – or at least that's how it felt.

A creepy-looking short fat vampire approached. His stringy, grey hair flowed down over the shoulders of a standard black Dracula cape. He briefly fixed his bulging light-green eyes on me before extending his hand to Devereux. As he reached out, his cape fell open, exposing naked, wrinkled flesh. 'Master Devereux, I am honoured to have been summoned for this ritual and to have been entrusted with the creation of the powerful ceremony we will participate in tonight.' His unidentifiable accent was so thick I could barely understand him. Of course, the fact that his fangs were fully extended, causing a lisp, didn't help. He smiled at me, and I hoped the movement of my lips resembled something friendly in return. His belly was the biggest I'd ever seen on a vampire. His transformation must have happened suddenly, because I couldn't imagine anyone choosing to live for centuries as an undead smelly, greasy-haired street-person version of Santa Claus.

Devereux grasped the rotund man's hand. 'Prospero, my friend. Welcome to my home. I would like you to meet Kismet, the one for whom I have been waiting.'

The greasy fellow flipped the edges of his cape behind

him, giving me the Full Monty, and my gaze shifted to his crotch in spite of myself. Unlike most large midsections, his bulged out like a pregnant woman's rather than the droopy, cover-the-penis kind of flabby flesh, so his substantial pride and joy was evident for all to view.

Obviously noting the path of my gaze, he grinned and winked.

Ewwww.

Executing a theatrical bow, he lifted my hand and kissed it. 'We all rejoice at your arrival, m'lady.'

'Prospero? Isn't that the name of one of Shakespeare's characters in *The Tempest*?'

'Yes.' He chuckled. 'I heard he featured me in one of his little tales. I absolutely must read it one of these days.'

He dropped my hand and addressed the small crowd. 'Take your places in the circle.' Giving me his attention again, he flicked the cape completely off his shoulders and it pooled on the floor at his feet. 'Follow me.'

I glanced at Devereux, who was trying unsuccessfully not to smile. He nodded in the direction of the flat buttocks swaying ahead of us. I was amazed by Prospero's ability to remain vertical with nothing to balance the back of his body.

'Prospero is a very powerful magician,' Devereux whispered to me. 'He is my friend, but never be alone with him. His weakness for beautiful women is well known and he has a remarkable ability to entrance. Women have been known to fall at his feet after one glimpse of his fully erect organ.'

I stifled a grin and whispered back, 'I'll make every effort to control myself.'

Even if his fully erect organ breaks into song, I'm not going near it.

As we approached the waiting circle of vampires, I noticed the familiar floating candles and the fact that everyone had undressed.

Wait a minute.

Prospero glided over to me, surprisingly graceful. 'Allow me to assist you, m'lady.' He started tugging my sweater over my breasts.

I grabbed the wool, pulling it into place again. 'Hey! Knock it off! What are you doing?'

Prospero backed away, shocked.

Devereux had peeled off his T-shirt, and was unbuttoning his leather trousers. 'The ritual Prospero has created requires bare skin to be most effective – I apologise if I forgot to mention that.' He didn't sound in the least sorry.

I didn't know which stunned me more: the fact that Devereux actually thought I'd get naked in front of a group of strange vampires, or his effortless ability to lie through omission. Did he think being the Master gave him *carte blanche* in his dealings with me?

'Stop!' I pointed to the zipper he was lowering on his trousers. 'You're out of your mind if you think I'm going to take my clothes off in front of all these strangers. Hell, even if I *knew* them, I still wouldn't take my clothes off. Don't you know me any better than that?'

Okay. There was one part of me now who was more than

willing to get naked whenever possible, but for whatever reason, she hadn't recently tried to force her way out, and I wanted to keep it that way.

Devereux stepped towards me. 'If Prospero believes nudity will enhance the power of the ritual, I trust his judgement enough to follow his recommendations. I will be here to watch over you. The ritual will be brief.'

He simply wasn't listening to me. So what else was new?

'Why do you think a ritual is going to help, anyway? Isn't it clear that Hallow can do whatever he wants? Nothing anyone has done so far has kept him away. What is the point of this?'

'The point is that each new ritual brings more power to our defences.' His voice floated over me, attempting to soothe. 'We already have the building well protected, which is why Hallow could only transport himself to the roof.'

'What?' A chaotic collage of images crashed into my brain and I slapped myself on the forehead, any calming effect of Devereux's voice completely negated. '*Shit!* How could I have *possibly* forgotten to tell you about the most horrible part of my evening? What's the matter with me? How can I have repressed the horror of watching Hallow rip the head off one of my clients – *in front of me?*' My voice was shaking with emotion. 'You think he can't come into your building? That your incantations and rituals are effective? My office is a bloody mess – and poor suicidal Jerome, who actually was about to drain me dry so you would kill him, got his wish: death by maniac.'

Devereux stared at me, frozen, his mouth open, before he wrapped his arm around my waist and pulled me against his chest. 'Come.'

CHAPTER 19

Stale air blew against my face as we transported to my defiled office. It was worse than I remembered. Jerome's headless body lay crumpled where Hallow had thrown him, blood congealing in a wide circle under the ragged edges of his neck. I had no idea how much blood a formerly human body contained, but whatever had been left in Jerome's corpse after Hallow had drunk his fill had soaked into the blue carpet, leaving horrible brown-red stains.

Jerome's head, his eyes wide, staring like a macabre Hallowe'en mask, had rolled under an end table. Death had restarted his ageing process and he now looked much more his true age, which was at least seven decades. His usually slicked-down hair was white and it spiked up in all directions, as if he'd been electrocuted.

The stench in the room reminded me of a similar vampire-created scene some months earlier, when my previous office had been defiled by another young male body. I pressed my hand to my nose and mouth to filter the worst of the odour.

Devereux navigated us next to my desk, where we weren't directly in the bloody remains but still had a bird's-eye view of the destruction. He was strangely calm. He released me and surveyed the carnage. After a couple of minutes he turned to me, his usually entrancing voice flat, and said, 'You were correct: our rituals are meaningless. From now until Hallow is disposed of, you will not be left alone. I will no longer depend only upon magic and vampire powers. Now it must be the force of my will against his.' He stared off again, lost in thought.

Hearing the almost hopeless tone of Devereux's words frightened me more than anything. Without acknowledging it to myself, I had always assumed he'd prevail somehow, conquering the challenger and restoring my normal life, but his voice told a different story. Maybe he was no longer sure he could defeat the fiend – or perhaps he'd finally come to the conclusion that I wasn't worth all the trouble. What if Hallow really could capture me? Had all the choices in my life brought me to this dark crossroads?

I started to wonder what I should have done differently. It was easy to second-guess myself about my involvement with the hidden world of the vampires. The minute I realised the ramifications of my new career choice I should have closed up shop and relocated. My life was much simpler – not to mention safer – before I blundered into this parallel universe.

But that was all blood under the bridge.

Devereux slid his finger along my cheek, drawing my gaze back to his. 'The fear is radiating out of you. I swear you will not be harmed. We will find a way to destroy Hallow.' His voice had reclaimed its polished texture and it flowed over me, the once-again assured sound calming my anxiety. He pointed at Jerome's body. 'Your client must have been relatively young as a vampire, for his body did not immediately crumble into dust when Hallow decapitated him. The older the vampire, the quicker the body decomposes; in this case it will disintegrate over the next few hours. If you watch closely, you can see the process beginning.'

I followed his pointing finger to the grey substance gathering at Jerome's feet and shook my head. Devereux was good at raising issues in order to distract me from dwelling on unpleasant realities; it was gratifying to realise how well he knew me now. As long as I had something logical to hide behind – a cerebral topic to discuss – I would be able to maintain some semblance of composure.

'I didn't know that.' Okay, we could stand over Jerome's remains and discuss the mechanics of vampire death as if it were just another seminar topic. I was great at denial. But I probably wouldn't ever be comfortable with the cold, calculating, analytical view of death most vampires held – they didn't really attribute much value to life of any kind. Devereux was more in touch with his emotions than any male I knew, alive or undead, but even he was able to compartmentalise his feelings. 'The only other vampire I saw die was Bryce, after I cut his head off. He disintegrated into dust right away.'

'Yes, I imagine he did,' Devereux said. 'He was very old.'

I scanned the room, becoming aware of splashes of blood on the walls and the ceiling. 'What should I do about poor Jerome and the ruined carpet? Is there someone I can call?' Thinking about cleaning duties reminded me that I needed to read Jerome's file to check for relatives and friends to contact. I'd never lost a vampire client before, and I wasn't sure what the proper etiquette was. 'Is there something special we can do for Jerome? A service, or something?'

Devereux tilted his head, studying me. 'What would be the purpose of a service? He was dead before he was destroyed. I am sure all his human friends and relatives are long since departed, and vampires don't require those kinds of ceremonies.' He saw me frown. 'But if you would prefer, we can bury his ashes. I will have his remains collected and you can tell me what arrangements you want. As for the carpet, it will be replaced immediately, and the room will be restored to its previous condition. There is nothing for you to do here. I have already mentally summoned the necessary assistance. Let us return to the penthouse.'

He circled my waist with his arm, gathered me against him and we rematerialised in the penthouse living room. The naked vampires stood talking in groups, like an undead cocktail party.

Prospero strode over, arms spread. 'Devereux, is it true? Has the monster breached our defences? If that is the case, I must rethink our ritual.'

Devereux laid a hand on the rounder man's shoulder.

'Yes, my friend, it is unfortunately true. It is important now that I concentrate on other methods for keeping Kismet safe. I would be most grateful if you and all those gathered here would continue the ritual on our behalf. As always, I welcome your wisdom and assistance.'

'Consider it done.' Like the director on a movie set, Prospero leapt into action, discussing strategies, assigning positions. Once again, I was surprised by his grace and agility.

Devereux fetched his discarded T-shirt and slid it over his head. It was a shame to cover that chest, but I took his action as verification of a change of plan, though I didn't know what I was supposed to do. What was my role in the war of wills?

A low buzz emanated from the participants in Prospero's ritual. Each vampire in the circle stood with his or her arms straight out in front, palms up. Perhaps my eyes were playing tricks on me, but I could have sworn the air around the group began to shimmer, reminding me of waves of heat rising off the asphalt in August. I was so fascinated by the subtle phenomenon that I startled as a raspy voice rumbled within inches of my ear, 'Master, there is a human downstairs – a dame – who claims she's a friend of Doctor Knight's. She insists on speaking with her. Shall I erase her memory and send her away?'

I expected to find a big, hulking body to match the meaty tone, and almost laughed out loud at the short, slender man dressed like a gangster from the 1930s. A fedora hat sat at a jaunty angle and an unlit cigarette dangled from his mouth, the rolling paper obviously stuck to his lower lip, allowing him to speak without dislodging the obviously well-used prop.

'Who is it?' I asked the messenger.

He continued to speak to Devereux instead of acknowledging me. 'She says her name is Maxie – I've never seen white hair on a young dame before. She's quite a babe. Rattled, though. Nervous. What do you want me to do with her?'

Devereux shifted his attention to me. 'Do you wish to see her? I am not sure it is wise to bring her into a penthouse filled with vampires. After all, she is a reporter.'

'Yes, she is, but she's also a friend – a very persistent friend.' And a member of a very small club, indeed. I thought for a moment. 'Is there a room we can use that's separate from the rest of the area? Somewhere she won't see your guests?'

'You may use the library.' He pointed. 'It is isolated from the rest of the penthouse, and accessible only from this recessed alcove.' He walked to a wall-panel near the front entrance. When he touched an intricate pattern etched into the rich wood, a door slid sideways. He extended his hand, inviting me to investigate. 'I keep many rare editions of my favourite books in this room. Some of the documents under glass are so ancient and fragile that exposure to the air would destroy them.' I poked my head inside the open door. 'It would be best if your friend did not spend much time viewing the contents of the room. She might have questions about how a humble club owner managed to collect such priceless books and artefacts.' He smiled and gave a quick bow of his head.

'"Humble club owner"? I don't think anybody, reporter or otherwise, sees you in that way. In fact, Maxie told me you're widely considered to be a powerful mob boss.' I chuckled. 'And after seeing the fellow doing the Sam Spade impersonation, she's probably more convinced than ever.'

'Mob boss? No wonder I draw so much media attention. And I thought it was merely due to my good looks and personal charm.' He gave a little-boy grin.

He certainly had those things in abundance. The sweetness of his smile took my breath away. How was it that he'd been a vampire for eight hundred years and such innocence could still shine forth from him at the most unexpected moments? Vampires were supposed to be evil – at least, that was the common assumption.

What I still didn't know was if Devereux was the exception and the maniac Lyren Hallow the rule.

'Ralph, please bring Doctor Knight's guest up to the library. There is no reason to entrance her or erase her memory. Escort her directly to this room – but be vigilant. I understand she is very curious, and that she does not have much use for authority.'

I smiled. That was a pretty good description of Maxie.

'Shall I await her arrival and introduce myself, or would you prefer me to leave the two of you alone?'

I remembered I'd promised Maxie she could meet him if an opportunity presented itself. Would it be dangerous for Devereux if I exposed him to Maxie's relentless quest for a story? Maybe she would be so caught up in thinking he was involved in organised crime she'd miss the bigger scoop.

'Would you like to meet her?' I decided to leave it up to him. He probably had better things to do – or, if I was honest with myself, I didn't want to take responsibility for any of the ways the situation could go to hell.

'I admit to being curious about the woman who persuaded you to befriend her. I would enjoy meeting the white-haired swimsuit model.' I elbowed him in the ribs and he chuckled. 'Ah, here they are now.'

Ralph held Maxie's arm, clearly restraining her rather than politely guiding. 'Here ya go, doll.' He nodded at Devereux, and moved back towards the elevator. I'd half-expected him to say something Bogart-ish, but he probably wasn't even aware he was impersonating anyone. Thanks to my father's obsession with the actor's noir films, I knew more than I wanted to.

Maxie wore tight jeans and an equally snug white T-shirt with the words *fuck you* printed across her braless breasts. Her wild mane flowed loose down her back. Yes, definitely swimsuit-model material.

She shot me a fierce glance, annoyance written large on her face as she shook her arm, obviously trying to restore the circulation. The shaking came to an abrupt halt when she noticed the tall, blond leather-clad god who'd moved to stand in front of her. Devereux was only a couple of inches taller than Maxie in his boots, and she was able to meet his eyes directly as she grinned at him, extending her hand, all bad temper forgotten.

Devereux offered one of his beguiling smiles.

'Wow.' She grasped his offered hand, throwing her

shoulders back to better present all her assets. 'The famous Devereux, world-renowned entrepreneur, billionaire and major stud muffin. You're way hotter than your sizzling photos. If you ever tire of my conservative friend here, I'm happy to send in the second team. You're so cute, I'm downright speechless.'

He bowed. 'All evidence to the contrary.'

'I'd really love to interview you sometime. Come to think of it, I have a few minutes now if that works for you. Maybe we could go find someplace comfortable to talk.' She took a step closer. 'You're really a hot tamale. I bet you're awesome in the sack . . .' Her voice drifted off as she stared at him again.

I waved my hand in front of Maxie's eyes. 'You wanted to see me?'

She blinked and slid her gaze to me, a lost expression on her face.

Devereux kissed my cheek. 'If you will forgive me, I have business to attend to.' He nodded at Maxie, his gaze lingering a few seconds. 'It was . . . interesting to meet you. I trust our paths will cross again. Have a fruitful visit.'

Ever graceful, he walked away, and Maxie's mouth sagged open as she watched his slim hips and firm rear end exit the hallway.

I poked her arm to get her attention. 'Let's go in here.' I pointed in the direction of the chairs in the library.

She shook herself, snapping out of Devereux's trance. 'Shit, he's a *hunk*!' Her eyes tracked the rows of ceiling-high shelves filled with old books, artwork, and antiquities. 'Jesus – he's got a frickin' museum in here.'

She wandered over to the glass cases Devereux had specifically asked me to keep her away from and I followed her, took her arm and tugged her over to one of the leather couches scattered around the centre of the room.

'Hey, what the hell?' She glared at me with total focus this time as I dropped us both onto the cushions. Her anger took a curtain call.

I braced myself for whatever she'd come to talk about, already emotionally wiped out. 'What are you so pissed off about? What's happened?'

After a brief pause, she blurted, 'So he's one, isn't he? Nobody human is that beautiful.'

Shit. 'He's one what?'

She sneered. 'Don't give me that crap. No wonder you laughed when I said he was into organised crime – you knew he was sucking the lifeblood from innocent humans. He tried to entrance me and it almost worked. Some fucking friend you are – you knew all the time. The Vampire fucking Psychologist: you *knew* they existed – you *lied* to me. That's what happened at the amusement park, isn't it? Isn't it? Damn . . . damn vampires took me.' She was so upset she stumbled over her words.

I had to know how much she'd discovered – I couldn't betray Devereux and my clients, not based on something she might know only a little about.

'Maxie, stop, please. Tell me what happened? I can't understand what you're talking about.' I laid my hand on her arm and she threw it off.

'You can stop lying now. I *know* – the whole, miserable secret is out.'

'What secret?' What the *hell* happened?

'You're probably worried that I'm going to tell the world about your vampire lover – and wouldn't it just serve you right if I did write about him? His entire operation would have to fold – he'd have to skulk off into the night with the other bloodsucking fiends. Maybe someone would even take him out with a sharp stake. Hey, fuck that – maybe I will.'

'Maxie! *Breathe*. Tell. Me. What. Happened.' My heart was pounding against my chest and anxiety twisted my gut. I wasn't afraid for Devereux as much as I was terrified about what he'd do to Maxie if she really did have the goods on him. I hadn't ever asked him how he dealt with humans who discovered his existence. Did he kill them? Oh, wait – no. I forgot. He could simply erase her memory. I let out the breath I'd been holding. Maybe everything wasn't lost after all.

Well, since he could make her forget anyway . . .

We sat glaring at each other for a few seconds until I broke the ice. 'Okay. Tell me how you found out.'

Her eyebrows shot up. She gasped. 'What? You're not going to deny it? You're not going to use some psychobabble on me – some therapy-speak – to convince me I'm delusional? You aren't going to tell me I'm hallucinating?'

'No. Tell me what happened.'

She'd apparently expected a lot more resistance and it took a few seconds for her to regroup. 'Well, okay then.' She briefly grabbed my hand, surprise and scepticism flashing across her face. 'Are you saying there really are vampires, then? You're admitting it?'

'Yes.' I thought she might calm down faster if I kept things simple.

She opened her mouth in a silent *ah*. 'Holy shit. I hoped I was wrong.'

Settling into full therapist mode, I stared at her, waiting for her to say whatever she needed to say.

'You're going to stare at me until my brain explodes, aren't you? I had a nice head of steam going. There I was, all self-righteous at being lied to, and now that I've got what I wanted, I don't know what to say. Give me a minute to sort out my brain cells.'

I waited.

'Damn, that staring thing is creepy, Doc. It's a wonder your clients don't off themselves right in your office just to get away from your eyeballs.'

I slowed my breathing to help calm her.

'Okay, okay. After I tried to tell you about Devereux and you didn't believe me, I went back to The Crypt a couple of times to do a little creative eavesdropping. Mostly all I ran into were wannabes with their pitiful play-acting, but while I was sitting there I saw this really studly guy doing his goth thing, but he didn't look like the other wannabes. Did I mention he was exceptionally hot? Anyway, he took a woman into one of the private areas upstairs – the little cubbyholes covered by thick curtains.' She jumped up and started pacing in front of the couch.

'I'd heard that you could find pretty much anything at

The Crypt: drugs, sex, cults, Satanism, torture, bondage, cutting – you name it. I followed them and stood next to the
curtain, and there was a space between the curtain and the
wall, so I could see them clearly. They got naked and were
fucking their brains out and I watched for a few minutes . . .'
She stopped in front of me and held her hands out a foot
apart, palms facing each other. 'This guy was hung like a
stallion!' She resumed pacing. 'Anyway, I was just about to
return to my listening post downstairs when the guy rears
up and sinks his fangs – fake, I thought – into the woman's
neck, and she screamed and pushed at him, which caused
him to lift his mouth for a minute, and blood gushed out
of the holes he'd made.'

'That's horrible! Devereux needs to know what's going on
in his club—'

'Yeah, yeah, as if he doesn't. So the victim was flailing and
carrying on and he grabbed her head to hold it still, then
he stared into her eyes and said something I couldn't hear
and she went limp. He resumed sucking on her neck and
had a magnificent, grunt-filled orgasm.' Maxie must have
burned off sufficient nervous energy because she reclaimed
her seat on the couch next to me.

'As soon as he was finished, he stood and started getting
dressed – then quicker than I could see, he slashed the curtains back and smiled at me, and I saw his bloody fangs
slowly retracting into his gums. I went to run away and he
grabbed me and pulled me inside the cubby.'

'Shit, Maxie – were you attacked?' My mouth dropped
open and I clutched my chest.

'Almost. He asked if I was a vampire groupie. He said if I wanted to donate some blood, he'd be happy to take advantage of my offer. He said he had a creative suggestion for a new moisturiser for my hair – and all of a sudden, I got super-dizzy and started thinking what a good idea it would be to have that guy suck on some part of my body. I almost took my clothes off – and I would've, too, if the woman lying in the booth hadn't groaned and sat up, and that snapped me out of whatever the guy did to me. I bolted down the stairs and out of the club.'

'Oh. My. God.'

'I know, right? The bouncer – that really tall, skeletal guy – at the door must have seen me run out – oh, holy shit, I just realised! That isn't a costume he's wearing – *he's really like that*! He sent someone to follow me out and I thought at first the guy, a real cutie, a Johnny Depp clone – I thought he wanted to make sure I was okay, but right away he started trying to lock eyeballs with me, so I knew he was trying to control my brain and make me forget what had happened. I managed to run away from him too and I came right here—'

I really hoped Devereux didn't know how many predators were using his club for feeding purposes, but that was probably more delusional thinking on my part. I knew vampires didn't have anything like human ethics.

'I'm glad you came here,' I said, stroking her arm, hoping human contact would calm her down. 'I don't blame you for being freaked out, but I have to ask: how do you know the fangs weren't fake and the stud wasn't just a sick psycho who enjoys torturing women and drinking their blood? Lots of humans are that screwed up. What made you assume he was a real vampire?'

'Yeah, that's the million-dollar question, isn't it, Doc. As the most sceptical reporter in the universe, that was my first assumption – but it was just the strangeness of it. The surreal texture, like I was in a wide-awake nightmare. I know that doesn't sound like me, but it's true. I just knew I was with something *other*.'

'So does this mean you'll be doing an exposé about the vampires of Denver?' I searched her face for clues about her intentions. 'If you do, you'll destroy everything Devereux has built here, and force my clients, many of whom were transformed against their wills, to go into hiding again.'

'Time out, Doc. Don't try to make me feel guilty for exposing these undead predators to the human world. Sure, maybe there are a few who aren't monsters – or at least not complete monsters – but others are, I know that for certain. Are you going to try to convince me that all these vampires are just humans with fangs?'

'No, they definitely aren't that, but they aren't all killers, either.' I thought about Hallow, the one who was, and I sighed. 'What are you going to do?'

'I don't know. Your reaction threw me. I thought you'd tell me more lies, so then I could get pissed off and write the biggest story of my career, but you had to go and screw up my plans. I still want to know one thing: did you lie to me to protect Devereux? Or just because you didn't trust me?'

Since she wouldn't remember any of our discussion later, I figured I might as well stick with the truth.

'Both, actually. What would you have done in my place if you met a tabloid reporter hunting for a juicy story? Someone you liked, but hadn't known very long. I couldn't take the chance that you'd write about me and Devereux, or that you'd expose my clients. And then there was the equally important issue of keeping you safe.'

'Keeping *me* safe?' She sat up straighter. 'What are you talking about?'

'I'm still new to this whole bizarro world, and the last thing I wanted was to draw someone I liked into the madness. The less you knew, the better – it was the only way to keep you out of danger. As you said, vampires aren't just humans with fangs.'

'What do you mean – is there some kind trouble? Is that why Devereux's watching you like a hawk – er, bat?'

When I didn't say anything, she shook her head. 'Still don't trust me, eh? What do I have to do to prove I'm in your corner?' She held out her wrist. 'Do you want me to take a blood oath that I won't write about your main squeeze?'

'Don't be flashing any veins around here. You never know who might drop in for a snack.'

She frowned and scanned the room, not quite sure whether I was kidding or not.

'No blood oaths required,' I reassured her. 'And it isn't that I don't trust you. It's that the hitman you heard about in the club – the one you thought Devereux hired to kill his manager – is an undead psycho-fiend, inexplicably obsessed with me. Remember the guy at the amusement park with the long hair wearing the genie trousers? The tall, pale, handsome one?'

'Yeah . . .'

'That's him.'

'Wow – no shit? He's a vampire?' She threaded her fingers together, then cracked her knuckles. 'I'd let him suck on my neck anytime.'

I clutched her arm, trying to let her know I was serious. 'You wouldn't say that if you knew what he's like. He's already kidnapped one of my friends and I don't want him to take you, too.'

She thrust her chin into the air. 'I can take care of myself, Doc.'

'Not against this monster.' I shook my head. 'He's crazy.'

'Yeah, but he'd make a great story.'

Damn. She just didn't understand how dangerous Hallow was – but how could she? No wonder she flip-flopped so fast from anger to eagerness. Once a reporter, always a reporter. It wouldn't surprise me if she sought him out on purpose. It was definitely time to have Devereux blast her with some laser vampire eyeball voodoo so she'd forget everything we'd discussed. I hoped whatever he had to do to make her forget wouldn't hurt.

'Well, if you won't believe me, maybe you'll listen to Devereux.' I rose from the couch. 'I'm going to get him. I'll be right back.' I hurried out of the room before she could ask any questions.

As I entered the hallway, Zoë's voice shouted, 'He's gone, Luna! We must tell Devereux.'

CHAPTER 20

'Tell me what?' Devereux appeared from somewhere and strode over to the two women.

'Master! Tom is missing.' Zoë grabbed onto Devereux's arm, quivering as she delivered her rapid-fire monologue. 'He was sleeping on the couch at Doctor Knight's townhouse when I went out to feed and when I came back, he was gone!' Her chest was heaving, as if she'd forgotten breathing was optional. If she hadn't been a vampire, I'd have diagnosed hysteria.

Devereux spoke in a soft, soothing voice. 'Zoë, I understand you are protective of him, but why would you immediately assume that Doctor Radcliffe is missing? Perhaps he awoke and took the opportunity to escape from what he considered his captivity? I am sure he will turn up eventually.' He patted her hand before stepping aside, allowing her fingers to gently fall away. He turned to me. 'Doctor Radcliffe seems the type of individual to place his own needs at the forefront in any situation. Would you agree?'

'Yes,' I said, studying the overwrought woman. 'Why are you so upset, Zoë? What aren't you saying? You know Tom – he'll do whatever it takes to get what he wants. He's probably off searching for another vampire to bring him over. What's really bothering you?'

Luna stepped out from behind her companion. 'When Zoë came to The Crypt and told me Doctor Radcliffe was gone, I thought it wise to come to the Master. It can't be a coincidence that first Victoria went missing, then the doctor, both of whom are close to Doctor Knight.'

Devereux's eyes were cold, his voice hostile. 'If you have something to say, just say it.'

The corners of Luna's mouth trembled slightly and she lowered her gaze. 'I believe it's possible the Slayer has them both.'

Zoë gasped and grabbed Devereux's arm again. 'Oh, Master – is Luna right? I've heard things about Hallow, very bad things. Do you think he has Tom and Victoria?'

Devereux softened his expression. 'There is no denying that Lyren Hallow is a monster, but I am not convinced that Doctor Radcliffe was taken against his will. In our short acquaintance, he has shown himself to be self-motivated and single-minded. In fact, it would not surprise me to find him on his way here, preparing to make another attempt to convince me to see things his way.' He shifted his gaze to Luna and, still addressing Zoë, added, 'There is no reason for anyone to fill your mind with fantastic speculations.'

Luna was behaving strangely, even for her, and I wanted

to know why she sounded so certain. 'Why do you think Hallow has them, Luna? Do you know something we don't?'

The expression on her face reminded me of the joyfully evil smile worn by the Grinch as he stole Christmas. 'I know many things *you* don't know, but my opinion is based on the fact that I know Hallow.'

'You *know* Hallow?' My voice came out much higher than usual.

She ignored me and spoke to Devereux. 'If you would like me to search for Doctor Radcliffe, to see if he has gone to any of his usual haunts, I will do so, but my gut tells me he didn't leave under his own power. I don't have your tracking abilities, but I usually find what I seek.'

Something about Luna's odd energy set my teeth on edge. I was sure Hallow had taken Victoria, and it wasn't beyond the realms of possibility that he'd snatched Tom as well. He'd probably figured out that we'd do whatever we could to get them back.

Luna shot her attention to me, glaring. 'Don't you care what happens to your so-called friends? Aren't you worried? Why aren't you offering to search for them yourself – are you really just another useless, stupid human?' She threw her words at me like knives.

What the hell had I done to make her hate me so much?

I took a step forward, opened my mouth to address her questions and bumped into Devereux.

'Enough!' He locked eyes with me. 'Do you wish me to search for your friend? I still have my doubts, but if you believe he is a pawn in Hallow's game – that he is in danger

– I will accompany Zoë briefly back to the townhouse and pick up the trail.'

I didn't know what I believed. Five minutes ago, I hadn't given one thought to Tom's whereabouts, but now that Luna had raised the possibility of Hallow's involvement and Zoë was so upset, I couldn't ignore the heaviness in my gut.

'Yes. Please go.' I stroked my hand down Devereux's chest. 'Taking Tom is exactly the kind of thing Hallow would do. I've seen him kill people twice now – he actively enjoys it. I should have considered that he'd try to control me by hurting my friends. Please find them.'

Face serious, he gave a curt nod. 'As you wish. But you' – he raised my chin with his finger – 'will stay here in this room full of vampires until I return. Swear it.'

I made an X over my heart with my finger. 'Cross my heart and hope to – er . . . not die.'

He spoke to Luna. 'I am giving you an opportunity to redeem yourself. You will be personally responsible for Doctor Knight while I am gone. She is never to be out of your sight. Do you understand?'

She nodded solemnly, eyes downcast, but I was sure I saw her lips twitch ever so slightly in the beginning of a smile before she brought her face back under control. I started to tell Devereux I didn't want to be babysat by the Queen of the Damned, but he took Zoë's hand and they vanished before I could get the words out.

A burst of sound filled the air as the vampires in the circle switched from the soft hum they'd been offering for the last few minutes to a full-bodied 'ohm' and my brain waves began to scramble until I thought I would dissolve into the tone. I distanced myself from the chanting, hoping to clear my mind, but something was niggling at me.

Shit – Maxie!

In the drama of the last few minutes, I'd forgotten about her. I headed towards the library, and heard footsteps behind me.

Luna caught up with me. 'Where the hell do you think you're going? Didn't you hear the Master put me in charge of you?' She grinned a mirthless grin.

'Dream on, Vampira. He didn't put you in charge of me. He said you were *responsible* for me – so be a good bodyguard and walk three paces behind. I have a guest to check on.'

She fell back and hissed, the sound much closer to my neck than it should have been.

I sailed into the library, the hostile Amazon almost literally on my heels. The room was empty.

Luna laughed. 'Was this guest an imaginary playmate or a ghost? Or maybe another kidnap victim? You don't hold on to your friends very long.'

I went through the room, opening every door, exploring every hiding space, while Luna leaned against the doorjamb, smirking.

'She must have left,' I said aloud, more to myself than to Luna. If Maxie had overheard the conversation about Hallow, she was probably on her way back to her office to file a career-changing story. I hated to think about what would happen if she mentioned Devereux.

Or maybe she was still in the penthouse somewhere,

watching the naked vampires, believing she'd hit the jackpot.

I headed back towards the circle and the chanting increased in volume. The sounds were so loud they repelled me. I pressed my hands over my ears to mute the vibrations and hurried up the hallway, bypassing the noise, and retreated into a room filled with Devereux's art.

'What's the matter with you?' Luna snarled from directly behind me. 'Are you too good to stand with the vampires who are trying to protect you? Does their nudity offend your tender human sensibilities?'

I am so tired of her attitude.

'Not even close. The chanting is giving me a headache.' That was true as far as it went. I didn't owe Luna any explanations.

I walked along the paintings until I came to one of my favourites: a self-portrait Devereux had created hundreds of years ago. He wore clothing from that earlier century and his hair flowed down over a black fitted jacket. The blue-green of his eyes sparkled from the canvas like precious gems.

Luna stood next to me, studying the image. 'He is very beautiful.' Her tone was disdainful. 'Too beautiful for the likes of you. If you truly love him, you will go away, let him find someone more suited to his station.'

I spun on her, determined to get to the root of her problem with me. 'Someone like you, I suppose?' Had it really been simple jealousy all along? 'You think you're better for him than I am?'

She laughed, and the sound was sharp enough to slice

my ears. 'I think the short fat vampire with the big dick would be better for him than you are.'

Even though she was laughing at my expense, I couldn't help but notice the gleeful explosion made her face even more attractive than it was when she was glowering or frowning. Her elaborate Cleopatra makeup was flawless tonight; she was every bit the sexy, otherworldly villainess of any horror movie. I wouldn't have blamed Devereux for lusting after his personal assistant. I still didn't understand why he was so uninterested. What was the problem between them?

'You didn't answer my question. Do you think if I'm out of the picture, he'll suddenly find you irresistible?'

She closed the space between us, bringing her face within an inch of mine. A musky scent wafted from her skin and mixed with the coppery tang of her breath, creating an intoxicating aroma. She must have fed recently. 'You know nothing about me or my relationship with the Master.' She lifted her upper lip, exposing the tips of her fangs. 'I told you I knew Hallow. Do you want to know how I knew him?'

My heart pounded. Out of nowhere, Luna's energy suddenly became manic, almost dangerous, as if she were in the grip of something more powerful than herself. Was Hallow controlling her, too?

I took a breath to calm myself. There was nothing to be frightened of. I was safe in Devereux's penthouse, surrounded by scores of vampires in the other room. But if that was true, why was my body on red alert?

'Yes.' I couldn't force any more words out of my mouth.

Luna's aura was suffocating, dark and thick. 'I belonged to him. I was one of his women. He calls us his *lýtles*. He was my *everything*.'

He was her everything? Devereux's addiction reference was more literal than I thought. 'I don't understand.' I licked my dry lips. 'Devereux said Hallow drains all his women. He uses them up, sucks their life-force as well as their blood. How could you still be alive if you used to be one of his slaves?'

'I'm alive because Devereux's clean-up crew rescued me. They found me, along with several corpses, in a field. They didn't know it was Hallow's dumping ground. Then Devereux made me his own. I didn't want to leave Hallow, but I was happy to give myself to Devereux.' She raised her palm and smoothed it down my hair, petting me like a doll.

Why didn't I see this about her before? Hallow created an addict and she just switched her drug of choice.

'Do you mean Devereux made you a slave, too?'

Does he know she's addicted to him?

'No, you stupid human.' She dropped her hand. 'Devereux *claimed* me. I was still mortal, near death, and he brought me over. He gave me his blood and a new life. He became my Master – my reason to exist. Hallow has never forgiven Devereux's vampires for taking me. I was supposed to die for Hallow, to be added to what he is so he can continue. I would have gladly sacrificed myself – and even now, I'd give up everything for one more touch from him.'

Jesus Christ. She's lost.

'So why aren't you with Hallow then, if you feel that way?'

She bared her fangs and heavy energy radiated from her

as she pressed her body against me. 'Don't you think I would if I could? I am of no use to him since I'm no longer mortal. He isn't like Devereux; Hallow needs the raw power of abnormal human women. Even though he won't touch me, I crave him still. I *ache* to have him inside me, to sense him in my mind. I *yearn* to have him pierce my veins with his sharp fangs.' She trembled, her eyelids fluttered. 'Once you're gone, Devereux will be truly mine, as Hallow was.'

No wonder she hates me. I'm standing in the way of her drug of choice.

Since she was in such a talkative mood and she hadn't hurt me yet, I pushed on. 'Why has Devereux been so angry with you? What happened?'

'It's my fault that Hallow is here.' She gave a skin-crawling smile and slid her finger along my lower lip. 'A few weeks ago he mentally contacted me, and I told him about you – about how Devereux is so obsessed with you. About how I *hate* you. He told me he would take care of it. I couldn't shield my thoughts from Devereux, so he discovered my fantasies. And he found out I had spoken to Hallow, which he'd forbidden. Since then, the Master has been trying to reject me – to cut me off. He said I couldn't remain in his coven if I didn't let go of my plans to kill you. But he will forgive me once you are gone. I am sure I can make things right between us.'

Oh. My. God. Kill me? She's even crazier than I thought. She wants Devereux to become what Hallow was to her. Does he even have a clue?

She pressed me hard against the painting on the wall and

as the edge of the frame jammed into my lower back I gasped with pain. Her voice became lighter, almost singsong, as she spoke directly into my ear. 'I know where Hallow is holding your friends.' She leaned back to watch my face. 'I can tell you where they are, and you can save them.' She smiled wide, fangs glinting.

I caught a flash of white out of the corner of my eye. Was that Maxie? If it was, I hoped she wouldn't do anything idiotic. She certainly wasn't any match for Luna. Was she stupid enough to sneak up on a rabid vampire? I shifted my eyes from side to side, searching for my friend, but I didn't see her again.

'Don't you want to be a hero?' Luna purred. She tilted her head and batted her eyelashes. 'They'll die if you don't rescue them.'

'You need help, Luna.' I stared at a point between her eyes; I knew better than to fall into her gaze, especially if she was connected to Hallow. She'd paralysed me once before, and the memory was still painful. 'It isn't your fault – you're an addict. Hallow did this to you.'

The evil grin slid across her lips again. 'The only thing that will help me is for you to go away. Permanently.'

'You're helping that monster kill people – do you really think Devereux will still want you when he finds out you've been helping Hallow?'

'I don't care about the fate of puny mortals; they mean nothing to me. Since Hallow won't take me back, Devereux is my only hope. No one else is as old and powerful. I need him. He will one day understand how things are.'

'I understand now.' Devereux's voice surrounded us.

He grabbed the back of Luna's shirt and pulled her away from me, slamming her against an empty wall on the other side of the room. The chanting vampires fell silent.

'Master! I wasn't expecting you back so soon—'

'I never left,' he snarled. 'Despite Hallow's efforts to block me, I have mastered the magic necessary to override his manipulations. Now I can easily read his influence in your mind.' He leaned into her – if she'd been human, her lungs would have imploded. She made a satisfied groaning sound, as if she enjoyed having him so close, no matter what the cause.

'You have betrayed me. I thought Hallow came to exact his revenge on my coven for taking you. I never suspected you had summoned him here to bring me pain.'

'No, Master – no! I would never do such a thing. You are everything to me now. I adore you. Just let him have her and everything will be good again, as if she never happened. You will forget her – she's only human.' She tried to wrap her arms around his waist and he grabbed her wrists, elevating them over her head.

I'd been slowly inching to where Devereux had Luna pinned, trying to stay out of her line of sight, but as soon as she saw me, she laughed. 'It's too late, anyway. Hallow has chosen her. He has already begun to feed from her. Don't waste your time. She isn't worth saving.'

With lightning speed Devereux released her wrists and clutched her neck in a stranglehold, lifting her off the ground. His features hardened as his body shook with rage. 'You will die for this.'

She made gurgling noises, flailing her arms and legs in a futile effort to escape – but though she was a powerful vampire, she was no match for Devereux.

Before he could crush her throat, I moved next to him, trying to wedge myself in between the enraged bloodsucker and his prey. My personal opinion of Luna didn't matter now; I understood why she'd always resented me, and why her attitude had become even more toxic since Hallow's arrival. She wasn't in control. The sickness had taken over.

Devereux could swat me aside like a fly any time he wanted, but I was pretty sure I was in no danger from him. Surely he'd want to know Luna hadn't *consciously* betrayed him? I knew him well enough to be sure he'd torture himself if he destroyed Luna for something she had no choice about, no matter how inflamed he was now.

'Devereux, wait!' I pulled at his free arm. 'She can't help herself. You were right about Hallow's effect on the women he uses: he makes them crave him, just like any other drug. She needs help – she doesn't know what she's doing and she's definitely under the influence right now. Please, don't do anything you'll regret.'

He was silent for a few seconds, staring up at Luna, still holding her in his steel-fingered grip. Then he dropped her to the floor, hard enough to break human bones. 'She must be punished for bringing the madman into our lives. I do not care why she has done so. It will be impossible for her to remain here now. I do not wish to see her face again.' He scowled at me. 'You will not interfere in this. It is beyond what you are able to understand. Your defence of her is more than she deserves. We are vampires. We have different rules. Rules I create and uphold. There is no known cure for an addiction such as you describe, and she must be taught a lesson. I have no intention of rescuing her yet again.'

Devereux's harsh tone and rigid body language spoke volumes about his ability to shut off his feelings. He'd retreated into an alien, nonhuman place inside himself and I couldn't follow.

Luna wrapped herself around Devereux's legs, clinging to him.

She glanced up at me, and to my amazement, she smiled.

Devereux had just bent down to untwine her fingers from his calves when I was pulled forcefully backwards. Cold, strong arms snaked around me, holding me immobile.

'I couldn't have planned things any better,' Hallow said. 'Thank you, Luna. Finally, one of my *lýtles* has proven herself worthwhile.'

'Hey!' Maxie poked her head inside the room. 'You're the guy from the amusement park. Kismet says you're a real badass vampire.' Visibly vibrating with excitement, she hurried over to Hallow. 'I've hit the jackpot. You're going to make my career—' She reached out to touch him.

He uncoiled one arm from around me and punched her in the chest, sending her flying through the air. She slammed into the far wall, the impact splitting her head open. Blood gushed from the wound as she slumped onto the floor, out cold.

'Maxie! Oh, my God – she's hurt! You demented son of a bitch!' I struggled against him, to no avail.

Snickering, Hallow tightened both arms around my body and dragged me over to Maxie's collapsed form. Tucking me under his arm, he bent and drank the blood dripping from her head. His mouth was stained red as he stood. 'If I have time, perhaps I'll return for your friend later, in the unlikely case that she doesn't die. One can never have too many worshipping females.' He glared at Luna and slowly licked my cheek. 'I am sure my new slave Kismet will surpass all who came before. The pickings have been very slim for a long time.'

Then as if a switch had been thrown, several things happened at once. At the touch of Hallow's tongue, Lust jerked into wakefulness in my psyche. She strutted nude from the shadows into the centre of my awareness and laughed. Screaming, I tried frantically to wrestle my way out of Hallow's arms. Devereux roughly peeled Luna from his legs. He lunged towards my captor.

'I've just commanded all your ritual guests to join us, Devereux, whether they want to or not.' Hallow shouted, and at his words, the vampires from the circle swarmed into the small room, blocking Devereux's path and impeding his access to me, while Luna speed-crawled through the herd of undead arrivals, burrowing towards her former master.

With a hysterical laugh, Hallow tightened one arm around me, grabbed Luna, and the three of us blinked out of Devereux's penthouse.

CHAPTER 21

After what felt like a trip through a wind tunnel, Hallow
released me and I fell onto my knees on a filthy red rug. My
landing stirred up a cloud of dust and I sneezed. I sat back on
my heels, keeping an eye on him. He was dressed all in white:
loose, flowing trousers and an Indian-guru-type silk shirt. His
feet were bare. Deceptive innocence – a beautiful demon.

Luna, who'd had no trouble keeping her feet, threw her
arms around Hallow's neck. 'Master, I knew you'd come for
me.'

He grabbed a handful of her shining black hair, yanked
her head back and riveted his eyes on hers. Her muscles went
slack, and when he let go of her hair, she made a gurgling
sound and crumpled to the floor.

'Is she dead?' I whispered.

'Of course she's dead,' he sneered. 'But you're asking if
she's *truly* dead – no, not until it suits me. I hoard my
resources.'

Watching them together made me wonder how I could've missed the strong resemblance. He truly must have clouded my perceptions. The same long, black hair and silver eyes – had she looked different before he found her? Was the similarity a consequence of their parasitic relationship?

Devereux! Can you hear me? I knew Hallow could intercept my thoughts, but it was worth the risk to contact Devereux.

The unfairly handsome monster sauntered around, his arms spread wide, hands palm-up. 'I have to give credit to my current *lýtle*. The old thing managed to find the perfect lodgings for my Colorado visit. I must thank her before she is called up to make the ultimate sacrifice.'

Ultimate sacrifice? I scanned the area. 'Where is this 'current *lýtle*'?' The word made me think of a female version of Dr Frankenstein's hunchbacked assistant, Igor. What kind of horrid creature did Hallow have in thrall?

He flicked his hand in a dismissive gesture. 'Oh, I'm sure she's around here somewhere. She knows better than to show herself before I call her. She's really quite disgusting. You'd be appalled.'

Do I even want to try to imagine what he means by that?

The large room had three windowless walls decorated in faded wallpaper; the fourth was brick – not the kind of trendy brick displayed in modern designer homes, but the sloppy, hastily slapped-together type generally denoting something hidden in a hurry. The air was heavy, musty – lifeless. It felt like all the emotional vibrations of the former occupants had coalesced into a psychic fog and lain undisturbed for a hundred years. The only light in the room came from cracked, sooty kerosene lamps on old gaming tables. A thick layer of dust covered every surface. Whoever had walled in the abandoned space was obviously not much worried about housekeeping.

With his hands on his hips, he surveyed the area. 'It doesn't have the charm of a Paris tomb or a Transylvanian castle, but I've always loved historical sites – especially disreputable ones.' He strolled the area, sounding disturbingly normal. 'This place was an underground gambling house and brothel, with a secret tunnel, complete with train tracks, leading to the Brown Palace Hotel,' said the tour guide from hell. 'Apparently, Denver's finest gentlemen got their rocks off in this forbidden place. Right now we're deep beneath the busy streets of the city – so removed from civilisation that the world could end and we wouldn't notice. I am the first new customer to enter this establishment in a century. How appropriate for such an infamous soul.'

Devereux!

Hallow fanned the air in front of his nose. 'It's a good thing I don't need to breathe, though, because I'm sure I'd find the foul smells unappealing. Water must be leaking in somewhere. And there's the unofficial graveyard I discovered a couple of levels down, of course. What a perfect place! I can only imagine how my human guests are coping.'

'*Human guests?*' Chills prickled my arms.

I was the only human in the room that I knew of.

He feigned surprise, slapping his palms against the sides of his face. 'What a poor host I am.' He reached down and grabbed me by the hand, pulling so hard I flew into his arms instead of merely coming to my feet. 'Ah, you're so affectionate. What a pleasure you'll be.'

Lust gave a thumbs-up.

I pushed against his chest, and he released me. 'I'll never be affectionate to you. It won't be long before Devereux discovers our location and you'll have to deal with him. I have nothing for you but pity.'

He stepped close. 'Even Devereux, clever lad that he is, won't find this place – and if by some astonishing chance he does, I've a special surprise for him.' He grabbed my hair, anchored my head in place, leaned in and kissed me roughly. His breath had a sweet, earthy odour. Lust swooned. He raised his mouth just enough to speak, his voice a low rumble. 'It doesn't matter what you feel for me. After you've tasted what I have to offer, your body will do whatever it takes to acquire more. I am highly addictive, as you've no doubt discovered from talking to lovely Luna.' He gave an exaggerated sigh. 'I wish human bodies lasted longer. It's so tedious having to restock so often. I hope you aren't another disappointment.' He clasped my hand and tugged me to a formerly invisible door in one of the regular walls.

He swung it open, exposing a wide, carpet-covered staircase. Stale, cold, nauseating air flowed against my face, making me gag. Dim light flickered at the bottom. 'Let's take a shortcut.' He wrapped his arms around my shoulders and I closed my eyes. He thought us to the bottom of the stairs and then standing on solid ground again, I raised my eyelids – and sneezed. The air was even thicker here; it hurt to breathe.

He released me and I hugged myself, shivering from the cold.

Soft illumination sparked from candles burning in tall, standing holders, showcasing a large, colourful pentagram painted on the dark floor. Esoteric symbols filled the outer rim of a drawn circle and a female body marked the centre. She was very small in that large space, lying naked and spread-eagled, her limbs tied to posts pounded into the ground.

I would have recognised those golden curls anywhere.

'Victoria!'

I broke free of Hallow, ran to her and dropped onto my knees. Her eyes were closed and her head drooped, slack-jawed, to one side. I pressed my palm on her cold chest, trying to detect a heartbeat, and was almost overwhelmed with relief when I found one.

'What have you done to her?' I demanded. 'Why is she tied up? What's *wrong* with you?'

Devereux! He has Victoria!

Hallow loomed over me, staring down at us with an amused expression on his face. 'Well, let's see if I can answer those in the right order, shall we? What have I done to the powerful witch? I drank some of her succulent blood, giving her the orgasm of her life. While she was entranced from my bite, I commanded her to instruct my *lýtle* in setting up a ritual circle. This part was ingenious, if I say so myself. Victoria's magical skills are superior even to Devereux's. I'll bet you didn't know that. Before she came back to her rational mind, I made her cast a spell to keep this entire room safe from intrusion. Only those I have selected can enter; everyone else is magically repelled.' He snorted and slapped his thigh. 'How clever of me to use his own witch against him.'

He polished his fingernails on the front of his shirt in a gesture of self-congratulation. 'Why is she tied up? I'd say that one's obvious. In order for the magic to work, the witch must remain in the circle. She was so overwhelmed after her last orgasm that she just passed out, which was the best thing that could have happened to her. If she'd kept up the screaming for much longer, I'd have had to slit her throat, despite her spell-casting skills. And, what is wrong with me? My dear doctor, I'm a very naughty boy. We'll have plenty of time to decipher all the quirks in my vampiric psyche – you'll have the benefit not only of my bite and my body, but you will be able to psychoanalyse me to your heart's content. What more could a woman want?'

Ignoring the madman leering down at me, I stared at Victoria, grimacing. He'd left ample evidence of the savagery of his attack all over her body: dried blood on her chest and pubic hair, multiple ragged fang holes in her neck, on both breasts and across her thighs. She never had a chance against the sadistic bastard. My stomach pitched, and it took all the self-control I could muster not to gag, because I was sure he would have enjoyed my revulsion. My throat was so tight it was hard to speak. Victoria's skin was tinged blue. My teeth were chattering, so she had to be in danger of hypothermia.

'Let me cover her up. She won't be any good to you if she freezes to death.'

He tilted his head to the side, studying Victoria. 'Hmm. Cover her up? No, I don't think so. I like her like this: all that provocative, voluptuous flesh. I especially love the way her breasts slide down on either side, making her nipples point in opposite directions. Very erotic – a Rubens painting come to life. And you needn't worry about her being cold. As long as she's entranced, she probably feels nothing.'

As my eyes adjusted to the dim light, I scanned the rest of the room. The echoing cavern had obviously been some kind of communal brothel or sleeping area. I'd guess brothel, because tattered curtains hung from the ceiling, marking off 'private' spaces. A pile of bed frames had been shoved into the far corner, leaving evidence in the dust of their previous positions. I couldn't make out the artwork on the walls in the deeper shadows, or any other furniture.

I suddenly remembered the other missing person and jerked my head in Hallow's direction. 'Do you have my friend Tom? Have you hurt him?'

'More questions?' He smiled condescendingly. 'Well, I suppose that's a psychologist's prerogative, isn't it. Yes. I have your chatty, obnoxious friend. Quite frankly, he was so irritating that I wasn't even tempted to take his blood at first, let alone anything else. I finally had to command him to sleep. How in the world do you endure such a person?'

I stood, squinting to see in the faint light. 'Where is he?' I was almost afraid to know.

Hallow pointed to the beds in the corner. 'I stashed him as far away from me as possible, just in case he wakes up and starts talking again.'

'I don't have your vampire eyesight. Can I have a candle so I can find him?'

His evil grin quirked his lips. 'Very clever, my good doctor: asking your captor for the means of his own destruction. I hate to disappoint you, but I meant what I said about my indestructibility: even if you did manage to set me on fire, I'd get little more than a temporary tan.' He chuckled and winked at me. 'I'll fetch a candle and escort you back there myself.' He strolled to a shelf near the wall, picked up a candle and lit the wick. 'Follow me.'

Hallow had been right about the stench. Now that I had a moment to process the secondary horrors, foul smells assumed a larger presence. This room reeked: a combination of mildew, bodily wastes and death. I was tempted to hold my breath, but I wouldn't have been able to manage long enough for it to make any difference.

My jailer led me to a bed in the darkest corner. Tom lay sprawled naked on top of a soiled mattress. I sat on the edge of the bed and grabbed his wrist, searching for a pulse, and was relieved to find one. His heart beat was much stronger than Victoria's. My initial relief was quickly replaced by anger at the vampire for hurting another of my friends. I had a quick thought about Maxie probably being dead, but that was too horrible to contemplate, so I focused on Tom.

'Why is Tom naked? Do you just enjoy humiliating everyone?'

He shrugged, unconcerned. 'Is nudity humiliating to humans? I'd forgotten. I took his clothing so he couldn't run away. It's cold outside. I didn't think he'd want to parade through downtown Denver naked.'

I almost laughed. 'You obviously don't know Tom.'

An angle of the candlelight caught two still-bloody fang holes in Tom's neck. *The lying psychopath.* Fear surged through me. What if we couldn't hold on until Devereux found us? 'I thought you said you didn't take his blood.' I slid my finger through the congealing liquid. 'Why bother lying?'

He grabbed my finger and sucked it clean. 'Not that it matters, but I put him to sleep before taking his blood, so technically I told the truth. It's not as much fun if they're compliant, but blood is blood, after all. I just had a little snack before popping over to collect you.'

He assumed his now-familiar stance, the candle-free hand on his hip, his legs apart: lord and master of all he surveys. 'Your friend is of no consequence. His only purpose was to serve as added incentive to get you here. I'm confident that Luna would have persuaded you to rescue your fallen comrades, loyal trouper that you are. But Devereux came back faster than expected, so I simply stepped in, shortened the intermission and raised the curtain on the final act.'

I tensed. 'What final act?'

He cocked his head. 'Even after spending so many months with cold-hearted bloodsuckers, you're remarkably naïve, Doctor. There is no pretence in you. You sincerely have no idea what is about to happen, do you? I don't think I've ever met anyone with as many innate abilities as you possess who is still so astoundingly mentally pure. You actually believe the world is rational, that an explanation can be found for everything. You expect a homicidal vampire – yours truly – to tell the truth. It's a mystery. I have absolutely, as the miners who once thrived in the Queen City would say, hit the mother lode with you.' He laughed and his body rocked with the strength of his hilarity.

I wasn't quite as naïve as he assumed, but if allowing him to think so gave me any advantage whatsoever, I'd gladly play along. 'What do you mean?'

'I'll walk away with the strongest, most pure *lýtle* I've stumbled upon in many a century, and your friends – well, let's just say they obviously won't be making it through the night.' He reached out and grasped my hand and pulled me up from the bed. I knew it wouldn't do any good, but I resisted, trying to delay the inevitable as long as possible. He grinned, not deflected in the least. 'Jolly good, Doctor. You'll find I enjoy a vigorous struggle. Unfortunately, the fight usually goes out of my *guests* much too quickly. So, please. Go ahead, arouse me. Soon you'll be just another docile slave. While it is my intention to suck the life force out of you, I will also miss it when it's gone. One of the little paradoxes of my existence, but never fear. I plan to savor you slowly.'

He must have noticed my shivering, because he gave me a surprised look. 'Once again I have been a poor master. Since temperatures don't affect me, I had totally forgotten you might find this room a bit *brisk* for your tastes.' He grinned. 'I can rectify that.'

Pulling me along behind him, he traversed the room, holding his flame aloft, and paused every couple of feet and ignited the wicks of row after row of tall candles until the entire space was ablaze with light.

'The witch told my *lýtle* to provide lots of candles, and my slave is nothing if not obedient. We might as well ignite them. I do want you to enjoy your last few hours in Denver.'

Huge paintings depicting various sex acts sprang to life on the suddenly visible walls of the subterranean den of iniquity. Hallow pointed to one in particular and chuckled. 'That should give you a glimpse of your future.'

The scene he'd indicated was of a woman on her knees in front of an abnormally well-endowed male who held her hair clasped tightly in one hand while he forced his obscenely large organ into her mouth with his other.

I gagged in sympathy, and cringed as Hallow slid his hand up my arm.

Taking advantage of his relaxed grip, I jerked my arm away. 'You'll never force me to do that – I'd rather die.'

He laughed as he reclaimed his grasp. '*Force* you? On the contrary, my dear doctor, you'll be begging me.'

I shuddered in trepidation, fear crawling up my spine, as Lust danced a celebration boogie in our shared inner sanctum.

Devereux, we're under the city, downtown.

'All the comforts of home,' Hallow said as he propelled me towards a fireplace carved into the back wall. He bent over, touched his candle to a clump of newspapers in the hearth and the fire caught.

Black smoke billowed into the room before it was sucked away and I started coughing. The fireplace must have a chimney leading up to the fresh air. I hadn't noticed if the room we'd landed in earlier had a fireplace, but there had to be one on the topmost floor. Hope momentarily glimmered. Wouldn't someone notice smoke coming from this supposedly empty place?

My optimism died as I remembered all the businesses above us. Nobody would have cause to think anything about smoke coming from a stray chimney. What was unusual about that? Many of the buildings in this area had been made into lofts, purchased by Trustafarians or Internet millionaires – not the kind of residents who devoted a lot of time to pondering the goings-on of the neighbours.

Hallow dragged me back to the circle and gave me a shove, causing me to fall onto Victoria's cold, still form. I quickly crept away from her, not wanting to make her any more uncomfortable, or cause any more pain than she'd already endured. The monster gazed at me with his hypnotic eyes.

I tried not to meet them.

'Are you as excited as I am?' He cocked his head and adopted a serious expression, as if he thought I'd actually answer his ridiculous question. 'I have one last task to complete and then your new life will begin. Since your friends aren't brilliant conversationalists tonight, you can spend the next little while contemplating how you can be of greater service to me.' He leaned forward, his veil of dark hair swinging down in front of him, and gave a maniacal grin. 'Think hard, now. There'll be a quiz later.

'Oh, by the way, you can stop trying to contact Devereux telepathically. The witch's marvellous magic stops everything, including communication.' He gave an exaggerated frown. 'This just isn't your day, is it?' Ear-splitting laughter burst from his throat before he vanished, and the sound echoed after he was gone.

I'd already figured out the futility of trying to contact Devereux, but that didn't matter. It wasn't going to stop me from flinging message-filled bottles out into the cosmic sea.

Searching for escape routes, I noticed the entrance to the staircase was only a few feet away. Either the fiend was absolutely confident I wouldn't try to leave, or he'd arranged it so I couldn't. Only one way to find out. I jumped up, climbed the stairs two at a time and smashed into a cushion of solid air at the top – or maybe the outer layer of the invisible beach ball I'd been trapped inside.

I slid my hands along the oddly pliable magical forcefield protecting the upstairs room. It gave when I pushed on it, but it wouldn't allow me to move forward. This must be what Hallow meant when he said he'd compelled Victoria to use her abilities to seal the area. Of course, the maniac could pop in and out at will. Too bad I couldn't—

'Hey!' I yelled down to unconscious Victoria. 'What if he forgot he gave me a ticket for Air Vampire?' Was I still able to transport myself? I quickly retraced my steps and moved towards the circle, visualising the interior of Devereux's penthouse, then froze. Wait – it couldn't be that easy. Hallow was insane, but he wasn't stupid. What if I was able to blink out, but smashed into the plastic beach ball again, only this time at the speed of light? Would I be pulverised into unrecognisable atoms?

How could I help Victoria or Tom or anyone if I was dead?

I glanced from one friend to the other and I realised it was a no-brainer. I simply had to try.

I closed my eyes, picturing Devereux's dining room. I recalled the wonderful breakfast buffet his helpers had prepared for me a couple of mornings ago, and sighed at the memory. I imagined the aroma of the coffee, the taste of the fresh baked goods, the sweetness of the strawberries, melons and grapes, and waited for the familiar sensation of freefall.

Nothing happened.

I filled in even more details and tried again.

Nothing.

Imagining myself in my own townhouse had the same result.

Damn.

My flight had been cancelled.

'Fuck.' I stood for a moment, hugging myself and trying not to panic. I ran to the fireplace, dropped to my knees in front of it, and tried to project my voice up the chimney flue. 'Hello? Hey! Can anybody hear me?' I grabbed a piece of wood from a pile on the hearth and banged it against the brick. 'Please call the police. 9-1-1!' I shouted, repeating every emergency phrase I could think of before the smoke from the small fire made me cough and my eyes water.

Using my sweater to blot the mascara-tinged tears running down my face, I backed away and hurried to the wall, moving clockwise around the periphery, checking for any sign of light or air. I climbed over abandoned furniture and broken sculptures, looking for anything that could be used as a weapon.

I looked behind the paintings and found nothing but insect nests, dislodging several bugs. I fanned them off as they headed for my face. 'Yuck! Now to add a cherry to the shit sundae, there's going to be a plague of locusts.' I would have laughed at myself if the situation wasn't so terrifying. After circling the room several times, I plopped down next to Victoria, laid a hand on her cold arm and worked to clear my mind. I couldn't allow myself to be overcome by fear. 'I'm sorry, Vic. I don't know what else to do.'

Suddenly Victoria groaned and pulled against her restraints, and I gasped as pain knifed through my body – *her* pain – as sharp as if it were my own. We had similar psychic abilities, so I guessed proximity had made the sensory connection between us even deeper than it usually was.

'Victoria?' I scooted close, angling my head so my ear was near her mouth. Overwhelmed by the magnitude of the torture Hallow had inflicted upon her, I had to take a few deep breaths to remind myself that I should distance myself emotionally – that I wouldn't be any help to her if I became further enmeshed in her misery. Almost like a physical act, I mentally pushed myself back from the waves of pain. My nose clogged up, and it took all my control not to cry.

She groaned again, and her eyelids fluttered, then slowly opened. Her beautiful exotic eyes were bloodshot, the pupils dilated. 'He's not' – the tip of her tongue struggled to moisten her lower lip – 'what you think,' she whispered.

'What do you mean? Who's not?'

She coughed, wincing with pain.

Shit. She was in bad shape.

I raised my head, scanning the area to see if I'd missed anything helpful – water, blankets – but I didn't really expect to find them. Unless they were accustomed to spending time with humans – live humans – the undead rarely took our needs into consideration, and even less so if the bloodsucker in question viewed humans as fast food.

Victoria kept trying to speak, even though it was taking a lot out of her.

'Hold on a minute, Vic. Let me see if by some miracle I can find an old tapestry or something to cover you with. You're freezing.'

I sprang to my feet and rushed through the tall candles, widening my search until I reached the edges of the room again. Along the far wall I reinvestigated the bounty of old couches, chairs and tables which had been piled together. On top were a few heavy rugs of varying sizes.

'Yes! I found a couple of small rugs, Victoria,' I announced breathlessly. 'They're filthy, but they'll keep out some of the draft.'

I'd just grabbed the rugs to retrace my steps when my eye caught sight of a can sitting on the floor. I lifted the half-full container. Diet Coke. Why would Hallow have a half-empty can of Coke? I'd never heard of a vampire ingesting anything but fresh blood. I sniffed the contents. It smelled like Coca-Cola. I tipped the container so the light would shine on the surface to make sure there was nothing floating there, that no one had used it as an ashtray, but it appeared to be cigarette-butt-free. I finally took a tiny sip. It really was a flat-tasting Diet Coke.

There was no telling how long it had been sitting there, but it would be better for Victoria than nothing.

I crushed the rugs to my chest, tightened my grip on the can and hurried back to the circle. I set the can safely out of the way, then spread the rugs over her. Retrieving the Coke, I slid my arm under Victoria's neck, and lifted gently. 'I know this probably is going to taste horrible. You're not much of a soft drink fan as it is, but it's wet, and judging by the lack of dust on top, it hasn't been sitting here very long.' She nodded and parted her lips to accept the liquid.

I could still pick up her anguish like a background hum.

She swallowed a few times, then cleared her throat. 'You have to resist him,' she whispered. 'He can only take you if you offer yourself freely. It's all a lie.' She tried to lift her head, but the effort was obviously painful because she gasped and closed her eyes.

I hovered, worried. 'Victoria? Please don't close your eyes. I'm afraid you won't open them again if you do—'

She slowly opened her eyelids again and gave me a trembling smile. Her voice was thin and hoarse. 'Don't worry; I'm not going to let any bloodsucking asshole take me out.' Her expression grew serious. 'Remember what I said: he's cursed. Not what you think. Don't choose him.'

Choose him? Why would she even suggest such a thing? Hallow had probably given her something to cause her pupils to dilate and make her say such strange things. 'I promise I won't choose him,' I said gently. 'You never need to worry about that. I know he's a monster.' I studied her eyes. 'He gave you a drug, didn't he? That's why you're so lethargic.'

'No.' She coughed. '*He's* a drug. His bite—' She went still except for her eyes, which shifted back and forth as if tracking something. 'He's coming.'

'How do you know?' I whispered, scanning for any signs of the crazed vampire.

'My body knows – it craves him. It can feel him approaching. Hide the can. I'll pretend to be asleep.'

I grabbed the drink, hurried to the nearest piece of furniture against the wall and thrust it behind, then I ran back and collapsed onto my knees by her side, whispering frantically, 'Can you release the magic spell you created? Is there something I can do to help?'

Almost immediately, I was startled by Hallow's enticing voice. I leapt to my feet. 'Well, what have we here? Pretending to be asleep, is she?' He materialised nearby, clutching a semi-conscious Luna under his arm. '*Tsk-tsk*, my dear doctor. I see you've misbehaved. Didn't I tell you to leave the witch uncovered?' He barked out a laugh. 'As if the rugs will warm her while she lies on the equivalent of a block of ice.'

I gazed down at Victoria. Her eyes were huge, lips parted.

Hallow dropped Luna, who fell to the ground with a loud *thunk*. He squatted next to Victoria and stared into her eyes. She lost consciousness again, her head flopping sideways. 'I can't have her screaming again,' he said, sounding very matter-of-fact. 'I would hate to lose control of myself and kill her before I have made full use of her.'

He stood effortlessly. 'I brought you some company.' He pointed at Luna. 'Letting her watch the finalé is the least I can do, after her recent service.'

Luna roused herself enough to wrap her arms around Hallow's ankles, whining, 'Master, please! You *need* me.'

He glared down at her. 'I haven't had a slave who was worth a shit in centuries.' Leaning down, he lifted Luna by her shirt and flung her across the room. She landed near Tom's bed. She was no longer whining.

He cast a glance back over his shoulder. 'Oh, yes, speaking of slaves – I have a surprise for you.'

He stepped aside and as he laughed again, sending chills down my spine, he sailed his arm through the air in a wide arc, pointing to the person I hadn't noticed waiting patiently behind him.

Maxie.

I gasped, pressing my hand against my wildly pounding heart. 'Maxie? Jesus!' My brain spun, unable to cope with the fact that Hallow had kidnapped yet another of my friends – another mortal he could drain. Blood covered her forehead and coated her tangled white hair. Dark circles underscored lifeless eyes in her pale, blank face. She stood silent, her *fuck you* T-shirt half-untucked from her jeans, her shoes missing. But at least he hadn't killed her back at the penthouse.

'What have you done to her?' I demanded as Hallow leaned in to study the expression on my face. 'There was no reason for you to capture anyone else. You've already got me.'

It was strange; he seemed to be overly interested in my reaction to his newest insult. I inched towards Maxie, wanting to touch her, to let her know she wasn't alone, but Hallow stepped in front of me.

'No, not yet. Let me get comfortable first.'

'Comfortable how? For what?'

Chuckling, Hallow jumped over Victoria, fetched a chair from against the wall and placed it where he could see both Maxie and me. When he sat, he sent a cloud of dust into the air.

'All right. I'm ready. You can continue now.'

Something was wrong. He was even more pleased with himself than usual. I studied his face, trying to figure out what kind of trap he intended to spring, but his wide smile told me nothing. I gazed back at Maxie, who stood silent, empty.

Had he already drained her and somehow animated her corpse to fool me into thinking she was still alive? Was that even possible?

I reached out and touched her arm, and immediately, her face blurred. As I watched, her features shifted, melting like wax. The pale skin, dead eyes and dark circles morphed into her usual flawless skin, bright blue gaze and silly grin. Her blood-free white hair was once again perfect.

She laughed. 'Good ta see ya, Doc.'

Instinctively, I jerked back.

What the hell just happened to her face?

'Maxie? Are you okay?'

Am I hallucinating?

She slid her gaze to Hallow, who got to his feet, strolled over and threw his arm around my shoulders. 'I don't believe you've been properly introduced to my current *lýtle*.'

CHAPTER 22

My brain started spinning, my mouth went dry and I stopped breathing. His words struck me like a verbal punch to the gut. All I could do was stare at the smiling woman in front of me. It took for ever before I could speak, though it was probably only seconds.

'Your *lýtle*? *Maxie*?'

Hallow cocked his head and made a *tsk* noise, faking sympathy. He patted my shoulder. 'Oh dear – I can't even begin to imagine how betrayed and disappointed you must feel. Allowing yourself to make a new friend, only to discover she's been spying on you all along – *using* you, taking advantage of your good nature – what an evil creature she must be.'

A tear rolled down my cheek before I even realised I was crying, but once the weeping began, I was overcome. I didn't even try to hold back, or worry about what an unprofessional image I might be presenting – what was the point? As I sobbed, I wiped my nose on the sleeve of my sweater.

It was clear that from the moment Hallow had entered my life he'd been in control. Nothing Devereux or anyone else did, especially me, had had any effect on the lunatic's actions. I would have laughed at my own stupidity if his machinations hadn't been so horrifying.

Being set up and sucked dry by an insane vampire wasn't where I had expected to be at this point in my life.

My heart ached as I thought about Victoria and Tom, and what Hallow would probably do to them. I cried hopelessly for Devereux's good intentions, and the pain he would experience after I was gone, and for all the possibilities that would die along with us. And I wept for Maxie's deception, for I had started to trust her, even though I'd known her only a short time – some judge of character I was. And so much for my intuition.

My knees gave out and I sank to the filthy ground. I still couldn't accept that Maxie had meant to hurt me – even now, with the huge, ugly proof grinning down at me, I couldn't make myself believe that our connection had been a complete lie. I had obviously been under Hallow's control for far longer than I had realised.

Were there signs I'd missed? Inconsistencies I'd refused to acknowledge?

Of course there were. And as I figured them out, they'd haunt me for as long as I was able to retain independent thought.

'Hey, Doc – you're doing that weird staring thing again.'

I gazed up at her through my tears, unable to speak. Did

she really think I'd respond to her, that I'd play this hideous game with her, now I knew that's all it was?

Suddenly there was a building-rattling crash, so loud that it startled even Hallow. Were we having an earthquake in addition to everything else?

Several more explosions thundered around us in all directions.

Hallow laughed. 'I take it your hero and his vampire cavalry have arrived.' He danced around the candleholders, clapping his hands after every new assault like a demented child. 'It will be entertaining listening to them take the building apart, only to discover they'll be stopped in their tracks when they hit the impenetrable layer created by Devereux's very own sorceress!' With a malevolent grin on his face he said to Maxie, 'I simply must go and watch. Witnessing their frustration is just too big a temptation to pass up. You stay here and guard your replacement.'

'Master!' Maxie groaned and threw her arms around his neck. 'Don't say things like that. You'd never replace me. You love me. You promised I'd be with you for ever.'

Hallow shoved her away so violently she fell, her head hitting the hard ground with a sharp crack. She landed next to me and he leaned over both of us, snarling, his long fangs glistening in the candlelight. His mercurial eyes narrowed. 'You *will* be with me for ever.' The sound of his laughter resonated long after his body had disappeared.

Maxie was as addicted as Luna and I didn't know whether to be disgusted or sad, or one of the myriad other reactions wrestling in my brain. I chose horrified. Was I getting a glimpse of my own future?

I found myself wondering why I was less compassionate about Maxie's addiction than Luna's. Maybe it was because I'd let my defences down with her, something I had never done with Devereux's bristling assistant.

Maxie sat up and rubbed her head. She yelled to be heard over the demolition sounds, 'I'll be glad when all my humanity is gone. It's irritating to still be so breakable.' She scooted close and stared at me. 'It wasn't personal, you know. I really did like you.'

I sniffled a couple of times to clear my clogged nose. 'With friends like you, I apparently didn't need any enemies.'

'Yeah, well, I can't blame you for being pissed off, but here's your chance to ask all your questions. Once Hallow returns, there won't be a lot of time to talk.'

She said the last in such an ominous tone that my stomach clenched. 'What do you mean? What's going to happen?'

She leaned back on her elbows. 'He'll take some of your blood, give you some more of his and begin the process of making you one of us.'

'Some *more* of his blood? What are you talking about? I never drank any of that psychopath's blood.'

'I'm not surprised you don't remember. He didn't share all the details, but one time I know about for sure.' She raised her eyebrows, as if she was waiting for me to ask what she meant, so I obliged her.

'Well?' I asked impatiently, 'are you going to tell me?'

'I just wanted to see if there were any traces left of the feisty doc I know and love.'

I frowned and pressed my lips together. She was making it easy for me to hate her.

'Okay, okay – I guess I am being an asshole. It's hard for me too, ya know. I didn't expect to like hanging out with you. No matter what you think, I'm not totally heartless. Anyway, do you remember when I gave you that brandy at the amusement park?'

'Brandy?' Our trip to the deserted funhouse was so long ago that I had to mentally recreate the evening step by step, starting with crawling under the fence. It took me only a few seconds to get to the bit where Maxie was insisting that I drink some brandy after my encounter with an invisible hand – and then I remembered the strange aftertaste that had made me assume it had been in her car for a long time.

'The light bulb over your head just lit up.' She smiled. 'Yeah, that's it: there was a little of Hallow's blood in the flask.'

The idea of drinking Hallow's blood was so disgusting that I scrambled to my feet and started pacing back and forth.

Maxie rose from the floor behind me and I faced her. 'Why put blood in the brandy?' I asked bitterly as I inched backwards. 'Was it just another way to prove you were in control?'

'Well, yeah.' She shoved her hands into her jeans pockets. 'There was that. You needed to acclimatise by drinking small amounts of his blood – it'll save time during the big trans-formation ritual, and it'll keep you from overdosing and becoming worthless to him. Putting it into terms you can relate to, Doc, you're connected to him now at levels much deeper than body or mind. We're in the realm of metaphysics or even quantum physics here. He has begun the process of joining his aura with yours. Soon you'll be an extension of him.' A huge smile curved her lips. 'Like me.'

Another crash sounded overhead and my stomach roiled and my breath caught. The notion that I already had some part of Lyren Hallow inside me was frightening. Even if Devereux did somehow manage to break through the magic and free us, I'd still be under the psychotic's control. All I could hope was that Devereux would get to Victoria and Tom before they were killed.

Knowing that Devereux was near should have been reassuring, but since nothing about Hallow was in the least bit rational, I was afraid to hope there might be a way out of this nightmare. Talking to Maxie was probably another dead end, but she had more information than I did and I was willing to repress my true feelings and appear interested, in the hope that she would reveal something I could use to help my friends.

I pointed at her head. 'So Hallow's the reason your hair is white? There was no mystery about your transformation?'

'Nope. I knew all along.' She winked. 'Sorry about fucking with you. You were so compassionate, it was easy to make up this shit.' She gathered the avalanche of white into a ponytail. 'But, yeah, the hair is a side-effect of becoming Hallow's *lýtle*. Turns out the progression is different for every woman. You probably figured out that his twin over there' – she pointed at unconscious Luna – 'only resembles him because they didn't get very far along in the transformation process before Devereux's vampires interfered. If they'd continued, her hair might have gone white, too. I heard it happened to others.'

'What about your face changing?'

She laughed. 'I wondered if you were going to mention that. The transformation gives each of us special abilities. Mine is that I can alter the appearance of my face and body so every person who looks at me sees what he or she wants to see. It's great for going undercover to get a story.'

Did she honestly expect me to believe she really worked for that tabloid? But she answered before I could ask the question.

'Yeah, I really do work there – although I've only been in the Denver office for a few months. Being Hallow's slave isn't a 24/7 kind of gig – a girl needs other interests. And if you're remembering what I told you about visiting the amusement park when I was a kid, I actually did live in Denver earlier. I wasn't lying about that. At least, not totally.'

I'm so relieved she didn't totally lie. Yeah, right.

'So who was it Hallow came to *harvest* if it wasn't Luna?'

Confusion clouded her face for a few seconds before she broke into laughter. 'Oh yeah, the *harvest* thing – it turns out Hallow's a pretty creative liar, much better than me. It was you he came for all along.' She smiled in apparent appreciation of her master's cleverness. 'He really got into the game here, littering the ground with bloodless bodies just to tantalise the vampire community and to keep them out of his way. Brilliant.'

Well, that explains Mr Roth's dead vampires.

From the way Maxie was talking, it was pretty clear she either didn't believe I was her replacement, or she was in denial. Devereux had told me the monster had a harem. I hadn't seen evidence of that and I might regret raising the issue, but I wanted to know.

'I thought Hallow had a lot of female slaves. Where are all the rest?'

Her good humour vanished. 'I don't know about how it used to be.' She raised her chin in the air. 'Since he's had me, he hasn't needed anyone else.'

'Until now?' I crossed my arms over my chest.

'I'm not sure why he wants you.' She frowned. 'I tried to convince him that three's a crowd.'

Ah, the seeds of discontent.

'It wouldn't be three. He said I'm your replacement.'

Her eyes narrowed and her hands clenched at her sides. She stood rigid and shouted, 'Shut up! You don't know anything – he won't replace me. You couldn't possibly be enough for him. He's just fucking with my head. I told you my boyfriend was an asshole.'

She didn't appear to believe what she said any more than I did, but addicts could be masterful at self-delusion. *How far can I push her?*

'Maybe he's tired of you – or maybe he's just a lying bastard who manipulated you the same way he did me. You probably don't mean any more to him than any of his other women.' I gave an exaggerated laugh. 'I'll bet you thought you were special.'

I must be suicidal.

Her lips curled into a malevolent smile and she took a step towards me. I cringed from the almost palpable anger radiating off her, when an entire portion of the wall collapsed behind us. Bricks and lumps of cement tumbled into the room like a chunky mudslide.

My gaze shot to the huge hole, and the sea of pale faces appearing. Devereux had brought reinforcements, and they were all trapped behind the unseen magical boundary.

'Kismet!' Devereux roared, and he threw himself against the invisible forcefield, speaking in the strange language he often used. After a few seconds, he slammed his fist against the barrier in obvious frustration and shouted, 'I must know which spell Victoria cast so I can dismantle it. Revive her!'

I took a step towards Devereux to ask him *how* to revive Victoria, as Hallow had knocked her out with his vampiric gaze, but Maxie grabbed my arm, holding me in place with unexpected strength. 'Nope, sorry, Doc. No conjugal visits today.'

'That's right,' a low voice rumbled directly behind me, and Maxie and I swung around to see Hallow.

'At least, not with your knight in shining armour.' He swept Maxie's hand away from my arm and said brusquely, 'Sit with the witch. Be prepared to do whatever I ask.'

She sank to the ground next to Victoria.

He lifted me into his arms and smiled. 'Now that the audience is in place, let the show begin!'

On the other side of the barrier Devereux raged, 'You will pay for this, demon!'

Hallow threw back his head and laughed theatrically. 'I almost wish I had time to finish you off before I claim my prize – killing one such as you would bring me great pleasure. But if I have learned anything after all these millennia, it's that a juicy human in hand is worth two – or multitudes – of vampires in the wall.'

His body shook with mirth. I struggled to free myself from the steel bands his arms had become, but my efforts only made him press me closer. 'Hallow,' I cried, 'why are you doing this? You already have Maxie – you don't need me. What's the point of this?'

He stared at me. 'You honestly don't know, do you?'

What the hell was he talking about? 'Know what?'

He licked his lips, exposing the tips of his descended fangs. 'You have strong abilities, and I shall be gorging myself at the smorgasbord of your talents for – well, for as long as you last.'

Great. We're back to the 'strong abilities' crap again – and I still have no idea what these so-called abilities are.

He walked us to the far end of the room, to the pile of beds where Tom was lying, still unconscious. Holding me easily with one arm, he snagged another of the dirty mattresses and dragged it over to Victoria's circle. When he dropped it, a great cloud of filth filled the air.

Shit – this is bad. I've got to keep him talking.

'Wait a minute – what abilities? Vampires keep saying that, and I still don't know what any of you are talking about.'

'You mean your golden magician hasn't told you?'

Devereux glared at Hallow as he continued mouthing incomprehensible words. If he was trying to cast a spell of his own, it obviously wasn't working. His vampire companions, at least a dozen of them, kept up an ongoing clatter of shouts and threats, making such a commotion that I didn't think anyone but I could hear what Hallow was saying.

'I think we've already established that I don't know what the hell *anyone* is talking about. Since you're so enamored with the sound of your own voice, why don't *you* tell me?'

He grinned. 'Glad to. You're gonna love this. Drum-roll, please! You're a vampire.'

I raised my eyebrows and pursed my lips. 'I'm a vampire?'

Well, what did I expect from an insane immortal killer? Devereux said Hallow's mind had mutated over so many centuries, so who knew what kinds of weird neural pathways were etched into his brain? His insanity aside, the longer I could keep him distracted, the longer I'd avoid whatever psychic lobotomy he had in store for me.

The entire situation was becoming more surreal by the second.

'You are indeed – oh, not the blood-drinking variety like your warrior vampire over there, nor even like me – but you are a vampire nonetheless. You, my dear doctor, are an emotional vampire.' He smiled, waiting for my reaction.

I frowned. 'We usually call those people psychic vampires, and I'm not one.'

He shook his head. 'No, it's not the same thing at all. Those pitiful humans live off the crumbs from the psychic table. You are different: you are a magnet; you literally *attract* emotions. And the fascinating thing is, you don't even know you do it! All those psychic emanations float in your aura like a vibrational buffet. And not only from your current life, but from endless others. For someone like me, you're a feast.'

Vibrational buffet? Endless other lives?

He paused for a few seconds, a huge grin sliding across his face. 'Devereux probably never told you the big secret about who you used to be, did he?'

'Who I used to be?' How much crazier can this madman get?

I opened my mouth to ask about those ludicrous assertions, but he shook his head. 'No, don't even bother asking. I'm going to keep that bit of information to myself for the time being.'

I'm arguing with an insane vampire. Time to switch techniques.

'Well, okay, so assuming I believe anything you just said, what's that got to do with you?'

He was still gripping my arm with his strong fingers. The heavy smokiness that had cleared slightly when Devereux punched the opening in the wall had returned, making my eyes water again and my lungs ache from breathing in the thick dusty air.

'Why, you'll just keep on drawing in resources from the human environment and I'll be well fed – what a glorious arrangement. Of course, your physical body will eventually give out, but by that time I'm sure I'll have found a replacement or two.'

He twisted my body so Devereux, whom I could clearly

hear still roaring unfamiliar words over the clamour of the other vampires, had a clear view. He stepped behind me, his hands following the curve of my waist to fondle my breasts.

I sucked in a breath, suddenly terrified. Hallow must have subdued my mind earlier, to keep me from sensing the depths of his vileness, but whatever he'd done to mute his usual predatory energy had shifted and the thing pressing himself against me was now horrifying and alien. The ancient vampire's power washed over everyone.

My gaze slid to Maxie, whose eyes were wide, her lips parted. She sat limply, her shoulders slumped, still entranced. Victoria remained locked in her own silent world.

Devereux pounded against the invisible forcefield, his expression a mixture of rage, fear and grief. The cacophony from the vampires around him had reached eardrum-shattering levels.

Hallow cupped my breasts, squeezing gently, his voice, soft silk in my ear, the resonance relaxing my muscles and disarming my resistance. 'Let's begin.'

He continued stroking me, whispering psychotic endearments, and as he spoke, my mind began to fragment. My perception split and I clearly saw in my psyche the two now-familiar aspects of myself, standing together in my inner world, waiting. The part I thought of as my professional self – reserved, shy, even cautious – was diminishing in size. I – who was I? – wanted to call out to her, to warn her she'd been deceived, but my vocal cords weren't functioning.

The primitive aspect, Lust, stepped forward, shining with raw energy. She responded to Hallow's unspoken invitation, excited to become whatever he demanded of her, and I experienced that same dissonant sensation as before: being both parts of myself at the same time, this time knowing the primitive was about to take control.

Hallow spun me around to face him. He stared into my eyes and his irises began to flicker and then swirl. My knees softened. The sounds of the room receded and the temperature warmed.

Like an hourglass flipped upside down, I transitioned from one personality to the other inside myself. It was a curious sensation, and I found myself simultaneously revelling in the growing strength of one aspect while grieving the decline of the other. Reality began to lose its crisp edges, morphing into an altered state.

Is this a dream?

He smiled.

I studied his face, which had become even more beautiful, more unearthly. His sculpted features, full lips and lustrous hair fascinated me, and all I could think about was touching him, tracing his naked skin under my hands.

In answer to my thought, Hallow pulled his shirt off in one seamless movement. His soft hair flowed down his body and I buried my fingers in it, sliding the long, dark strands across his muscular, pale chest.

He wrapped his arms around me and brought his lips to mine. A wave of heat pulsed through me, creating an odd melting sensation, as if my very skin were dissolving. I felt myself merge with Hallow as his aura consumed mine. Intense sensations rocketed through me and I heard myself scream – I recognised the sound, but I knew it couldn't be coming from my physical mouth, since my lips were still pressed to Hallow's. My heart pounded double-time, the rhythm so hard and fast I expected the sharp pain that would signal an impending coronary, but it didn't come. Bright images, like a film on fast-forward, bombarded my brain: scenes of death and destruction, visions of bloodless corpses and ancient graveyards. Were these Hallow's memories?

He deepened the kiss, sending electricity pulsing through my frame. I wasn't sure if my muscles spasmed or if I only imagined they did. He slid his tongue into my mouth and I tasted blood.

Then he suddenly disengaged; he reared back and stared at me for a few seconds, his eyes exerting an almost-physical pull, and without thinking, I raised my chin, exposing the throbbing vein in my neck.

Fast as a serpent, he struck.

In that moment, a door slammed in my psyche, locking away the only part of me with any hope of resisting the beautiful monster, once again sealing her in the soundproof glass cage.

I shuddered in orgasmic bliss. The commonsense, rational part of me could no longer interfere and the primitive self was enraptured. My entire being ached with need. As Hallow sucked on my vein, my body convulsed, one climax building into another.

When he lifted his bloody mouth, I groaned and raised my neck again in invitation, already craving what only he could give me.

He chuckled. 'That was only the prelude. The finalé is yet to come.' He tugged my sweater over my head and tossed it onto the rugs covering Victoria. 'Turn around so your ex-lover can see what is no longer his.' I slowly faced the hole in the wall where Devereux stood. A sad expression shadowed his gorgeous face. I had forgotten he was there, but as soon as I saw him, I smiled and waved. He was so pretty – I didn't see any reason why he shouldn't come and take part in the fun.

Hallow unhooked my bra and I shook it off, happy to be free of it, oblivious to my nakedness.

He stroked my breasts and pinched the nipples, making me moan with pleasure.

As he slid his hands across the chain of my protective necklace, he groaned. 'Oh yes – such powerful magic in this trinket.' He clasped the silver pentagram in his hand. 'And it would work beautifully, if I were merely what Devereux believes I am.' He laughed. 'But I'm not!' He tugged hard on the chain and the necklace came free in his hand.

'Hey – that hurt!' I yelled, raising a hand to rub the welt at the back of my neck.

He threw the necklace across the room.

Still massaging the sore skin, I glanced down at Maxie. She'd raised herself onto her knees. Her brows were contracted, her lips a tight, thin line. I couldn't understand why she was so upset. We were all going to be together, weren't we?

Distant noises floated into my ears. Devereux appeared

to move in slow motion, exaggerating his enraged expression. Why was everyone so angry?

Hallow unfastened my jeans and started to push them down my legs, leaving me standing in my white bikini briefs. 'Get rid of them,' he ordered.

I stared at the jeans lodged around my ankles, but I couldn't figure out how to discard them. The portion of my brain that was in charge of such things wasn't reporting for duty. I tried lifting one foot, then the other, but the jeans wouldn't budge. Watching myself march in place made me giggle, and laughing felt so good that I began swinging my hips.

'Stop!'

I froze in place.

Hallow turned to Maxie and barked, 'Help her.'

Maxie crawled around Victoria and knelt in front of me. She pulled my jeans off, one leg at a time, and threw them out of the circle. I leaned over and stroked her hair and her head jerked up. She looked surprised.

My bare feet were so pale against the dark floor. Hadn't I worn shoes? I tried to think about that for a few seconds, but became distracted by Hallow's loud voice.

'Move away.' He kicked out at Maxie, and she flinched and returned to her original location.

'I told you there was fantasy sex in our future.' He smiled at me. '*My* fantasy, of course.' He tugged at the drawstring waist of his flowing trousers and the tie came open. The silky fabric pooled at his bare feet and he stepped out of it.

I was struck by Hallow's fantastic form: white marble skin

over well-toned muscles and a huge erection jutting out from the dark hair between his legs. I couldn't tear my gaze away, nor stop my hand floating in that direction.

He laughed and assumed his favourite spread-legs, fists-on-hips stance. 'Patience, my good doctor – or whoever you are now. I can assure you I am worth waiting for.' He pointed to the filthy mattress. 'Lie down.'

I stretched out on the thin pad, unconcerned about any-thing but persuading Hallow to suck on my neck again. I knew there were other people in the room, but they were only faint blips on my radar now.

'I'm ready! Bloody Marys for everyone!'

Hallow knelt at my feet and said dryly, 'How charming. I'll have to do something about getting the rest of you back – this mindless part of your personality is becoming a mite boring. Who knew your psyche would be so fragile?' He smoothed his hands up my legs, hooked his fingers into the elastic band of my panties and pulled them off. As he crawled up my body, his soft hair sent pleasure ripples along my skin, and when he completely covered me I lifted my head, offering my vein again.

He grabbed my hair, lining my lips up under his. 'Don't skip ahead,' he scolded. 'You'll make me lose my place in this tedious ritual.' He glanced at Victoria. 'If it wasn't for the hag of a witch who originally cursed me, we'd be off to the next adventure by now instead of making me jump through all these ridiculous hoops. Since the crone – who is long dead, and by my hand, I can assure you – stuck her warty nose into my business, turning my usual process into a Wiccan fairy tale, we'll have to accomplish this the slow way. Not that you'll be complaining, of course.'

'But don't you want to bite my neck?' I whined.

He pressed his lips against mine in a rough kiss which lasted only a couple of seconds. 'Shut up and pay attention.'

He licked and kissed his way to my breasts and as he focused on one nipple, then the other, my body trembled. His rumbling chuckle vibrated my stomach as he finally shifted lower, moving glacially slow. He spread my legs and knelt between them. 'Bend your knees,' he ordered.

My body's quivering escalated as my breathing hitched, making my heart flutter in my chest like the wings of a hummingbird. A continuous low moan escaped from my throat.

'Do you freely choose to become my slave, my sweet Kismet?'

I'd just taken a breath to yell, 'Hell, yes!' when Hallow's face slammed into my crotch and something heavy landed on top of me.

'No fucking way!' Tom screamed.

CHAPTER 23

All hell broke loose. I gasped after being squished by an unidentified flying object, and then screamed, before focusing on Hallow and Tom wrestling each other.

'Hey! Come back!' I sat up, pissed off that my fun had been so rudely interrupted, but they ignored me.

In the blink of an eye, Hallow pinned Tom to the ground and grabbed a handful of Tom's hair, exposing his neck. He paused briefly, flashed his long, sharp fangs, then sank them into the frantically pulsing vein. Tom shrieked and wailed, wildly flailing the limbs that weren't trapped under the vampire's body.

Hallow's loud sucking sounds entranced me and I stared, unable to shift my gaze away, until a rush of movement on my other side drew my attention. I was surprised to find Maxie crouched over Victoria and slapping her face, demanding, 'Wake up!'

The white-haired *lýtle* glanced at me before leaping towards one of the four thick wooden spikes that secured the leather straps restraining Victoria. She wiggled the spike back and forth, still trying to rouse the unconscious woman. 'Wake up, damn you – Hallow really is going to replace me with her!' She jerked her head in my direction. 'I agree with your dickhead ex-boyfriend: *no fucking way*! Wake up, Witch, and tell the blond stud how to tear down the magic bubble. Hallow will be pissed off, but he'll get over it and I'll have him all to myself again. Wake. The. Fuck. *Up!*'

Victoria groaned and pulled against the leather straps. Maxie must have loosened the first spike enough because Victoria's arm came free. She coughed, then licked her lips. 'Yes – Devereux,' she mumbled.

While Maxie crawled to the next anchor, Victoria took a deep breath and almost sang some foreign-sounding words, her voice weak, '*Patefacio veneficus, patefacio veneficus.*'

I glanced over at Hallow, who was now licking Tom's neck like a bloody lollipop, then boomeranged my gaze back to Maxie.

'Louder, Witch!' Maxie ordered as she dislodged the spike binding Victoria's other arm. 'Before the master comes out of his blood-trance.' She edged closer. 'This is going to hurt.' She pushed off the rugs, slid her arm under Victoria and heaved her into a sitting position. Victoria gasped with pain. 'Again, Witch! Louder.'

Victoria licked her lips and chanted, '*Patefacio veneficus, patefacio veneficus, patefacio veneficus . . .*'

She paused for breath, but before she could take up the chant again, a deafening crash reverberated from all directions and I saw a blond blur heading towards Hallow, followed by a stampeding herd of vampires.

Tall candles toppled like downed trees as the newcomers swarmed across the room. I watched for a moment to see if anything would catch on fire, but the ground was little more than hard dirt, so there was nothing to ignite.

Devereux pointed at Luna and yelled to the nearest vampire, 'Take her back to The Crypt. I will deal with her later.'

A Jean-Luc Picard look-alike swooped over to Luna, gathered her into his arms and they vanished.

Devereux interrupted Hallow's feast by wrapping his arm around the fiend's neck and pulling him off Tom. The two vampires faced each other, snarling and hissing.

Devereux's undead storm troopers spread out in a loose formation around the combatants, calling out graphic suggestions for subduing the dark-haired bloodsucker. 'Do not interfere,' Devereux roared at his companions. 'He is mine.' He removed his coat in a smooth movement and tossed it behind him. 'You will pay for this, Slayer.'

Hallow spread his bloody lips in an evil grin. He laughed and made a 'come and get me' gesture with his hands. 'This night just keeps getting better,' he announced and leapt at Devereux, lethal fangs extended.

Blood spurted from the bites and gashes they inflicted upon each other. My heart pounding, I sat up to get a better view of the fight, and my gaze caught the limp, bluish-white body sprawled on the floor. Tom didn't look so good – in fact, he looked dead. A strange, sad feeling coursed through me. I tried to shift my attention back to the two vampires, but I couldn't stop staring at Tom. Some distant voice in my head kept insisting I had to do something to save him – *save him? What the hell? How was I supposed to save him?* I was just waiting for one of the gorgeous long-haired guys to finish what Hallow had started.

'Hey!' Maxie said, and I rose to my knees and jerked my head towards her voice. 'What are you doing?' she asked Victoria. She grabbed the witch's hand, which was tugging at the straps tied to her ankles.

'Let go – I need to help him!' Victoria pointed to Tom. 'He's dying—'

'No, he's not dying. He's dead – drained dry. Toast. There's nothing you can do, Glenda.'

'You're *wrong*.' Victoria wrenched her hand away. 'I can still sense him.' She squinted her eyes and stared at Maxie. 'He's more alive than you are – whatever you are. You're not a vampire, but you're not human, either.'

'Yeah, looks can be deceiving.'

'Not to me. I see you – or what's left of you. And I see Hallow, too.' Victoria locked eyes with me. 'I have to make Kismet see before it's too late.' She slid her gaze back to Maxie. 'If you really want to make sure Hallow doesn't claim her so you can keep him for yourself, you'll help me.'

'I did my bit,' Maxie snorted. 'I helped you give Devereux the key to unlock the spell. The rest is up to the blond Sir Galahad and his knights of the round coffin. But just to be clear, I wasn't helping *you*. I was helping *me*.' She gave a bitter laugh and nodded towards me. 'Yeah, as if anything we do will keep her from giving Hallow whatever he wants.

He's been controlling her a lot longer than you think. She's basically one giant libido at this point.'

'I'm not a giant libido.' I planted my hands on my hips. 'I'm just the right size. Why are you two talking about me like I'm not here? What is it you want me to see? *Hey!*' Devereux and Hallow tumbled into me, knocking me face-first to the ground, and my forehead bounced on the hard surface with a jolt of pain. I scrabbled sideways towards Victoria, trying to escape the frenzied fight. She'd managed to dislodge the last two stakes holding her legs and now she rose painfully to her knees.

Devereux yelled to one of his vampires – a refrigerator-sized undead linebacker with a tight cap of wiry black curls named Basil – and pointed at me. 'Move her to safety.' But the second Devereux shifted his attention to Basil, Hallow kicked out at Devereux's shoulder. He struck with such force that Devereux flew through the air and punched a deep indentation in the far wall before he crashed down into a pile of stacked-up furniture. Devereux's bellow of rage was accompanied by the sound of wood splintering.

Time stopped.

Hallow moved unbelievably fast and appeared next to me, dripping blood. Covered in the red liquid, he looked like a cartoon demon. The thick smell made me gag. He wound his wet fingers into my hair and pulled my head tight against his sticky leg, yanking so hard that it felt like my hair was being wrenched out by the roots.

I wailed, 'Ow, dammit – that *hurts*. Let *go*.'

'Shut up,' he snarled. 'We have unfinished business.'

He spun to face Basil, who'd just stepped up beside me, pushed his fingers into the linebacker's chest, and before the huge vampire even had a chance to notice the wound, grabbed Basil's heart and crushed it in his dripping hand.

Basil slammed to the ground.

As his warrior's body disintegrated into dust, Devereux reappeared. Growling, he flung off the tattered remains of his bloody shirt and took a step towards Hallow, then looked down at me and stopped. The other vampires closed in around us.

Hallow tightened his hold on my hair. 'Yes,' he said silkily, 'I thought my hostage might get your attention.' Keeping his eyes on Devereux, he dragged me backwards a couple of feet through a pool of Basil's blood. 'As delightful as this interlude has been, I'm afraid my new slave and I have to complete the ritual and be on our way. Of course, I could simply wait until the sun comes up, watch you and your minions die for the day and then finish you off. You wouldn't feel a thing, but that would be incredibly kind and well, *humane* – of me, and I can't have that. No, better that I allow you to observe while I complete my business with your former significant other, and then I'll destroy you all personally and painfully, the way it should be.'

He tugged me to my feet, wrapped his arm around my waist and snugged me against his body. As soon as he pulled me close, his limp organ stirred to life.

Devereux stared at me and as I met his beautiful eyes, a crackle of energy arced across my forehead. I heard, 'Come to me.'

That sounded like a great plan to me, so I stepped towards him. *Yeah, Fang Boy—*

Hallow yanked me sideways, breaking my eye-contact with Devereux. 'Nice try, my boy, but you simply don't have the juice to override my control of the delightful doctor. And if you keep trying, her mind will simply collapse upon itself – but of course, that's your call. It won't bother me if she's a vegetable. She'll still be able to attract emotions like a magnet, so her mental state is of no concern to me.'

Hallow strengthened his grip and spoke into my ear, and his voice sizzled across my skin. The achingly ecstatic tone melted my bones, slowed my heart rate. I was beyond relaxed. 'Do you choose me, Kismet?'

I wanted to say yes, but I couldn't form the word. My lips wouldn't work. I was unable to make any of my muscles do my bidding.

He shook me roughly. 'Fucking sensitive human! Even my voice is too much for you! *Speak, slave.* Do you freely choose me?'

I coughed, trying to clear my throat, and a hand suddenly reached out and grabbed my leg, shooting a quick burst of electricity through me.

'*Aspicio!*' Victoria screamed.

The strange word hit me like a lightning strike, sending a trembling wave sparking along my skin. I jerked my gaze down to Victoria as she yelled again, louder still, '*Aspicio!*'

Holy shit!

I slid bonelessly out of Hallow's grip and fell to my knees, staring into Victoria's wide eyes.

'See the truth, Kismet! Take my hand and see what I see.' She held out her hand, palm up.

'Silence, Witch!' Hallow commanded. 'I will make sure you remain obedient to me – and this time, there will be no traitorous slaves to intervene.' He reached for her golden curls and Devereux leapt over me. He smashed into Hallow, pushing them both backwards and knocking over more of the tall candleholders, all the while snarling and growling.

Maxie, a silent observer on Victoria's other side, suddenly stood. One of Devereux's vampires moved in to restrain her, clutching her arm in what must have been a painful grip. 'The Master told us not to interfere in his fight with Hallow.' He smiled wide, displaying one perfect fang and a chipped one. 'That includes you – I think you've caused enough trouble for tonight.'

Devereux and Hallow continued their battle behind us to a soundtrack of guttural growls and rumbling hisses and the ripping of flesh and wrenching of bone: grisly background music for the surreal confrontation. The smell of fresh blood saturated the smoky air.

I was staring blankly, unable to move, aware of everything around me but frozen, when Victoria reached over and took both my hands, squeezing hard. '*Aspicio! Excito!*' she cried, and my head flopped back and my mouth gaped open. Then my chin thumped forward onto my chest as Victoria's words reverberated like a cattle-prod to my brain. Electrical impulses radiated through all of my nerve-endings and energy danced along my scalp. My toes cramped.

Slowly, I lifted my head and met her gaze. My eyes felt twice their normal size.

Her expression intense, she leaned in close and whispered, 'Keep hold of my hands and focus on Maxie.'

The worst migraine I'd ever experienced threatened to explode my skull. I blinked and licked my lips, then shot my attention to Maxie, who was struggling to break free of the snaggletooth vampire's grip.

'Stop, Witch!' Maxie yelled. 'Don't do this!'

Maxie was as she always was, right down to her cynical smirk. Her long hair flowed down her body like silky snow; her model's figure was showcased in her tight T-shirt and jeans.

Confused, I turned back to Victoria, not sure what she thought would happen.

She squeezed my hands again, so hard I felt the bones crunch together. '*Aspicio! Excito!*' she repeated, and my body twitched like a frog in a high-school biology class. A loud buzzing filled my ears, like white noise times a thousand. I tried to raise my hands to block the annoying sound, but Victoria held them in a death-grip.

I glanced at Maxie again, and her face blurred. The blue eyes I was accustomed to seeing morphed into green – then brown, then silver – and her features melted, gel-like, creating a double-exposure image. I blinked several times to clear my vision, then opened my eyes as wide as possible, but the ghastly transformation continued until the beautiful woman with the quick smile no longer stood in front of me. Instead I stared, uncomprehending, at a tall, brown, dried-up husk with vaguely human features, except for the empty holes where eyes should be. The figure was surrounded by a murky, dark greeny-grey energy field, bubbling and churning like chemical sludge in a toxic waste tank.

The hideous sight so shocked me that I gasped and slumped back against Victoria, who encircled me with her arms.

'Look at Hallow,' she demanded, and everything slowed. My eyes watered and my vision fuzzed. The pain in my head hammered relentlessly, pressing with such intensity against the bones of my skull that I knew I couldn't possibly survive. I must be dying – this had to be death. Victoria's voice was very far away.

'Kismet! Look at Hallow!' She grabbed my face and angled it towards the two vampires fighting.

Hallow and Devereux floated in the air, their mouths yawning wide, their fangs displayed menacingly. They were both covered with blood from the gashes and lacerations crisscrossing their bodies. For a second I thought Devereux had embedded his powerful fingers into the skin of Hallow's neck, but then Hallow, the beautiful man I'd so desired, faded from my sight, and something unbelievable appeared.

Devereux was levitating inside a massive energy-field filled with thousands of skeletal shapes, all slithering around and through each other like bony serpents, each with huge, bulging eyes. It looked like a vast, loathsome amniotic sac – the fluid thick, nebulous, and toxic – containing the partially formed embryos of a demonic breeder. Or the undigested remains in the distended stomach of a psychic cannibal.

He didn't seem to notice anything out of the ordinary as

his grasping hands floated in a thick, dark, bloody liquid, which made up an inner layer surrounding an emaciated, contorted, charred-black thing in the center.

My attention had been so transfixed by Hallow's grotesque form that it took me a few seconds to realise that Devereux appeared the same as always – maybe his skin was a touch whiter, a shade more corpse-like, but I couldn't see any other changes.

So why was Hallow such a monstrosity?

The soulless creature in the holographic nightmare had no face that I could make sense of, but still it glared at me.

The torment in my head built to a crescendo and I screamed, and suddenly, as if I were watching several movies simultaneously, each featuring one of my scattered sub-personalities, the pictures speeded up. The volume cranked. Certain my head was about to burst into flames, I braced myself to scream again, when it all—

—*stopped*.

There, standing alone on the centre stage of my inner world, waited the part I've spent most of my life considering 'me'. Her eyes were closed. The aspects who had splintered off during Hallow's take-over of my mind wafted in like metaphorical ghosts and merged back into the physical form of the main personality. My psychic skin stretched as if to accommodate the gossamer reintegration.

Lust sauntered over slowly. 'I'm stronger now. You can't sweep me under the carpet. Everything is different.'

She fused into me, and all my puzzle-pieces locked into place.

Heat rushed through my body, and I reeled, as if I'd been hit by a truck. Victoria shook me and yelled again, '*Aspicio! Excito!*' and at her words, something snapped inside me. A lifetime's worth of repressed rage splashed over the crumbling metaphorical dam in my psyche, and suddenly I was drowning in anger, so lost in outrage that I could barely catch my breath. My fists clenched as I thought about all the risks I hadn't taken, in the name of being somebody else's idea of a good girl – the perfect rule-follower.

My mouth went dry with the fury of truths unspoken, desires swallowed. My body shook with the wrath of allowing myself to be bullied and dominated my whole life. I'd become so disempowered, so afraid of my own wisdom that retreating into my intellect was the only safe place. Bitterness rose in my throat, as relentless as fiery magma, building towards eruption.

An unknown darkness awakened inside me.

'Yes, that's it,' Victoria whispered in my ear. 'Feel his blood in your veins – let his evil fuel your resurrection. Turn it against him.'

I opened my eyes in time to see Hallow's form flipping back and forth between the beautiful demon and the metaphysical cancer reaching for me. He'd managed to momentarily stun Devereux and now he rushed over to retrieve me, his *prize.*

He yanked me to my feet and pulled me against his body, which stayed humanoid for only a few seconds this time before the illusion gave way to the grisly aura it had been superimposed upon. I fought against him, jabbing my elbows into his gut, enjoying his grunts of irritation.

Victoria struggled to her feet, thrust her bruised arm into the air, fist closed, and screamed, '*Expugno!*'

The hairs at the back of my neck prickled and chills rippled over my skin. I didn't know what she'd said, but the word rattled the air.

Now that I could see exactly how monstrous Hallow was, my stomach twisted and my skin went clammy. I had to remind myself to breathe while he pressed me against him. I closed my eyes and cringed as I thought about what I was really immersed in. My intuitive radar was wide open now, and I could sense every foul nuance of his alien nature. He was sickeningly obscene.

'Enough of this nonsense.' He grabbed my hair, tugged my head back and exposed my neck. He began repeating the same phrase, over and over, in his enticing, hypnotic voice: 'Do you choose me? Do you choose me? *Do you choose me?*'

I was becoming drowsy, and the edge of my anger was dulling. Several hundred pairs of eyes stared back at me from Hallow's incorporeal death camp. I screamed, my rage rebounding, and forced out the words: 'No! *No!* I don't choose you. *Let. Me. Go!*'

And as I screamed, Devereux tackled Hallow again, sending them both back to the ground. It seemed they'd been fighting for hours, but time had ceased to have any meaning.

My body was shaking now – even if I hadn't been quaking with anger, being naked in the below-freezing temperatures was taking its toll.

The vampires struggled, switching positions every few seconds when one gained dominance over the other. As

Hallow straddled Devereux, his sharp fingernails gouging out flesh from Devereux's neck, his voice rang out. 'I've changed my mind, laddie. You've been a worthy adversary. And I don't know how you managed to shake off my control, but you've become much more trouble than you're worth. Time to put an end to this.' He slid his hand across the floor and picked up one of the stakes that had restrained Victoria. He raised it over Devereux's heart, preparing to strike.

Devereux's vampires lurched towards him, but Devereux roared, 'Get back! He is mine.'

The useless bloodsuckers glanced at each other and stepped away. I couldn't believe they were just going to stand there and watch. The time had come to replace mindless obedience with common sense. Devereux was a force to be reckoned with, but it was insane to think that something as old and freakish as Hallow could be bested by anyone.

Hallow had become the quintessential symbol of every tyrannical person I'd ever allowed to override my free will. He'd put me and everyone I cared about in danger for his own selfish needs, leaving a trail of death and destruction in his wake, and I was not going to have it. I'd finally awakened from a long sleep and I refused to stand by, passively allowing Hallow to complete his foul plan.

We all sensed a turning point approaching. The air crackled with energy. Maxie managed to free herself from her dentally challenged captor and took a step toward the bloody battle. Except for her aura, which was still thick and dark, she'd transformed back into the beautiful woman I'd befriended.

After watching Hallow flash back and forth continuously between his two forms, I discovered if I focused on the likeness I was more used to, he would stay like that – but if I softened my gaze and viewed him with my peripheral vision, the horror show emerged. It was definitely less hideous dealing with the monster in his human shape.

Devereux had managed to slough off the demon sitting on his chest and they were both on their feet again, circling, Hallow brandishing the spike.

A couple of feet behind me, Victoria chanted.

'Bring me the witch!' Hallow yelled at Maxie, who startled at the harsh sound of his voice.

She pivoted like a robot, stomped over to Victoria and backhanded her with such ferocity that she fell back on the ground, unconscious. Maxie grabbed her arm and started dragging her towards Hallow.

Shocked by the savagery of Maxie's assault, I jumped in front of her and pressed my palms against her chest. 'Let go of her, Maxie,' I pleaded. 'You don't have to do this – don't give in. You're more than just his slave.'

'You've seen what I am.' She stared at me with wide, glazed eyes. 'I serve at his pleasure. I can't fight him.' She shook her head. 'I don't want to.' She raised her fist, reared back and hit me in the jaw.

The blow took me down. I'd never been struck in the face before and I was shocked at the violence. The punch radiated pain across the bones of my face and stunned me. I sat, dazed, on the cold earth for several seconds, rubbing my jaw, opening and closing my mouth, trying to gauge the damage.

Maxie dumped Victoria near Hallow and gave her a vicious kick to the ribs – and seeing her attack my friend shook me out of my stupefaction. Heart pumping, adrenalin surging, I leapt to my feet, took a running jump and landed on Maxie's back. I wrapped my arm around her neck and pulled hard, and I must've caught her by surprise because she lost her balance and we both crashed down a couple of feet away from Victoria.

Old ideas about my physical limitations combusted in the raging fire of my anger. I savoured the dark satisfaction of having a stranglehold on her throat. Who knew aggression could be so good?

But Maxie was by far the more experienced fighter. She sloughed me off, straddled my hips and pinned me beneath her. She braced my wrists over my head and smirked, keen intelligence once again shining from her eyes, replacing the entranced gaze she'd had moments before. Our unexpected trip to the ground must have altered the zombie-like trance Hallow inflicted on her.

I struggled, bucking my hips, and actually managed to shift her off my lower body and free one arm before she regained control.

'Gee, Doc, I'm impressed.' She raised her eyebrows. 'A little of Hallow's blood flowing in your veins and you turn into Wonder Woman.' Her expression became pensive and she leaned down to whisper, 'Your boyfriend's a little busy and I reckon he won't be riding to your rescue tonight, so I'm going to have to change the game plan. I guess I'll have to get rid of you permanently. Hallow will punish me, but we'll both get over it. He needs me.'

Delusional thinking. She needs a twelve-step programme, like Vampire Slaves Anonymous.

'He might need you, but he doesn't care about you – you mean nothing to him.' I laughed, trying to goad her into a strong reaction. 'You're an empty husk – why would he want you when he could have me? For a smart woman, you're pretty dense.'

She didn't disappoint. Her eyes narrowed and she gathered both my wrists into one hand.

Bull's-eye.

She reached over and grabbed another of the stakes that had held Victoria, pointed it over my heart and laughed. 'Say good-bye, Ethel.'

I twisted my body with enough force to bounce her off my hips, making her release my wrists, then rolled on top of her and grabbed for the stake, hoping to wrest it from her grip. We grappled. Evenly matched due to my newly enhanced physical strength, we both held onto a portion of the wood as it angled between us.

'How arousing,' Hallow crooned from above us.

Maxie lifted off my body and released her grasp on the stake, but I held on. Having the sharp weapon in my hand added to my illusion of control – sort of like carrying an umbrella in a hurricane.

We both stood, staring at the madman.

Hallow spoke directly to Maxie, his expression dark. 'Kill

my new slave and suffer a fate much worse than death, old woman.'

He'd apparently found a way to escape Devereux long enough to grab Victoria's unconscious body from the dirt; he was cuddling her body against him. Quick as a cobra, he pierced her neck with his long, sharp fangs and drank deeply before raising his crimson mouth from the holes in her skin. He licked his lips. 'Ah, yes. Elixir of the gods. The perfect pick-me-up when battling a jealous bloodsucker.'

Devereux stood in front of Hallow, unmoving and silent. His blood-covered chest was still, breathing unnecessary. His gaze locked on his adversary.

'I'll have to reconsider my plans to be rid of the old in favour of the new,' Hallow observed as he studied Maxie and me. 'In fact, I've decided to take this voluptuous witch along for the ride too – after all, she *is* powerful, and one simply can't have too much blood available.'

He bent down as if he were dipping Victoria in a macabre dance, preparing to sink fangs into her neck again.

I couldn't let that happen.

He turned his back to me and I lunged, my spike poised to impale – but with unnatural speed, Maxie streaked by me and leapt in front of Hallow. My momentum had decided the course of action and there was no time to pull back. The spike pierced her skin, slicing through bone into organs. Vibrations radiated up through the wooden weapon.

I screamed, 'Maxie, no!'

CHAPTER 24

Maxie's body crumpled to the ground, blood gushing from the gaping hole between her breasts.

My stomach churned and I fought back vomit as her physical form disintegrated within seconds, leaving a semi-transparent puddle of dark greeny-grey sludge that oozed like an extraterrestrial life form into Hallow's death-aura.

Hallow retracted his fangs from Victoria's neck, pushed her away and snapped into a rigid posture, his spine ramrod-straight. He shrieked, the sound rising into the register probably only heard by dogs, and his face transformed into a mask of fear and outrage. He tore at his hair and growled. Blood dripped from his fangs.

Devereux's arm slid around my waist from behind as he pulled me backwards, away from Hallow. 'Come. It is over now, my love.'

'Over?' Shock and confusion overwhelmed me. 'How could

it be over? Insane Hallow is still here.' Did Devereux think Hallow cared that Maxie was dead? That he'd stop his homicidal behaviour to mourn her passing?

Victoria opened her eyes and groaned at Hallow's feet.

Devereux freed his arm and wrapped me in a thick blanket that suddenly appeared before pulling me against his bloody chest again. I didn't know where the warm cover had come from – Devereux must have mentally contacted one of his vampires – but I wasn't going to turn it down. A muscular male popped up next to us and hurried over to Victoria. He removed his own heavy woollen cloak and threw it over the wounded witch before lifting her into his arms.

'Take her to the penthouse,' Devereux ordered.

'No, Devereux – wait. Not yet. I need to witness the end of this nightmare,' Victoria urged, her voice barely audible.

At Devereux's curt nod, Victoria's rescuer moved to stand beside us.

My head spun as I remembered the wet, thick sound of the spike penetrating Maxie's chest. I couldn't have killed her – no, this had to be another horrible nightmare. I'd reacted without thinking when I went for Hallow – I couldn't stand watching him suck the life's blood from Victoria. But why had Maxie got in the way? I didn't really need to ask that. I knew the answer: she couldn't help herself. Protecting the source of her addiction was all that mattered to her. But after her years with him, she had to know that Hallow couldn't be killed. Had she *wanted* to die?

I didn't understand why we were all just standing there, staring at the madman. 'Why is the fighting over?' I whispered to Devereux, fear clenching my stomach. 'Tell me what's happening.'

He pressed me closer. 'Watch.'

I made myself stare at Hallow. I'd been so caught up in remorse about Maxie's death that I hadn't noticed what was happening to him.

His terrified face reminded me of *The Scream*. His silver eyes were abnormally wide and his high-pitched keening wail had descended the frequency scale and could once again be heard by human ears. While I watched, his beautiful body – or rather, the image he'd projected – began to blister and swell, as if he had been dipped in acid. Within seconds the familiar façade was gone and all that remained was the grotesque spectre.

Frightened by the fog of impending doom permeating the air, I glanced up at Devereux again. My mouth went dry. 'Am I hallucinating?'

He gave me a gentle squeeze. 'The Slayer has lost his tether to the physical world.'

What?

Devereux rubbed his cheek against my hair. 'From what I just read from his mind, he cannot remain without a slave to feed from. You have bested him.'

'*Bested* him?' I said, distracted by the horror show in front of me. 'You aren't making any sense – I don't understand any of this.'

Hallow's vast, malignant aura pulsed and writhed, oscillating around the distorted, twitching thing in the bloody centre that looked like a gangrenous cell. The holographic image shifted as I studied it from slightly different angles. Hundreds – no, thousands – of bony creatures swam or floated in thick, slimy liquid – or maybe it was heavy, noxious air. All the lost souls trapped in Hallow's metaphysical hell stared at me, wide-eyed and desperate, somehow communicating terror without having actual faces to express anything. Lightning-like energy arced throughout the putrid sac.

The entire energy field began to spread, mimicking the shockwave around a nuclear explosion, and my heart pounded as the edge of the toxic mortuary rolled towards me like a foul tsunami. I raised my arms up to cover my face and braced myself for the impact as I waited to be swept inside Hallow's psychic abyss—

—but nothing happened.

I lowered my arms to discover the grisly aura deflating, almost as if it were in the throes of birth contractions. As it transitioned from one dimension to another, it pushed itself through an invisible fissure, becoming translucent. A face – the only one I'd seen in there – floated into the remaining section of the sac and as I watched, Maxie's familiar form appeared. She gave a sad smile before dissolving back into the sea of death.

With a deep rumble, the Hallow-thing vanished.

A heavy silence fell in the underground asylum.

What had just happened? If others hadn't been present to witness the incomprehensible delirium, I would have feared for my sanity. A chill ran through my body. Could it really be over?

A deep voice boomed, 'Master, the human is near death. Do you wish me to transport him to the penthouse?'

The human?

I gasped and stared towards the vampire squatting next to a very-blue Tom. We'd all forgotten him, and now he was freezing to death on the chill ground.

'Tom – please, no!' I broke free of Devereux's arms and ran to him. Even through the haze of my previously altered state, I recalled the fight between my rarely courageous friend and the monster. He'd tried his best to save me.

Devereux knelt down next to me and hugged me against him. 'I can barely hear his heartbeat. He has little time left.'

My body went cold inside the warm blanket. I grabbed Devereux's arm. 'Can't you do something? Transport him to a hospital? Cast a spell to heal him?' For the second time that night, I cried, but these tears were not caused by anyone's influence; they were pure grief.

Devereux touched his head against mine. 'I am not able to bring back the dead, my love. I am sorry.'

I jerked away and turned to him, excited. I grasped his arm, my fingers pressing into his cold skin. 'Yes, you are – you *are* able to bring back the dead! He wanted to be a vampire – you can transform him. *You can!* Please, Devereux – I don't want to lose him this way. There has been enough death and misery tonight.'

Devereux laid a hand on Tom's chest and closed his eyes, then he lifted Tom's hand and met my gaze. 'I would not do this, not even for you, if I had not seen him take extraordinary action on your behalf. You must understand that there is no guarantee. Not everyone survives a turning of this sort. He is weak already, and he might not withstand the challenge.' He stroked his finger down my face. 'Are you sure you wish me to make your friend one of the undead? He will not be the man you knew, not for a long time – perhaps never again.'

No, I didn't want him to transform my oldest friend into a bloodsucking creature of the night, but since Tom had made his desires known, and he was nearly dead already, I didn't see what other choice I had. I simply wasn't ready to let go, not when Tom was dying because of me.

'Yes,' I whispered, 'I'm sure.'

Devereux stood and spoke to the vampire still crouched at Tom's head. 'The dawn is less than an hour away. Take him to the penthouse and prepare him. I shall follow.'

The vampire gathered Tom into his arms and they vanished.

Then Devereux ordered the vampire holding a limp Victoria, 'Take her.'

As they vanished, I stared down at the ritual circle in which Victoria had been held prisoner. The colourful symbols and letters looked so benign in the remaining candlelight, but the last few hours had been a nightmare – one I would never forget. Even while the sane part of me had been locked away, I'd still been observing everything – every hideous detail was seared into my brain.

Maxie was dead.

I'd killed her.

My mind was numb, empty. 'How can I simply go about

my normal life as if the last few days haven't happened?' I asked myself, out loud.

'Do not torture yourself, Kismet.' Devereux enfolded me in his arms again. 'The responsibility for the death and destruction of the recent past can be laid at Hallow's doorstep alone. It was his abuse of his *lýtle* that caused her willingness to die.' He tightened his grip. 'Come. I must attend to your friend before the sun rises, and you must sleep.'

I relaxed my head against his chest, closed my eyes and felt the familiar sensation of freefall. Soft air blew against my face as we transported from the hidden gentlemen's club under the streets of Denver to Devereux's high-rise penthouse. When Devereux released me, I opened my eyes.

He stepped in front of me, looking like a war casualty. His hair was so saturated with blood, it appeared brown instead of blond, but nothing could dim the brilliant green-blue of his eyes. 'My staff is here to assist you in my absence. As always, my home is yours.' He held my face in his hands and gently kissed my lips. 'I will do what I can for Tom.'

He disappeared.

Several unfamiliar women swarmed towards me, startling me – they'd been so quiet, I hadn't noticed them. I pulled the ends of the blanket tighter around myself.

A tall, elegant, dark-skinned woman stepped forwards and offered a warm smile. No fangs. 'Welcome, Doctor Knight. I'm Carolyn. You must be exhausted. Devereux said you usually prefer a shower, but we thought, after the night you've had, you might enjoy soaking in the tub, so both are available. We've also prepared food and drink for you, when you're ready.' She tilted her head, waiting for my response.

'Are you vampires?' They didn't feel like vampires to me, but I wasn't sure how keen my awareness was at the moment. It would be a while before I trusted my instincts again.

'No.' She chuckled. 'Garden-variety humans. Devereux has hundreds of human employees, although not all of them are aware of his true nature. We' – she pointed to her companions – 'have been with him for years. He's a wonderful man.'

She didn't refer to Devereux as master. That was one point in her favour. I didn't ask what they were employed to do.

'He also asked me to get your permission to call the clients you have scheduled for today and tell them you have a personal emergency and will need to reschedule. Is that all right?'

My first reaction was to insist I'd see my clients, but that idea quickly deflated. A traumatised, grief-stricken therapist certainly wouldn't be at the top of her game, so for all intents and purposes, I was temporarily useless to them. 'Yes, thank you. If you would tell them I'll call later . . .' I paused. 'Just out of curiosity, when exactly did Devereux tell you all this? He's been with me for the last several hours.'

'Devereux communicates with me telepathically. He told me shortly before you arrived here. Shall we go?' she asked.

I started to say I didn't need any help – that I could run my own bath and find my own food – but I realised that simply wasn't true. I was exhausted, and my heart was so filled with pain, I could barely breathe. Help would actually be great.

Carolyn led the way and I shuffled along behind her with the other women bringing up the rear, like an impromptu royal procession.

After a hot bath, a small meal and a glass of wine, I let them tuck me in.

Sleep sucked me under.

The smell of coffee once again caressed my nostrils and enticed me to rejoin the land of the living. I was beginning to associate Devereux's penthouse with the aroma of high-quality java.

I put on a comfortable bathrobe and wandered out to the dining area, expecting to find another breakfast buffet, and I wasn't disappointed.

Victoria sat at the end of the table, drinking a cup of tea. She was dressed in one of her lovely goddess gowns and she smiled as I approached. 'I could get used to this.' She chuckled as she flicked a hand towards the feast.

I hurried over and pulled out the chair next to hers and sat. 'Are you all right?' Her neck and cheek were a mass of multi-coloured bruises and her lip was split and swollen. My stomach tightened in anger as I confronted the damage Hallow had inflicted on her.

'Yes – I'm better than I would've expected, considering.' She sounded surprisingly perky. She patted my hand and added, 'And I'll be even better by tonight, after my coven has performed a healing ritual on me.' She took a sip of tea.

'You're welcome to come, you know. I think it would be good for you to deepen your occult knowledge and practice your skills. And we could help heal that terrible bruise on the side of your face.'

I stared at her until she sighed and dropped the false cheerfulness. 'Okay, it was *horrible*. I feel defiled and broken – *slimed*. I'm almost sorry he's dead – or whatever he is – because now I can't take my revenge. I can't make him *pay* for what he did to me.' Her breathing was coming fast and ragged now, and her face was flushed. 'I'm left with all these layers of hatred, with nowhere to put them.'

She started to cry, and I scooted closer and hugged her.

We stayed like that, silently holding each other, for several minutes, until Victoria sniffed and wiped her eyes on her sleeve. She shifted back in her seat, and I took that as a cue to give her more space, so I moved my chair back and poured myself a cup of coffee while I waited for her to continue.

'When he came into the lobby yesterday morning–' She stopped, then said, 'Was it really only yesterday? Anyway, I was so shocked by what he really was that I hesitated too long. I should have pressed the alarm button under my desk, but my brain froze. I couldn't think. And before I even realised, he'd transported me out of there into that disgusting, freezing-cold underground pit.' She gave a cynical laugh. 'I did manage to fight him off for about two seconds before he entrapped me with those demonic eyes. I think I pulled out a handful of his hair.'

'Yes,' I said softly, 'I found one of the strands on your desk. That's how we knew he had you.'

She stared out one of the large windows framing a pan-oramic view of snow-covered mountain peaks. 'I was so afraid his plan would succeed, that he'd control you to the point where you'd do what he wanted – it almost worked. He's incredibly powerful.'

Fear washed through me. 'What do you mean? You said he *is* powerful. He's been destroyed, hasn't he?'

She brought her gaze to mine. 'I don't think whatever he is *can* be destroyed. He lost his connection to the physical plane when Maxie sacrificed herself before he could claim you, and I want to believe he'll exist for millennia like that, as that abhorrent energy field we saw, unable to take form in our world . . . but he's like no other. He defies everything I know about the laws of physics and the nature of vam-pirism. All we can do is strengthen and educate ourselves.' She took my hand. 'I was serious about inviting you to my coven. We are a large circle of strong, dynamic witches, healers, seers and teachers. You need to acknowledge and sharpen your abilities.'

'Abilities?' I frowned. 'I'm so tired of hearing that word, Victoria. I just don't understand – I know I'm intuitive and empathic, but I don't consider those to be special things – they're normal, everyone has them to some degree. And I can see a few ghosts – but so what? What are these *powers* I'm supposed to have?' I paused, then said, 'Hallow said I'm an emotional vampire.'

'Not powers,' Victoria said, shaking her head vigorously. '*Abilities*. Powers implies something beyond the range of the species.' She smiled at my confused expression. 'You know, like comic book superheroes, shooting fire or webs from your fingertips, bending steel with your eyeballs, being able to fly, that sort of thing. You simply have an exceptional amount of your particular abilities. For example, everyone can sing, right?'

I was on safer ground now; I knew where she was going with the story because I'd used this example myself to explain intuition to clients. 'Well, most people have average singing abilities, some can't carry a tune to save their souls, and a few have extraordinary talent. It's the same for everything: all vampires have the same abilities – mind-reading, tele-portation, immortality – to a greater or lesser degree. Devereux has added talents thanks to his magical lineage – but none of those things are *powers*, per se.'

She sipped her tea. 'People misunderstand witches, too. We're often accused of having powers when we really have skills, abilities, talents, wisdom, and, in some cases, common religious beliefs. You told me you learned about Wicca in a comparative religions class in graduate school. See? Nothing strange about that.'

'Okay – but so what?' I still didn't get it. 'Being empathic and intuitive comes in handy with my work, but sometimes it's a curse, sensing things I don't want to know. What I don't get is why so many vampires are interested in my so-called *abilities*?'

It was her turn to shrug. 'I only know what Devereux told me. You're a gifted human. That's what he said when he first met you, that something about the level of your innate tal-ents is unusual. He suspects that you've accumulated them over many lifetimes – a bit like adding chords to a basic melody.' She laughed at my expression. 'Yes, I know, you're not at all comfortable with the notion of reincarnation yet – but after all you've seen, isn't it silly to resist something as widely accepted as past lives? Many ancient religions take reincarnation for granted.' She pointed a finger at me. 'Put your Inner Scientist to work on it and do some research.'

I chuckled as she continued, 'The way Devereux described it was that there's something about the texture of your abilities that enhances him. You act like a crystal, concentrating and expanding energy – or maybe a tuning fork, holding all the notes in his aural spectrum. Ask him. He'll tell you.'

'Crystals, reincarnation, vampires, wizards? Tuning fork? Aural spectrum? The texture of my abilities? How much more weirdness is there? I'll be banned from the psychologists' club for sure.'

She laughed, and laughed a bit more as my stomach growled loudly, and I realised I'd been sitting in front of all that delicious food without eating any of it. I helped myself to a bagel and some fruit and chewed thoughtfully for a few minutes. There was another question I hadn't asked her yet.

'Before I killed Maxie and Hallow went wherever he went – I know—' I held up my hand in a 'stop' gesture in response to her mouth opening. 'I know I didn't kill her intentionally, but I *did* kill her. I have to accept that.' I sat up straighter, trying to calm my heartbeat and rein in my mounting anxiety. 'But before that happened, you said something about me using his blood flowing in my veins. And Maxie said I drank more of his blood than I knew about. Since he's gone, does that mean the effects of his blood are gone, too?'

I must have looked as frightened as I felt. 'I wish I knew,' she said, smiling compassionately. 'My guess is that whatever changes his blood made to your psyche, your physiology and your abilities, they'll be permanent, but you're still in charge of how they manifest in your life. I hate to sound like a broken record, but it's Devereux you need to ask. He is the only one who could possibly advise you.'

She was right, of course.

We ate in silence for a few minutes and then she pushed her chair back from the table and stood. 'I need to return to work – to take control of my life again.' She grinned. 'I know I'm not irreplaceable, but things certainly do get chaotic when I'm out of the loop!' She rested her palm against the side of my face where Maxie hit me. 'We're in this together, my friend. We'll figure it out.' She leaned down and kissed my forehead. 'I'll see you tomorrow.'

She limped slowly out of the room and headed to the elevator.

I topped up my coffee and sadly studied the beautiful scenery through the glass. Nothing would ever be the same for me. No matter what long-term effects Hallow's blood had on me, I was different. I'd seen too much. Victoria had been right about that, too. I couldn't hide behind my professional defences any longer.

So many things had happened. Tom was dead, or in the process of becoming a vampire. Devereux's addicted assistant, Luna, had proved to be less than trustworthy. My brief friendship with Maxie had ended tragically. I'd been the target of yet another mentally ill vampire, and he might still show up anytime. My blood was contaminated by something that had no logical description.

What if Devereux doesn't have any answers?

After my talk with Victoria, I dressed in comfortable jeans and the blue blouse Devereux had painted in the mysterious portrait he had created of me some eight hundred years ago before driving back to my townhouse. I desperately needed to create some semblance of normality.

Rescheduling clients, answering e-mails, catching up on paperwork and doing household tasks filled the remainder of the late afternoon, and reminded me of life before vampires. I'd just poured myself a glass of wine and clicked on a rerun of a Harry Potter movie when Devereux appeared in my living room.

His face and body were flawless, as always, giving no hint of the ferocious battle he'd waged less than a day earlier. His shiny, platinum hair flowed down his chest, begging to be touched. He wore a snug aqua silk T-shirt, a perfect match for his flashing eyes. He was a total feast for the senses.

He opened his arms and I rushed into them, allowing myself to be held for a few seconds – to feel safe, to pretend the events of the past few days had been a bad dream.

We finally pulled apart and he cradled my face in his hands, leaned in and pressed his warm, soft lips against mine. I opened my mouth for him and he slid his tongue inside. A rush of heat flowed through my body, and my heart raced. It was so wonderful to simply kiss him because I wanted to.

He broke the kiss and stroked his hand along the colourful bruise on my cheek. I hadn't even tried to cover it up.

'How are you?' he asked, his voice gentle.

'Better now.' I smiled and tugged him over to the couch. We sat silently for a few seconds while I avoided asking what I was afraid to hear the answer to. 'What about Tom?' I said at last.

'We performed the ritual of transformation for him. I gave him my blood. What happens now is unknown. He will either pass through death and be reborn, or he will truly die. We will not discover the outcome until his soul makes its choice.'

'Thank you, Devereux.' Relieved, I leaned over and kissed his cheek. 'I know you wouldn't have tried to save him if it weren't for me.'

'There is nothing I would not do for you.' He smiled. 'In fact, I wish to grant another of your wishes.' He stood in a fluid motion and extended his hand to me. 'If you will indulge me?'

My expression must have reflected my doubts about whether or not I was ready for any more surprises, because he laughed. 'All is well, truly. You will enjoy this.'

He extended his hand again and I took it, letting him pull me up from the couch.

'You might wish to wear a wrap. We are going to a high altitude.'

I just stared and he laughed again, his eyes sparkling.

'Wait. I shall fetch it.' He vanished and was gone a few seconds before returning with my heaviest coat. He held it out, waiting for me to slide my arms in. I couldn't figure out the danger, if there was any, so I did as he asked. My suspicious nature wasn't likely to change any time soon.

'Excellent.' He slid his arm around my waist and we travelled, cold air flowing against my face.

CHAPTER 25

We landed in an extraordinary room.

My mouth fell open as I scanned the huge space. I'd never seen anything so astounding.

It was a palace carved out of stone. Gorgeous paintings and beautiful tapestries adorned the walls, interspersed with colourful illustrated tiles and gemstone murals. Beautiful sculptures, some that looked very old, anchored the room. Plush rugs on top of some sort of thick matting softened the floor. The room was illuminated by tall candles in ornate holders. A spicy aroma wafted from incense-burners, and a fire blazed in a magnificent fireplace. Classical music floated from invisible speakers.

My gaze was drawn by a huge gilded four-poster bed on one side of the room and a shiny black coffin on the other. I moved around the cavern and had to swallow a few times before I could speak. 'Where are we?'

'You wanted to know where I spend my daylight hours.'

Yes! He's finally opening up.

'You live in a cave?' *Maybe he really is the vampiric Batman.*

The corners of his lips curved. 'No, not a cave, per se, although we are deep inside a mountain.' He waved his hand through the air. 'This is my private place. It has been so for centuries. Sometimes I come here to be alone. Or to time-travel.'

Yikes. A time-travelling hideaway. I am so out of my league.

'Are we near Zephyr's vampire library in South America? That's inside a mountain, too.'

And what an incredible place – books, papers, antiquities and entire buildings stored in an area vast enough to boggle the human mind.

'Zephyr's collection *is* amazing. But no, I created this fortress in what were formerly the Druid lands of my mortal birth in Europe.'

My throat tightened, holding back all the words I wanted to say. I was touched and flattered that he'd finally shown me his secret lair, overwhelmed that he was willing to be so vulnerable to me.

'Well, then I'd better thank you. This time for trusting me.' I peeled off the heavy coat and dropped it. Then I walked to him, looped my arms around his neck and kissed him.

He pulled me close and deepened the kiss.

We stood with our mouths pressed together for a couple of minutes before my head spun and I broke away. My heart pounded so fast and loud I could barely catch my breath. He smiled, well aware of my reaction and his ability to cause it.

He's a walking aphrodisiac.

Needing a few seconds to regroup, I strolled over to the sleek black coffin. Even though he couldn't entrance me any more under most circumstances, he still held the key to my libido. All the keys. But after my experience with the primitive part of myself, I was no longer sure what would happen if I let myself become overly aroused. It was definitely time to change the subject.

'Do you sleep in here?'

He joined me, caressing the smooth lid with his pale long-fingered hand. 'Sometimes, if I am feeling nostalgic. Mostly I enjoy the comfort of the bed.'

'You use the bed if you have company?' I didn't know why I asked that question, but since I had, my stomach tightened in anticipation of what he would say.

His expression darkened, his brows contracting in the middle. He took my hand. 'I have never brought anyone here in all the centuries since I created this place. You are the first. The only.'

That stunned me. I encircled his waist with my arms and pressed myself against him. 'I'm honoured.' And I really was – honoured and touched that he was willing to let me inside his defences.

He kissed the top of my head. 'I have wanted to bring you here since we met, but there was always one drama or another preventing us from taking time for ourselves.' He scooped me up into his arms and walked us to the bed. 'Let us be comfortable.'

That sounded like a fabulous idea to me.

He deposited me into the exquisite softness of the multicoloured duvet, then quickly crawled on top of me. His soft hair tumbled onto my face before he flicked the sweet-smelling mane behind him and licked my lips with his warm tongue.

I opened my mouth in invitation and groaned.

We kissed for a long time, stroking each other's bodies and shifting positions for better contact. Pressing our lips together triggered the same exquisite reaction I'd had before – the sensation of us melting into each other, body and soul.

Eventually he raised his head and gazed deeply into my eyes. 'I want to make love to you.'

'Oh, yes!' I wiggled underneath him, causing his erection to twitch. This would be the perfect distraction from the insanity of the recent past. Surely I could enjoy our regular intimacy without losing control of myself. At least I hoped so.

Seconds crept by, but instead of getting on with things as I expected, he continued to stare at me.

'What?' He definitely had something on his mind. I hoped he wasn't going to talk about that whole 'mate' issue, because I wasn't ready. He hadn't been nearly forthcoming enough about that topic. I had no idea what I would be getting myself into, and until I did, there would be no more metaphysical ceremonies.

He kissed the tip of my nose. 'You have been through a horrible experience. Your mind and body were taken over. By all rights you should be traumatised, but you appear calm. Are you repressing your true feelings?'

That was a good question. I thought for a moment. While it was true that I'd been numb and exhausted most of today, now I felt . . . neutral. Not depressed or anxious, as I might have expected under the circumstances. 'Calm,' I said. 'That's a good word. I don't think I'm repressing anything, and I'm usually pretty good at stuffing whatever I don't want to face. Maybe because as terrible as it was to be under Hallow's control, he never really made me do anything totally outside my nature. I was simply an uninhibited version of myself, and I probably needed to cast off some of my introverted shackles, anyway. I actually feel pretty steady.'

'Perhaps that is Hallow's influence, as well. His blood.'

'Maybe. I don't have a clue about how he changed me long-term. I won't pretend to be blasé about that, but for tonight, I'm glad to be here with you and am ready for some up-close-and-personal time.'

'That is music to my ears.' He sat up, pulled off his boots and tossed them onto the floor. Then he stood and gazed down at me, an unfamiliar – almost hungry – expression on his face. 'Since that is the case, I would like to share something new with you.'

'New?' *What now? More paranormal delirium?* 'Well, don't keep me in suspense.'

He gave a slow blink. 'I was recently surprised and pleased to discover that there is a lustful part of you that enjoys being restrained. That appreciates sexual games, and likes to play . . . rough.'

My cheeks warmed. Even though I hadn't sorted out those desires yet – or the sexually aggressive part of me that liked that sort of thing – I couldn't deny them. If he only knew what I *really* fantasised about . . . At least he wasn't inviting more naked vampires to perform a ritual around the bed. I hoped. 'That's true. I was surprised by those urges too.'

He tugged his shirt over his head, and threw it across a chair, baring his sculpted, smooth chest. 'And were you pleased?'

Even without the enticing view of his muscles, the sensuous tone of his voice sent shivers down my body. My nipples hardened and my toes curled. I sat up. 'The jury's still out about that. Why?'

He lowered his voice. 'You have often mentioned the fact that I am domineering and *bossy*.'

'Yeah, so? I think everyone who knows you would agree with that.'

'Are you familiar with dominance and submission?'

'What?' *Yikes!* My brain froze, but my traitorous body immediately reacted, becoming so acutely turned on that my breath caught.

'Breathe, Kismet,' he whispered.

I blew out a deep breath and tried to calm my pulse. 'Dominance and submission?' Totally flummoxed by my own dissonant emotions, I gave a hysterical laugh. 'Is that a new video game?' I began practising the mental hum so I wouldn't blurt out any more ridiculous words. Cerridwyn's mystical sound-healing tool came in handy, not only to keep vampires from damaging my brain, but to relax me.

'Answer me, Kismet.' His voice shifted subtly and now held a dangerous edge. 'Do not deflect. Are you familiar with the terms?'

I cleared my throat and licked my dry lips. I'd seen Devereux in his Lord and Master persona many times, but there was something extra dark and unsettling about his behaviour now. *What's up with him?* 'Yes. I have many clients who explore the lifestyle.' I sat up straighter. 'Why are you talking about this?'

'I am excited to unexpectedly be in a position to talk about it.' Charm once again permeated his tone. 'Until the events of the last week, I had not given much thought to the topic. Previously, you gave no indication that you were interested.' He combed his fingers through his hair, pushing wayward strands back from his forehead. 'As it turns out, I have quite a bit of experience as a dominant – a *dom*. My need to control is likely why I chose to be a master vampire. I find the role enjoyable and arousing.'

Oh. Shit. A dom. My brain sputtered. Devereux's secrets were apparently endless. 'What's this got to do with you saying you want to make love to me?' As if I didn't know.

'I thought it might be time for us to push the boundaries of our sexual relationship, since you have opened the door, so to speak.'

Push the boundaries? Terror and excitement wrestled for control. 'What does that mean, exactly?' Why was I being coy? I knew precisely what he meant.

He gave a wicked grin. 'It means I would like to tie you up, have passionate sex with you, and then partake in a little blood-play. And I would like you to struggle. Merely a simple introduction to another level of pleasure. If you are emotionally able, that is.'

I sucked in so much air, I bent over in a coughing fit.

He watched as I hacked, then moved to a nearby cabinet and retrieved a bottle of water. 'Drink this,' he ordered.

'Thanks.' I took the bottle and drank. Oh. My. God. This was a dream and a nightmare all at the same time. It was true that my sexuality had recently ratcheted up a few notches. Okay, so more than a few. But what would happen if my Inner Nympho took over and humiliated me? How could I ever look Devereux in the eye again if I made a fool of myself? He'd never be able to respect me. Besides, I knew very little about dominance and submission, really, just some basics. I hadn't even read any of the recently popular books.

And what about my professional reputation? Who knew what would happen if I didn't keep my newly uncovered desires on ice?

'Are you all right?' He'd reclaimed his gorgeous fallen angel demeanour.

I coughed a couple more times to clear my throat. 'Yes, I think so.'

He held his hand out for the bottle and I gave it to him. He set it on a table.

'You can, of course, decline to participate. The submissive always has the power in the interaction. She – or he – sets the tone. If you are not ready for this level of exploration, we can revisit it in the future. But I must admit I have been eager since you introduced me to your more prurient aspect.' He watched me for a few seconds, then popped open the button on his waistband.

My eyes followed his hand as it slid down the outside of his zipper, stroking his erection through the leather.

Moisture pooled between my legs and I swallowed loudly.

'Would you like to play with me?' His blue-green gaze bored into mine, spellbinding beyond tolerance.

Another wave of heat rippled down my body. In all the times Devereux and I had been romantic, he'd never been so blatantly sexual, so *raw*. Sweat broke out on my forehead, my heart kicked powerfully against my ribs and my muscles clenched. If I got any more aroused, I'd burst into flames.

'Play with you?' I took some deep breaths. 'What did you have in mind?' My imagination had already dived into the deep end of the pool. If the reality proved to be better than my visualisation, I might not survive.

His lips spread in a slow, devilish grin. He glided over to a large brass trunk and opened it. Bending down, he retrieved something from inside and walked back to the bed. 'I will show you.' He held out several lengths of black silk rope.

I eyed the bindings, anticipating what was coming.

'I will restrain you. If you give permission.' He watched me, twisting one of the ties in his hands. 'We will begin slowly and gently. You may tell me to stop at any time.' He studied me for another moment, frowning. 'Something troubles you. What is it?'

I hated to rain on our parade by bringing in reality, but I had to be honest with him. 'As exciting as your suggestion sounds, I don't imagine it's something a psychologist ought to be doing.' I tried to visualise my oh-so-respectable thera-pist Nancy in handcuffs or suspended from the ceiling and couldn't. She wouldn't act out like that, would she? Wasn't there something . . . *wrong* . . . about it?

'Why ever not? Are you first a woman, or a professional?'

I actually had to think about that for a few seconds, since I'd never made the distinction before, which was an odd realisation. I'd mostly thought of myself as the latter. But I wanted to change that. 'A woman. Definitely.'

'Well, then . . .'

Maybe I'd regret opening this particular Pandora's Box, but for now, the entire inner team was cheering. There was no reason to pretend his suggestion wasn't outrageously tempting. 'I won't be telling you to stop.'

He snapped his fingers and several of the candles in the room extinguished, leaving the bed in shadows. 'I was hoping you would say that.' He stepped back and dropped all but one length of rope. 'Take off your clothes,' he ordered, now fully in his *dom* role, his voice a deep rumble.

Burning to oblige, I jumped up on the bed, peeled off my shirt and bra and tossed them onto the floor. Watching his hot gaze skim my breasts made me moan. Pleasure chills cascaded along my skin and suddenly, all I wanted to do was leap on him, pull him onto the bed and have my way with him. 'Hey, who says *I'm* the submissive? Why not you?'

He laughed as if that was the funniest thing he'd ever heard, then tackled me. Immediately he stretched my arms above my head and tied them together at the wrists. 'I do not have that particular orientation.' Almost faster than I could see, he had reached down next to the bed, collected another piece of rope, and secured my restrained wrists to the headboard.

I tugged against the ties. 'Hey, no fair. I can't touch you.'

'No.' He grinned. 'Not until I tell you to. In fact, for the next few hours, you will do nothing unless I will it.'

The next few hours? I almost had an orgasm just thinking about that. 'Oh, yeah?' I remembered what he'd said about wanting me to struggle, so I put some energy into twisting from side to side. 'I can do whatever I want. You're not the only one who gets to make up the rules for our little "vampire captures the psychologist" game.' *And this time, I'm participating voluntarily.*

He strolled to the end of the bed, eased his leather trousers down his legs and stepped out of them. He gave me a glacier-melting look. 'I am indeed the only one to make up the rules. And you will obey.' With that, he reached over and tugged off my jeans and panties.

Hmmm. We'll see about obeying.

I had a difficult time dragging my eyes from his naked body to his face. 'Well, then. Why don't you come over here and teach me the rules?'

He studied me. 'Are you so eager to be dominated, my little psychologist? Perhaps I will bind your ankles as well. There is no hurry. We have all night.'

I could have argued, but I got sidetracked again by the notion of having *all night*. My mouth went dry.

He made a return trip to the trunk and retrieved several longer lengths of the black silk rope.

'What else do you have in that trunk?' I raised my head

to see. One of my clients had brought in a BDSM catalog and had shown me some of the merchandise, most of which I'd found amusing then. But now chills broke out on my arms as I contemplated the intriguing possibilities.

'Many wondrous things, and I will show them all to you.' He returned to the end of the bed. 'But for tonight, we will start slowly. You need a safe word. Do you know what that means?'

'Yes – one of my clients says he keeps forgetting his word, which is why his partner brutalises him.'

'That is unfortunate. We will experience no such thing, but it is good for you to have a boundary. I am not aroused as much by your pain as by your captivity, and my power over you. I can be very creative. So, what word do you choose?'

'I don't know. I'll have to think about it.' Was I supposed to come up with the perfect word on the spur of the moment?

He flicked his fingers, dismissing the topic. 'Let us not waste time intellectualising it. I shall choose it for you. Your safe word is "portrait".'

'Portrait?'

'Yes: a meaningful word for both of us. If at any time you become uncomfortable, just repeat it and all action will stop.' He leaned in and grabbed one of my ankles, tied the rope around it and secured it to the nearest post. Then he did the same with the other foot, giving a quick tug to make sure I was firmly held.

Instinctively, I fought to bring my knees together and couldn't. Having my legs forced open and exposing myself caused an avalanche of emotions – helplessness, fear and arousal primary among them. I was at his mercy. Feverish with need, my nipples stood rigid, my clitoris swelled with desire.

He watched me struggle for a few seconds and all my muscles tensed. If he didn't touch me soon, I'd go mad. 'Devereux, please.'

'Please what?' He crawled onto the bed between my legs and began sliding his hands along my skin, which had become a pulsing erogenous zone.

Something like electricity flooded my cells. I craved his fingers on me. And in me. 'You know.'

He eased his body up mine, holding himself away by his hands and feet, as if he were performing a sensual push-up.

His silky hair brushed against my breasts and I gasped.

'Please what?' His warm lips replaced his hair, and he slowly sucked one nipple into his mouth and pulled roughly on it. He repeated the action with the other, leaving both aching with need.

'I want you.' His tongue on my breasts was having a direct effect on my throbbing clitoris.

'Not yet.' He kissed his way down my stomach to my wet folds and when his tongue reached its hyper-sensitive destination, I bucked my hips and screamed as an intense orgasm tore through me. But still he didn't stop. He captured my legs with his arms to hold me in place while he sucked and licked.

The sounds alone pushed me over the edge. It was as if his mouth was everywhere at once.

Since I was tied by the ropes and restrained by his grip

on my legs, I couldn't move away as he forced me to have one orgasm after another. I had no idea a body could sustain such rapture. I was certain I'd eventually pass out from the bliss, but all I could do was whimper and try to breathe.

Finally, he lifted his head, rose onto his knees then lifted my ass onto his thighs. He grabbed my hips, pushed himself roughly into me and began thrusting. 'You are so tight and wet, if I were not able to control the duration of my erection I would have already exploded inside you. And I will soon.' His voice flowed like auditory silk. 'I am going to take you again and again, until the sun rises. You are mine. Your body belongs to me. Say it.'

'God, Devereux!' Another pleasure rush surged through me.

He pulled back just enough to be able to thrust even deeper and I screamed. It felt so good.

'Say it!' he ordered.

'I'm yours,' I gasped, spasming in ecstasy.

He moved his hands to my upper legs and tightened his arms around them as he pounded into me, my body sliding up and down the bed from the power of each thrust. Lucky the sheets were high quality, or I'm sure the motion would have worn the skin off my lower back.

Writhing, frantic to touch him, I yanked at the ropes holding my wrists, trying to break free.

He slid his hands back to my hips again and lifted me, forcing his erection even further inside. 'Tell me what you want,' he demanded, his voice ragged.

'I want—' I bucked, all my muscles contracting in another spine-bending orgasm.

'What?' He thrust harder.

'I want you.'

He touched a place inside me I'd never experienced before and I almost shot out of my skin. 'Do you *choose* me?'

I gasped and stared up at his beautiful face and his god-like body. Unlike when Hallow asked that question, the answer was clear. 'I do.'

That must have been a good answer, because Devereux moaned and came with a wild shudder.

Overwhelmed with sensations, I tugged at the ropes holding my wrists to the headboard. Thanks to the enhancements I'd got from Hallow, they broke free. I looped my tied wrists around Devereux's neck and pulled his mouth to mine.

We kissed passionately for an eternity, then softened the kiss before he raised his head.

He gazed down at me, his incredible eyes shifting colours through the blue-green spectrum. 'You look like a satisfied woman, Dr Knight.'

With a groan, I released my arms from his neck, licked my lips and cleared my throat before giving him a big smile. 'I am. You're pretty pleased yourself.'

'I am indeed. I have great hope for our future together.' In a flash he was off the bed, his long, lean body moving with his usual athletic grace. He untied my ankles from the posts, and released my wrists from the ropes.

I tested to see if my limbs were still functional, half-expecting screaming muscle cramps, but apart from some red skin where the rope had been and the area between my legs being numb and tingly at the same time, I wasn't any the worse for wear. I stretched out, boneless, appreciating the afterglow.

He handed me the water bottle from the side table. I sat up and drank, breathing hard, as if I'd run a marathon, and uphill at that.

'After our next activity, you may rest in order to gather your strength. Although you might not have a problem in that area, as evidenced by your strength in pulling the rope from the headboard. Quite an impressive feat, that. We will discuss what to do about Hallow's *gifts* at a later date.'

Unwanted, frightening gifts.

'You want me to take a nap?' I chuckled.

'No, just a brief reprieve. Part of my job as a dominant is to keep you happy and well. You have no doubt discovered that I am very good at that task.'

'There's an understatement. So what's this next activity? I was pretty fond of the previous one.'

He grinned. 'As was I. The next one is special. Blood-play is my favorite.'

'Blood-play?' I envisioned us painting pictures on each other's bodies with Devereux's dinner.

'Yes. I will carve your skin with my fangs and drink your blood.'

'Wait a minute.' I tensed. 'Carve me?' So not finger-painting after all.

'Yes – superficially. It will not be very much different from what we usually do, just a little bloodier.'

'Well then, why bother?'

His expression became serious. 'Because I love to watch the blood bubble up from the scratches before I lick them clean and heal them. It is very arousing.' He glanced down at his erection, which once again stood at attention. 'I wish to share all of my *interests* with you. And it gives me ultimate control over you and your pleasure. But never fear. I *will* bite you. Everywhere. I will penetrate all of you.'

Oh. My. God. My body shifted into ecstatic overdrive again. I hoped I wasn't drooling. What was wrong with me that the thought of blood-play turned me on so much? 'My pleasure?'

His wicked smile was back. 'Oh, yes. In my skilful hands. You can trust me.' He ran his tongue over his fangs, the points of which had descended. He bent and retrieved the ropes again.

So aroused I could barely talk, I flopped down onto the soft bedding. I cleared my throat a couple of times, allowing my gaze to track up and down his gorgeous frame. I trembled with excitement. 'You're going to tie me up again, bleed me, drink my blood, and then . . .'

'Take you in ways we have not experienced before.'

I couldn't think of much we hadn't already tried, but what came to mind took my breath away.

'With your permission, of course.' He leaned down. 'Do I have it?'

'Oh, yes . . .'

EPILOGUE

Looking back, I don't know which of the recent events was the more life-changing: surviving Hallow's sick agenda, witnessing the deaths of people I knew, helping my friend Tom join the ranks of the undead, discovering the depth of Victoria's skills and abilities as a witch, or exploring new sexual interests – mine and Devereux's.

It's definitely a toss-up and I don't expect to sort things out for a long time.

A few days after his death, local police launched a search for Carson, the radio show host. His mother, an alcoholic hoarder, had alerted authorities that her son was missing. Apparently, he lived with her and she only noticed he was gone when the beer ran out. He was discovered by law enforcement after receiving an anonymous tip (it was the least I could do) that his body could be found in the funhouse at the abandoned amusement park. Despite what he'd said, Hallow had left it there. A lot of publicity surrounded the grisly reveal, and Carson enjoyed a few days of national fame before the media moved on to the next story. During his fifteen minutes, the horrors of his childhood were brought to light, and I became angry all over again, thinking about Hallow victimising Carson one more time.

To my great relief, Tom survived the transformation process from human to vampire and has been sequestered away until he can be trusted to be around the living. I understand that could take decades. Zoe tells me she intends to wait for him. It's good that he'll have a welcome-committee-of-one to celebrate when he re-emerges. Needless to say, the Dr Sex show is on hold. I'll be old and grey before he's safe, so who knows if we'll ever reconnect. The Tom I knew is gone, anyway. I'll miss him.

Luna has been banished to a secret vampire enclave for observation. Devereux says her addiction to Hallow changed after the demon morphed out of our dimension. But her fixation on Devereux still remains. He hasn't decided yet what to do with her. He's convinced there's no treatment for this kind of obsession in the vampire realm. I'm not so sure, and will continue my research. Even though she isn't my favourite bloodsucker, I can't pass up an opportunity to expand my knowledge base about all things undead. But it's okay with me if the bloodsucking supermodel who tried to kill me isn't allowed to return. I'll have to see if there's any such thing as a supernatural restraining order.

Victoria came through her ordeal stronger than ever and continued to nag me relentlessly to join her coven until I finally gave in. I have been enjoying the company of powerful women, in addition to utilising the structure of the magical group to explore my innate abilities, as well as the new items on my Hallow-created menu. Victoria was right when she said I'd likely hold onto the changes – at least in some form – caused by ingesting the monster's blood. *Priestess In Training* was never a title I expected to pursue, but I'm grateful for the coven's support and encouragement. Victoria feels like the big sister I never had. Her relationship with Winston thrives and they're adorable together. I guess I met him originally at The Crypt the night Lust was in charge, but I don't remember. Regardless, we've been officially introduced since. I tease her about turning into a love-struck teenager around him. Devereux and I are going on a double date with them soon.

I dream about Hallow. At first I thought the nocturnal visions were a normal reaction to having gone through a traumatic experience. And I'm sure that's true. Not only did he upend my life, but because of his immunity to Elder protections, he was able to tamper with my brain. I'm lucky to have any functional neurons left. But the dreams are like the one I had while he was controlling me – the one where we're standing in the beautiful, white-columned scene. I don't know why I remember it, but I do. Odd, since I forgot so much else from that time-period. He talks to me in the dreamscape, once again appearing as the beautiful man he was before showing his ghastly truth. He insists he's the only one who can assist me with my enhancements. So far, I've avoided thinking about the alterations to my psyche and his *gifts*. I'm just not ready. But worst of all is his claim that he'll return to the physical, and that I'll be his doorway. That's too terrifying to contemplate.

Devereux and I have grown closer since spending that night together in his secret lair. Sharing his predilections built a deeper connection between us. We've since become more creative, but he understands that I'll always like the basics – in every sexual category – best. I prefer long, lingering kisses and slow caresses to toys and techniques, but everything has its place. I'm thrilled to be integrating more aspects of my libido – using Jung's expanded definition – into my personality. Neither of us has mentioned the *mate* issue. I think he's finally willing to be patient, although who can say for sure when discussing such a *dom*. He left a gift for me a few nights later – a beautiful Celtic bracelet. He says it's a replica of a Bonding Bracelet and he swears my accepting it brings no terrifying or life-changing consequences. I'm giving him the benefit of the doubt.

All the anger I reclaimed shows up in unexpected ways. According to those around me, I have a bigger temper than I thought. And a shorter fuse. Learning to regulate the new layers of my emotions is proving challenging, but expressing everything I feel is better than all the repression I'd previously practised.

The question for me now isn't *who am I?*, but rather, *who do I want to be?*

I wonder what the answer is.

THE END

ACKNOWLEDGEMENTS

Many thanks to the staff at Jo Fletcher Books/Quercus Books, UK, especially amazing editor Jo Fletcher. She has been a patient, kind and compassionate teacher throughout our time together, and I've learned so much from her. My series is much, much better for her participation. I'll be forever grateful.

Thanks also to my agent, Robert Gottlieb, chairman of Trident Media Group, for his ongoing efforts on my behalf. I appreciate you!

Special thanks to my brainstorming, writing and critique partners: Betsy Dornbusch, Esri Allbritten, Julie Kazimer, Laurie Hawkins, Lynn Rush, Helen Woodall, Donna Tunney, Cora Zane, Nancy Adams, Diane Schultz and Jessa Slade. Your input was invaluable.

And gobs of appreciation to all my friends and readers – in-person and online – who encourage and support me, and who love Kismet and her world. I wouldn't be here without you.

Lynda Hilburn
Colorado, Spring 2013

THE VAMPIRE SHRINK
Lynda Hilburn

As a rational scientist who knows full well vampires are all hokum, Kismet Knight is the perfect choice to counsel troubled wannabe vamps. That is until she meets Devereux: a sexy, mysterious man who claims to be a real – and immensely powerful – 800-year-old vampire, and she is pulled into a whirlwind of inexplicable events that start her questioning everything she once believed about the paranormal.

Kismet Knight is about to achieve her dream job – but becoming the Vampire Shrink is going to change her life. Forever.

Jo Fletcher
BOOKS

www.jofletcherbooks.co.uk

BLOOD THERAPY
Lynda Hilburn

Kismet Knight is the Vampire Shrink. She's capable, intelligent and grounded, and she knows exactly how to handle her patients, whether they're vampire wannabes – or the real thing. But when it comes to her love life she's on less steady ground. Devereux, her mysterious and sexy-as-hell vampire lover, has become preoccupied and possessive.

Needing a break, Kismet heads to the American Psychological Association's annual conference in New York – but it's not long before her new life intrudes. The monster who stalked her three months earlier reappears, her bloodsucking clients won't leave her alone, and there are ghosts haunting the hotel.

So much for Kismet's nice, ordinary life . . .

Jo Fletcher
BOOKS

www.jofletcherbooks.co.uk